I0658371

Faith's Fate

A novel by

H. Avery Chenoweth, Sr.

Copyright©2015, PPP&K/B Inc.
ISBN: 978-0-9846883-1-9

Cover art by the author

The following literary works are by the author:

ART OF WAR
Eyewitness U.S. Combat Art from the Revolution
Through the 20th Century.
Barnes & Noble, 2002

SEMPER FI:
The Definitive Illustrated History of the U.S. Marines,
Barnes & Noble, 2005 & 2010

TO BANBURY CROSS
and Other Wagging Tales:
Kindle & Nook, 2011

THE FINAL BATTLE:
An Epic Trilogy of the Early 21st Century:
Kindle and Nook. 2012

GUIDEBOOK FOR "Z" GENERATION GRADS:
Amazon and CreateSpace POD; Kindle, 2014

PICCOLO THE PAMPERED POOCH
Amazon and CreateSpace POD; Kindle, 2014

ALL OUR YESTERDAYS:
Growing up in the 1930s and '40s
Amazon and CreateSpace POD; Kindle, 2014

LEST WE FORGET
Extraordinary Episodes in Often Forgotten
Military History.
POD CreateSpace & Amazon 2015

DEDICATION

To my dear wife of almost thirty years,
Lise LaHaye,
who is not portrayed in this story
in any way.

CONTENTS

Chapter 1   Hallelujah!

"Praise God! Praise God, brothers and sisters! Will ya' all rise and let's sing to the Lord! Hallelujah! Ain't it wonderful to serve Him? Whew! Makes you jist want to shout and sing!"

A surge of hand clapping and Hallelujahs began to sweep the banquet room of the Holiday Inn as Stephen followed the leading of the speaker and the rhythmic response of the now standing, clapping and swaying audience.

"Glory to God!" someone to Stephen's right at the speaker's table yelled out, followed by another's, "Praise the Lord!" . . . echoed by dozens more throughout the now vibrating room. The piano in the corner tinkled a barely audible tune which the master of ceremonies at the microphone picked up in a robust but slightly flat, nasal baritone as the audience joined him. "Aa- MA-zi-ing Grace, aa–ma–zi-ing Grace," he bellowed, lifting his hands slowly in a majestic gesture toward the ceiling which simultaneously triggered the closing of his eyes and the tilting back of his head. Stephen, standing on the leader's right, had turned in his direction. For a split second, this sight had appeared to him like that of a ventriloquist dummy he had had as a child whose eyes rolled back the same way when he pulled the strings inside the chest cavity. Quickly he dismissed the thought as irreverent and joined in the singing, slowly surveying the assorted group of men and women at the tables below the

7

podium. He mouthed the words instinctively as his thoughts wandered, watching the others.

Who were these people? Same as at all of these meetings: a cross-section of the community, school teachers, businessmen, ranchers, oil men, day laborers, housewives, old, young, some decked out in their Sunday best, some in work clothes. They were all supposed to be business people; one active member of the organization bringing a non-member. But, no doubt, the popularity of this sort of "prayer" breakfast in this rural community had drawn more, Stephen mused. Look how simple and ingenuous most of them seem. A glow of happiness on their faces—most of them that weren't bewildered, the old-timers anyway. God, they're beautiful in that faith of theirs! No class distinctions; all brothers and sisters in the Lord Jesus Christ and in His Kingdom of Heaven on earth! Stephen's enthusiasm began to approach the audience's as the speaker segued them into the next song.

When the last song for this interlude subsided amid hand-clapping and shouts of Hallelujah, Praise God, and Praise the Lord, the emcee added his own energetic praises over the public address system, turning to grab the man to his left who responded in a mutual Holy Hug with manly back-slapping as they disengaged. Next, he turned to Stephen, who responded in like manner, who then turned to the woman on his right and embraced her in a discreet, lightly touching gesture. At this point everyone all over the room was doing the same, creating a din of mingled ecstatic shouts and laughter. "That's it. Give one another a Holy Kiss, as the Bible says!" came the booming voice over the PA system, for a moment engendering in Stephen's mind how the voice of God must have sounded on occasion in the Bible—especially at the river Jordan, after John baptized Jesus, and the Holy Spirit came down from Heaven in the form of a dove and alighted on Jesus, as the voice of the Almighty was heard to say, "This is my beloved Son, with whom I am well pleased." *He wondered if that voice had sounded to the astonished Jews that day like this electronically amplified one.*

"Folks, ain't God good?"

A thunderous response of Amens and Hallelujahs ricocheted around the stark, partitioned walls that formed this area created out of a larger one in order to seat the two hundred or so diners at the long rows of tables crowded toward the front where the raised podium with six places on each side of the rostrum was. The buffet tables were stretched along the back wall in usual hotel fashion. Two waitresses were struggling up and down the rows doing their best to satisfy the requests for more coffee.

As the emcee waxed inspirational with all the expected catch phrases that Stephen—and most of the audience—knew so well, his mind began to drift away from the moment. Not looking up to his left but every now and then in order to appear attentive, Stephen let the sound of the speaker's voice revive memories of recent events. Doctor Luke Parsons was in his element now, his broad smile and twinkling eyes had infected his listeners. They seemed to be unconsciously imitating him in eager, emphatic mimicry.

Stephen admitted to himself an admiration for this medical doctor whose life had so drastically changed when he "came to the Lord" ten years ago. As he thought about Doc's testimony, the speaker's words fell in tandem with his thoughts *and he chuckled to himself becoming aware that he had heard it so often—or was it that it had become so automatic and rehearsed?—that in a way it was losing its impact?   But, then, maybe his own testimony was, too.* Stephen glanced politely at Doc who was really getting worked up—the audience right in the palm of his hand. Stephen knew they were in for a good, long time of it and allowed his thoughts to wander again. His perfunctory glance had made him aware of the get up brother Doc had on this morning: a silk multi-colored shirt with a garish, impossibly mismatched wide silk tie over which hung a heavy silver chain with a thick, gnarled, slag metal "Jerusalem" cross which rested on the bottom

9

of the tie which rested comfortably on the protruding belly that hung out over the big metal buckle in the shape of a stylized fish with greek letters spelling "ichthys" attached to the belt that somehow kept his Levis up. Over his shoulders, arms and back, but obviously of no use to his front since there was no way it would ever meet to button across him, was a western leather jacket with padded shoulders and fancy stitching across each side of the chest. The wide lapels looked like banners of dangling ornaments: on the left one was the gold outline "dove," which is the standard badge of the "charismatic" or the Pentecostal. To other charismatics, this automatically means that you, too, have received the "Baptism of the Holy Spirit." Of course, Stephen thought, they mean "Baptism IN the Holy Spirit." But, there are a lot of things that he is a stickler for and others are not, so what difference does it make? Looking up at Doc again, Stephen couldn't help but think of a neon sign. *Tacky? The epitome; but he must stop this disrespect. He was letting his snobbery—no pride, as the believers call it— creep in. After all, he now was one of these people. His Ivy League background that fostered these types of thoughts had been rejected several years ago when the "Born-Again" experience had happened to him . . . as he would tell about for the umpteenth time again later in the morning's program.*

He had to hand it to Doc. Here was a guy whose life had gone to pot —literally! *He was an MD, a surgeon, and had gotten hooked on something, some kind of drug which was never mentioned in the testimony. His kids were on pot or worse, his wife was a bitch—whoops, forgive me, Lord. Family life a mess. Medical practice declining. Then—miracle! God touches him in a wonderful way and, whap, Jesus comes into his life and he gets baptized in the Holy Spirit and right away his whole life changes. He straightens up, digs into the Bible, shares it all with his wife, who "accepts" and gets Born Again and Spirit-filled and the kids, one by one, do too. No denying that's a powerful testimony to the power of the Lord! And, his practice began a turn-around. He got to praying over his patients first, and in some cases they were healed by the power of God through the "laying on of hands" instead of surgery.*

10

So, old Doc follows what the Bible—or what Jesus commanded: "Go ye into all the world and preach the Good News of Jesus Christ." And, he does it all the time. He's a self-styled, non-ordained, evangelist whose personality and zeal for the Lord is so strong that he goes forth boldly, just as the Bible commands true believers. Stephen unknowingly shook his head. How does he keep up with the medical field? He's got to read volumes of medical journals each week just to stay current. Maybe one of his gifts from the Holy Spirit is the ability to keep abreast of things. Stephen hoped so, reminding himself that Doc had performed the vasectomy on him. He recalled asking Doc before the operation in his office how such surgery fit in with Biblical teachings. Was de fertilization, if that was the word, going against God's law just as abortion was? After all wasn't there "life" in the semen just as there is in the egg? Or, is there only life after the union of the two? Stephen reflected and then put it aside in his mind; that is something he would want to pursue at some length some day. But, for now, he was absolutely sure, as was every other charismatic, that abortion at least was the great sin, the "murder" of a living child, an act that will be punishable by God to persons and to nations that permit it as well. "Murder." He pondered the word. Why can't the believers and the non-believers ever get it right? The Bible doesn't say, "Thou shall not kill." It says in the original Hebrew in the ten commandments, "Thou shall do no murder." Lord knows He told the Israelites to go out and kill often enough. Of course, the various translations have glossed over the distinction and generalized it so there is now a knee-jerk response. That doggone King James version is what misleads—some think that if the King James version was good enough for Jesus, it's good enough for them! Stephen caught himself; there I go intellectualizing again. Must stop. Why challenge these things? God wants us to be simple in our beliefs, not to go around challenging every jot and tittle. That's what the Pharisees did. They were what legalists are today.

A loud "Glory to God" from directly below and in front of Stephen broke his train of thought, if it were a train, and caused him to look a bit startled. He hoped no one noticed and deftly combined it into a smooth reach for a sip of coffee. He was aware again of Doc's words, now coming down from the climax of his experience with the Lord and easing into the subsequent and now rote lines of his mental script. And Doc milked it for all it was worth; voice now subsiding, almost hushed, leaning forward over the microphone in order to become more intimate in this triumphal moment of sharing with those out there the meaning of this great experience. And, how they could have it, too. Just like the Doc. And, get their lives cleaned up and put back in line. In line with the Word of God, which is Jesus, and when He lives in your heart, that's what it's all about. You become like Jesus. Jesus lives in you! And, we all become like Jesus. And, we all become brothers and sisters in Jesus. We become Jesus' "body," with Jesus the head of the body . . . the body of believers! Hallelujah!"

The pitch was picking up again. The room reverberating with Amens, Glory-to-Gods, Hallelujahs and here and there a babbling of unintelligible utterances. These seemed to swell and Stephen let himself go with it, letting a flow of sounds come from his mouth that could pass for a foreign language of some sort, with a particular cadence and staccato that might favor punjab Indian or Thai. It was the particular "tongue" that Stephen had received as a "gift" in his Baptism in the Holy Spirit experience and he liked to speculate on it as his mind became totally detached from the sounds and any seeming thought that might be ordering them forth. The whole room was chanting a cacophony of sounds which blended strangely into an overall harmony that was as beautiful as it was inexplicable. Stephen felt a warm glow come over him from head to toe in the midst of this familiar experience, as this "praying in tongues" often evoked. *The Holy Spirit is really moving today*, he thought, as well as did many others no doubt.

Doc abruptly ended the spontaneous pouring forth with his customary, "Praise God," and deftly steered the proceedings back to himself. *Whoops*, Stephen thought to himself, *that got a little too much. Tends to scare the guests and newcomers who have never seen or heard about praying in tongues. These Full Gospel meetings are getting to be more like church services than businessmen's testimonials. Doc must have sensed that, too.*

It was now 9:45. The breakfast had started at eight. Stephen was scheduled to give his testimony at nine but he had become used to these things going on a lot longer than planned. *After all, these people loved to spend time in church. They'd think nothing of two- and three-hour services. They got fed by the Word—the Word of God—and their appetites were ravenous. This morning was no exception; what better thing to do on a Saturday morning?* A couple of people got up to leave. *Maybe it's a bit much for some of the guests, traditional Christians who think a 20-minute sermon is too much. But, these people—the true believers, that is, have all had similar experiences with the Lord and they never tire of hearing that of others. It helps to reinforce their own and reassure that it really was what they think it was. Otherwise, mightn't it fade along with their faith? No, not if it gets fed constantly,* Stephen knew. *I guess this is the part of the meaning of Jesus' Words, "Man does not live by bread alone, but by every Word that comes out of the mouth of God." Or, by the chorus of saints in Revelation, "We shall overcome by the blood of the lamb and the word of our testimony." Good enough reasons, both, he reasoned.*

Finally it came time for the main event on the program, Stephen's testimony. Several short testimonies had been given, many announcements and sing-and-praise sessions, the sole purpose initially of the this Fellowship. . . which is basically to expose businessmen to what the Lord has done for those businessmen who have given their lives to Jesus . . . and how that has brought them to peace and prosperity at work and at home. He looked intently at the sea of smiling faces; *they sure didn't fit the stereotype businessman, or business woman.*

Doc made some appropriate remarks and turned the lectern over to Pete "Rock" Weller, who looked like he could be a businessman. He is.

He is the president of Agape Oil Company of Tulsa. *A giant of a man, a bit rough around the edges after years in the oil fields but he at least put on a business suit this morning,* Stephen thought—*along with his stetson hat*—as his close friend Rock strode to the mike to introduce him.

Rock's Gary Cooper-like demeanor as he casually sauntered to the microphone seemed to exude authority and commanded an immediate sense of respect from the audience, which settled back comfortably for the main event. Rock was a master at this; he shuffled a bit and stretched his long arms out to grasp the corners of the lectern, slowly surveying the group while allowing a big, friendly smile to creep across his craggy face . . . finally erupting in a tooth-filled laugh that had his viewers imitating before he yelled out like a coyote on the range: "Ya' love JEE-sus?"

The ensuing pandemonium and cheerful replies gave brother Rock time to shift into his "aw-shucks," foot shuffling, humble attitude that was so familiar to everyone. He had been a pro football player for the Dallas Cowboys a couple of decades or so ago; not very distinguished as a running back but enough to keep the memory fresh in introductions and conversations. He had been an oil field roustabout, a roughneck, a boozer, womanizer, general all 'round hell-raiser, you name it. He'd been in the Korean war, too, was wounded and came back with a bunch of medals. In the oil business for almost twenty years now, he'd had his share of ups and downs like most until he found the Lord. Or, the Lord found him . . . in a gutter in Oklahoma City. But, that's another story. Rock had made his usual well-chosen, down-to-earth remarks about the oil business and how he owed it all to the Lord and how he and the Lord were working together to His glory as he tied it somehow right into the introduction of the guest of the morning, Stephen.

"Hey, saints, I want you to know we got us a feller here today's got a testimony you ain't gonna believe. I know this brother . . . and he's one of us!" Applause and amens erupted from the tables.

"Hit don't matter he's some eastern dude." Stephen winced but was used to it. "We cain't all be perfect!" The audience roared. "But, I oughtta take that back. He is perfect— we're all perfect in Jee-sus! At least we're a tryin' ta be." Murmurs of agreement echoed. "Who said God cain't do miracles? This here guy . . . " and he made a sweeping gesture with his right hand toward Stephen . . . "went to Yale you-ni-ver-sity." He repeated university, exaggerating and drawing out the "U" until it was embarrassing, at least to Stephen—not to the believers. They ate the ridicule up. "Yup. This here dude from one of them big U- (and he made fun of the word again drawing another round of guffaws and giggles) . . . ni-ver-sities over east, there, where all them commies and liberals teach . . . and get inta the gova'munt . . . and mess us all up . . . and take prayers out of the schools, an' OK abortion . . . and mess up the oil business . . . " The crowd roared approval, punctuating with a cacophony of Amens and Hallelujahs that could surely be heard as far as the lobby. "Whoa! Don't lemme git carried away, folks. I ain't the speaker. It's this here good brother in the Lord . . . this here Okie now— he's junked all that eastern stuff—who you folks might not know, but a lot of folks should know, 'cause you see what he does on your TV all the time . . . I'm talking about him bein' the guy what runs the Christian TV station outta Broken Arrow, KXAO TV, channel 21 . . . 21 is three times seven, get it? That's God's number. 'X' stands for Christian. 'A' and 'O' is for the Alpha and the Omega, the beginning and the end, praise God. That's the station we all oughtta be watchin'. You can take your NBC and your CBS and whatever—Satan's got them—we got God's station!" Hearty applause.

Doc's voice could be heard in a stage whisper to hurry up. "Folks, I could stand here and tell you all sorts of good things about my brother, Stephen Trevelyan, but it'd take too long. We go a long ways back, him and I. But, I'll jist let him tell you his own story his own way. Brother Steve."

A round of polite applause sprinkled with the customary exclamations and amens broke out as Stephen rose with a broad grin just as Rock wrapped him in an all-but smothering bear hug.

Leaning into the mike, Stephen did a theatrical aside, grimacing, "Hey! A Holy Hug is one thing, brother Rock, but I think you snapped two ribs!", he said feigning an examination inside his coat with his right hand. The audience welcomed the light interplay and Stephen felt that it was the ice-breaker he needed to start with. Which by now, seasoned as he was, he seemed always to be able to come up with somehow.

With a display of polished ease that served to eradicate the previous contrast between himself and Rock, Stephen let it come forth naturally, since it was a part of him now, "Praise God! We don't need these lights in here—I see Jesus shining in your faces out there. Hallelujah!" 'Amen, brother,' came like a chorus from the room. "Want to see a miracle?" he continued. "Ever see an Episcopalian . . . from Yale raise his hands to the Lord?" The crowd cheered. "Most Christians out there, who don't know Jesus like we do, go around like this" Stephen stalked in a clumsy circle, arms close to his sides, head down, a sad look on his face. "They don't know what 'joy in the Lord' is! Do they?" A thundering 'No' from in front of him. "But we do, don't we?" Again, the response, the amens. *He was getting them where he wanted. After all, the preceding were some pretty hard acts to follow.* He shut the thought off and got back on track.

"You know, I was like them. No, I wasn't even like them before I met Christ, my Savior. I was worse. I didn't even go to church, 'cept maybe Easter with the kids. I didn't really believe in anything. Can you imagine that? I was almost forty years old and I hadn't ever read the Bible! Oh, yes," he corrected himself, following his mentally imbedded script now with its practiced pauses, reflections and intonations. He only had to adjust now and then for particular audiences; a little more down to earth for ones like this one, a bit more restrained and proper for the civic and business clubs . . . and churches, occasionally. "Yeah, let's see . . . I seem to remember I had to read a chapter in the Bible for an art course at Yale back in fifty-nine to see what all this 'Nativity' business was all about." Friendly snickers from in front of him. "That was so I could understand the Biblical pictures we were studying." He had caught himself and said pictures instead of paintings, not wanting to sound highfaluting and too cultural. He had them with him and he did't want to screw it up with some turn-off phrase that would lose them. "Well, I didn't learn much about the Bible from that. I sure hadn't learned anything about it in that Episcopal church I grew up in." Heads nodded in affirmation, punctuated with low amens, like 'isn't it so?' "Fact is. You know the only thing I learned in Sunday school in that Episcopal church?" He paused, watching their facial expressions exude anticipation. "It was—I've got to admit—one of the most important things I ever learned in my life. 'Cause I use it every day. You know what it was?" (the pregnant pause) He stepped to the side of the lectern and thrust his foot up on the edge of the dining table where half the group could see. "I learned how to tie the best doggoned double knot in my shoelace . . . " The room filled with shrieks of laughter, as he knew it would . . . and he played it for all it was worth. Chuckling aloud with them, Stephen composed himself and stepped back to the microphone. "No, really. I can thank that Episcopal Sunday school of mine down there in Atlanta, Georgia, for teaching me something that has lasted me a lifetime." People turned to one another, amused, obviously relishing a new story against the dead church of the end times that they hadn't heard before.

"But, before I get to the part you really want to hear," purposely delaying and manipulating his audience at will, Stephen launched into the story he'd told endless times. "You know, at one point in my life I was deathly afraid of the future. Things hadn't been going so well for me up there in that world of Madison Avenue in New York. Ever heard of Madison Avenue? "Just in case some hadn't, so as not to lose them, he explained, "Well, that's where all those advertising agencies are. Up there in Satan's paradise, that evil, fun (derisively) city—sin city —New York. That's where the real Babylon is today! Amen! That's where all those people make all those TV programs that you and I don't want our kids watching. There and Hollywood. Right? That's where the 'Humanistic' networks . . . (*oops, better back up on that buzz word*) . . . that's where those liberal, Godless networks and magazines spread all that filth into our homes from. Or, at least, try to . But, Praise God, I don't let 'em come into my home any more!" Hallelujahs from the audience, as expected. "Amen? Well, there I was, with my Yale U -niversity (he stretched out the 'U' as Rock had done) degree right in the middle of all that sin, turning it out like all the rest. Not knowing right from wrong!" Stephen had things going so well at this point that he felt complete control. He had long picked out those in the room for direct eye contact, smiling at them in turn as if to share this intimate secret specifically with these chosen handful. And, he had built the cadence of his words toward an undulation that elicited the Amen and Hallelujah responses almost at will.

"My business life wasn't right. My home life wasn't right. I don't even remember my kids ever growing up; I was always gone at the crack of dawn, commuting into the big city from Connecticut. I never saw them in the morning, most of the time I never saw them at night when I came home . . . for two reasons. One, I came home so late. Boy! What a rat race that kind of life is. Second," and he paused dramatically, slowly scanning the room; then, letting it drop, "Because I came home drunk . . . or half drunk most of the time!" The reaction as expected: cries of sympathy, shock, a mumbling of quick acknowledgments of those who affirmed their first-hand knowledge of such things and who, of course, had overcome it, too. "Yep. I was an alcoholic . . . and didn't even know it. Know why they call liquor 'spirits'? That's what it is . . . evil spirits . . . that'l grab you and ruin your life. I know!" Heads nodded in agreement.

"Well, knew something was missing from my life and I began to think about the future. Would it get better? Could I avoid some of the big mistakes I had been making if I could foresee the future? So, where did I turn?" Laying it out in deliberate measures, he let it drop: "Horoscopes!" A spontaneous eruption of clatter came from in front of him and from both sides; praying in tongues and interjections of the Amens and Hallelujahs.

"Horoscopes! Witchcraft ! Would you believe I let these things guide my life? Remember, I wasn't a believer at this point. How could I have known?" Stephen pulled a wallet-sized pocket calendar from inside his coat and held it up. "See this? It's a little calendar and it ruled my life. I had dug up my old horoscope my mother had done when I was born—is that what the Episcopal church taught? And, I went to a guru of sorts up in New York state, some guy who read your horoscope . . . and I tape recorded that. Then, I went and had a computer outfit make one up for me. Well, you're not going to believe this, but I studied all those horoscopes and I outlined them and I made charts and calendars . . . to see if they all indicated the same thing. Well, when I had done this, I took out my pocket calendar and marked the whole year out. I'd use a little arrow pointing up for good days, an arrow pointing down for bad days, and an arrow at an angle for so-so days." (Chuckles from the audience) "But, you know what? This little thing got aholt (Stephen found himself dropping a few more affectations as he went along) of me and it soon had me! I couldn't do anything or make any decision without checking the calendar. I'd get a phone call. 'Hi, Steve, I've got something very important to discuss with you. Can we meet Thursday?' I'd say, let me check, and I'd open my pocket calendar to Thursday and there the arrow would be pointing down!" ('Ughs" from the audience) "Uh, Sam, I can't make it Thursday; how about Friday? See? The thing had me. And, I didn't know it." The listeners were in rapt attention.

"Well, to make a long story short, I had to go down to Atlanta to shoot a commercial or something. And, my younger brother Tom and I were out at dinner. I was only into my first martini when he started talking about an experience he had had." (More murmurs and heads nodding knowingly) "It turned out that he had gone through a particularly tragic time in his life and a friend had asked if she could pray for him. She first told him some things that he could not really understand concerning the Bible and something about Jesus, and all that. But, after she laid hands on his head and prayed . . . nothing happened. Until later. He said he woke up suddenly in the middle of the night and experienced a warm, glowing feeling all over him . . . and he felt the presence of someone with him, he wasn't sure whether there had been a light or anything, but he was sure something had happened to him. That was two years before and the experience was not only still with him, but it had grown in intensity . . . and he fed it daily by reading the Bible."

"You guessed it. This was too much for me. I knew my brother. He is OK but no intellectual. And, of course, I was," said Stephen, deliberately puffing himself up to the delight of the on-lookers. "After all, I had graduated from Yale . . . and I had been an officer in the Marines." He clicked his heels and saluted in self-mockery. This was the part he particularly liked getting into; how pompous he used to be, an intellectual know-it-all, conceited to the point of absurdity. Flattening this image of a stuff-shirted non-believer always won him over to his audiences. The charismatics never tired of iconoclasm (*there's a term I'd better never mention!*), deriding those 'above them,' knowledge and U—niversities. "Speaking of Marines," he interjected, "You know, there is only one adjective in the whole Marine Corps? It only has four letters and it's used to describe everything," he said knowingly, addressing some of the men in the audience, to whom some whose wives leaned to them for further explanation. But, this was always a tricky one and he had to be careful and let it go over the heads of those who missed the innuendo. "Well, suffice it to say that I was used to cussing worse than anything you have ever heard—even around the oil rigs!—'cept you guys who were in the Corps, too!   Bad thing was, I cursed—cussed—at home, around the children, everywhere.   It was a wonder I wasn't thrown out places!" (Ooohs and aahs from the audience).

     "So, my brother Tom and I got into a deep, deep discussion that night. I didn't even finish the martini. (Hallelujahs and Amens) I pooh-poohed what Tom was telling me. I used the old arguments, like religion was the opiate of the masses, like Karl Marx said.   (A few raised eyebrows, otherwise blank expressions) And, I told him that it was all just a crutch for those who could not cope with reality.   And, furthermore, you don't expect me (breaking into the wide smile again) an intellectual from Yale and a combat officer in the Marines to go for this Jesus nonsense, do you? (Laughter; the listeners straining forward to hang on to every word.   They were with him; the Fellowship regulars had gone through something like this themselves, which made listening to someone else's testimony all the more intriguing, to see in what mysterious ways God was continually working) Well (*for a split second Stephen was aware that he had lapsed into an overuse of 'well,' a habit, once started in a talk, hard to overcome. Oh well, who's going to care—or count them—anyway?*) I must have argued with him until well into the early morning, Sunday.   We didn't start filming until Monday, so he said, 'Steve,' you're not doing anything this morning.   How about going with me   to church?   I said, 'what church?'   (The cautious tone of his voice evoked titters)   'Oh, just an Episcopal church near here.' I figured no danger in that! (Loud guffaws)

"I didn't have anything to do so we went together to this typical Episcopal church—ya' know, fake English-looking. Only it wasn't exactly typical. Everybody was friendly. (Laughter) And looked happy! (More laughter)   And in the service, they lifted their hands up in the air! (Hallelujahs and Praise Gods) I didn't know much about it, but I woulda thought I'd wandered in a Baptist church. (Gales of laughter)

Stephen began to change pace now. "And, you know? Something began to happen to me during that service. Now, I had been to church on and off and since I was a kid and could not tell you one thing I ever heard from a pulpit. I doubt if any traditional church-goer can either. But, when one of the priests started reading from the Old Testament lesson, reciting the ten commandments . . . when he came to the one about not taking the name of the Lord thy God in vain, those words suddenly caught my attention. And, they hurt, sort of. (Amens) Then, there was a reading from the Epistles—I'm telling you what all this reading was from, now, 'cause I know it, but at the time, I didn't know what an Epistle was!   (Hallelujahs and laughter from the floor) Well, there was something about there not being any condemnation for those who are in Christ Jesus . . . which passed over my head. (Chuckles) But, then, when the reading got to the Gospel story about the blind man meeting Jesus, and Jesus making the clay out of his spit and putting it on the eyes of the blind man and telling him to go wash in the pool of Siloam, something started to happen to me."

The hush over the room was punctuated by soft Amens and Praise the Lords.

"It was as if the scales started to fall from my eyes and I could see for the first time . . . just like the blind man!" HALLELUJAH! There was an agitated stirring all around the room, then a hush so Stephen could continue.

"That wasn't all, but that got me to thinking. From then on I began to pay attention to what was happening. Then the sermon came. Well, that was not much to be worried about . . . if you have ever heard an Episcopal sermon! (Shrieks of laughter and applause) But, this one turned out a little different. A retired minister got up to give it and he said something about this being the third time this morning he had given the sermon. But, for some reason, he was not going to follow his outline now. The Spirit was leading him—and I had no idea what he was talking about (laughter) —leading him to preach something else. He looked right back at me in the last pew and said there was someone, someone he'd call Joe, who was lost, who was floundering, who was seeking a deeper meaning in life. Can you imagine how I felt? He was talking to me ! And, as he kept preaching, the words kept cutting deeper and deeper into me like a sword. (Amens and Hallelujahs) Each time he would make a point . . . which seemed strangely to answer every one of my arguments the night before with my brother, I would sink down, deeper and deeper . . . " and here Stephen would slump in stages behind the lectern to the glee and laughter of the audience, " . . . with my ol' Jesus freak brother poking me in the ribs as I sank lower and lower!" Howls of laughter, and Stephen stopped and looked around contentedly to the right and left of the head table, giving ample time for the story and the visual punch to be savored by all. Then, quiet again and anticipation as Stephen continued.

"Well (*doggone it*, "well"—*again!*) . . . by the time I was down as far as I could go on that hard, wooden seat, I asked myself—or God—or somebody, 'What's happening?' Fortunately the night before, in our discussion, Tom had made a big to-do over confessing one's sins, repenting, asking forgiveness and accepting Jesus to come into one's heart. (Praise Gods and Amens) So, there, slumped down in that pew, with my eyes closed, and all those words searing into me like a hot iron, I heard myself saying, 'OK, God, I give up. I don't know what this is all about, but, if You'll forgive me for all the bad, stupid, wretched things I've done wrong in the past—and, You know, there're a bunch of 'em— and give me a chance at a new life with You, I'll now ask Jesus to come into my heart."

The room erupted with thunderous applause and praises. People got to their feet, some holding their hands aloft, murmuring softly in tongues. While they were thus, Stephen's strong voice thundered over the PA, "And, you know what happened then?"

"Praise God, what?", shouted someone.

"A change came over me!" The room began to quieten and everyone resumed his seat. "Remember, I didn't know the Bible, or Jesus, or what you or I know now. I was just a middle-aged, non-believing, intellectual, Yalie Marine, who was a total mess . . . and this something happened to me! You know, I've thought about this constantly since it all happened and I know it happened . . . and you do, too! But, right then and there. in that crazy Episcopal church, I became a new person in a flash! (Praise Gods and applause) Of course, I didn't know what it was but I was Born Again ! Right in the last row of an Episcopal church! Talk about miracles! (Near pandemonium in the room)

Stephen paused long and dramatically. "Well, sir, that's the only way it could have happened to me. A total, overwhelming experience. Not by intellectualizing, not by some persuasive argument by some preacher or someone. No, I had to be wiped clean of everything, all that intellectualism. My mind felt like it was a blank. And, it was 'cause I didn't know a word of the Word of God. The only thing I knew was that

24

before I was blind and now I could see! (Amens) I found out later as I studied that God expects you to come to Him as a little child. Well, that I was. I didn't have a single thought in that new, empty head of mine. (Roars of laughter) That's why I've been trying to fill it with the Word of God ever since!" Amen!

Instead of ending, to the audience's delight, Stephen continued. "You're not going to believe this—yes you are!—but I walked out of that church a 'new creation in Christ.' I had the silliest grin on my face (more laughter), and a total feeling of joy! Man, there wasn't anyone happier than I was. And, I still didn't know or realize the full impact of what had happened to me. But, one thing stood out: when I had walked into that church I had been a bitter person, full of hate. You know the kind, ya' get behind the wheel of a car and somebody cuts in front of you," Stephen demonstrated by grabbing an imaginary steering wheel in front of him, forming a snarling glare of hatred and turning the imaginary wheel this way and that, "You so-and-so, I'll run you off the road. (Loud guffaws and Amens) Well, when this experience happened to me and I walked out of that church, I saw all these beautiful people! I had never really looked at people before except as targets or annoyances, things that got in my way and I hated them mostly. Suddenly, they all looked so beautiful (laughter) . . . and I felt that I loved them (more laughter). I couldn't believe it: I actually felt that I loved these people that I didn't even know! I went around with a dumb look on my face staring at them like some visitor from outer space who had never seen human beings before. (Praise God and Glory to God and Amens ad infinitum)

"Another thing happened, too. I wasn't aware of it for some time, until, I think, when my little daughter remarked that I didn't cuss anymore. (Praise the Lord) I didn't. I had stopped altogether, and nothing seemed to be able to get me to do it. I could stumble, hurt myself, of something could go wrong and I'd come out with, 'Praise God!' " Applause.

"And, there was another aspect: the drinking. I asked my brother how Christians handle liquor, since I knew there was some drinking of wine in Biblical times. He said that everything was done in moderation and to ask the Lord about it. To make a long story short, I cut down to one martini a day, after work. But, then, I'd get to thinking about that martini all day and race home to have it. But, I'd allow myself only the one ! However, I started putting it in a larger glass! (Laughter) So, one day I just said, 'Lord, will you just take the taste away from me?' He did and I haven't had a drop since, Praise God!" Echoed by approval from the audience.

"Hey! You'd think this is the end, wouldn't you? (Audience shake heads negatively) Nope. I had to go on and get the second course. I had been Born Again and knew that was real. Now, I wanted the "Baptism in the Holy Spirit" that I had heard about but wasn't quite sure what it was. So, the next night my brother Tom took me to the service of a famous evangelistic team, the Happy Hunters   (knowing laughter and approval) . . . right in the same church. I didn't know what to expect but, when the time came, I went forward and received instruction in how to ask for the Baptism. Now, you know this is not the water baptism, this is different—the real baptism of the power of God. When all was done, the Hunters came down the line and laid hands on each one of us, and each one would collapse onto the floor. I wasn't prepared for this (laughter) and when my time came, darned if my knees didn't buckle and I went backward, caught and eased to the floor by someone standing there. When I gathered my wits, I got up and a string of what they said were 'tongues' came out of my mouth like came to the apostles at Pentecost, whatever that was. (Laughter) I had been 'slain in the Spirit' and had received the power of the Holy Spirit to work in my life and had received one of my 'gifts,' the ability to pray in tongues—my own special prayer language that only the Holy Spirit understood.

"Well, I don't have to tell some of you, I had the full course in two days!   And, from that Monday, I must have floated three feet off the ground," Stephen exclaimed, measuring the three-foot height with his right hand.   "Brothers and sisters, you talk about somebody who was up in the air, that was me ! It was unreal. I never experienced such joy and happiness.   Of course, the moment I could I started filling that empty head of mine with the Word." (Laughter)

"So, it was only later that I found out what had happened to me: I had been Born Again, just as Jesus had told the Jewish Pharisee Nicodemus in the third chapter of the Gospel of John.   Anyone who wants to see the Kingdom of Heaven must be Born Again.   And Paul tells more about it in his letters. But, I didn't know at the time that I had been justified, that is, my blot of original sin had been wiped away and I had been reconciled with God and He was now going to treat me as a son and brother of Jesus, His Son. I had been forgiven and I was 'saved,' that is, I have God's promise of salvation, of going to heaven instead of burning forever in hell.   I had received the power of God through the Holy Spirit coming to dwell within me when I became baptized in Him.   And, those gifts of the Holy Spirit which Paul lists in the 12th chapter of First Corinthians   (Stephen's tempo picked up and he rattled them off without hesitation): wisdom, knowledge, faith, healings, miracles, prophesy, discerning of spirits, tongues and interpretation of tongues. The greek word for these is 'carismata'—and I didn't learn that at Yale! (Laughter)   That's why they call us Charismatics.   We have these gifts through the receiving of the Baptism of the Holy Spirit . . . just like the apostles at Pentecost in the book of Acts.   And, these gifts work in our lives. Ya' see? This is the full gospel—the power and the gifts to make things happen—the things they don't teach you in the mainline churches!

"Follow? I didn't realize at first that I had been made new, that my spirit was now activated to control my soul and my body—and my body had now become a dwelling place for the Holy Spirit as Paul says in the 6th chapter of First Corinthians. The temple of the Holy Spirit. And, it was paid for with a price . . . the price of the blood of Jesus shed on the cross, once for all . . . for you and for me. We are now cleansed by the blood of the Lamb!"   Amens and Hallelujahs swelled from the tables, but Stephen felt to continue in this vein would end up in a preaching exercise that would dilute his testimony. He brought it to an end.

"Brothers, sisters —and any of you out there who does not know Jesus Christ as your personal Savior and who would like to have Jesus come into your heart . . . and you who want to go forth in the power of the Holy Spirit and turn you life into one of love, joy, peace, forbearance, kindness, generosity, fidelity, gentleness and self-control, as Paul says in Galatians 5:22 . . . then, come forward. Any of the brothers or sisters here—or anyone in the room—will be glad to assist you. We want you to share what we have found in the Lord. Now is the time; tomorrow may be too late. That's it, step forward. Come on. Receive Jesus into your hearts. Receive the gifts the Holy Spirit has been waiting to give you. Amen, Amen Amen .

Chapter 2   The Man at the Well

Stephen pulled out of the Muskogee toll gate and headed back to Tulsa. He had come alone to the Full Gospel Businessmen's Fellowship International breakfast this morning on purpose. It was Saturday and he wanted to stay away from the TV station, and it might be a good opportunity to drop by and take a look at some of the wells. He figured Rock would be going over to Henryetta and down to Seminole to check on some of his. Stephen had a couple of investment units in one of the Seminole wells but it wasn't doing too well. He winced at the pun.

It was midday and the Oklahoma sky was bright and clear. Stephen never tired of the beauty of the vistas around him as he drove. *Strange state*, he mused. *Looks like 'anywhere USA' from Tulsa south to Dallas; trees, rolling hills, pastures – set someone down in the middle of this place and you couldn't tell it from Tennessee, Georgia or Pennsylvania. Connecticut, yes. Wasn't at all like I expected Oklahoma to be, I guess because of the musical. But, when you get over west of Oklahoma City it does get flat and barren and treeless and windswept and looks like the stage play. North and west of Tulsa it starts to get sparse and prairie-like. Anyway, I like the wide open spaces out here. You don't get that crammed-in feeling like the New York-Boston corridor.*

That corridor. Connecticut seemed like another world to Stephen now, three years after he'd left it. All that Ivy League and New York stuff

29

was far behind. So were Diana and the kids. That was the main thorn in his side: Diana and Gloria and Michael.   The new life in Christ with Faith was maybe not as perfect as it should be, but he could account for the former marriage not having been so, either. After all, it had been a secular one.   Neither he nor Diana had been true believers. How could they possibly have had a happy, Christian marriage? He had really loved Diana all those years, he reminded himself. And, the kids. Gloria going on thirteen, Michael, just turned ten.

"God, I wish I could see them . . . and while You're at it, God, please heal that scar I have caused them and let them some day understand and forgive me."

He had introduced Gloria and Michael to Faith in Atlanta the first Christmas after the divorce and it hadn't clicked.   *They were too young to understand.   Of course, Faith is about as opposite from their mother as you can get. It's like going from Junior League to car hop. He knew they all thought he just went through the typical middle age male menopause – and took out after the first broad who came along. That's what Diana told their friends. How can they ever know that it was God's timing and answer to prayer that He sent this angel to me? After all, Diana had flatly refused to leave Darien and move to Tulsa.6*

Stephen was passing the turnoff to Coweta and he glanced at the familiar antenna farm to the west where channel 21's antenna was side-mounted on one of the thousand-foot towers.   The countryside was glorious in the warm sunshine.   He contemplated turning off at the Broken Arrow exit and going back down 61st street to the apartment to see if Faith were there . . . or of going on out to Skiatook to see how the Logos wells were pumping. They'd been watering out and it looked like nothing but trouble. Maybe Rock had gone up there.

Figuring that if Faith were not at home, he'd just go down to the pool and waste the afternoon.   And, if she were there, they'd just go up to the Woodland shopping mall and waste the day anyway and end up going across to Chi Chi's to share a mexican pizza, which wasn't bad – even if they didn't have a Dos Ecces to go along with it.

Ahh, beer! When was the last time he had tasted one? Too long to remember. Back around his coming to the Lord, almost four years ago. But, he reflected a moment, *he hadn't really missed drinking since he became a new creation in Christ. He had totally quit the hard stuff, but before meeting Faith he had had an occasional beer or a glass of wine. Certainly Jesus drank wine. But, with Faith there was no reasoning, no compromise. She was an Evangelist and had a ministry herself, and no alcohol was ever going to pass her lips. And, neither was any going to pass his if he married her and became a part of her ministry. It was not a hard bargain to live up to. God had simply removed that taste, too, from him and he had no desire whatsoever for a beer or wine or anything else alcoholic. Much less, he and Faith never went into places or around with people who drank* – *everybody was just like him and her.* He thought, too, *how repugnant it was now to pass a bar or tavern and look in and see all the unhappy, lost souls sitting there, drinking, trying to find companionship, trying to find love and the meaning of life through alcohol and smoke. He thought how easy it was to turn away from that sort of wasted life by coming to Jesus.* Often he had wanted to just step inside one of those places and start talking to someone at the bar about Jesus. *But he knew he'd cause a scene and be thrown out. Shoot, he'd be accused of trying to reduce the bar's sales and thus run it out of business. He'd leave that to others* – *like Faith. She'd just as likely charge right in and start button-holing the drinkers. With her looks, they would give her their undivided attention masking a different intention. No, somebody must have warned her that she can't legally do that, so sometimes she and her cohorts wait outside bars and pounce on people as they leave. Got to hand it to her, she's always turned on for the Lord and is bold to give the message of the Gospel at the drop of a hat . . . to anyone, anywhere, at any time. And, she lives what she preaches.*

Stephen was cruising his Bronco leisurely below the speed limit. He had decided not to turn off at Broken Arrow and was now on the turnpike rounding the curve which gave what he always considered a magnificent view of the skyline of downtown Tulsa twelve miles in the distance . . . rising like the emerald city of Oz. Not exactly green but glistening with glass. This was part of the turnpike where traffic started piling up every morning just as bad as the Connecticut turnpike from Darien down into the city. *Can you imagine? Way out here in this wide open country, so much traffic into a fairly small city that's it's as bad as major metropolitan centers? He guessed that's what the world everywhere was becoming. And Tulsa has such a spacious look and feeling to it – except at drive-to-work and drive home time. The major streets are laid out along the mile square sections of the original land surveyor's rectangular grid system. Six square miles equals a township.*

Stephen prided himself that, having associated himself with some oil men and investing in a handful of units he had picked up some of the jargon. But, Stephen detested jargon droppers; he had made sure that he learned the terminology correctly . . . and what it all meant. In fact, in a short time he had surprised some of the more seasoned pros in the oil business by asking some probing questions and showing he was no dummy. He liked to pat himself on the back that he could thereby spot the phonies a lot quicker. And, there are a bunch in this business; they come on and throw the terms around and you find out later that the guy was driving a delivery truck six months ago. But, then, the oil boom had attracted a lot of people – drifters, promoters, opportunists, and outright crooks. When the price of a barrel went up to over $27, that made shallow-well drilling profitable . . . which is how Stephen got into his investment in Limited Partnership units for wells less than two thousand feet deep. The one thing he was always quick to tell anyone who complimented him on his knowledge of the oil business was that while he had a pretty good grasp of the land leasing end of it and the drilling and the completion and marketing, he'd always leave the choice of site to the geologists. A few times, he had to admit to himself, he had crossed over the line when he, Faith and other charismatic investors –

including Rock Weller, too – had prophesied and walked over the land and prayed over it and had cast out all demons, especially lingering Indian spirits, and had laid hands on the earth and commanded the oil to flow forth "in the Name of Jesus." Of course, naming the wells after biblical passages was the added fillip to assure God's blessing and providence.

He passed the intersection at Garnett with its landmark modern multi-story buildings clustered on the north side, the most eye-catching, the all mirrored exterior at 4500, which housed Rock's Agape Oil Company's lavish office suites. "Agape," the greek word for the all-encompassing "love" of God. And, God had surely bestowed his blessing on Rock's drilling.

Next he made the turn onto Route 169 and headed up the more scenic route north through Collinsville, then over to Skiatook.

As he crossed under Route 75, his mind turned to the wells just north of where he was, the Genesis Field that had totally watered out. *More salt water than you'll find in Long Island Sound. Why hadn't the prayer worked? And all the exorcism? And, all the positive thinking and the "calling forth, in the Name of Jesus?" The "believe, and it shall be given you?" Why was our group any different from what's his name on the board of directors at Rhema Bible school? He just walked over his ground with his driller and pointed to spots to drill – despite what the geologist said, and his driller said. This man of faith had said God told him to drill right at that particular spot. They did and seven producers in a row came in! And, he went on to some fifty or sixty more, all with God's direction. Why didn't God honor ours? Every investor had lost everything! Even at two-thousand dollars a unit, these God-fearing, God-trusting folks couldn't afford to lose that. Stephen had lost $12,000 himself – in the name of the ministry!*

As he approached Skiatook, Stephen scanned the horizon for the rocking-horse-like pump jacks that indicated producing fields. They were sprinkled all over the place along with the cows and an occasional buffalo grazing inside the long, neat post and barbed wire fences. Nothing better for a farmer than a couple of producing wells on his property, just-a pumpin' that royalty money out of the ground day and night, night and day. They were mostly shallow wells he could tell by the size of the jack; of course he knew that most of them around here were less than two thousand feet in depth anyway. The field had been explored back early in the 1900s and abandoned as not productive. Now though, what with today's price per barrel, if you produce one at ten barrels a day, that'd make anybody rich. *Imagine just having ten wells producing ten barrels a day,* Stephen mulled over the same, familiar figures in his mind that he used time and time again when explaining oil investing to neophytes. *That's a hundred barrels a day . . . times thirty days in the month . . . equals three thousand barrels . . . times, let's say a net after windfall and other taxes, of twenty dollars a barrel times three thousand . . . and that's a cool sixty thousand a month. A month ! After you pay back your initial $30 to 40,000 costs in six months, the rest is gravy, even if it costs you fifteen or twenty thousand a month to operate — which it won't. He thought about Homer Sikes' eight wells off a mile or so to the south . . . just-a-cranking out that oil! Thinking about the Genesis field once again, Stephen spoke out loud as he often did when he was alone,* "Lord, how come you let us come so close to the hundred-fold return you promise . . . and then let it become a disaster? Is it that I'm doing something wrong? Not walking totally with You? I believe I am. Is it the divorce? I stood on 1st Corinthians 7:14, 'If the unbeliever leaves, let her depart, the believer is under no obligation to continue . . . ' the marriage. After all, I prayed to You about it and You seemed to have given me a clear answer, and You brought that angel, Faith, to me later for the perfect Christian marriage I thought You wanted."* This was almost getting to be a recurring argument with God, no doubt because Stephen felt under the surface that the passage he quoted did not line up with Jesus' Words in the Gospels forbidding divorce except for adultery. "But, Father," he pleaded aloud, "Your good and faithful servant Jimmy Swaggart, himself, printed an article on just that passage of Paul's from the first letter to the Corinthians, which finally convinced me. Now, I know Swaggart is walking with You and You must certainly be instructing the Holy Spirit to tell him what to say. And, You are certainly blessing his ministry. And he's even in the Assembly of God church which is about as tolerant of divorce as the Catholics are. Is that it, God? The divorce?"

By now Stephen had instinctively turned down the gravel road between the wells, leaving a light gray cloud behind him that obscured everything in his rear view mirror. This was the new Logos field. The "Word of God" field, which Rock and Faith and a whole host of other investors and prayer warriors had walked all over, around, across—and under, if they could have— praying and consecrating the oil and gas to the work of the Lord and casting out or binding all forces of evil that would try to come against this field . . . in the Name of Jesus. And, the field had come in pretty well—good , he chuckled.

Spotting a figure over at the well head of number two, Stephen pulled the Bronco onto the shoulder and stopped near the gate behind a dusty, beat-up pickup. He was still in his business suit, so he yanked his tie off, got out and pulled off his suit coat and rolled his shirt sleeves up a couple of turns. He bent back into the vehicle and reached onto the back seat for his straw cowboy hat, which still looked a bit too new. Slapping it onto his head, he knew he would convince no one; he was obviously not one of them. But did it matter? These guys were used to all kinds of investors and odd balls coming around. Lifting the bent wire off the nail behind the gate post, he nudged the wide strutted aluminum gate and allowed it to swing open, then closed it back. *These farmers sure make a fuss when their cows get out. Can't blame them.*

He walked along the tire ruts past the brackish sludge pit with the several bluish rainbows reflecting from the film of oil floating on top of the water, along with a couple of half-submerged beer and soft drink cans, shreds of packing material and paper milk cartons ice berg-like, protruding just above the scummy surface. There was also a fairly good amount of cow droppings, which required his keeping his eyes on the path ahead.

"Howdy," Stephen hailed. The other figure looked up and made a responding gesture with his head, keeping his hands tightly gripped on a wrench handle. "Who you with?"

"Sooner." Stephen guessed as much. Sooner was the gas gathering system for this part of the county. Half of these wells had come in gas instead of oil, which required the laying of a plastic pipe line from each well into the main conduit which would carry the gas several miles to the pumping station for further distribution. If they had come in oil, a truck would simply come by and pick up the full oil drum and replace it on a regular basis.

"Think we got a good one?"

"Shee-it!" came the reply. "Yew kain't never tell with these goddam things."

Stephen winced at the language. *Had he become a prude*, he wondered? "I was here when it came in," he volunteered, "Sounded like ten freight trains roaring over. We figured we were getting three and a half million cubic feet."

"Yea? That ain't bad. Could be a good little sucker, then."

"This ought to be a good field. Give you guys a lotta business."

"Yeah, but, I ain't never rilly seen one 'ud come in at three and a half million that'd produce near that."

"Figure half that . . . or a third that . . . it's still all right," countered Stephen.

The wrench dropped onto the concrete pad as the man jumped back to avoid getting his toes smashed. "Christ, damn summbitch! Jee-zus!"

The elation of the morning's events had not left Stephen. Before he realized it, he shot back with, "Hey, brother, you're talking about my dad, you know that?"

The man turned to him with a puzzled look. "Yore dad?"

"God is my Father. And his last name is not 'damn.' "

The man turned back to his work.

Stephen pressed. "And do you know that the name of my brother, Jesus, is the name above all names? That at the name of Jesus, every knee shall bow, those in heaven, and on the earth and below the earth? Even Satan, the devil, bows his knee at the name of Jesus! So, it grieves me when I hear my Dad's and my Brother's names used that way."

No response. A long silence. Stephen broke it.

"No offense, brother. Say, it doesn't sound like you know Jesus. Would you like to be introduced to him?"

"Look, fella. You some kinda preacher? I ain't got no use for preachers."

"Nope. Just a guy who's invested in these wells. But, I know Jesus as my brother and friend . . . and He saved my life." *Feeling he was not warming up to his pitch quite right and keenly aware of how much better Faith would be doing it—but, then, who wouldn't stop and listen to a good-looking chick—true, older chick, but still a head-turner—maybe, after all, he, Stephen, just isn't cut out to preach salvation to the lost. That isn't his gift.* Reaching into his shirt pocket, he pulled out a fold-over tract from Faith's ministry, Living Waters. "Look. Take this and read it. It's easy to do and it could change your whole life."

The man took it and stuffed it into his pocket. Stephen moved a step or two toward the gate.

"God bless you anyway."

Driving back down the road, he ran through the event in his mind. *How could I have botched that up so? I just don't have an ease about unloading the born-again story to some one like that under those circumstances. Now Rock could have done it. Faith could. Why can't I? He remembered a long ago prophesy: "Didn't You say through the gift of prophesy, Lord, in that prayer meeting back in Darien that I would speak boldly in Your Name and bring many into the Kingdom? Or, did I actually plant a seed just then?"*

Stephen switched on the radio. A gospel rock song came on abruptly in the middle of a bar. *Shoot, that's just as bad as regular rock! Why in tarnation do Christians want to copy the world? Yeah, yeah, I know . . . to get to the kids who can't be reached any other way.*

He turned the dial until the comforting strains of classical music came through. Aah. Beethoven. Piano. Piano concerto. Then, a familiar passage. The fourth! God, there just isn't anything as beautiful as that. The majesty and ecstasy of the piano concerto sustained him blissfully all the way back to the apartment.

Chapter 3　　Renewing Faith

Stephen swung into the empty space next to the Ford van, which meant that Faith was here, unless she had gone off with someone. Not too likely; she did most of her galavanting around in the van. Irrepressibly gregarious, he often thought, part and parcel of an extroverted personality. What an Evangelist needs, for sure.

As he mounted the stairs, he could hear her quite pretty voice singing along to one of those orchestrated tapes without vocal that most singers nowadays take with them in lieu of a group of musicians. It allows every would-be vocalist to imagine he or she is 'big time' talent. Faith's not bad, though, for an untrained voice. In fact, her singing was one of the first things that had attracted her to him. His own voice was not bad, either, and he had harbored vague thoughts of their doing some duets perhaps. But he came to realize in short order that he had more Sigmund Romberg, 'Make Believe' and other light operetta in mind—which would have been fruitless to suggest to Faith. He couldn't come up with any religious duets, and, of course, the Messiah and heavier 'classical' things like that were out.

He turned the key in the lock and opened the door as Faith twirled, mike in hand, continuing the song, singing now to him. She was barefooted, in a simple, thin wrap-around dress, which made no pretext of hiding her full and buxom figure. Her eyes were sparkling as they always did when she talked or sang about the Lord, and even without makeup, she was still a thing of beauty—for a woman of forty. Her face had perfect features and fully made up, sometimes she resembled Marilyn Monroe, a fact that she consciously or unconsciously capitalized on, often threatening to peroxide her long dark hair to see if she really would look like her. She closed her eyes, swaying as she sang, turning back toward the picture window that overlooked the magnificent view toward the river, experiencing the words as she mouthed them, imbuing them with every ounce of her being until the customary tears began to stream down her flushed cheeks. Stephen knew not to interrupt and stood motionless, really quite enjoying it. Since the windows were open, he hoped the neighbors were too.

As she came to the end, he timed his steps so that the final note coincided with his arms enveloping her in a rear embrace flowing naturally into a kiss on the side of the neck as he wrapped his right hand around to rest tenderly but firmly over her left breast. He knew she loved it. They stood locked in this manner for a few moments after the tape clicked itself off. Still keeping the body contact, he turned her around facing him, locking his hands at the small of her back, becoming slightly aroused. She was smiling. "Hi, Babe. Miss me?"

"As long as I have Jesus, I don't miss anyone!" she teased.

"You don't fool me. You can't live without me."

She disengaged, which signaled to Stephen that this would not end up in a delirious, passionate romp on the floor as he was in a mood to welcome.

"Glad you got here when you did, Hon. Oral's speaking at the chapel tonight. Richard'll be singing and Stephanie, too. Leah and Matt want us to join them. We can grab a burger at Braum's afterwards. OK?"

Stephen was amenable, although he would have preferred that romp on the floor. Later, maybe. It hadn't occurred just now, not because she wouldn't have liked to—she loved it and was almost always ready—thank God in her Christian zeal she had come to the correct conclusion about sex: God created it and He created it for Christians to enjoy! Think if she had gone the other way and had become a prudish, pure and holier-than-thou sex-is-sin preacher, the usual movie stereotype . . . not just movie, maybe like Leah. He really did think these charismatics had that part of it right; they're probably all terrific in bed! No, Faith has this thing tonight at ORU on her mind, which typically will block out any distractions.

They took the van. It was more comfortable with its upholstered captain's chair seats and lush, custom interior; more important, with no need to verbalize, vans were the badge of the Evangelist. The peripatetic Evangelist, going all over the place with the ministry name for all to see either painted on the sides or rear, some times with biblical passages like John 3:16, Mark 9:23, or, as in their case, with Living Water Ministry, Inc., Tulsa, OK emblazoned in three colors on the exterior rear tire cover with what is called in advertising a signature line, Jesus: "If any man is thirsty, let him come to Me and drink." John 7:37.

Stephen switched the ignition on and backed out while Faith was still leaving the apartment. He turned the radio to the classical PBS station and caught the finale of the Lizt *Les Preludes*.

Faith opened the door and swung into the passenger seat at the same time giving the radio selector knob a hard blow, silencing the music. "Demonic! That's all garbage. Full of demons. Only God's music counts."

Stephen let it go. There was no reasoning with her. Her judgment was final and irrevocable. Here she was, musically inclined, yet totally tuned out to the great classical music of the ages.

"If that had been the Messiah, would you have turned it off?"

"Whoever wrote the Messiah was not spirit-filled—no discussion!"

As they drove along, Stephen wondered whether she had ever been exposed to serious music, or art, or anything before she came to the Lord. Of course, she had never gone to college. Just a typical high school type he suspected, cheerleader, that sort of thing. Faith and Diana were miles apart; perhaps that's what had attracted him. The contrast. Unburdened with all the baggage of college, Junior League, the Driving Club in Atlanta, Darien, New York. All those impediments. Life with Faith was a return to simplicity, to following a simple faith in the Lord, so much as could be accomplished with the other foot in the TV station.

Stephen swung through 61st Street where it bordered the lush Southern Hills country club and golf course (of which, he had been told, Oral was a member, albeit an honorary one) on the left and the lovely ranch type homes, with a few colonials here and there, in amongst the tree-lined lanes on the right. He loved this part of Tulsa, perhaps because it reminded him somewhat of Connecticut, without the steep hills, though, and although all of Tulsa seemed to have a beige cast to it rather than the green he was used to. The homes were elegant, obviously in the four and five hundred thousand price range, like his own and the neighborhood back in Darien. Tulsa, to Stephen, was really one of the most beautiful cities he believed he'd seen. Spread out, clean and airy. All the rich new homes toward the south from Interstate 44 down along the east bank of the river to Bixby smacked of money. Not old money, like in Connecticut, nor the old oil money, but evidently new—and a lot of it! Gosh, the square mile sections just go on and on with expensive homes. Homes beautifully tucked in among the gentle rises. Newer ones certainly in the three to five hundred thousand range. No doubt a result of the present oil boom, despite the unpopular Carter windfall profits tax. Stephen wondered if when any of the wells he had invested in ever came through, he would once again be able to live like this. He could bet Faith would torpedo any such idea, though!

Stephen turned left on Lewis and headed south. The setting sun over the Arkansas river to his right had painted a breathtaking panorama in the evening sky. "God's quite an artist, isn't He?" he remarked to Faith who had been uncharacteristically quiet.

"Honey. The Lord's telling me to go again. I don't know just where yet. Maybe over to Texarkana—or El Reno. I've got a stirring in my spirit and you know I've got to obey." She looked out at the sunset again, her mind—God knows where—wherever it was being led by God.

At the flag-lined entrance to Oral Roberts University, Stephen made a left. He never could suppress that first impression every time he saw ORU that it looked like a "World's Fair." The ultra-modern design, the glistening brass geodesic domes less garish now in the golden rays of the setting sun; the sharp, jagged spires and rhythmic colonnades of the main academic building reminiscent of an abstracted Parthenon. Maybe that's what the Japanese architect had in mind. Parthenon—a pagan temple. Well, many early churches turned pagan temples to their use. The center of the cluster of odd-shaped structures, and certainly meant to be its focal point, was the so-called "Prayer Tower," a round flying saucer-like construction seemingly balanced fifty or sixty feet above the ground on a giant slim pedestal in the midst of a sunken garden. Radiating out in 360 degrees from the row of windows that circled the saucer were sharp spokes stabbing the air. The top of the crown tapered up to a spire capped with an "Eternal Flame."

"Doesn't just seeing ORU just thrill you? To see God's work through Oral?" Faith said quietly.

"It always strikes me like an imitation World's Fair. The architecture is bizarre— not first class at all. Those golden domes are downright tacky, wrong gold, too brassy. Like a stylized McDonalds. Motel modern."

"Careful. You're criticizing God's anointed."

"No, I'm not. I'm not criticizing Oral especially—just his architectural taste. Or lack of it!"

"Hon, I worked up in that prayer tower. I know what it's like."

"Well, to me it looks like a flying saucer or a revolving restaurant perched up there in the air on a not too steady needle."

Faith was silent; she brooked no ridicule of any of God's work. She was also incapable of differentiating between Oral's work and the style of architecture, which is what Stephen had only been trying to point out.

"I hear that eternal flame on top of the needle is actually a direct line from one of the six or seven wells Oral has on the property. But—the sharp spokes radiating out from the windows? Come on now!"

"They're supposed to represent the crown of thorns on Jesus' head!"

"They're more like oriental points to impale evil spirits."

"Hon, you've got to change your attitude."

"Sour grapes, I guess. Since they turned me down for the faculty post when I first came out here."

As the van swung to the right toward the giant pillbox-shaped double auditoriums, the big and little "Maybee" centers, the sight that no one could help but marvel at appeared between the main campus and the Maybees: the three-tiered skyscrapers of the "City of Faith" teaching hospital and medical center in the near distance. The tower—or towers — were breath-taking. Awesome! The central building was sixty stories high, the tallest building in Oklahoma. Oral had said why shouldn't

God's building be the highest? (Shades of the Tower of Babel?) It topped the bank building downtown by five floors. Glory to God! The giant statue of praying hands rising out of the ground in front of the buildings (supposedly after Albrecht Durer's 16th Century drawing) always disturbed him, however. What the sculptor must have done was to stick his own hands down into wet plaster to mould them for the original cast, then, forgetting that gravity would fill the veins and cause them to swell, enlarged the result and turned it upside down—or rightside-up for what he wanted. When you hold your hands up in prayer the blood drains back down and the veins do not protrude. He was not about to bring that detail up, you can bet!

He drove the Living Water van into a slot in a row of at least a dozen other similar vans with markings all the way from large signs and banners praising Jesus to just simple bumper stickers, like, "Honk if you love Jesus!" Almost all had the fish or dove symbol of the charismatic, either on the windows or the license plate.

Faith grabbed Stephen's arms and pulled herself close to him as they walked across the little bridge and up the concrete walkway to the chapel. This kind of display of affection was not for effect or occasion. They walked this way almost everywhere they went. Stephen loved it; Diana used never to get close to him. In fact, he couldn't ever remember Diana putting her arm around him. Others were strolling in the same way; this was one of the very appealing aspects of the life in the Kingdom— unabashed display of marital and "Agape" love—the Divine Love that charismatics all acquired as a result of the Baptism in the Holy Spirit.

"Hon, don't walk so straight. You look like you're full of pride."

"What?"

"Pride cometh before a fall."

"That's not biblical."

"Well, 'pride defileth a man.' It's 'wicked,' it's 'of the world,' it's 'of the devil,' it 'comes from the heart,' it 'hardens the mind,' it is 'hateful to Christ,' it is 'hateful to God'"

"Good grief," Stephen interrupted. "Just because I walk erect? That is pride? I've always walked straight, shoulders back. I was brought up to stand erect. Five years in the Marine Corps, drilling, an officer. What do you expect me to do? Slouch around? Is that what Christians are supposed to do? Wear ashes and sack cloth and slouch around? I don't see Oral or Richard, or Kenneth Copeland—any of those guys doing that!"

"Honey. Think about it. Examine yourself. Ask God to remove every last bit of sinful pride from you. Pride was the greatest sin. That's what God's greatest creation, the angel Lucifer, developed when he formed the rebellion in Heaven and as a result was cast out, with a third of the angels who sided with him when he tried to put himself above God. He and they, ya' know, became Satan and demons. You have got to get right with God!"

Stephen seethed. He never won at this sort of thing. Never even held his own. When Faith got something in her craw—forget it!

Matt and Leah spotted them and all exchanged the customary round of hugs and kisses. Matt was a nice enough guy, a former minister now turned carpenter-evangelist. Stephen never could get a conversation going with him, though. Maybe he was intimidated by Stephen; maybe his prideful military bearing made Matt feel enlisted or something.

Leah was a walking, living tape recording. She seemed to go on and off, even in mid sentence, talking in a stream-of-consciousness which passed for conversation and was so interspersed with Scripture that it was hard to tell what she was saying or meant. Stephen had written her off as so weird as to be avoided, which he did as politely as he could. She had the habit of putting her face right up to the person's she was talking to (possibly indicating myopia) which Stephen couldn't stand from anyone. That, and her thick scandinavian accent, plus her prophesying at the drop of a hat and telling you—especially Stephen, it seemed— what God was telling her to tell him, just drove Stephen up the wall. But, he tried not to let these feelings get the best of him; instead, he prayed under his breath in tongues and asked the Lord to give him the patience he needed to endure her onslaught. The fact that she still wore her hair in an outmoded bee-hive style, as so many of the charismatics persisted in doing, only made her the more obnoxious in Stephen's eyes.

Faith and Leah immediately enmeshed themselves in a rapid repartée that made them oblivious of everything else. They got seats about ten rows from the front, dead center, the talking women together between the two men, which was a relief to Stephen.

The chapel never ceased to fill Stephen with awe. Architecturally it was a marvel; esthetically it was, too, if you like stark unadorned, functional modern. It was filling up rapidly. The turnout here was always a full house, packed to the functional rafters. The class of attendee was a touch higher than at the Businessmens' breakfast that morning and at some of the other Spirit-filled churches around the area. These people were a bit better dressed, even if they still wore fifty dollar polyester suits and wide pastel neckties. At least there were not so many broad-butted middle-aged women with flabby cellulite under their upper arms squeezed into skin-tight shorts and tee shirts, their tummies protruding so you weren't sure whether it was obesity or pregnancy. No, these people made some effort toward decent appearance. Probably a bit more affluent overall and able to give generously when called upon — which called upon they would surely be!

After the usual milling about and the Holy Kisses and embraces and general camaraderie, a hush began to settle over the place and stirrings on stage began to augur the anticipated event. This was not to be a

47

particularly spectacular night, it was just a warm-up for the big show tomorrow over in the television studio where the full orchestra and the singers and the backdrops and the stage and the cutaway set and all were being readied at the very moment. Not all the big guns would be brought out. No, this was just a simple praise and-prayer for the faithful. Oral himself would be here and his anointed son, Richard, who was a handsome chip off the old block, and his new wife, Stephanie . . . all would certainly make the evening worthwhile. Worthwhile both prayer-wise for the faithful and money-wise for Oral. His disarming pitch, which would come at the appropriate time later on in the program, was bound to touch the heart strings and the purse strings of the attentive flock. As Richard broke into the first song with his rich baritone amid enthusiastic applause, Stephen's thoughts drifted to that earlier half-hearted attempt of his to see if he couldn't land a professorship in the TV department at the "university," sort of as a bargaining chip with KXAO at the time. He'd always wanted to teach and certainly had the credentials in this area, including a masters degree in communications from Columbia. *He recollected how the question of his divorce had arisen as a central issue, though, and how he had had to submit an essay explaining his actions for the Board of Regents' approval. He had stood on Scripture—à la Jimmy Swaggart. But, he had not pursued the matter when the KXAO offer had materialized, so he had no idea what the Regents' decision had been. Except that less than a year later, Richard Roberts himself —Oral's and God's own blessed son in whom 'they were well pleased'—up and announced his own divorce! And, shock upon shock, turned around and three months later married Stephanie! Wow! Talk about a quick revision of theology! Bet the Board of Regents crapped in their pants! Stephen unintentionally allowed a cynical smile to creep across his face. But that sure hadn't harmed Oral's ministry —or ORU—or Richard's and Stephanie's new joint ministry.* "Lord, You surely blessed them. They are all truly walking with You. They've received more than the hundred-fold blessing. You sure didn't hold divorce against them ! So, I'm going to stand on that— that You don't hold that against Faith or me. I proclaim in Your Name that You do not hold our divorces—neither Faith's nor mine—against us, either in our ministry, in our work, or in our investments. Thank You, Lord. Amen."

There was no rush to leave; it was more of a general reluctance for it all to be over. People stood up and chatted with those around them, others wandering to other parts of the chapel, grabbing hands, embracing, kissing, like one big family. True fellowship. Matt and Leah straggled out like the rest, hailing those they knew, exchanging pleasantries and inanities. Outside, the cool summer air filled their nostrils with faint wisps of daffodils from somewhere. The lighting on the building facades created a picture-book atmosphere, unreal yet so satisfying. When they reached the parking area, Stephen suggested they all go down Lewis to Braum's and have ice cream cones, figuring that would be a good enough spot and reason to part company from.

It was not yet eleven-thirty when they split, so Stephen drove back via the hill behind ORU, a favorite spot of his and Faith's. When they reached the crest and got out to walk, it was just as they knew it would be. The glow of downtown Tulsa straight north on the horizon, the ORU campus, now beginning to darken, immediately below them to their left. They entwined themselves and strolled a way down the road in silence, taking in the absolute beauty and tranquility of the night. The few clouds reflected the lights from the city below them while the space between them seemed illuminated almost as brightly by the millions and millions of stars that shone through the clear, black sky above.

"Honey? Wasn't that great tonight?" Faith finally whispered softly. Stephen knew it needed no reply. "You know? God's done a mighty work with brother Oral . . . and with Richard, too. And, it didn't come

49

over night. It took him eighteen years just to get started . . . just to get around to doing what God had been telling him to do. And, now his son is following in his footsteps. That's what I want to happen to my ministry. I want to build this vision God has given me and I want someone to follow after me to carry it on. Maybe it'll be Philip. I know he's not mature yet but I know he's got a true calling from God on his life. I feel it."

They turned and headed back to the car. Stephen knew it was his role to listen, to let her talk it all out.

"Honey, you know God has called me to this ministry to the prisoners. And, I know He has given me special powers to reach them with the Word and bring them into the Kingdom. I know it. I just know it down deep. It's all I want to do . . . and I must do it!"

"Go to it, Sweetie," came Stephen's transparently less than sincere response. He realized it and immediately gave her a squeeze lest she pick up on it and start the usual challenge that he was not in total sympathy with her calling and ministry. "I'll help you in any way, you know that."

"You love me, Steve?"

" 'Course I do—you know I do . . . ," he segued right into it, bending down on one knee, Jolson style, right arm back and forth from chest to outstretched. "Gimme, gimme, what I cry for. You got the kinda kisses that I'd die for . . . ," really belting it out into the still night air. "Fai-thy, Fai-thy! How I love ya'! How I love ya . . . my dear, young Fai thy..the world will know—that even down in ORU I love you . . . "

"You nut," Faith chuckled.

It was well after midnight when they parked back at the apartment. Instinctively they strolled the long way around by the pool, which was at the crest of the little hilltop and right on the edge. The small clubhouse hovered directly above with its large, dark picture window staring in blind dumbness. There were some low shrubbery lights and the underwater pool lights were still on. There was not a soul around.

"This is almost as pretty as up on the hill," volunteered Stephen, calculating his next move. "Why don't we take a dip? Want to skinny dip?"

" And get caught? No way! You can get your suit on. I'll just sit here a while. I don't think I'll go in . . . and, bring me a Diet Pepsi, will you, Hon?"

Stephen skulked off into the darkness back to the apartment to change. He really wanted to go in the water, it was a kind of muggy night and he hadn't changed all day. He slipped into some loose jogging trunks with no supporter, got two cans out of the refrigerator and went back to the pool.

At first he didn't see Faith. "Hi," came her voice from a dark area on the opposite side. She was in the water. He descended the wide steps into the cool water holding the cans at shoulder height as he waded and floated over to her. He handed her a Pepsi. "Did you take your dress off?"

She propelled herself upward to show, "Nope. It needs washing anyway."

"You're something else, Faith Chapelle-Trevelyan" Her skirt floated outspread near the surface as she bobbed down again, careful to keep her hair dry. As she did, Stephen reached out to grab at her panties, only to touch bare skin . . . much to his delight! "Aha! There must be a purpose in that!"

Faith placed the can on the edge of the pool and put both hands behind his neck, gently kicking her feet through the water until she could wrap her legs around his hips in a fluid motion, pulling her body close to his. "What cha' gonna do now, Mister?" she challenged teasingly.

Before Stephen could put his soft drink on the edge, too, Faith had slipped her hand up his leg into his crotch. "Hah! Looks like you were ready for something, too!" In this state of buoyancy, she deftly eased him inside her and pulled herself tight against him, looking into his face with a broad, knowing grin, delighting now to watch the expressions of ecstasy as they rippled across Stephen's face. They floated locked together and gently undulating in this suspended fashion out into the center of the pool. "I guess this is what the Bible means when it says they will become as one flesh," he whispered as if there were anyone to hear them.

Then, as the spasmodic moment overcame him and subsided, she floated away and he turned to chase her through the water, grabbing playfully at her bare bottom until they reached shallow water. He grabbed her in an embrace as they stood waist deep, pressing her groin into him with a hand firmly placed on her smooth buns.

"Ho, ho! Old man. Can't get it up again, can you?"

"Just you wait!"

As she climbed out of the pool she was even more erotic. The wet cloth clung to her nude body which was only faintly illuminated by the soft reflections bouncing off the ripples of the water in the pool and now off the puddles collecting beneath her.

"Wow. Aphrodite in her nightie!" chortled Stephen. "Whoops! Take it back. No pagan goddess, you. The woman at the well? No, she didn't get wet." He searched his mind for a biblical reference. "OK, so Debbie Reynolds in Singing in the Rain. No, that was Gene Kelly who got wet. Will you settle for Bo Derek?"

"Silly! You better get your mind back on the Lord."

Chapter 4   Alpha & Omega TV

Channel 21, KXAO-TV, was located in a small industrial park in Broken Arrow, primarily because the rent was a lot cheaper than adjacent Tulsa and it was a short straight microwave shot for the signal from the studio with no hops from the transmitter and the dish on the roof to the one on the tower eight miles away.

The station was not very impressive compared to the secular networks and indy stations in Tulsa—and couldn't hold a candle to ORU's nationwide TV operation.   The temporary sign with the call letters, channel number and "TV for Christ" was weathering badly. Even the gold stick-on letters from K-Mart on the window were peeling. It was, when you got right down to it, shabby.   Most of the so-called Christian television stations that were springing up around the country looked pretty much the same. Make-do situations with inadequate funds to operate properly, or make-overs of failed stations with inadequate funds to operate. They operated on faith, faith that the faithful Christian viewers out there would be donating generously. It was always hand-to-mouth, bailing wire and a "prayer" to get into the next month.   To Christians—at least to Charismatic Christians who seemed to be the group specially ordained by God and the Holy Spirit in these End Times to spread the Gospel through the visual air waves rather than the

Christian pioneers of radio—looks and surroundings didn't really matter. The only thing that did was getting the message out into the homes to counteract the secular humanism and the sin and pornography—and anti Christ-ness—of commercial networks.

It pained Stephen to think about it—the situation at channel 21. *Never enough money to operate right, even to keep the signal on the air most of the time. The crummy, second-hand, out-dated electronic equipment constantly having to be patched together. And, the staff and crew—bless 'em—doing their best, dumb and happy 'in the Lord,' most working below minimum wage, volunteering more hours than scheduled. Qualified for food stamps, their zeal to spread God's Word driving them on . . . knowing and confessing that their 'God shall supply all their needs according to His riches in Glory in Christ Jesus! Hallelujah!'*

Stephen felt the pinch as well. He had reluctantly accepted, after much prayer (and having virtually burned his bridges behind him), what he now considered a token salary of $25,000 a year—one-sixth of what he had been making on Madison Avenue. And, that with a final twist he realized now of the petard by brother Felix Toombs, Chairman of the Board, with whom he had principally negotiated. What with the drains by Faith to underwrite her ministry and the child support (he had generously given the house to Diana and everything in it), it pretty well dictated his present life style. The small apartment, burgers at Braum's. He had also shared his profit sharing from the agency with Diana, but with the investments in the wells taking a chunk out of what remained, things were awfully tight.

He walked through the glass doored entrance into a room that served as reception, with the phone system on a rickety desk, donated by one of the 'faithful,' and general catch all. An assortment of other tables and odd pieces of furniture filled the remaining space, every flat surface piled with stacks of papers, most waiting to be collated and mailed out in the never-ending drive for donations.

"Morning, brother Steve. The Lord bless ya' over the weekend?"

"Just like always, Praise God! Any messages?"

Taking the handful, he walked down the narrow plasterboard hallway to his office near the control room. Lydia Godsey, his secretary, Girl Friday—more like Monday through!—confidante, buddy, confessor, booster, chider, friend and indispensable ingredient holding the whole operation together, intercepted him.

"How'd the Businessmen's breakfast go?"

"You know how it went. As Always. I was simply great. No doubt I'll be one of the greatest prophets of this generation . . . singled out on that day when Jesus comes back in the air and all the world sees Him—on TV—Channel 21, of course!" There was nothing sexual at all in the kind of banter they carried on although it sometimes raised eyebrows around the station. Lydia had a husband and kids and they all went to the same fellowship, that of brother John Mark Fisher's Fishers of Men Fellowship. It was just a plain old comfortable, honest relationship with mutually engendered loyalty. "Oh, oh! There goes that doggoned pride again. Think God will ever humble me?"

"He will. You just wait and see."

"Gosh, you sound more like Faith every day. Sometimes I forget whether I'm at the office or at home. Hard to keep you two straight. Gotta remember, she's the brunette, you're the blond."

"Well, you're either on a high for the Lord or you've been popping pills. Better keep my eye on you. Bind those demons."

"What's the glitch report for the weekend? We stay on the air much?" Stephen, now seated, checking his calendar for the day's appointments, inquired half-heartedly, fearing the usual.

"Transmitter off four times, once for two hours. Saturday. And you couldn't be located. Six spots lost besides those during off-air, bad tape transfers or our quad is finally on its last leg. Shall I schedule it for 'last rites'?"

"If you can find a Charismatic Catholic priest who will buy us a new one after he administers Extreme Unction. You know, that two-inch quad machine was sounding its death rattle when we bought it from that used equipment outfit."

"Two spots screwed up. Never got on the air. This is a problem between sales and traffic—and engineering. It's either mislabeling the boxes or the reels. I don't know, but you've got your hands full trying to get that one straight. Only other thing . . . things: the soft drink kitty got filched. Certainly not by one of our crowd. Then, of course, brother Bobbie Joe is furious. He claims someone changed all of the lighting in the studio before his show and his crew didn't have time to reset. 'Course, they came in a half hour before air time."

"Curses! Can't production work that out with their crews? Do I always have to wet nurse 'em?" He lowered his head into his hands, waiting for the rest, dispiritedly reciting an old refrain, "If only we had some real professional people, could pay them decently, and do something that didn't always come off like a high school play in the sticks."

"Oh joy, oh rapture. You've got to start planning for the telethon. And, you'll be happy to remember, there is a board meeting Thursday."

"You sure the Bible doesn't allow drinking? You know, for situations like this?"

"Drink in His Word. Pray in tongues. Ask for peace . . . and the answers. Corinthians 10: God will not let you be put through trials more than you are able to bear— He will give you a way of escape."

"Lydia, you know how I feel about that passage. It's been mistranslated so much by you King James people that you miss the point," he said good naturedly, disguising some irritation.

She tuned out, having gone through this before. Her mind was made up; she was confident in her understanding.

"I've looked that word 'temptation' up in the original greek," he pressed, "and it means just that, temptation, just like sexual temptation. It doesn't mean trials and tribulations. One day I'll tell you what I think the 'way out of it' is. You will be mildly shocked."

"One last thing. Brother John Mark might not be able to host the midday show today. You might have to stand in. The guests are some evangelists from Antlers."

"Just great! Get a bunch of music tapes racked up. We've got to have something for our forty-six viewers out there!"

"Oh, ye of little faith," she chided as she turned to leave. She had been detecting a tone of bitterness creeping into Stephen lately. She'd turned it over to her prayer group and had interceded for him often in her own prayers. Certainly the station's daily prayer warriors were holding him up, too. Maybe the challenge and spark were going out of him. Could hardly blame him, what with the sloppy operation and the running battle with the board.

Stephen watched her leave. Lydia was full figured, tall, big boned—statuesque, if it weren't for her abundant *avoirdupois*. About twenty-five pounds too *pois*. *Why were there so many good Christians so overweight, preachers especially? They can fight the pride and the temptation, except when it comes to food. The proverbial sin of gluttony. Or, maybe in her case it's menopausal. She's his own age. Four children. He guessed that women just began to retain water and more cellulite around that age. Funny; not anyone in his family, nor Diana. Just as slim and tall as ever, still wearing some old skirts she had at Duke. Faith will probably bloat up; her mother was that way. It's all in the genes, as they say.* As Stephen's mind wandered in these thoughts, Lydia's head reappeared around the door frame.

"All right. I'm curious. You keep telling me about that passage from First Corinthians 10 . . . that you're going to tell me what it really means. So?"

Stephen could not restrain a smile . . . one with a bit of undisguised lasciviousness. "You sure you want to know? It might embarrass you."

"Well, well," she said, detecting something temptingly forbidden and closing the door behind her and taking a stance a few feet from his desk.

"Gosh," Stephen flushed, "This embarrasses me a little, too."

Lydia's eyebrows raised. She was all-attentive.

"Uh. Let's see. The word temptation . . . means just that. Sexual temptation."

"And, 'the way out'?" queried his secretary.

"Masturbation," he responded, studying her eyes intently for her reaction.

Lydia studied her boss for a few seconds. "And? How do you figure that?"

"Well, my dear Lydia, that term . . . masturbation . . . is a fact of life. It is an activity of both male and female of the species—and the lower primates . . . if you have ever been to the monkey cage at the zoo."

Lydia drew herself up defensively but made no attempt to conclude the explanation or to leave. She waited for Stephen to continue.

"Now, if one accepts that the functions of the human body are God-given . . . masturbation seems to be a rather natural one . . . just like copulation. I would venture to observe that the prohibitions against it are man-made . . . man-imposed . . . Church-imposed. Certainly in the

58

Catholic church where young boys are frightened into believing that they will end up going blind if they engage in it—or grow hair on their palms. Probably because the faggot priests get their jollies telling 'em about it—or thinking about it—then going off and doing it to themselves! Hah!"

"Stephen. How can you? The Bible forbids things like that . . . fornication . . . and . . . and . . . Onanism . . . isn't that what it's called?"

"Hate to punch the balloon on that one, my dear Lydia. No, the Bible says nothing specifically about—or against—masturbation. Many preachers, priests and evangelists try to stretch scripture and interpret certain passages to mean that Christians are not to play with themselves. And . . . this little story in the Old Testament about that hapless fellow, Onan! That is a real stretch to try to interpret his encountering a harlot on the side of the road and prevailing on her to have his way with her—then, before ejaculating inside her—I hope I am not offending you, Lydia — he withdraws and spews his semen upon the ground. And, God admonished him for 'spilling his seed upon the ground.' That, to me, is *coitus interruptus* . . . which, I think, was the original form of birth control. In fact, petting—heavy petting—like teenagers do . . . or used to do. Guess they do a bit more than just pet nowadays. Petting is *foreplay interruptus*, so to speak. Heck, the French . . . a lot of cultures do that . . . and it amounts to mutual masturbation. Better that than pregnancy! Furthermore, how do you think men can stand being away from their wives or girl friends, off on adventures, on ships, in wars . . . without, as the Scripture says, 'without a way out of temptation'? You know, men can't go for too long a time without some sexual relief. It's just the way God made us. I suppose women can't either, for that matter." Observing her reaction, he continued, "Of course, Faith does not share my interpretation. Have I convinced you?"

Lydia pursed her lips and feigned annoyance. "What a thing to be saying to a Christian woman—Lady! You ought to be ashamed of yourself, Stephen Trevelyan!" she concluded, struggling to stifle a smile.

Stephen raised one eyebrow in an unmistakable stage leer and he watched her turn and exit.

Charlie Goodpaster appeared at his door. "What we gonna do, boss? Lost nine spots over the weekend. For us, that's a lot of bread! Yea, and I know we can't live by bread alone, don't say it!"

"What can I say, brother? Got any ideas how you can get your department and traffic and engineering to coordinate so these stupid foul-ups don't happen? What'd we lose?"

"Three PIs, coupla car dealers and that new sports store account. You know, it's hard enough for us to get 'em—then, to goof 'em away! We'll run make-goods but it sure don't make our clients happy to watch their spots go down the tube, especially in the sports block."

"I know, Charlie. You think this thing will ever work? One foot in the Christian world, one foot in the commercial world?"

"You know how I feel, Steve. I'm as good a child of the Kingdom as the next. But, when we don't got the numbers, we don't got the business!"

"Tell me! Tell the board ! We're schizo! Trying to be an electronic church winning the lost out there to Christ and, at the same time, a wholesome, family station bringing programs into your living room that you won't be embarrassed for your kids to see. But, they are all ancient, cast-off reruns. Who's really watching 'em? Don't you get fed up with some of the goody-two-shoes crap sometimes yourself? Sorry, Charlie. I think it's getting to me."

"Yea, some programs. Who wants to watch all this black and white stuff anyway? Do we really know if there is anybody out there watching? We don't even show up in the ratings. How's my Sales department gonna sell if we don't got no numbers?"

"Charlie, that's a thorn in my side worse than Paul's. We just haven't got the money to promote like we ought to. We need newspaper ads every day. Billboards—dozens of 'em. Mail-outs, door-to-door. Where's the money coming from? We're running in the red each month as it is. All we need is PSE&G to cut our power off, and you know I plead with them every month. If Doc's brother-in-law weren't director, we'd be dark now."

Stephen admired Charlie. *He was a pretty straight-forward sort of guy. Knew his business; sold time for a radio station for years. Probably felt like he himself did: wished it could be a more professional operation, one professional to another. The rest of the staff had never been in broadcasting, except for some of the kids who worked camera over at Oral's studio. Nobody else knew the difference. God, he thought, this is one long way from Madison Avenue!*

"Sorry, Charlie. It's on the agenda again for the board meeting, but unless some miracle—the Hand of God reaching down and plunking a couple of hundred grand on this desk—I can't offer much hope. How're the agency buys?"

"Pretty shaky. Even the cartoon strips aren't keeping ratings above a 'one.' We need something like Little House on the Prairie against the network news."

"Got five thou an episode? Star Trek at least pulls the male audience."

"Too bad we don't have a large enough black market—black market, hah! You know what I mean, negro-black, like the markets back east so's we could run Jeffersons and Sanford & Son. They bring in the numbers, never mind whether its a target income market. Oh well, I'll just wait for your miracle . . . unless the rapture comes first. In which case, don't look for me!"

Stephen closed his door, hoping to cut down on the incessant parade in and out of his office. *'What office?'* he thought to himself. *'I've come this far in life, to give up career and family to serve the Lord, and He gives me this hole-in-the-wall, with no windows? Forgive me, Father. Pride again, I suppose.'* *But, as his eyes took in his surroundings, he could not help but think of his palatial— by contrast—office at 488 Madison Avenue. He had just made senior vice president and maybe had a shot at the top. Then the born-again experience and the luster of advertising began to tarnish. Advertising was no longer so stimulating, no longer such a challenge, or at least one that seemed so worthwhile. Giving his whole life and energy to a box of soap powder or headache pills . . . or anti-freeze. It was getting hard to even recall the accounts any more. And, the commuting had begun to take a real toll on him. Was that on account of his new attitude? His new walk with the Lord then that tended to make the commercial world ugly? He had hacked out a pretty good life for Diana and the kids, at least he had provided more than the basic necessities. A colonial house as expensive as any others in a fashionable neighborhood. Gloria and Michael had gone to good sub-prep schools and would be headed for Ivy League universities. So, it wasn't all bad. Or, was it? Certainly the charismatic experience had made him see things differently and he had tried to share it with Diana and even with the kids, but they were too young. None of them had bought it. Then, after a year, with a personality change that was even commented upon at the agency, he had made that fateful decision. Cast off the secular career at, perhaps, its height and head a Christian television station so he could do God's work. He had made sure, first, that he had maneuvered what he thought was a good position as General Manager here before committing and he confidently expected that it was God's calling for him to turn the station around—even though the salary was an insult—but it was what the board considered top scale until the station got on its feet, so to speak. No contract, just good faith and a handshake. Fortunately, Stephen's agency profit sharing fund was fully vested and he could let what was left after sharing it with Diana carry him over his initial adjustment. Diana's reaction, if he had stopped to consider, was the least that could have been expected. She was shocked and would have none of it. She had been acutely aware of the change in Stephen, but, just as Stephen failed to anticipate her reaction (perhaps because he really didn't want to), she failed to anticipate his. The proverbial breakdown in communications at this stage of so many marriages; thirteen years and they were total strangers. Trite but true.*

His train of thought was interrupted by a knock, followed by the door opening a crack. Rebecca, the midday live show producer, stuck her head in. "Hear you got the show today. Anything I should know?"

"You tell me . . . I'll just wing it. Gimme some background on these people and be sure I have accurate cutaway cues to music."

"Will do. You got ten minutes."

Is there ever going to be any way to do these things right? Too much to handle. Have to 'wing' everything. Trouble is, the viewers not only don't detect it they could care less anyway.

He went by what passed for the men's room and dressing room and combed his slightly graying hair, straightened his tie and pulled on his coat. His thoughts now turned to the program. He counted on the Holy Spirit's inspiring him with something, even if it only came as the camera lights came on. He was introduced to Brother Andrew and Sister Margaret in the studio as Rebecca filled him in on their ministry and went over the cues with him. She produced this and a few other tidbits and was also otherwise back-up typist, collator, sometime traffic stand-in and anything else that needed doing.

The guests had been seated on the double sofa to the right of the emcee's chair, and a crewman was adjusting their lavalière mikes, which in eight—no, nine—out of ten times failed to work properly. The set was ersatz living room, decorated in non-nondescript cast off. Stephen chided himself for being so harsh. It was just a matter of taste—his against a lack of any. No, the furniture had been donated by some furniture outfit whose owner claimed to be in the brotherhood and had donated it during one of the telethons. The thing that saves every set the crew tries valiantly to create is the foliage, fake foliage. If it weren't for the potted plants the set would resemble a bus station waiting room. Even though they never got the same ones in the same place two days in a row—or the dime store pictures on the walls either, for that matter. Having spent a life-time dealing in the perfection of television commercials and advertisements on the national level in New York with its painstaking design, and casting, and shooting, this all seemed like amateurs'-ville. Of course, a hundred thousand for a thirty-second commercial does make a difference, he reminded himself.

So, make the best of it, he thought as he adjusted the tiny mike onto his lapel.

"One minute!" someone shouted.

'Darn! Will they never learn to give me three-, two-, one-countdowns?'

Stephen sat forward and said in a commanding voice, "Let us pray." As he did so, he grasped the hand of the guest nearest him, who did the same to the others. The studio hushed, all eyes closed, at first anyway. "Father, we just come to you this day in humility and love of You, Father. And, we just ask that You bless this program this day which we hold up to You. And, we ask Your guidance and that You will direct our words so that they are the words You would have us to utter. (*The thought streaked across his mind that he was beginning to talk like them now, or was it just a growing affectation?*) Let Your Word go out over this, Your TV channel, to do the work that You have foreordained that it do this day. And, in the Name of Your precious Son, Jesus, I now bind Satan and all his demons and forbid them, in the Name of Jesus, from coming against us during this program. I forbid them to tie our tongues or our thoughts or to cause any technical difficulties that would interfere with Your Word. In Jesus' Name. And, I loose us from all things that would hinder us in our mission and I loose the powers of Heaven. "

64

"Ten . . . nine . . . eight . . . " Stephen looked over at the monitor as the title, "Midday Message" faded up on the screen with a radiant sun behind it, music under, and the announcer's voice welcoming the faithful viewers to the program . . . "and now to the host"— Cue!

"Praise God! Glad you all are with us out there today. We have a good program for you, two interesting guests whose ministry down in Antlers you'll want to hear about. Remember, we have telephone counselors standing by to receive your calls. Just call the number you see at the bottom of your screen and one of our staff or our volunteers will be glad to pray with you, talk to you, bless you . . . or whatever you need at this moment of your life. Now, I want to say something to you folks out there who might not know just what we are talking about," he confided, leaning forward as the shot tightened on his face. "If there is anyone out there right now listening to my voice . . . to this program . . . who would like to have a personal relationship with Jesus Christ. Who might be going through personal troubles right this minute, maybe there was a death of a loved one, a child on drugs, things just piling up so much you can't handle them any more. Whatever it is. Maybe you just have an empty feeling about life; you know there is something missing. Let me tell you how to find what is missing. The Word of God says, 'For all have sinned and fallen short of the Glory of God.' See? It's not just you. But, the Lord is 'quick to forgive.' He sent His only begotten Son that we might not perish but have life, and that abundantly. That's cause He loves you ! God loves each and every one of us. You think nobody cares about you? God does! And, you know how easy it is to get into right relationship with Him? Simple. Do just what I tell you right now as I am talking to you on the TV set in your home or wherever you are. Say after me, 'Father God in Heaven . . . I confess that I am a sinner . . . But, I am sorry . . . If you will forgive me and accept me as a child of yours in the Kingdom, I will repent of my evil ways and turn to You from

65

here on out . . .   I know You sent Jesus down here on earth to show us the way to You . . . and, as a sacrifice for our sins . . . to wipe them away. I believe on Your Son, Jesus . . . and ask Him to come into my heart and dwell there forever . . .   I have faith that He is my brother now and that I . . . have been reborn into the Kingdom of Heaven on earth and . . . I am a new creation in Christ Jesus . . . Born Again. Hallelujah!' "

The shot widened and Stephen addressed his unseen audience: "Welcome to the Kingdom, you brothers and sisters out there who just accepted Christ.   Now, you just telephone the station—that number right down there at the bottom of your screen—and one of our counselors will talk to you more about it and tell you how to start growing now in the Lord.   You know, He doesn't want you to just sit back now and pat yourself on the back. You gotta learn and grow as a baby Christian into maturity and be able to tell others about the glory of your new life in Christ.   Call that number, now!   We'll be back to meet our guests after the Archers tell us in song, "How Great It Is!"

Chapter 5   Coven of Witches

The sound of soft sobbing penetrated Stephen's subconsciousness. He turned and buried the other side of his head in the pillow, groggy between asleep and awake. He kept his eyes closed, hoping to drop back off to sleep. His sleep had been fitful lately; it was no use. He glanced at the illuminated digits on the alarm-radio. 3:10 a.m.! Bending his knee, he put his foot over to where Faith should be. Empty. He was used to it; she was talking to God in the dark living room. Knowing the pattern, he awaited the transition into tongues, hoping it would not be protracted this night so that he might fall back and get some rest. If she didn't sleep, he usually didn't, and he would be hopelessly insomniac until dawn.

The characteristic sounds in her word-like cadence always seemed rote to him, whereas when his tongues came, he never knew what to expect. His followed no predictable cycles. From the living room hers became louder with apparent anguish and then subsided into a sing-song melody that her voice carried sweetly. It lulled him back to sleep.

"Hon, wake up." The edge of the bed dipped with the weight of her body, almost rolling him off. He popped up wide awake.

"OK, what'd He tell you?"

Ignoring the slight derision or missing it entirely, Faith launched into it. "It's witches ! The whole coven!"

Stephen had become inured to it; perhaps he no longer bought it. "You're gonna attack Satan's kingdom, huh?"

"Don't make fun. You know the consequences." She stood and began pacing in the darkness. The glow from the breaking dawn outside the window silhouetted her alluringly in her short, filmy summer nightgown. The thought that flashed across his still unclear mind was quickly dismissed; *that would be a disastrous bit of mistiming,* he told himself and settled in for phase two, *'What God has now called His faithful and true servant, Faith, to do to combat the forces of the devil in this wicked world!'*

"Honey, it's been on my mind for some time and now I know why. You know the village of witches south of St. Augustine that I was telling you about? Casa Dega? Well, that's where coven after coven of witches are. I was praying in tongues for the Holy Spirit to give me His direction—to tell me what it was that has been troubling me for a couple of days now—and it came to me clear as can be. Wipe out Casa Dega and the entire southeastern part of the United States will be loosed from the grip of witchcraft!"

This stunned Stephen. Of all the things to come up with! He suppressed a desire to laugh but wisely kept his cool.

"Hon. God told me that that was the key. I've got to obey! I'm going to take Leah and Rachel and maybe Miriam, and we'll leave in the van as soon as we can. We shouldn't be gone more'n a week. Might stop by Pensacola and see mama on the way back. Or go up through Texarkana if the others feel the leading and preach to the prisoners, too." She picked up the phone.

"You're not going to call at this hour? What time is it?"

"It's six," she reported matter-of-factly, dialing a number. A pause, then, "Leah! Guess what? God just told me we're to go to Casa Dega! . . . Casa Dega, near St. Augustine . . . where the witchcraft controls Florida, Georgia, Alabama and who knows? . . . "

68

Stephen pulled himself wearily out of bed and headed for the bathroom. Might as well get an early start. No telling when she'd get off the phone.

Rock Weller waved his big, burley hand from the booth at the rear of the restaurant as he spotted Stephen come through the door.

"Howdy, brother," he hailed, struggling to get his husky frame up so as to give the proper charismatic hug. His big western hat stayed on his head the whole time, as well as during lunch, as was the custom. The rest of his outfit was westernized work clothes, checkered shirt with rolled-up sleeves, jeans, western belt and Dingo work boots rather than true western style. "The Lord a treatin' ya' good?"

"Jes' blessin' mor'n I can handle," Stephen retorted good-naturedly mimicking Rock's genuine colloquial accent.

They both scanned the menu, exchanging small bits of information about wives, how the station was doing, the upcoming Camp Meeting. They ordered and Stephen got right to the point.

"What's the story on Genesis?"

"W e e l l l . . . ," Rock dragged out . . . "In the beginning God created the heavens and the earth." This brought a groan from Stephen. "Into the latter of which, the earth, He put a bunch of this here oil and gas . . . knowing that in the latter times you and me—His faithful servants Peter Rock Weller and his brother Stephen Trevelyan—was a going to find it . . . and live like ol' Abraham with all the cattle on a thousand hills. It's already writ in the Book of Life that you'n me's His faithful servants and He's given us the hundred-fold return." It was Rock's way to get into serious things with a light, whimsical touch. His 'country bumpkin' facade masked a mind with a steel grip that matched his determination. Stephen had great respect for him and regarded his brother-in-the-Lord as nobody's fool.

"Well, how come I haven't seen that hundred-fold return yet?"

"Patience, brother Steve. The Lord's timing is not our timing."

"Yeah, His ways are not our ways, our thoughts are not His thoughts. Believe and it shall be given you . . . Let's get down to it. What's the situation?"

"We gotta keep the faith. Right? Well . . . " and he leaned back, tilting the brim of his hat back a bit. "Don't rightly know Steve. You know what the drilling engineer did completin' 'em. He estimated they'd be pumping ten, fifteen barrels, didn't he?" Stephen nodded in agreement. "Then Sooner messed around and didn't get their line hooked up for months—should have been two weeks! So, in the meantime, where there should have been a holdup of pressure there was watering. Man, you cain't tell about them formations. They're fragile down there . . . and we jist cain't go down there eighteen hundred feet in them holes and see what's wrong. We never did get ten barrels outta any of the oil wells."

"How come? Frac'ing? Cementing? Formation? What do you think?"

"Dunno. On the next batch, I'm gonna git this guy Bobby Howse. He's a big engineer type. Worked on the big stuff along the coast, before that, over in the Anadarko. He's been telling me the Genesis wells was completed badly."

"I thought as much. But, what can we do?"

"Well, I ought to have done the dang completion myself. You know, brother, when I   do it, it gits done right! Cain't count on these guys, they don't know their . . . " catching himself, " . . . way around their own britches! Most of 'em."

"So, what do we do? Make another assessment? The investors aren't going to take that. You know who these people are, the little

70

guys . . . ministers, evangelists, Logos and ORU people. They shouldn't have gotten in."

"Look, they knew what they was gittin' into. They was supposed to have read the prospectus; they should'a known what a Limited Partnership was. They was only two thousand a unit!"

"Yeah. But most of them didn't qualify financially . . . dipped into life's savings."

"Hey, they heard from God! Had one tell me he'd let me know how many units he'd take after he prayed. Called me back and said God told him to take four! That was probably all his savings. But, God told him, he had faith and figured that was how God was going to provide the means for his ministry. That was what most of 'em figured. And, that's what's happened to a lot of 'em—not with our wells, but, a lot of 'em's got a good income coming in from a bunch of little wells scattered around."

"Then, maybe there's still a chance for ours?"

"Could be. I ain't sayin'. We've got enough people praying over 'em. Let's just leave it to Him upstairs. But, He'd better hurry, the water haul-off's costing us eighty to a hundred dollars a well—a day !"

"Was that because we didn't have a heat treater? And no extra holding tank for after they were treated?"

Rock was waxing a bit irritated at this kind of quizzing by Stephen, even though he knew it was right on. "Yep. When we turned the wells off, they reversed and came back four times as much water as oil."

"There was money enough in the original subscription for enough tanks, pumps and all, wasn't there? Then, how come they weren't there when they were needed?"

"You tell me, brother. The engineer was supposed to have all that stuff working. I was off on another project—cain't be everywhere at once't."

"How long you figure this oil bust to last? The boom sure did go ppffft overnight, didn't it?" said Stephen, abruptly changing the subject. He had wanted to discuss this with Rock for some time.

"Steve, I'll tell it to you straight. The 'boom' was one thing—we all rode high, right? Man, last January there was more'n sixteen hundred rigs working. Remember how we used to have to fight to schedule drilling? Everybody was a going great guns—that's when you and everyone else jumped on this here oil bandwagon. Ain't that right?"

"The great opportunity for the little guy," Stephen chided derisively.

"Well, why do you think that 'bust' came last March? Forty thousand new wells a year, hundreds of new companies popping up everywhere, investors coming out of the woodwork, price of oil going up to $27 a barrel. Why the bust? Answer—the majors didn't want us minors in the business, that's why! So, they got together and in collusion with the OPEC countries dropped the price. Right? Down to $21. . . then $18. Now around fifteen dollars. After windfall and other taxes and costs, it gits to the point that it's not that profitable to the investor anymore. So, that's why we had an oil glut—we was had , brother! The majors did it to us right up the ol' gingo! You know how many rigs are looking for work? Dozens! They're beggin' for work, and they've dropped their fees by half. Biggest driller in Tulsa laid off four hundred people. More'n a hundred so-called oil companies already gone belly-up here. Somebody told me nine hundred in Houston! Only a fool would invest in an oil program right now—a fool or a Spirit-filled Christian!"

"Yeah, it's like the depression of the '30s out here, except the people back east haven't heard. Maybe the news media are in cahoots with the big oil companies. So, you are saying we ought to plug 'em up and walk away?"

"Nope. Not at all, brother Steve. 'Cause here's the kicker—after the majors figured they'd screwed the little guys and driven us off, what d'ya think they're gonna do? Answer?   Come back at $40 a barrel! That's what it's all about.   Some people figure $60.   I've heard predictions of up to a hundred dollars a barrel a year after the glut is declared a no-glut.   Especially if I-ran and the Russians block the straights of . . . what's it? Hor mooz?"

"Hormuz," corrected Stephen.

"Yeah, Hor-mooz. See? The majors have driven the little guys off the land; they come back, gobble it all up and walk off with the whole deck—at a hundred dollars a barrel! And, they can afford to clean them up and get them back into production."

"Then . . . if we can hold on, even the small amount our fields can produce will be worth a fortune."

"You bet. And, when Reagan de-regulates the price of gas— even that will help our shallow wells."

"Never thought I'd be on the side of higher prices. Easy to see, when it means more in your own pocket. Poor consumer." Stephen had detected less of the Okie twang as Rock's enthusiasm had increased; he wondered how much of it was pure put-on. "So, in the long run, it looks pretty good . . . if we can hold out, right?"

"Right, brother. We've just got to keep the faith."

That was not the kind of faith Paul had been writing about in the Pastoral Letters, Stephen thought, but it was applicable maybe.   "OK, what about the Skiatook field?"

"That outta be a good one. Better formation. Oswego . . . all under that Indian land."

73

"Hope Faith and her prayer bunch bound and cast out all those lingerin' indian spirits!"

"Amen. Stuff don't look bad. You know what that will mean? Got any idea, Steve, what kinda dollars we're talking about? Even at twenty bucks? "

"You bet I do. And this field has to produce . . . or me and a whole lot of folks are really going to go down the drain!"

"Faith, brother, faith!"

"Easy for you. You're a general partner. It's all of us thirty-two limited partners who've put up the money for each of these wildcat, test wells. We're the ones who're going to be out— "

—"Or, in—big!"

"Hope so. But, look at what I've lost already on Genesis, if that's what's going to happen. Sixteen thousand! You know, each drilling report—and I was out there with you, I saw 'em come in—ten, twenty, thirty barrels. Million, million and a half cubit feet of gas. So, we all just kept investing in the next well and the next, just a countin' what we were going to have coming in! I figured ten, fifteen grand a month. So, I kept rolling on . . . then, when they didn't produce. Bam! The bottom dropped out! You think they were drilled too close? Or, was that field just no good?"

"What can I say? Only the Man up there knows. But, look'it, you're into the Logos field for what, twenty thou? I've got a good feeling that they're gonna produce real good. And, when they do, you're gonna forget Genesis. But listen, I ain't had a chance to tell you about the really big one. You know that lease I've told you about over in Logan county, just west of Stillwater?" Stephen nodded. "Well, ma-an, am I going to put together a drilling program that'l knock the ears off a mule! It's gonna be a biggie! Sixty-five hundred feet! Rotary mud—no more of this air drilling. You know, that land has been locked up in an estate for years; nobody's been able to lease it for drilling. Well, I've been working on it for three years . . . through a brother in the business over there. And, we got the executor to sign without having to go through public auction in court—don't ask me how! And, we're puttin' together a program of just fifteen, selected investors. Most of 'em are lined up; rich brothers, too."

"How much a unit?"

"Forty thousand."

"Gulp!" Stephen clowned a reaction, demonstrating that was out of his league. *He had already sunk a total of thirty-five thousand out of the eighty thousand he had from his share left—after the divorce—from the agency profit-sharing trust. Forty-five left. To take forty of that—too risky.*

"You know what some of those wells over there hit? Eight hundred barrels a day! Eight hundred. You figure how much a unit will bring in, after expenses? Well don't try to do it, I've already done it: twenty thousand a month! How'd ya like bankin' that each month? Buy a lot a bread, wouldn't it? That's at twenty dollars a barrel—think if it comes back at eighty! A hundred a barrel?"

Stephen was silent, pondering. *This was no time to make a decision like this. How about Dad's trust? Maybe he'd call Tom and see if he could get him to invest for Dad and himself. The three of them could get a good chunk of that well.*

"Want to pray about it?"

"Yeah. I'll ask God how many units to buy," he chortled, masking a serious thought beginning to take shape in his mind.

The rest of the meal went quickly. More questions about the big well, which was to be called Revelation 22:20. Questions about Faith's ministry, about Rock's.

Stephen's mind was riveted on the twenty-thousand a month. *Even if it were only half that, he pondered, that wouldn't be bad, would it? Or, twice* that. That would recoup the other losses. Was it greed, though? Or was this excitement a leading of the Holy Spirit? He would certainly have to pray about it. Should he discuss it with Faith? No, it was, after all, his money that he had brought into the marriage, and he could darned well do with it what he pleased . . . that, and his dad's trust money, if it came to using that. Both he and his younger brother, Tom, had power of attorney, since his dad's stroke had left him incapacitated—and his mother had died. Only, would Faith's prayers be beneficial? Be needed? Maybe her pull with God would be the one thing that would assure success. Then, what about the other wells? Why hadn't her pull with God brought the sought-for prosperity? "When you intend to spud?"

"Hope by mid July. Figure twelve drilling days. Only got three units unspoken for, and one of those could go. One of your board members said he was serious. So, let me know soon's ya can."

"I'll get back to you. God bless."

Stephen drove back to the station with the radio off. 'This could be the one. Lose, and I'd only have five grand left. Maybe that's what the Lord wants me to do; step out in faith and not rely on that eighty thousand I used to have. Maybe He has been testing me to see how I react in adversity—losing a big amount—to test my faith . . . then, to reward me on the final test and have it come in big! Glory to God! Glory to You, God! And, You know that I would use the bulk of it for Your work. That's what it's all about, isn't it? Your putting wealth in the hands of Your flock to enable them to do Your work? Look how You have blessed Oral, and Kenneth Copeland, and Kenneth Hagin—and Norval Hayes— businessman with a Midas touch because of You! The money just won't stop flowing in! Well, Father, I just believe that this is the way you are going to have the money flow in to me and Faith so that we can do Your works and You lead us. And, for Tom and dad, that could mean paying all his medical expenses forever! Everyone would be blessed! I stand on Your Word for it, God, and speak it forth. Hallelujah!'

Chapter 6   Mass Slayings

Faith's voice responded as he identified himself on the phone.
"Hon. Don't forget. Tonight at Logos. I told you how good it was last night . . . you shouldn't have missed it."

"I did forget. What time?"

"Starts at seven thirty. I'm picking up Miriam and Phil. Meet us when you can. We'll save you a seat. Billy Bob's fabulous!"

Stephen hung up and uttered a sigh . . . more groan-like. *'Billy Bob Baxter! Another of God's anointed . . . out to fleece the flock. Oops, better watch myself . . . don't want to bring God's wrath for criticizing one of His anointed.'*

Logos Bible Training School was only five minutes away from the station, also in Broken Arrow. It was a complex of two good-sized attractive buildings of non-nondescript architectural style. But, they contained two enormous auditoriums and a dozen or so classrooms, everything fitted out neatly and nicely. Couldn't be a year old yet.

In Greek, *Logos* was the spoken, active, incarnate in Jesus Christ, Word of God, as opposed to the other greek word the formative, creative, conceptual Word of God, *Rhema*. The training school's founder, Brother Leo, was a contemporary of Oral Roberts and in many ways they were similar: both had begun as itinerant tent preachers in the midwest, back during the dust bowl days. Both had been afflicted physically as youths . . . and both had been miraculously healed by God—so

77

miraculously that the healings became the bases for their ministries. Both knew that only the power of God had healed them, and their lives had been at those critical points each dedicated to the work of the Lord in gratitude. Each had an army of ardent followers.

Stephen particularly liked Brother Leo because he would come out to preach, open the Bible to a particular place from which to launch into his 'teaching,' and go into that particular passage or verse so thoroughly and interestingly, and inspiringly, that he wrung the very essence out of its meaning . . . for the whole evening . . . and everyone clung to his every word. His interpretation of the simple meanings were not complicated, were not involved . . . he kept the simplicity, the message, but he was able to present it in a way never heard before and one which would never be forgotten. He was not given to histrionics, to showiness . . . he simply stood before his flock and held his worn King James outstretched before him and stated God's clear and concise case to all. His twangy voice would rise and fall with intonations and emphasis, but it was in the manner of a pleading for understanding along with him of what God was a trying to tell His folks here on earth. Brother Leo looked what anyone would type cast as a Baptist Preacher, well dressed— both he and Oral always wore dark, 'authoritative' blue or gray suits . . . three piece, of course— but Brother Leo, while he preached with the fire and zeal of any Baptist preacher as well, was totally charismatic. One of the old-time Pentecostals . . . irreverently dubbed Holy Rollers by unsympathetic outsiders. He preached the Full Gospel . . . with the power and the gifts of the Holy Spirit . . . and shared its joy and love. Stephen wondered how Baptists could be so fired up on the Lord and just managed to miss the true message? Come so close . . . and then not get there; preach so much hell-fire and brimstone and condemnation . . . and go around with frowns on their faces trying to convince others to join them. As one Spirit filled brother said, the Baptists take you through the desert and up to the Promised Land . . . but they don't know how to go down into it!   It is the charismatics who take the believer into the Promised Land, the Kingdom of God on earth, and into that promised realm of the fruits of the Promise.

Knowing that Brother Leo would not be going into one of his in-depth teachings tonight, but would defer to his guest, the peripatetic and beloved Evangelist Billy Bob Baxter, Stephen had drifted in a little late. Spotting Faith and her entourage seated mid center, he politely made his apologies as he squeezed down the row to the empty seat that awaited him.

Faith leaned over to him and whispered an up-date, informing him that he had gotten there just in time; right after the singing, Brother Leo was going to introduce brother Billy Bob.

Stephen sized up the good brother Baxter. Tall, good-looking . . . mid forties . . . handsome shock of graying hair . . . nothing hayseed about him at all. In fact, there was a bit of a dichotomy; except for the accent (*which Stephen wondered how authentic it really was*), he could well pass for a well-to-do business executive. Conservative, three-piece beige suit. And, contrary to the customary, a tasteful regimental-striped tie, setting off the white collar with gold tie clasp on his thin red striped shirt. *That's the kind of thing one sees more in the east than out here*, he thought.   His overall demeanor was dignified, almost refined, bordering on class . . . exuded a distinct charisma.   But if the name   Billy Bob hadn't spoiled the impression created, the first words that came out of his mouth did him in.

Stephen tuned out of brother Billy Bob early on. He seemed nevertheless the typical itinerant evangelist . . . with the typical message. Nothing new or interesting . . . or maybe it was the style of his pitch. Anyway, he just didn't snag Stephen. Faith hung on the edge of her seat, as did her cohorts. They nodded appreciatively at the appropriate spots; 'praised God' and 'hallelujah'd' periodically . . . and otherwise were transfixed and mesmerized as they were wont.

The problems of the station just would not leave Stephen's mind . . . nor would the failures of the Genesis oil wells. Four wells, named biblically, dedicated to the Lord . . . and they failed! Not a one came in. Oh, they sounded like they were coming in when they hit . . . like a dozen freight trains coming out of those holes . . . then—fizzle— nothing! He had invested in all four . . . to 'get his feet wet' in wildcatting . . . and he had lost a considerable amount. And, he was less than consoled by brother Rock. Nevertheless, he had gone ahead and invested in the Logos drilling program . . . as he was recounting all of these untoward events, he gradually became aware of brother Billy Bob . . . something about his change of cadence . . . a change in his approach . . . now almost crouching at the front edge of the stage . . . and his thoughts aligned themselves with the good brother's. He was saying something about the apostle Paul in the book of Acts when he traveled to Athens and was debating the philosophers . . . something about Paul on the steps of the Parthenon debating with Socrates . . . and getting the best of him!

'*Good grief,*' thought Stephen, '*Doesn't this guy know his history? Socrates had been dead three hundred years before Paul lived! . . . And the debate did not take place on the steps of the Parthenon . . . but in the debating circle in the Agora, the market place! God . . . another example of these half-baked, semi-educated Bible-thumpers!*'

"Brothers and sisters . . . God has been speaking to me . . . and, as I told you last night, He said to me that He was goin' ta' come right in this here very room . . . and perform a miracle right before your very eyes. Hallelujah! Right here! Right where you're all sittin'! Praise God! . . . Now He told me to git ready . . . ta' git you all ready . . . ready for when He comes!   Now last night He was preparin' ya' . . . by the Word He had me to speak to you . . . and now, tonight, He's gittin' me to speak His Word to you . . . again! And, you gotta take it to heart . . . take it into   your hearts . . . and prepare along with me . . . 'cause He's coming . . . I tell ya'!   Now, we'll all be here tomorrow night . . . and we'll all be here Friday night . . . and somewhere during one of these nights, He promised me He would perform a miracle before your very eyes. It could be tonight! It could be tomorrow night . . . or . . . it could be Friday night. He didn't tell me which one . . . He just said to be His faithful servant and to follow Him . . . He would give not the hour . . . nor the day . . . nor the time . . . but ye faithful, remain alert, for He will come when ye least suspect . . . like a thief in the night! Hallelujah!— and you will all be slain in the Spirit !"

As brother Billy Bob wound down and God seemed not to have selected this night to perform His promised miracle,   Stephen looked thankfully for the end of the evening.   He knew Faith and her clutch would be in attendance tomorrow night, Thursday. He would wait until Friday . . . and, If God performed His long-awaited *Deus-ex-machina* tomorrow, he would just have to listen to the 'playbacks.'   Something told him that this build-up was for the last night, Friday, anyway. One way to hold a crowd . . . no use hitting the climax before the final night and losing your audience—not to mention, your biggest revenue!

As the baskets for the offerings were being passed down the rows, Stephen took the opportunity to excuse himself and head for the apartment.

Friday night was jam-packed! Standing room only. Faith had insisted that they all get there early.   So, that usual routine of grabbing seats, practically front row center, stowing their bags and programs on them . . . then cruising about the auditorium seeing friends and acquaintances . . .

exchanging the Holy Kisses and hugs . . . the hearty greetings, the gleeful laughter and joyous banter . . . all augured an exciting evening.

The appointed hour was fast approaching. The room began to settle down . . . the warm- up singing and instrumentals had begun . . . and the faithful were shifting in their seats like groundhogs readying to hibernate. The anxiety and tension in the room was bordering on measurable. No one could quite sit still; there was continual nervous chatting and turning to one another with broad smiles and twitters. The musical numbers finished. One of the Logos staff ministers led a lengthy prayer and another led another round of song and praise. Brother Leo strolled in casually and took his customary seat at center stage along the back . . . but the chair for brother Baxter remained empty. This was immediately noticed by the faithful flock and elicited excited agitation. 'Where was brother Billy Bob?'

The program went on . . . and on . . . and still no brother Billy Bob. The tension was running at fever pitch. Had he forgotten? Had he been in an accident? Had the Lord taken him? Where was brother Billy Bob? He had to be here tonight! This was obviously the big night . . . since God had not performed His miracle any of the preceding nights. 'Brother Billy Bob had to be present for God to perform that miracle! Don't let us down, Lord! Bring Brother Billy Bob to us! Oh God, oh God! Where is he?'

At an opportune moment when the music subsided, Brother Leo rose and stepped forward. The ensuing hush was pregnant with anticipation! Slowly he selected his words, "My friends . . . Brother Billy Bob is not with us tonight . . . (groans, stifled cries of anguish, sighs from the assembled) . . . yet! I don't know where he is . . . he has not contacted me. I don't know if anything has happened to him or not . . . why don't we just bow our heads an say a prayer for him . . . wherever he might be . . . Father God, we hold up to You our brother Billy Bob . . .

Your faithful servant . . . and we just ask that You keep Your protective hand upon him . . . wherever he is. Bring him to us safely . . . so that he can do the work that You set out for him to do . . . We say this in the Name of Your precious Son, Jesus . . . Amen." He turned and indicated to the musicians to go into another song. There was a buzzing and mumbling throughout the auditorium as the perplexed faithful turned to one another with questioning looks and hand-wringing exhortations.

Midway through the song, a figure appeared off to the right of stage . . . and bounded up the six steps. Was it Billy Bob? It looked somewhat like him . . . but this man was dressed casually . . . in tennis attire! He even had a towel around his shoulders. He was sweaty; his skin glistened and he wiped his forehead with the towel and brought it over his head leaving the gray hair to spring back in its trained place. It was Billy Bob! Praise God! It was Billy Bob! The momentarily stunned audience had now gathered its collective wits and the agitation reached its peak. The din of chatter rose also, overtaking the music. Billy Bob smiled to brother Leo, then casually, as if it were the most normal thing in the world, gazed out over the audience with the same infectious smile. People instinctively smiled with him and at him, delirious that he was with them . . . that he was not injured . . . that he was there to lead them . . . that the Lord could now work through him to bring that long-awaited miracle tonight through him! Clapping began . . . then cheering . . . then the clapping and cheering overwhelmed the room and the music; people stood and cheered and praised and prayed in tongues until the rafters shook with the sound. The spontaneous applause went on and on . . . without surcease.

Finally, brother Billy Bob sprang to his feet and in a most uncharacteristically casual manner, sauntered over to the center of the stage. All were on their feet, clapping and chanting, their eyes alive with delight. In the midst of the tumultuous ovation, brother Billy Bob raised his right hand . . . as if to silence them . . . shouted at the top of his lungs, "God is with us . . . right here ! He is in this room! . . . Don't you feel His very presence? Hallelujah!" and, with that, he waved his hand from left of the audience to the right . . . and as his hand traveled, the standing figures under its spell crumpled to the floor, amid crashing chairs and fervent cries . . . from one side of the auditorium to the other. The whole room was a mass of bodies strewn onto the floor or slumped onto the chairs. The entire congregation had been slain in the Spirit ! . . . except for Stephen, and a handful of others. Faith, Miriam, Phil, and everyone around them had gone down. Ushers were straightening some of them out, pulling the ladies' skirts down modestly over their knees, that sort of thing . . . and attending closely lest there be any real heart attacks, strokes or serious injuries from the fallings.   Brothers Baxter and Leo were holding each other's arms with eyes closed in silent prayer. The music had resumed and with the melodic tones of the prayer tongues of the slain there arose a sound as angelic as a heavenly choir.

Stephen simply sat down at his seat and surveyed the scene. *'Unbelievable! Mass hysteria,'* he said to himself under his breath. *'Has the Holy Spirit of God truly moved upon this multitude? . . . or, have I just witnessed the most blatant demonstration of mass manipulation I ever hope to see in my life?   If it's the former . . . I'm out of the loop, Lord!'*

Chapter 7   *Little Bema* Judgment

Lydia strode over to Stephen's desk and put some papers in his In box. "There's your agenda for tonight typed up. Better check it."

"What for? We never follow it anyway."

"Then, how come the notes you take always track according to the outline?"

"Ever heard of creative writing?"

"Or, maybe, the leading of the Holy Spirit?"

"Whatever. Pray for me. Another crummy dinner; another long-winded meeting. You know, they're beginning to get to me. They constantly stick their noses into day-to day operation. The board ain't supposed to do that. They mean well, but, 'deliver me, oh Lord'!"

"Trinity Network is more than sixty days behind, thought you ought to know."

"Poor Paul Crouch. Must be going through another crisis. When's their next telethon? Shame. They were the first Christian satellite network, out there in L.A. Now, everybody's got a transponder. All three Christian nets and a bunch of others. The Lord sure gave the Christians a jump on the commercial guys. The secular nets have been trying to buy those satellite transponders back ever since they woke up. You know, Lydia, the PTL network was offered ten million for its?

Imagine; three of those birds just sitting up there over the equator, 22,300 miles high, just moving right along with the earth . . . beaming their signals down to thousands of stations and cable systems all over the U. S."

"Right," chimed Lydia. "What an amazing way God gave us to reach every part of the world in these end times to preach the gospel before Jesus comes again. Mark 16:15."

"Gotta talk to you about that passage sometime, remind me, will you?" Stephen began to arrange the documents needed for the evening meeting and reached for his briefcase. "But, you ever think whom He gave this mission to? Did He give it to the Baptists and the other fundamentalists? The ones He first gave radio to? Ever stop to think that most religious broadcasting up to now has been for forty years or so by the radio Bible Belt fundamentalists? And, so because of their good work did He give them television? No siree. He gave tele-vision to us charismatics. Maybe the Baptists and fundamentalists weren't preaching what the Lord wanted them to. So, maybe, just maybe, He created the 'Move of the Holy Spirit' in these times in order to accomplish His will through TV . . . by a group who He knew would follow actively the truth of His Word—the full Word with power and love ! Think about it; Trinity Broadcast Network, PTL Network, CBN Network . . . all charismatic. Tongue-speaking!"

"Amen! We've got the power of God working for us!"

"Sound like Faith again. But, you know that passage from Revelation? 14:6 or something. 'And I saw another angel fly in the midst of heaven, carrying the everlasting Gospel to preach to every nation, tongue and tribe and people'? You ever hear what they named the first satellite sent into orbit? Angel. Coincidence?"

"Praise God! I've only heard you tell this ten hundred times. But, praise God, anyway!"

Stephen got to the private room at the steak house early, as always. He left nothing to chance if he could help it. He the agendas and support material neatly put at each place.   Placed himself across from Felix Toombs; adjusting the place on his right to allow enough elbow room for writing. Although it was the secretary of the board's job to take notes, after the first meeting a year and a half ago, he learned he'd better do it himself.   He'd learned that lesson the hard way a long time ago in advertising: 'CYA,' cover your you-know-what in writing, especially with a guy like Felix as chairman. He'd never been known to put anything in writing, memos, directives, nothing . . . undoubtedly contracts in his contracting, real estate, tool equipment and other enterprises, but, of course, his attorneys did that. So, 'minutes' had to be accurate to pin him down and even this was not always successful. He just ignored what he wanted to. Felix Toombs was the power on the board—he was the board, except he and Stephen were the only ones who realized it. From some of the things that came out, Stephen suspected that Felix had tapped his office phone.

Barnabas Childs, a pediatrician, made his entrance, bellowing 'Praise Gods', followed by Alessandro Cabado. The usual 'Ain't God good's' and 'Love ya', brother' preceded the customary and ritualistic embraces. Repeated again when the other members arrived. Felix Toombs strolled in and was greeted warmly while maintaining a slight reserve, call it aloofness. As everyone got seated, the waitress began taking orders. Stephen told her that only one more was expected, the other three places would not be needed. This group, while orderly, was not one of the waitress' favorites—there'd be no two or three rounds of drinks and a paltry ten percent tip, except from Mr. Toombs.

They could hear him down the hall—the inimitable and irrepressible Doctor Luke Parsons, cheerfully greeting all the waitresses in the Name of the Lord; patrons, too. Then in he came—his always perfectly-timed entrance. His get-up as outlandish as ever. The loud greetings, praises, hugs of bodies and hands, the jovial smile, walking around the entire table and coming back to his place next to brother Felix. Doc had actually recruited Felix Toombs to be chairman when the Christian group was organizing to apply to the FCC for the channel. They had evidently needed a 'big' man—a monied man—in the community to be Chairman of the Board, somebody who could talk to the 'big givers', the 'big bucks.' Didn't matter that Felix was a Presbyterian, one of the 'dead' churches. Doc gave him the course—the full course: "born again' and 'baptism in the Holy Spirit.' Even so, Felix had always struck Stephen as being a bit uncomfortable with the 'Praise Gods' and 'Hallelujahs'; but the other members of the board either did not detect it or attributed it to the chairman's natural reticence. After all, what could you expect after all those years in a dead Presbyterian church? Stephen reflected, though, *that come to think of it, he had never heard Felix pray in tongues as they usually ended up in the big prayer-and-praise session that closed the meeting.*

The meeting was called to order. Previous minutes were 'approved as read', although they were not read. And the first agenda item of the night was addressed. Stephen gave the financial report.

The board members sat in glum silence, broken occasionally by fidgeting or reaching for a glass of water. No smoking, though, that was a 'no-no' with charismatics. Stephen often wondered if Doc really comprehended finances at all; probably didn't. The slow recitation by Stephen; the pause for questions as he went along. Trying to parry, trying to defend, holding off his attack until later. Wrapping it up, Stephen stated in carefully chosen words, "So, again, not a happy report. Still more out-go than in-come. The total amount billed and credited in trades, close to ninety-five thousand a month. Cash flow in—fifty three thousand. Not enough actual cash coming in to cover cash going out; we're running in the red ten, fifteen thousand a month."

"You gotta cut down on expenses," Felix sourly interjected.

"We're stripped to the bone now. What we should be doing is actually spending more . . . especially on promotion . . . and to up-grade production."

"Steve," asked Doc, "Don't we have a problem trying to be both a Christian station and a commercial station?"

"You've hit the nail on the head. You're absolutely right. We've got one foot in one world and the other in another. We can't get enough rating points to attract advertisers . . . or enough donations to cover the ministry and its programs. Fortunately, most of the Christian program buys are paying within 30 to 60 days, but one of the networks is now getting habitually late. We get thrown farther and farther back and we can't recover. Our only hope is to raise an amount large enough in the telethon to make up the deficit. But, that still won't give us the wherewithal to do what needs to be done . . . billboards, newspaper ads, car cards, flyers, direct mail-outs . . . You know, in the real world, when you're down, you don't cut everything down until you can't function. You do just the opposite, you promote. Make people aware that we're out here, get their attention." He continued, "improved production, up grading engineering. We lost two camera tubes last month. Nursed 'em as long as we could. Going to cost eight thousand to replace them."

"Hey, when you gonna give us some good news, brother Steve?" quipped Alessandro Cabado, puncturing the gloom that had been building up.

"The good news is that Jesus lives!" shot back Steve, for lack of anything better.

"Amen to that," said Doc nodding to others around the table who responded with the 'praise Gods' and 'hallelujahs.'

During the subsequent exchange of ideas and general discussion of many of the points of Stephen's report, Stephen studied Felix opposite him. He had liked Felix a great deal at first when he negotiated the position as General Manager and Vice President and board member. Then, as the station had gone on the air, the relationship had strained. Felix intruded too much; kept a tight grip on the purse strings, virtually had his own man take over the station's accounting. Stephen was CEO—at least that was what he was led to believe when he took the job, but, of course, it was a good faith, handshake deal, no contract. Felix had had other ideas; he saw himself as CEO, chief executive officer. And, he didn't know the first thing about television. They had had a few head-to-heads and Stephen had reminded his senior in years and position that TV broadcasting was not the construction business . . . or the real estate business. It was not a dictatorial thing nor a nuts and bolts thing. It was a very complicated and nebulous holding together of diverse talents and abilities, trying to perfect a less-than-perfect system of day-to-day operation and solving of problems, no two ever alike. It required tact, insight, leadership . . . all sorts of qualities that took a lifetime to acquire and hone. As tactfully as Stephen tried, the taciturn Felix never articulated any responses whatever. He was the type who never let the other know what he was thinking; it could also be a cover up of ignorance in an area Felix was trying to demonstrate expertise.

But, when he started reversing things Stephen had initiated, he became Stephen's nemesis. Stephen began to dread his too frequent visits to the station; he was fast losing his authority as general manager, and the personnel were aware of it. Lydia sympathized openly with him. The board was no help; Stephen had confided in Doc the problem he was having with Felix. Doc's reaction was: Felix is a millionaire. He's proved himself. The implication: 'and who are you? . . . making twenty-five thousand a year.' Doc then pointed out The Golden Rule : 'he who has the gold, rules ! Any question who we're going to side with?' Stephen had heard many stories of Felix' reputation in the business world —far from complimentary. He was thought a bastard . . . even after 'coming to the Lord.'   Stephen pondered author Robert Ringer's examples of the three types who win through intimidation: the one who says he's going to get you, and gets you; the one who says he's not going to get you, and does anyway; and, the one who doesn't know he's out to get you and ends up getting you anyway, too. He figured Felix was the second type. Only Felix now knew how to get all the chips with a smile and a 'praise God' as he skewered his opponents! Steven guessed he wanted to own the station and then sell it. Stephen's digression was abruptly ended by a voice to his left, Cabado's.

"Brother Stephen, I get a lot of flack at the church over Star Trek. Now, personally, I kinda like it. I don't see nothing real wrong with it, but some folks tell me it's full of witchcraft."

"Whoa, Alex, you're beginning to sound like my wife." Stephen had not wanted to get into this; programming decisions were his and he was darned lucky to have gotten the first reruns on Star Trek. The board was again intruding. Alex was a pharmacist, pretty limited in outlook, but, then, he was a sample of the audience profile of any Christian station. "She and I go 'round and 'round over this, too. But, look, space is a new frontier, it is adventurous, it has captured the imagination—and it brings up an audience. In fact, the only sizable numbers we've got! That's why I've stripped it from six to seven to compete with the news. It builds up our male numbers while holding the kids over from I Love Lucy and Hogan's Heroes, leading up, hopefully to our dumping them right into the 700 Club at seven . . . before the movie strip at eight."

"You get more witchcraft, if you think of the magic, and wizardry and supernatural and evil in the cartoons!" interjected Doc.

"So, what're you going to do?" Felix said dryly. "Eliminate everything?"

"That points out a real problem, brothers, " said Stephen. "Look, Star Trek, is nothing more than a form of literature, if you will . . . a 'Morality Play' in space-age dressing. 'Good' always wins over 'evil.' What could be better for us than that? One episode even had a reference to the central power of the universe as the Sun, spelled S-O-N! No, the real problem for all Christian TV broadcasters is that most of the programs produced since roughly 1975 have too much sex, violence, bad language, and plain humanistic values—not to mention promiscuous life styles . . . condoning of homosexuality, of unmarrieds living together— for us to program. As you know, the nighttime shows all step down to syndicated reruns. So, the afternoon strip and early evening are getting worse and worse from our standpoint. At least, witchcraft and all, the cartoons are keeping the kids away from the 'soap operas.' Have any of you watched them lately? They're about as porno as you can get and get away with it on TV!"

"I always said we should not have compromised. We should have stayed all Christian— none of the world's garbage. Maybe that's why we're having so much trouble. We allowed mixture, didn't go all the way God's way. Like Paul Crouch did with his station," piped up Doc in his usual litany.

"Yeah, but I keep pointing this out. TBN is in the third largest market in the U.S. His telethons draw from a ten to thirteen million population . . . so he's able to raise five, ten million two or three times a year from a couple of hundred thousand faithful supporters. Chicago, too. Their donations are probably over two hundred thousand a month. But, look at our population—or lack of it. And, the competition from the hundreds of ministries here, all begging, begging, begging. Too bad we're not like the Baptists. I know of a Baptist church down in Georgia, about six thousand in the congregation. They take in forty-five thousand dollars every Sunday!   And, it only averages about sixteen dollars a head."

"Well, us charismatics don't do so bad in giving," Alex offered.

"Right. Look at PTL and CBN. They're getting cagey now and don't tell the exact figures they raise.   But, I guess CBN's up there between eighty and a hundred million—but, that's nation-wide.   And, they've got a tremendously expensive operation to run and a lot of air time to buy on other stations—like ours."

"Praise God," exclaimed Doc.   "Ol' Billy Graham trailing at about thirty million. Think I heard Jerry Falwell brings in around fifty million. Anybody got any idea what Oral raises?"

No one volunteered. Stephen picked it up again. "You can use this argument, brothers, when someone criticizes all this money these TV and Evangelistic ministries are bringing in: all together they don't equal each year what Disney World takes in! How does that grab you? And, with EPCOT coming, I'll bet Disney tops five hundred million yearly. See where the world's values are?"

"Lordy, Lordy, praise God!" echoed around the table.

"Think about this," Stephen continued.   "When the three Christian networks saturate the cable market, or when direct home satellite receiving is available, look how they are going to be able to raise money. Figure the 700 Club membership—at fourteen dollars a month from each faithful member . . . times a million members . . . each month! 'Course, as we know, it costs a lot to maintain those big studios and staffs and colleges and all. But, brothers, that's another aspect of our problem in the future.   How viable are we—KXAO TV-21—going to be struggling day-to-day trying to get the message out, when people have a much better choice on cable? Or, when this new low power translator broadcasting comes along? You know, you'll probably be able to fully

93

automate one of those—put nothing but Gospel out at very low cost, covering a whole city. But, I will point this out, too: 'Independent' stations . . . Indys . . . have been doing very well against the network stations in a lot of markets. The first Indy to enter a market, that is. They program just what we are doing, the cartoon strips, sports and movies. No news, no live local programming; they run lean and mean . . . and they are making it, so I hear in the industry. Of course, they don't lose their audience every time a religious program comes on . . . and they pay good money for good, first reruns. But, they are getting competitive numbers against the entrenched network affiliates . . . and making money. We could do it, too, if we went all the way commercial independent, bought some new programming, concentrated on movies, have sufficient publicity and dumped the religious except for the traditional Sunday morning ghetto. But, I know we can't do this. On the other hand, we can't go all religious because of the limited viewership. It's like direct mail; you reach a lot of people for a few returns. But, the bottom line, I feel, is that somehow a 'wholesome family format with inspirational programs' should succeed! Wasn't that what we all believed was our direction from the Lord? And, isn't that what good, God-fearing Christians want in their living rooms instead of the junk they get now? You tell me !"

The meeting degenerated into discussions of these and other points presented during the evening. Again, nothing of any significance accomplished. Stephen was getting sick of the whole mess; there was really no solution to all their problems unless someone bought them out and came in with the necessary money and did it right. Toombs and the board had really 'backed in' to Christian television, without any depth of thought or analysis. As much as Stephen had valiantly tried he was unable to convince them to go at least second class if not first. They had elected tenth class; even so, debt service was more than twenty thousand a month.   He mused about what his position and prestige as general manager of a television station in a good-sized market would be like.   He tried to stifle thoughts that were coming to him more frequently: what had he given up to step out and serve the Lord?   He had discounted the position and prestige factors, and shucked the Ivy League image, when he took the job.   Those were, after all, just the world's dressings. Meaningless. We were all one in the Lord Jesus Christ. It was late and he was tired. He hoped Faith wouldn't be home yet; he wanted to hit the sack.

Chapter 8   Fisher of Men

After the call to come forward and receive salvation or the baptism in the Holy Spirit had ended and everyone had gone back to their seats, pastor John Mark Fisher held his hands outstretched to the unseen Father God and Jesus and the Holy Spirit who were with them at that very moment in the large, modern nave-meeting room of the Fisher's of Men Fellowship, and blessed the assembly of the saints in Christ, his faithful flock. The pleasant chorus of tongues and Hallelujahs swelled and then subsided into a silence that signaled termination of this night's midweek celebration of prayer and praise.

Stephen had first seen Faith here at Fishers of Men when he had just come out to Tulsa to accept the job with the station. He had been looking around for a church to join or 'fellowship in,' as the initiates describe it. Faith had been ministering as a guest preacher and had sung several songs. Both her looks and her voice had attracted him, and he had managed to meet her during the course of the breakup of the meeting. He had run into her shortly afterward and had asked her out for a cup of coffee. One cup had led to another, several more, and a good two hours had slipped by before Stephen had been aware of it. He spilled everything about his life, his testimony, his marriage breakup—all to Faith's tender and sympathetic ears.

And she told about her life in a secular marriage, her one child, who had stayed with his father. How she had had to go it alone—he had divorced her, for what reason Stephen thought it more polite not to ask, although he wondered—left her penniless, and how she had turned to God, had been anointed for her particular ministry, which was to fight Satan and cast out devils . . . and how eventually God had prospered her. She had all her needs in riches and glory in Christ Jesus, Hallelujah.

Stephen had been fascinated, so much so that he sought her out again . . . and again. Needless to say it got them both to where they were at this moment. He was sure that it was the leading of God, God's bringing to him an angel to be his true helpmeet in his quest for that righteous life to which he had dedicated himself now and for which he had given up his family. Brother John Mark had married them in the fellowship, insisting, however, that it be a small gathering and ceremony, Stephen suspected, because both of them had been divorced.

As they went out into the wide hallway that half encircled the large room, Faith spotted a crony. "Hon. There's Miriam and Phil. I gotta go talk to them. Listen, I'll just ride back with them and they can drop me off. OK? See ya later."

Left a bit unceremoniously, he began to search for familiar faces. Brother John Mark spotted him as he was disengaging from a small group. "Hey, there, brother Steve. Good to see ya'. The Lord treatin' ya good?"

Stephen allowed as how he would like to sit down and chat with the brother sometime. "Now's as good a time as any. I got a few minutes before I have to close up. Lemme jist git those folks over there on their way. Go on down to my office. It's open."

Stephen sat on the heavy Mediterranean style couch on one side of the rather good sized room. Was he subconsciously playing the patient role by selecting the couch? He gazed at the surroundings. Everything new looking, the fresh plaster wall, the blond stained wood trim, the picture of Jesus—the awful one with the long hair, eyes turned upward, hands clasped, praying, that some contemporary hack had turned out which had caught the fancy of the tasteless religious world— frame right out of Woolworth's. Jesus didn't have long hair; that was frowned upon by the Jewish customs of the times, and Jesus was a rabbi. Even Paul had admonished to cut hair short. It was this erroneous image based on an obscure nineteenth century second-rate romantic artist that the hippie generation had emulated. Oddly, as the hippies faded, the formerly crew-cut red-neck element males adopted the long hair and pony tails. Except for the stubble, mustaches and beards, most of the oil drillers looked like women under their hard hats. Funny, too, that this long-haired, unkempt, dirty look that came from the liberal left originally . . . shifted to the radical right, to the pistol-packing, tobacco- chewing, beer swigging, pick-up truck ilk. Talk about unintended iconoclasm! At least the Christian elements had cleaned up their act— cleanliness was next to godliness, as some mistakenly thought the Bible taught.

There were the other usual mementos, the color photo of the family group on the oversized desk, a brass cross on a pedestal, a container of pencils. All very neat; an 'unused' look about it. The photo reminded Stephen of the incident with John Mark's wife, shortly after they had all met. He and Faith were at some small get-together prior to the wedding and John Mark's wife, Mary—of course, Mary, what else could she have been named?—had shrieked with alarm when she took his hands in prayer! His ring! The ring on his third finger left hand—the only ring he had ever worn; a family heirloom, gold, his signet on it, over a hundred years old. He had always loved it. Didn't even take it with him to Vietnam; fortunate, too, because when he was wounded, he was stripped of everything during medical treatment. Mary had shouted that she felt demonic power coming out of that ring. She had drawn back in utter horror, shrinking from Stephen as if from something unclean!

Stephen had been totally flustered. He hadn't known what to do. Faith had stepped in and said that he must destroy it immediately.

With all sorts of conflicting thoughts racing through his mind, Stephen had ultimately consented to the directions of those whose leading from the Lord and whose special gifts were greater than his, and had gone out into the garage with the owner of the house, had gotten a hammer and had smashed the beautiful ring to smithereens . . . and tossed the bits of twisted metal off into the woods next door. Everyone congratulated him when he returned. Congratulations for having obeyed God and casting off those evil spirits. He had only managed to smile wanly.

Brother John Mark appeared. Like all these charismatic-fundamentalists, he wore his three-piece robin's egg pastel blue suit with the vest all buttoned up. If the suit came with three pieces, then, by dern, you wear all three pieces, a hundred degrees or not. Striding confidently (pridefully?) to the matching Mediterranean chair next to the couch, he settled in. "Well there, brother Steve, I ain't seen you in some time. How you gittin' along? You and Faith? And, good ol' KXAO-TV. But, you's the one what wanted to talk. So, lemme let you go at it. What's up?"

"Hey, things are going great, John Mark. They could be better, maybe. But, I just thank God every day for what He's doing in my life—and Faith's."

"Amen. Praise God!"

Stephen tried to warm up to what was troubling him but he felt uncomfortable. He had never felt any sort of real rapport with John Mark. John Mark was six years younger, 37, and there was a big gap in their backgrounds. There— he did it again, Pride. John Mark was his brother. A good, honest, God-fearing, righteous man of God. "Oh, I guess there are a few things going on I've been asking God about, to see if

He could straighten 'em out. They haven't been straightened out, so I don't know whether God is abandoning me or just testing me."

"You talked this over with Faith?"

"Not really. I don't get too sympathetic an ear there. She constantly harps on the fact that I have got to get right with God . . . whatever that is. I have thought everything all through and I honestly don't see that I am not 'right with God.' But, things are not going right, I'm beginning to think."

"How? What way?"

"Well . . . the wells and the TV station . . . and, the relationship with Faith, for that matter. You know, we get along fairly well . . . at least when everything is going her way, which it does most of the time because she is walking constantly with God, as she is quick to point out to me. So, if she is and I'm not, whose side do you think that puts me on? And, she's started something that I have no control over . . . I guess I should say, don't know how to counter. She accuses me of sending forth demons of sexual lust! Not toward her—our sex life couldn't be better—but we can be out with a group, or strolling arm in arm around Woodland Mall, and—suddenly, she'll turn to me with a fierce look in her eyes and outright accuse me of demons of lust! In a firm stage whisper, 'I saw those demons of lust for that woman! You better ask God's forgiveness!' and, I'll be stunned. Stopped dead in my tracks. 'What woman?' 'That woman we just passed, in the short shorts and halter top!' I can protest until my breath gives out—that I never even noticed such a woman! But, it does no good. She has picked up on the demons of lust coming forth from me—I guess her particular sensitivity to the spirit world— and there is nothing I can do to counter it. No protest, no renunciation of any such idea—nothing. She then closes up, convinced in her total being that I have emitted demons of lust toward some woman I never even noticed. OK. If it ended there it might not be so bad, but she carries it on, drops an invisible shield between us, separating the righteous from the sinner, the saint from evil . . . and it goes on and on! And, I mean she doesn't let up! We walk out of wherever it was and she is still carrying on about my demons. We get into the car. It goes on. Her mind is like a steel trap on the darned thing. It won't let go."

"What do you do during all this?"

"When I get over the initial outburst and protestations in self defense, I sometimes try to tune out—which is impossible—and I now try to counter her by praying in tongues and praising God . . . which only turns her diatribe into scolding me for blaspheming God with such irreverent prayers, saying God will not honor such prayers of one under Satan's power! God! How do you win against that?"

"Then, what?"

"Then . . . I wish I could say it fizzles out . . . but it doesn't! She keeps this up day and night, sometimes for three and four days! Can you believe it? This kind of incessant condemnation going on without my being able to get as much as a word in edgewise? Of course, after a while, I get a bit ticked off and shout at her to knock it off . . . which only feeds the fire . . . and she comes back with more fervor than before. It's insane! After a day or so of this, sometimes I can't take it any more and I yell my head off at her, call her crazy, sometimes let a cuss word slip out . . . "

Interrupting, brother John Mark warned, "Be sure you don't blaspheme the Holy Spirit—you lose your salvation if you do that. That is the unpardonable sin. God will forgive others, but not that!"

" . . . Well . . . we get into some real shouting matches . . . as I'm sure the neighbors can attest. Then, when I reach one of these almost uncontrollable pitches . . . she seems satisfied, tapers down . . . seems to let up and goes into a quiet, self-absorbed mode . . . apparently relishing some sort of victory in her mind. I guess she figures she has won another victory over Satan—me !—and it's over.   For her, that is. She goes off, humming and praising the Lord and gets right back into whatever God is telling her to do next. Me? I'm a wreck! I frankly don't know how to handle this . . . and it's beginning to get to me, to say the least!"

"Hallelujah . . .   mena..shem-nachet-ivnitennishamma-halla-danna-shanna-ma-ha . . . " John Mark drifted off to himself with his eyes closed and remained in that state for an embarrassing length of time. When he came out of it, he asked, "What about the station . . . and the wells."

Feeling that unloading about Faith was enough to dump on the brother in one session, Stephen tossed the other problems off. "Yeah, there are a lot of things going wrong with the station— mostly stuff that money could take care of. The wells, though, they're something else. They're going down the drain, so to speak. Watering out. Nobody's getting the hundred-fold return . . . with all that prayer and casting out of evil spirits. And, still they don't come in . . . and they are all dedicated to the Lord . . . Genesis, Logos, Hebrews.   And, He knows that the money from them will go to his good works. So, I don't know. 'Course, Faith blames it all on my not being right with God. Why always me ? I'm always the one not in tune with all the rest. I've prayed about it . . . and frankly don't know what else to do."

"Well, brother Steve,"   brother John Mark leaned over and extended his hands to take Steve's. "We got a heap of battling to do against the forces of darkness . . . Hallelujah . . . praise God! lumma-has-o-kee-at-ta-she-ho-kee-ah . . . . Lord, I just lift my brother up to you this night, feeling Your presence with us . . . as you said when two or more are gathered in Your Name, You would be in their midst . . . Hallelujah . . . I bind, in the Name of Jesus, those forces of evil that would come against my brother, Steve, and I stand on Your Word, Lord, that my words will loose him from any bondage that Satan might have on him. And, I ask that You show him Your guidance so that he may follow Your voice and Your ways . . . getting 'right with You' . . . so that his particular gifts and ministry can continue to go forth and save souls in this evil, destitute world. And, Lord, I ask You to bless his wife, Faith, and her ministry and to give her the proper insight and wisdom in Your word to discern those spirits that are un-Godly. And, Lord do Your healing work in this marriage so that they can both go forth in the harmony of Your Word . . . and Your mission for them. In the Name of Your most precious Son and Savior, Jesus Christ. Amen!"

As he drove back to the apartment, Stephen went over the session with John Mark in his mind. He was uneasy about it still. He had the feeling that John Mark had not exactly sided with him. It was as if John Mark was sure of Faith's calling and not so sure of his, Stephen's. That was really a cop-out prayer. One that would offend neither party. John Mark was playing both sides—or was he playing God's mediator? He would chew on that.

Chapter 9   Miracle at the well

Lydia's voice sounded from the other room, "Rock's on the hook for you, Steve."

"Howdy, brother Steve, thought you'd like to know, we spudded Logos number five this morning at eight. She should come in some time after midnight. Wanna come on out and watch th' fun?"

"Wouldn't miss it for anything.   Be out there around ten. Thanks, Rock."

"Shore 'nuff, brother. She ought'a be a winner!"

Stephen had heard that before. He hung up and dialed Faith. If she weren't sunning at the pool, she just might be at the apartment. Faith picked up on the second ring. "Jesus loves you! Hello."

"Hi, hon, it's me. What are you up to?"

"Getting ready for the trip.   Both Leah and Miriam are going. God is so good! We're gonna leave Sunday."

"Good.   That means you can come with me tonight to pray Logos number five in. Want to?"

"You bet. When's it due? Maybe Rachel and Andy and Ben and some of the others will want to be there, too."

"OK. I'll be home around seven. We can take a swim, eat, then go out to Skiatook around ten."

"Sounds good. See ya'."

After a round of nachos, which they shared at Chi Chi's, they headed back to the apartment to get into more comfortable clothes. It was past the middle of summer and the hot weather was settling in with its usual vengeance. They could begin expecting one hundred and seventeen to twenty degree days. The nights remained rather cool, though, so they took light jackets along. Stephen gathered up a sheet and the pillows off the bed. There were bound to be periods during the drilling when she or he would want to sack out in the back of the van. They'd get some soft drinks on the way.

They got to the site a little after ten. The work spot lights served as a beacon once they rounded the turn off the main highway. With the windows down, the noise also shattered the otherwise still night. The gate to the field was open so Stephen drove the van up to the cluster of other vehicles in the tall grass. The thirty-foot mast of the drill, which was attached to the rear of the drilling truck, shuttered with the impact of the intermittent pounding, raising, dropping, and pounding of the rotating 'kelly.' Several large vehicles were nosed up to the drill rig and connected to it by hoses and lines, looming like large pachyderms. Generators added their loud and low rhythmic cadence to the scene. The flexible blouie line from the hole to the dark fluid in the sludge pit spit large gulps of water and mud raising its level. The pit had been bulldozed a short way from the drill site with the dirt banked up on the far side like a small mountain. The compressed air turned the kelly on the drill pipe with unrelenting force, while the water pump engaged in counter point with the coughs of the blouie pipe. Water and mud circulated in, water and mud—and hopefully oil—circulated out.

Stephen doused the van lights and he and Faith got out into the muggy summer air. Rock bounded toward them.

Faith embraced Rock in the charismatic manner then stood with one arm around his waist. "How's it going?"

"Great, sister Faithy," Rock shouted above the cacophony around them. "We're a gonna have us another winner here, Praise the Lord! We're down to fourteen hundred feet and the samples show a hundred percent phosphorescence—smells like ol' Ben's auto shop, too! Figure we'll hit TD— total depth—around twelve thirty, one o'clock. Think you wanna stay?"

"Hallelujah! That's what we came for!" interjected Stephen.

"Amen, brother!" Catching a signal from the drilling engineer, Rock excused himself and strode over near the toolpusher's shack.

The headlights of a vehicle illuminated them as it bumped over the ruts before turning and parking near the van. Andy and Rachel Bartholomew got out and joined them. "Hey, folks! She come in yet?"

"On the way," came Faith's cheerful reply reflecting the ecstatic smile that seemed to radiate through the darkness. "And, Praise God. I know it's going to be a biggie!"

"Sure hope so," Rachel added, grasping Faith's arm as she kissed her on the cheek. "We've got two units in this one, one for us and one for the kids. Life savings, you know, but we've stepped out in faith."

"Amen, Rachel. Believe and it shall be given," Andy admonished, hugging Stephen then turning to Faith to do so also.

Dutifully, Stephen stepped to Rachel and embraced her. He was not too fond of brother and sister Bartholomew. Andy, he considered, as his children would have put it, a bit of a wimp. He was on the ORU faculty, making even less than Stephen, praising God and believing He was providing—or was about to with this oil well investment. Faye was the stronger one; had her own ministry like Faith. Going off all the time at 'the call of God.' Of course, the husband was always the head of the household—the Bible says the man is the head of the woman and Christ

106

Jesus is the head of the man. But, with this couple, one might wonder. Andy had evidently reached a point of accommodation and now operated in quiet acquiescence. Stephen wondered if people thought of him and Faith the same way; he supposed that he, too, would have to reach what amounted to an accommodation (*resignation?*) to Faith's Living Water ministry. *But, acquiescence? He wouldn't go that far.*

The women stepped back out of earshot to converse animatedly, thinking the increased distance would lessen the decibels of the drilling. It didn't, of course.   Conversation with Andy was difficult enough anyway, through the din of the drilling it was fruitless. They both just stood and watched.

An hour passed. The monotony of the surging and pounding of the kelly and the incessant gurgling and belching from the blouie pipe lulled the senses . Samples were pulled every ten or fifteen minutes as new deeper formations indicated more hydrocarbons, which were placed under a crude ultraviolet light in the driller's shack.   The phosphorescence glowing in the wet mud under the light indicated the probability of oil or gas at each depth in each formation. They were going for the Mississippian stratum down around seventeen hundred fifty to eighteen hundred feet. The formation was most likely not perfectly horizontal but undulated like a river current, now in sediment form, formed, as the geologists liked to say with authority, several million years ago in the Cambrian Age.

The charismatics scoffed at this among themselves, confident in their revealed knowledge from God that there was no such thing as 'Evolution,' and that these alluvial deposits were created by the great flood during Noah's time, around three thousand B.C.   Only, they wouldn't have been able to articulate it as such. Stephen had come to believe this as well. His deep interest in the two extremes—evolution and the God-creation belief—had prompted his study of contemporary Christian writers, particularly Dr. Henry Morris and his group of scientists who were Christians (as differentiated from Christian Scientists !) at the Institute of Creation Research in San Diego . . . who were proving scientifically that the phenomena in the Old Testament were indeed astronomical, geological, and physical events that have left proof, if only investigated scientifically. Stephen had also read the controversial Immanuel Velikovsky, who has been effectively stifled by the self-appointed scientific community for also advocating such an approach . . . all of which denies that the earth is more than about ten thousand years old. This would be something he would like to get into on one of the talk programs at the station . . . but, usually such deeper discussions turned off the more simple-minded audience. *It's their doggoned irrational abhorrence of 'knowledge,'* Stephen thought.

Rock interrupted this reverie by asking if anyone would like to go get coffee and something to eat for everyone. Faith volunteered and she and Faye drove off in the van.

Andy and Stephen were invited into the driller's shack, which was the enclosed back of a truck, a sort of grungy, make-shift office. It was connected to the drilling platform by a wide four foot board which allowed the toolpusher access back and forth without having to slosh around in the sea of mud which the whole area near the well head had become. Andy and Stephen lifted their legs carefully over the big throbbing blouie pipe and climbed up into the shack. After looking at the samples, they reversed their steps and went back over to the spot near the parked vehicles. The driller had remounted the rig and was greasing down the section of drill stem pipe that was about half way down its twenty-foot length; Rock was walking toward Stephen and Andy—

"—Whoooom!"—

The shock of the sudden explosive sound and the fourfold increase in noise level sent Rock and others sprawling onto the ground; Andy and Stephen instinctively drew back. The toolpusher cleared the rig in one gigantic leap and landed shin deep in mud a good ten feet from his former perch. The roar was deafening! The blouie pipe was like a gyrating fire hose with an undulating stream of fluid whose force began to eat right through the dirt mound on the far side of the pit!

"Blow-out!" yelled Rock in their direction as he scrambled to his feet and scurried to a safer distance. The driller and the engineer all convened with Rock where Stephen and Andy were crouching.

"Dang! Knew we should'a had that blow-out preventer!" lamented the driller. "It's gonna be one big job stopping this baby now!" he shouted above the din.

Stephen and Andy were stunned. What did this mean? Each afraid to ask the question aloud. Rock, seeing their bewilderment and sensing the question, broke in, "We just got us a little temporary problem, brothers. Nothin' to worry 'bout. We'll have this sucker shut down afore ya know it! Must a hit a gas pocket!"

Each of the crewmen cautiously crept back—or as close as he could—to his duty position. The main concern was to get mud back down the hole to stifle the gas pressure or they'd lose the whole thing. The water and mud hose connections had been broken by the sudden pressure of the gas. They'd have to be replaced at the same time everything was being forced up out of the hole. Everything would have to be done without creating a spark, which could set the whole thing off. The gas and pressure was going both out the blouie pipe and now up the drill string. Residual gas settling back around the surface could conceivably find its way to the generator motor—or metal against metal —and that'd be it! The whole show would be over. These things Rock disclosed later; at the time the on-lookers had no inkling of the seriousness of the consequences. The crew, the engineer and Rock were soaked to the skin with mud and grit, struggling with the heavy connections and hoses. Dark silhouettes darted back and forth in the nightmarish scene illuminated by the stark floodlights. The noise did not abate; the fury raged on!

The frenzied scene had been going on for almost an hour when Faith and Rachel came back with coffee and donuts, soft drinks and chips. "Glory to God! Did we hit?" were Faith's words of greeting.

"Sure hit something! A gas pocket . . . and blew the well out," offered Stephen with self-conscious authority.

"Does that mean it's a disaster?" Rachel asked excitedly.

"Don't think so yet—if they can cap it in time," her husband replied.

"Well, come on in to the van and let's have some coffee or whatever. Stephen," Faith instructed, "See if any of the guys can stop for refreshment. Wait, take a couple of cups with you."

Stephen took a cup in each hand and stumbled over to where the action was. Rock spotted him and came over to him, taking the cup that Stephen offered. Rock was strangely exhilarated, like a quarterback called to the sidelines to confer with the coach—only he was the coach, too. It was the result of increased adrenaline in the face of mortal danger, like a combatant during a lull in the fighting. This was hand-to-hand combat and neither side showed any signs of yielding. Rock's face was almost unrecognizable, sweat, oil, mud; his shirt was hanging in shreds. He had lost his gold Rolex watch, Stephen noted. "Some fun, eh, brother Steve?" he shouted above the noise, which had now dulled everyone's senses to the point where it seemed to have abated.

"Straight talk, Rock. What does it look like?"

"Right from the shoulder, brother, we ain't gonna give up. I ain't gonna lose this sucker. Satan may think he's gonna drag us down, but I guaran-dam-TEE ya he ain't! Not as long as I got a breath in me and God with me! We gonna drown that sucker with mud then drop a casing string down through the formation and drill deeper to see if the pay zone is right below it. It could be a gas pocket on top of the Mississippian . . . or, we could just have us a good gas well. Jus' got to get 'er under control and see what we got!"

One more hour passed. Rock and the crew were making a superhuman effort but the blowout continued unabated.

The third hour. Exhaustion would be the decisive factor now. Two thirty a.m. came. Three a.m.

Headlights shone from the gate, increasing in illumination until they veered off and extinguished. A car door opened and closed in the darkness. Stephen followed what appeared to be a pair of light trousers walking ghostlike toward him. As they came within range of the work-lit area the dark jacket and black skin atop the pants completed the commanding figure of brother Hamilton Washington. "Praise God, fellas, you shore are making enough noise!"

Stephen clasped the stately brother in the hug and Rock, spotting him, bounded in his direction making as if to do so too—all grimy and nasty. Ham let out a roar and stepped back.

Rock shouted good-naturedly, "What kinda black brother are you? Won't have anything to do with a dirty honkey, huh?" Then, noticing Ham's attire, "Whatchu been doin'? Playin' golf all night?"

Hamilton was a natty dresser; always elegant slacks, light gold sweaters, his usual gold braided golf cap, trim white loafers. His

111

handsome, dark face was chiseled with regular features set off by a gray mustache and short gray afro. These on a six foot-three muscular frame caused many a stare wherever he went. He was reported to be a millionaire with a chain of restaurants out in the Los Angeles area. He dropped famous names with an ingenuousness that never turned people off; quite the opposite. He and his wife, Crystal, and their three children had come out here when the Lord told him to go to Kenneth Hagin's Rhema Bible Training Center in Broken Arrow. The so-called academic life, so far, did not appeal to him and he spent much of his time in good weather on the golf course.

Rock explained the situation and Hamilton excitedly broke in, "I knew God was telling me something! I woke up about an hour ago and something told me to come out here; I had really forgotten you were drilling today. So, I just obeyed, got dressed, got in the car and here I am. You people been praying?"

"Faith, Andy and Rachel have been over in the van for a couple of hours doing that," offered Stephen.

"Well, brothers, I came out here praying in tongues all the way . . . and I didn't even know anything was going on! At least bad, that is."

Faint shouts over the cacophony caught Rock's attention. He bounded to the rig, hopped over several overturned boxes and debris and pulled himself up onto the platform, bending into the action with the two other figures already there.

There was a slight reduction in the noise level; then, after a few minutes, even less noise. And, less. Someone eased off on the blouie valve and the stream that had bored a deep gully through the other side of the sludge pit backed off like a fire hydrant being turned off. It was as if total quietude were pervading the scene but the noise was only returning to its original level . . . a little less since the drill had stopped

112

rotating. The generators and the mud and water pumps were still going. "Hallelujah!" came Rock's voice along with the others'. "We got 'er!"

Faith, Rachel and Andy had come out of the van when they became aware of the change in the noise level. Spotting Hamilton, everyone had a round of hugs and Hallelujahs.

"Praise God! He answered our prayers," shouted Faith.

"Yeh, and I think He sent His servant Hamilton here, too," said Stephen to them, going into detail how Ham had been aroused out of sleep and had followed a strong leading to come out here at this time of night. "And," he reminded them, "It wasn't but a few minutes after Ham got here that they got the thing back under control! How's that for God's timing?"

"Praise God," said Rachel, tears coming to her eyes. "He used Ham to save this well from Satan's grasp!"

"Maybe. Along with the prayers of all you prayer warriors," added Hamilton tactfully.

Faith remained silent.

Chapter 10

Keeper of the Aquarium

Things were getting out of hand. Stephen felt pressured from all quarters. Faith had returned from Casa Dega, having saved the entire southeastern portion of the United States from Satan's domination and was off on another mission for God. The station limped along and he felt impotent under the circumstances with more unsolvable problems than he could handle—than any one person could be expected to handle. The board—or at least Felix—was breathing down his neck and he was picking up signals that something was brewing. There were reported meetings of board members to which he was not invited, which, if in any way official or binding, was illegal and he could call them on it. Even Doc Parsons treated him a bit diffidently when he saw him and quickly glossed over Stephen's inquiries.

Stephen felt he had to get a break from all this. Get his head screwed back on. He realized he had no real, close friend out here, no one with whom he could talk frankly—like he used to to his blood brother, Tom. No one who would drop the praises and hallelujahs even for a moment to engage in ordinary, honest, down-to-earth intelligent conversation. The closest individual who might fit that description was, of all things, the Episcopal priest of All Saints in downtown Tulsa, whom he knew slightly, Father Paul Masters.

He telephoned him and said he just wanted to drop by and chat. Sometime at Father's Paul's convenience.

It was Thursday afternoon that they had agreed upon. Stephen simply left the station, told Lydia he had somewhere to go, and she had the good sense to understand and cover for him.

As he walked around the gothic-style church, which was probably built right after the First World War when that kind of stone-crafting was still being done well, into the adjoining Parish House of similar style, he was struck by a strange touch of nostalgia. This was so much like the one he had attended as a boy in Atlanta at the corner of Spring and Peachtree, where his scout troop was. And, it was like the one in Darien that he, Diana and the kids had attended from time to time. He sensed that there was, after all, comfort in tradition.

Father Paul Masters had seen him from his window and went to meet him in the hallway. "Steve, this is an unexpected pleasure."

"Thank you, Paul. You'll be pleased to know that it feels kind of good to be back in familiar traditional surroundings. Some admission for a wild charismatic, isn't it?"

"If you're looking to joining the All Saints' congregation, I'll sign you right up." He motioned Stephen to a leather stuffed chair in the conversation nook in his book-lined office study-conference room. Stephen had never been in it before. It smacked of Yale; the gothic stone window treatment, the leaded mullions and the fired, imperfect glass panes, the shelves with rows upon rows of volumes. He diverted his direction toward them, feeling comfortable, strangely at home. Instant rapport with his surroundings as well as with his host. Stephen scanned some titles, conscious that Paul was studying him.

115

"So, my friend, what brings you to this humble sanctuary of the dead, liturgical church of the end times? Isn't that what you Holy Spirit-filled tongue-speaking charismatics refer to us as?" he said, smiling engagingly. "The lukewarm church of Laodicea . . . from Revelation?"

"Ouch. You've got my number."

"Don't forget. We ministers of the traditional church—some of us, anyway— are not so dead or, at least, lukewarm as you suspect. You know, I know Terry Fullam up there in your country."

"No, I didn't know that," Stephen said taking a book off the shelf and opening it. "After I was converted to Christ I used to go over to Greenwich to Fullam's Episcopal church. Really charismatic! The Spirit really moving. The people really turned on to the Lord. I loved it."

"Terry and I are old friends. And, we are pretty close theologically."

Stephen turned. "You don't mean you're charismatic, too?"

"Could be. Although if I am, it hasn't manifested itself in quite the same way as with you folks."

"Hmmm. Interesting. You know, I was converted in an Episcopal charismatic church in Atlanta. I think I might have told you. John Bellman's church.

"We're a small fraternity. Yes, I know John. He and I overlapped at Sewanee Theological Seminary. '55."

"Talk about a small world! I went to Sewanee Military Academy. Where'd you do your undergraduate?"

"Princeton. V-5, class of '45."

"Pret-ty good. You've covered all bases—northern and southern Ivy leagues—liberal and conservative. Did you go into the Navy?"

"Took a reserve commission. War was over . . . until Korea. Then I got called up. Stayed stateside. Then, decided on seminary. And you?"

"Yale, '60. Liberal arts, english major. Real practical, huh? But, it was no drawback later getting onto Madison Avenue, that and my military experience. Got a PLC commission —Platoon Leaders Class— Marines. Liked it; was able to go regular . . . which was a little unusual in those days."

"How long did you stay in?"

"Seven years. Made captain, commanded a rifle company in the 5th Marines in Vietnam. Got shot up—mortar shrapnel—smashed hip. By the time I got out of the hospital, my usefulness to the Marines was, to put it practically—zilch ! I'd married Diana about that point and with a contact or two I landed on the Marine Corps account at J. Walter Thompson advertising in New York."

"I spent some time in New York, myself, right after Princeton. Got into early television, back when the ad agencies were producing the shows . . . worked on the early oratorios and opera-concerts televised from Carnegie Hall. Exciting times."

"Well, Praise G'—listen to me. It just comes out now. I'm around them all the time"

"Nothing wrong with that. We should be doing that, too, in the Episcopal church. I suppose we are dead or lukewarm in that respect. Respect—too respectable to let ourselves go and really enjoy the Lord. No. We are that— respectable— if nothing else— snobbish, if you really get right down to it. Unfortunately, either we Episcopalians are or are perceived to be a social church. You know only too well that you find the community leaders, the monied—old money especially—seem mostly to be Episcopalians."

Stephen cut in, "But aren't a lot of converted Jews Episcopalians, too? Don't they usually become Episcopalians, I guess, because they want to move with the 'right' crowd? Or, they join the Unitarians? . . . whose lack of particular beliefs, especially concerning Jesus—the usual stumbling block for Jews—and Unity's monotheism present no obstacle to them . . . nor does Episcopalianism, for that matter."

Paul allowed him to continue without commenting.

"As to lukewarm . . . ," Stephen continued, "that's basically what the charismatics have against Episcopalians—all mainline, liturgical churches, for that matter. Revelation 3:14 or so? . . . something to the effect of . . . *'Woe to the church of Laodicea . . . you are neither hot or cold'* . . . "

Paul picked up on it, . . . *So 'because you are lukewarm, and neither hot or cold, I will spit you out of my mouth. Because you say, I am rich and have become wealthy, and have need of nothing!'.* . .

Stephen finished it, "and 'you do not know that you are wretched and miserable and poor and blind and naked!' Say, we ought to try team preaching!"

Paul smiled. "So, the Episcopalians, and the Roman Catholics, and Presbyterians, Lutherans, Methodists, and so on— not the Baptists, of course—are the church of Laodicea of the end times that Jesus finds wanting, whereas, you charismatics who have rediscovered the early simplicity, power and love of Jesus' teachings are His church of Philadelphia of the end times, whom He loves. It might be so. You people certainly seem to be causing a worldwide awakening of the Holy Spirit. Of course, there have been numerous such revivals, especially in the nineteenth century, but certainly nothing on this present scale.

"And, you know what has occurred to me?" continued Paul, now caught up in the direction of the dialogue and finding it refreshing that he could express some innermost thoughts without the fear that they would be misinterpreted and spread around the flock. "It began about the same time at the turn of this century that Zionism did. You know, biblical scholars haven't associated the two things as yet to my knowledge. But, just think: what if God really did cause Hertzel to stir up Zionism so that the Jews dispersed all over the world since Roman Emperor Titus destroyed Jerusalem in A.D. 70—as Jesus had predicted would be done— to bring the Jews back to the Holy Land, to Jerusalem—which happened in 1948 thanks to the U.N.—and, at the same time, brought forth an outpouring of the Holy Spirit in order to prepare the Christian world for the dry bones of Ezekiel's Israel to come back to life and to prepare Christians for their part in the Second Coming of Christ!"

Stephen interjected, "Which will be seen by all the world at one time—How? On TV, of course. Christian TV."

"Hadn't thought of it exactly that way . . . "

"You aware that the satellite up there carrying all this Christian network broadcasting was dubbed Angel ?"

'And I saw another angel fly in the midst of heaven, carrying the eternal gospel to preach to all the earth, and to every nation and tribe and tongue and people.'

"You see? That's where Christian satellite television comes in, why God created it and gave it to us. The gospel has to be preached to all the world before Christ will come again! That satellite 'footprint'—all those footprints of the signals from dozens of transponders—can conceivably cover the entire globe! Paul, there are many things coming to light in biblical teachings . . . by Oral, Hagin, Copeland, Robertson . . . all of these people. New interpretations, hidden things now revealed to those truly anointed with the Holy Spirit."

"Fulfilling the prophesy of one of the last chapters of Daniel . . . *and in the last days men will go to and fro and knowledge will increase.* Not very impressive in its usual context —except when looked at in line with our phenomenal progress today . . . jet travel and the computer, high tech, space age. Knowledge certainly doubles itself every decade. I've given up even trying to keep up."

"That's partly why this charismatic thing is so attractive," observed Stephen. "With life so complex, so hectic, so overwhelming— what a comfort it is to come back to the simplicity of the Bible and its assurances of all the things, the peace, the joy, the hopes, the protection . . . that nothing else can give a person."

"You're right about that. And I've got to hand it to your group. They know how to get it across and make it work—come alive." Paul asked Stephen if he would like a soft drink . . . or something harder. Both offers were declined. "So, Steve, what is it that really brought you here?"

Stephen stretched his legs forward and slouched down a bit, getting himself more comfortable. "Guess I got a lot on my mind these days. And, I'm not here to unload them on you as a counselor . . . you get enough of that, I can imagine. I really just wanted to talk to someone intelligent, learned. Faith would accuse me of pride, but I honestly sometimes cannot abide all these people and their Bible-thumping all the time. They don't think, don't allow themselves to; everything is ingrained in them. All rote. None of them read newspapers, books or magazines; they certainly don't watch secular television! . . . I don't have any idea what Faith thinks—she doesn't think, the Word is so ingrained in her that her every response is a quote or paraphrase from scripture. I realize I have married someone I don't actually know at all! She's a tape machine on a continuous loop. So? What have I gotten myself into? *'Left house and wife and brothers and parents and children for the sake of the kingdom of God . . . who shall receive a hundred times as much and in the age to come, eternal life.'* I stood on that. Gave up wife, family, job . . . to step out in faith . . . and I can't figure out whether God is still testing me . . . or I'm just not one of His chosen. But, I don't want this to turn into an analysis of my marriage . . . or my problems with the station. Now that I'm so involved in this part of religion that they like to call the fishers of men as opposed to the keepers of the aquarium , the traditional church I left . . . I'd sort of like to stand off and take a good, objective look at them both. Try to fathom the whole thing."

"I'm afraid nothing will ever be objective in religion. But, you tell me. How do you see them differing?"

"Basically, it's one group— yours—holding up all assembled together to grow, worship and, I suppose prosper. But, there are no real works with it . . . .The other are the Evangelists— the charismatics, fundamentalists—who have taken God's command in Mark 16 to go forth into all the world and spread the Good News—the Gospel—of Jesus Christ to all creation. Those who believe and are baptized will be saved, those who do not will be damned. So, the second group are 'doers.' They bring the lost into the kingdom of heaven on earth."

"Those verses of Mark, chapter 15, verses 15 through 18, have probably caused more trouble than any others in the Bible. They are spurious; most scholars are of the belief that they were added into that Gospel at a much later date and therefore are not the actual words of Jesus. And, so much spurious theology has been built around them, especially about handling serpents and you will not be bitten, that sort of thing taken literally by some sects . . .   And around a lot of other mistranslations, especially from the 1611 so-called Authorized King James version."

"I know, it's somewhat pathetic. 'Authorized' by good ol' King James, of course, not Jesus, as the fundamentalists think . . . You can just hear them now . . . 'praise God, if the King James was good enough for Jesus, it's good enough for me!' The astounding ignorance in all this is staggering. Yet Hagin, Copeland—all swear by it. Those Elizabethan 'thees' and 'thous' seem to set the Bible off into something a bit removed from the ordinary . . . yet, Jesus, it seems to me, wanted His Word to be simple, to be understood by everyone. Especially not just by Ph.D's of Divinity, deigning to interpret for us unwashed."

"Like yours truly?"

"No offense. But, what do they teach in theological seminaries?"

"A lot of things . . . outmoded things, ancient thinking, church structure, ritual, cannon law, the prayer book. And, a little Bible thrown in for good measure."

"Someone who dropped out of a Roman Catholic seminary told me that he was actually chastised for reading the Bible; the Catholic hierarchy wants the story told their way. And, how come you can go into a Baptist church and find a Bible at every seat . . . and hear the preacher preach the sermon directly from it as the congregation follows? . . . and you can't even find a Bible in the Episcopal church except the giant one on the lectern at the altar?"

"Alas, alas, you have hit on a troubling truth. Aside from the short readings from the Old and New Testaments, we Episcopalians use the prayer book as our Bible. More of us fight over that and how to use it and how to change or not change it than fighting the real issues of living a righteous life in a sinful world."

"But," reflected Stephen, "take the Baptists. They, of all the backbone denominations . . . of all the traditional churches . . . they are just in between the dead liturgical keepers of the aquarium and the fishers of men, the latter which they profess to be. And they believe in the literal Word of God as that of every word of the Bible—King James version, of course. But, they just can't quite see it either—they just miss! They go out and preach the gospel and gather the lost sinners and lead them to Christ—they think— getting them 'born again' and baptized by immersion in water. But, they get the lost soul there by threat, by scaring him with fire and brimstone and eternal damnation otherwise. They don't realize it but they teach the old burden of 'burning in hell fire for sins' if you don't confess and ask forgiveness. They don't preach coming to the Lord in love—for love. It's like taking the flock . . . taking themselves . . . through the ordeal of the desert, of wandering in the wilderness and then standing on the ridge overlooking the Promised Land— but they never go on down into it . . . like the charismatics do. We preach 'coming to the Lord' in repentance and love, but we are able to really 'live a life in Christ' as it was meant to be lived because we are not only born again as new creations in Christ but we have been baptized in and have received the power of the Holy Spirit . . . so that we can operate in power—good things happen to us, miracles, the gifts of the spirit. And, of course, the upshot of all this is that we charismatics truly find the 'fruit of the spirit' . . . "

" . . . Galatians 5:22 . . . *love, joy, peace, patience, kindness, goodness, faithfulness . . . gentleness, self-control.* Does your life exhibit these fruit, my friend?" asked the Episcopal priest..

" . . . well, I guess I'd say . . . most of them . . . for the most part . . . most of the time. Who am I kidding? But I'm striving for them, and I have the power through the Holy Spirit to attain them," defended Stephen. "But, the Baptists miss it in their literal interpretation of the Bible in one place and that screws them all up—First Corinthians chapter 13—the beautiful Love chapter . . . verse 10 . . . *'but when the perfect comes . . . tongues will cease . . . knowledge and gifts will be done away with'* . . . something to that effect. Poor souls, they interpret 'perfect' to mean the final writing down of the Bible, so they think the power of the Holy Spirit is no longer needed with all His gifts since the Bible was written. They don't realize that perfect refers to Christ, Jesus. He is the 'perfect.' And, no, when He comes again, we won't need the power of the gifts. But the Baptists just don't get it . . . and they loose so much of the teaching . . . not to mention that their lives are always only half-fulfilled as a consequence. As Jesus said, '*I am the Way*' . . . *meaning out of bondage* . . . '*I am the Truth*' . . . meaning the law, the new covenant of the Spirit . . . and 'I am the Life' . . . meaning the new life in the promised land enjoying the fruits of the Spirit. See how that all makes sense? And, how the poor Baptists miss it? As do many other fundamentalists who are not imbued with the Pentecostal power of the Holy Spirit . . . "

"If you level such charges at those good Baptist brothers, goodness knows what else you would have to say about us poor, almost heathen-by-comparison Episcopalians! At least they go about carrying their Bibles and trying to live as the Gospel requires. No, an Episcopalian—anyone from a liturgical church—doesn't go around totin' a Bible."

"Hmmm. Brings to mind, to change the subject a bit, now I hear that the Episcopal church is ordaining women. Next thing you know, it'll be homosexuals! How do you feel, Paul, about ordaining women? We have beaucoup women ministers and preachers in the charismatic movement, and they are truly God's instruments."

"Rather than answer that directly, let me put it to you this way: how strongly do you feel about Apostolic Succession?"

"I've heard the term but I'm not sure exactly what it means."

"It means that starting with the name of the Episcopal bishop of this parish, one can trace back in the records—in history—every preceding bishop all the way back to Peter, the Apostle of Christ, in the first century. The names of every one in the succession, the unbroken chain directly from Saint Peter. Now, if you think that is important, that is something you will want to preserve. There have been no female names in that line. Recall that in the Old testament the line of succession was always through the male; Abraham begat Isaac . . . and so and so."

"You've got a point there. How important is it? If you are traditional, conservative, you want to preserve that rather than be the first

124

to break it and destroy the whole thing. I know the Roman Catholics think it is very important."

"Well, today we are faced with the ever increasing forces of 'liberalism,' up-dating, modern thinking, or what have you. As you are aware, even the Bible is being re-interpreted in the light of liberal thought. Things that have heretofore been sacrosanct are caving in under so-called enlightened scrutiny. Just like the recent attack by the hippie generation on our hallowed institutions, some of which crumbled without so much as a fight. To wit, as a result we now have a society that has virtually abandoned the Bible, certainly the organized churches; prayer has been taken out of the schools, the family has disintegrated, divorce is the norm, sexual promiscuity is rampant, drugs have replaced Christian teachings, violence has replaced the peace and tranquility of our cities."

"All the predictions of the end times coming true? . . . *'and upon the earth dismay among nations, in perplexity at the roaring of the sea and the waves, men fainting from fear and the expectation of the things which are coming upon the world; for the powers of the heavens will be shaken.'* Luke 21."

"If any of your charismatics have picked up on that 'heavens,' it is in Greek, *ouranon* . . . any connection with 'uranium,' you think? Hydrogen bombs? I would have thought your people would have carried that to the goal line."

"Indeed they have, many of them preach on it: that the coming confrontation with the Soviet Union will be that Armageddon that will ultimately usher in Christ's second coming. You ought to hear Pat Robertson of CBN go to town on that!"

"So, back to Apostolic Succession," steered Paul, "even when Henry VIII broke with Rome and the Anglican Catholic branch—based on adultery, I might remind you—came into existence in purer form without the trappings of Mary and other impedimenta, it has been

125

somewhat of a backbone right on down to the American Episcopal offshoot. To now eliminate that, or interrupt it, or to bastardize it . . . well? Is that important in the scheme of salvation?"

"Speaking of that break with Rome that came shortly after Martin Luther's in Germany, the charismatics— and, I'm sure all the fundamentalists, too—regard the Roman Catholic church as a cult, a vile perversion of the true church."

"It would be politic of me not to engage in this line of reasoning."

"I'm just telling you what they think; I haven't made up my mind about it yet. But, they think that when emperor Constantine adopted Christianity in one fell swoop, and made the empire do likewise, that it was not by conviction but was just a covering over and continuation of paganism. Even Christmas was a cop out. Constantine had to keep his troops happy, and they were happy with and would not give up their bacchanalian Mithraic cult of ritual and debauchery, especially on december 25th. So, Constantine just adopted that date for the birth of Christ and everybody celebrated whatever way they wanted on that date . . . and it was finalized at the Nicean Council in A.D. 323. Then, the thought goes, the Roman church started growing and, instead of following the simple precepts of the simple Christians that had been beaten up on and who now were tolerated, added on layers of hierarchy and dogma so that in time the Roman church became as powerful as a temporal state—more powerful in many cases."

"History is rife with examples of that."

"And, as the top bishop held power as Peter's direct successor, as Pope, Christ's simple teachings took on trappings and tangents never imagined in the Gospels."

"Fortunately, the Anglican church dropped most of those corruptions."

"Enlightened Roman Catholic charismatics do also, thank God! . . . but, to continue, everybody knows of the degradation, the degeneracy and vile perversions of the Papacy after the turn of the first millennium and for a long time afterwards . . . the Papacy became a house of prostitution, of Satan worship, of gambling, of all sorts of wickednesses and perversions and crimes . . . the excesses go on and on."

"Pretty rough times, all right," Paul confirmed.

"Not to digress, but I came across an incredible history of the Crusade of Pope Innocent III, not over to the Holy Land as the previous ones had been, but into southern France to wipe out the Cathars, a sect that was trying to maintain Christ's simple teachings and a populace that was trying to live the good Christian life in the early 1200s. The atrocities in the Name of Christ on the part of the crusaders make the Holocaust look like a picnic! Read some day about the massacre of French Christians at Mont Ségur! Sickening that such things could be done in the name of Jesus!"

"They weren't. They were done for political power. And, atrocious they were. Think about the Catholic Inquisition. Look into that one. Defies belief."

"Of course, the charismatic-fundamentalists also blast the cult of the Virgin Mary and all the Catholics' praying to the dead, to their saints —which the Bible strictly forbids— and rewriting the Bible to create the Immaculate Conception , which most protestants think refers to Jesus' virgin birth. But, no! That refers to Mary's virgin birth also . . . and the Assumption of Mary, not dying but simply ascending!—only Jesus ascended, He only rose from the dead—which they made up, along with the 'sacred heart' business, purgatory, having to 'work' your way into heaven and a whole bunch of nonsense inflicted on the gullible to keep them in line. Total thought control. Like confession to a priest. The Bible says '*confess your sins to God and He will hear you; you need no   intercessor between yourself and Christ Jesus.* And, Jesus expressly admonishes about calling any man 'father' except your Father in heaven . . . and it goes on and on—worse than the Mormons!"

"Relieved to get some of that off your chest? Want to tackle the Jews? Off hand, though, I'd say you've done a good share of serious reading and thinking but you could use some organizing and balance."

"I guess I'm just rattling off. I don't know what I really wanted to get out of this session. Guess I just need to bounce some, as you noticed, disconnected things off some sympathetic, understanding—or corrective ear."

"How about a small glass of sherry?"

"You know, that would just be great. I swore off all that stuff, but sherry is wine and Jesus drank wine, seemed pretty well to have condoned it, since He turned water into it. And, what safer place to imbibe than in the sanctuary of the church?"

Paul poured them each a glass. "Here's to your good health . . . as my predecessor and namesake, Saint Paul, wrote to his faithful pupil, Timothy, *'be sure to take a little wine; it is good for the stomach . . . and your frequent ailments.'* Steve, I hope you will take this bit of advice—leading of the Lord, if you will—from one older than yourself and one who has been doing the Lord's work a lot longer than you have—dead, lukewarm, or whatever. Read and study the two letters to Timothy. I think you will find some much-needed insight and guidance in them. Something pertinent to avoiding worldly and empty chatter and the opposing arguments of what is falsely called knowledge."

Stephen held the glass up in acknowledgment . . . swirled it ever so slightly to let the setting sun's rays from the window irradiate the nut brown liquid . . . and slowly savored the first taste of alcohol that had passed his lips in four years.

It went down smoothly and warmly.

Chapter 11   Revelation

Stephen picked up the phone.

"Hey, there, brother Steve. This here's Rock. Lord a' treatin' ya all right?"

"I haven't checked this morning . . . but I'm still kicking."

"Good to hear it. What I'm calling is . . . you gonna buy in on Revelation?"

"The Lord hasn't spoken to me on that one yet. How's the completion of Logos five?"

"Coming right along. Sooner's connecting it to th' others and then they gotta make the main connection to the main line. I'll keep ya' posted. Meantime . . . les' you'n me go on out to the Revelation 22:20 site . . . so you'kn git th' feel of it. Brother Ham wants to go too. I'll swing by in half an hour."

"OK. Might as well. Not much I can do here except muddy the waters."

Rock pulled up in his fancy new Toyota pick-up. "How are we all going to get in this?" asked Stephen.

"Brother, we ain't going all the way in this. You watch."

After a ten-minute drive they pulled into a nice new subdivision with a light brown brick entrance way. The houses were neat, attractive and in the hundred and fifty thousand range. As they turned into the driveway of a ranch style house with a beautifully kept lawn, brother Hamilton Washington strode out, neatly dressed, as usual.

"Hi, there, brothers—Hey, how do you expect us all to squeeze in there?"

"Nothin' to it," quipped Rock, "Just take a deep breath, squeeze in and keep your knees together!"

"No way, Jose! Not for a two-hour drive each way. C'mon, let's take my Caddie."

Rock winked at Stephen. "What'd I tell ya?"

Stephen chose to sprawl out in the back seat and enjoyed the scenery as he tuned in and out of the animated conversation in the front seat. This part of the country as they headed west became more barren but still fascinating. He could imagine indians roaming these plains with the scattered scrub brush and clumps of stunted trees. Imagine them charging on horseback chasing—or being chased by—U.S. Cavalry troops just like a cliché out of Western movies. Or, the pioneers of 1890s who lined up to charge forth in their covered wagons with their families and possessions when the signal gun was fired to grab large plots of ground and stake claims for homesteads which the federal government would give them for free ! Many of them succeeded; many succumbed to the unexpected rigors of plains life. Opportunists, or those who were not yet ready to settle, simply staked a claim and erected a portion of a mud brick wall with the indication of a window frame, which was all the government required to keep the claim. Of course, many of these large spreads that were plain to see now stretching to the horizons came from that homesteading, and the descendants generations later were fortunate enough to enter a second phase of bounty when oil was discovered underneath their land. Their rights went to the center of the earth, virtually, so they ended up with a royalty right to whatever lay beneath them. All they had to do was sign a lease that some landman had drawn up after diligent research in the county seat, which would allow for so-and-so to drill at a particular spot on their land—at driller's expense—and, if they hit, the landowner, heirs and all, would receive a twelve percent royalty on the proceeds that gushed forth. Many a rancher's or farmer's oil royalties exceeded his crop or cattle income. It was all fascinating to Stephen—so utterly different from the life he had known, been brought up in. Such a far cry from Yale and Madison Avenue.

At an opportune moment, Stephen broke into the conversation and asked Ham how he had come into all this Logos and oil business . . . with the Lord.

"Whew! That's a long story, brother." Ham replied, eyes concentrated on the roadway, and pausing to gather his thoughts. "Guess it all started back in Detroit. My dad worked at the River Rouge plant, one of the few blacks that made it. By the time I came along and was growing up, he'd somehow instilled in me something—a desire to be better, maybe—that kept me off the streets, away from the gangs. Guess the fact that I played good football in high school . . . on the fringe of one of the better neighborhoods . . . put me in good stead with my peers, both black and white . . . "

"Shoot, man," Rock interrupted, "With them good looks of yours . . . back then, you musta had all them chicks—black and white—a fallin' all over ya'!"

"Hey, man. Whose tellin' this story? . . . So, I managed to stay out of trouble . . . went to a junior college a couple of years, studied business, accounting, that sort of thing. Then, an opportunity came along and I went into the restaurant business. Did pretty well. Started saving some money, got married to Crystal, the children started coming . . . and I got the break of my life. Fred Price—you know the black evangelist brother in Los Angeles? . . . "

Rock and Stephen both echoed acknowledgment of Fred and his ministry.

"Well, to make a long story short. Fred came to Detroit, I went to one of his revivals . . . and got hooked on the Lord. Brother Fred took a liking to me and we, our wives and all, got together . . . and he proceeded to lead me on through the process . . . .the born-again bit and the baptism in the Spirit as well. No need to tell you that that did something to my life. I don't think I was off on the wrong track or anything . . . was just going along trying to do my best, earn a living and raise a family . . . so, I didn't have one of those 'God striking you' things . . . or anything like that; I just had a nice recharging of my batteries . . . So after that, Fred and I kept in touch and he would give me a call when he was in the area . . . and we got to be pretty good buddies . . . buddies in the Lord, if you will.

"Praise God! That brother Fred's really with the Lord, ain't 'e?" added Rock irrepressibly.

"Then, one day I get a call from brother Fred and he tells me about an opportunity . . . a business opportunity out there in LA . . . a restaurant up for sale by a friend of his. He thought I might be interested and why don't I just pop on out there and check it out? . . . I did . . . I liked the deal . . . the brother was a Christian, the one selling it—you know you gotta be real careful in this business; supply, trucking, liquor licenses and all, the underworld gets mixed up in all this and sometimes you don't know what's what . . . know what I mean?"

"Hallelujah, brother," punctuated Rock again.

"The upshot? I bought the restaurant, prospered, made enough money to buy a real good one in Santa Monica . . . then another one near Malibu. And, I was living pretty well . . . and attending Fred's church there . . . and tithing pretty heavily.   But, somewhere along the line there was some sort of screwup, my CPA didn't do something right— or at least the IRS didn't think so . . . and, I guess to them, the restaurant business is suspect to begin with, especially the ones making a lot of money. So, I had audit after audit . . . to the point I felt they were deliberately harassing me. Matter of fact, I think they still have their boys tailing me . . . even out here! Well, they were giving me such a hard time that I was practically driven out of business. My accountants argued with them, we appealed, but the cost was getting so that I just said pay off the bast—you know what I mean—and let's stop this battle. Fred then suggested that I get a change of pace and scenery and come out here to Brother Leo's Logos Bible Training set-up. Good thing I had my brother—blood brother—and oldest son who could take over things for me . . . So, here I am driving you two crazy charismatic brothers out here in the middle of nowhere—in Oklahoma !—going out to see a piece of dirt and dig a hole in it."

"Brother we don't dig oil wells—we drill oil wells. You dig water wells—dig me?" Rock corrected good-naturedly. "You gotta shake off all that yankee talk. Don't wanna sound like this dude, Steve, back there, do ya'?"

"Thanks a bunch, pal." Stephen retorted. "What does it take to get accepted here, anyway?"

They left the four-lane divided highway and traveled down a scraped dirt road. "Hope we aren't gonna need that four-wheel drive in your pickup, Rock."

"Naw. Nothing to worry 'bout, 'cep getting red clay dust and crud in this here fancy white Caddy-lak! Tell ya', hit's a gonna be red by the time we get back. Sure rides good, though. Beats that little Jap buggy of mine."

Rock directed Ham to turn off toward a low hillock. "This here dome-like hill we're on is probably what we gonna find down six thousand five hundred feet down there, 'cept we're a hopin' there's goin' ta' be a pocket or a pool a oil at the top of it, floatin' on a pool or river of water. If that sucker's big enough, or it's a river of oil itself, we gon' git us our eight hundred barrels a day!"

"Holy Lord! Eight hundred?" exclaimed Ham.

Rock went on, thoroughly relishing the telling as much as the drilling. "This ain't goin' to be like them other shallow wells . . . this here is 'big time.' You ain't seen a rig like we gonna use on this one . . . or the heavy stuff, frac'ers, cementers . . . man, this place will look like a truck stop. And, you ain't seen no sludge pit like we gonna have . . . big as an olympic pool . . . Man, we'll be in the big leagues! Wait'll ya see the drill pipe! . . . and, you know, this is gonna be one big, big operation! We gotta drill down there . . . gotta put a big outer casing over the drill stem all the way down . . . to keep the sides from caving in . . . gotta get way down there . . . down to the pay zone . . . gotta cement the casing so it and the formation will stay in place . . . then gotta replace the drill stem with tubing so the oil can come up through it . . . then gotta frac' the formation so hit don't cave in or tighten up . . . and then stand out of th' way and let 'er come! We got to gather all that oil, 'course, and get it trucked outta here constantly . . . they'll be a big holding tank . . . but them tanker trucks is a gonna be coming in and outta here like the Tulsa freeway at rush hour! Lordy, what a sight this is gonna be!"

"Man! Wish I could buy into it," exclaimed Ham. " Afraid I can't, though."

"Well, just ask the Lord to lead. That's what Stevie boy is doing right now. Right, brother?"

Stephen glanced at him then started walking around the site. Beautiful. Somewhat of a clay shale ground, small, crushable rocks.

Scrub trees, not pine, but he couldn't identify them. He was deep in thought and prayer. *'Lord, is this the one that You are finally going to bless me with? I need a strong leading from You. A definite sign.'*

"Pity civilization had to come to this part of the world. Think of the wildlife, game, fowl, that roamed these open spaces," reflected Stephen to no one in particular.

"And, the Indians," Rock added.

Stephen looked at him. "Anybody prayed over the site yet?"

"Don't think so. Les' us do it," suggested Rock.

"I could use Faith here right about now. Casting out demons is her schtick." Seeing Rock's eyebrow go up, he continued, " . . . her special gift. But, let's give her a try, brothers . . . *'where two or three are gathered, there He will be in our midst.'*"

They joined hands, forming a circle, heads down, eyes closed. "Father God," Stephen began, " . . . You see us down here calling upon You to hear us in the precious Name of Your Son, Jesus . . . and we just ask that You honor our request as we stand on Your Word and sanctify this land to You, to Your works . . . and, in the Name of Jesus, we rebuke Satan and all his demons . . . especially lingering indian spirits—that were not of You, Lord . . . and we bind them in Jesus' Name . . . and cast them out, Hallelujah, in the Name of Jesus. Lall-sa ya-sab-athach-tha-na-so-we-eela-tha . . . We stand on Your Word. We have bound and cast out of this land whatever would come against You, Lord, against us, Lord, who are going forth in Your Name . . . and we just claim that this oil well . . . that has been named Revelation 22:20—Yes, I am coming quickly. Amen. Come, Lord Jesus—after Your Word . . . will come in successfully . . . that it will produce eight hundred barrels—no, we, Your humble servants, will put no limit on it—we place our trust in You, Lord, knowing that You will bring forth the fruit of the land and prosper us all with Your riches . . . so that we may do Your will. And, I just thank You,

Father, that You have chosen us . . . to do Your will. And, we praise You and sanctify You, and give all the thanks to You, Oh Lord. In the Name of Your precious Son, Jesus. Amen! . . . and Amen . . . and Amen. Hallelujah!"

That evening Stephen called his brother, Tom, in Atlanta. "How're things going? How's dad?"

After getting an update of the status quo, except for the fact that Tom was having to give more of his attention to dad, which was affecting his home life and his job adversely, things were as expected. Dad could barely hobble around on his cane, holding his right arm tightly to his body and dragging his right leg, not able to utter intelligible speech. Tom described him as terribly frustrated over his condition, and it was virtually impossible to communicate with him, even after long, protracted efforts at sign language, pointing, articulating thoughts . . . only for dad to shake his head.. no, that was not it and then retreating into himself and virtually giving up. Tom thought that the nursing care might not be enough; he might have to be put in a nursing home.

That sort of news unnerved Stephen. It undermined what he was calling about. Finally, working his way circumspectly around to the wells, he reported the condition of the Logos field and the possibilities of success for number five.

Tom had been enthusiastic about the first several investments, feeling as Stephen did, that the leading was truly 'of the Lord.' Now, however, since so much money had had apparently been lost . . . down a bottomless hole, so to speak . . . he was having second thoughts. Doubting the wisdom—even the leading of the Lord—in the investment. Stephen reminded him that he, Tom, had stepped out in faith just as he had.

Stephen explained how Revelation was going to be 'big time' drilling. How much more complex it was going to be, and, therefore, more costly. But the payoff was so much higher . . . eight hundred barrels a day! That would mean about thirty-two thousand per share per month! Roughly $385,000 a year. Three shares . . . and that's over a million-one a year! Think what that could do for dad! . . . for all of us . . . our children . . . the ministry!

"How much a share?" Tom resignedly asked.

"This limited partnership is limited to just fifteen partners . . . each share $40,000. I'm buying one for myself out of what I've got left. I'm thinking two more, one for you and one for dad, both out of the estate—joint tenancy, you and dad."

The silence on the other end of the line was not unexpected. Tom finally came back on and in an even voice said, "You know, of course, what that will do to the remaining estate?"

"I know. I've thought it all out . . . and I have had a strong leading from the Lord. I believe the foregoing was just the Lord testing me—or us— and that now we are to step out in our biggest test yet. I'm going for it . . . and I won't even have five thousand left afterwards— but, I might just well have over a hundred thousand a year coming in, too!"

"I'll have to think it over, pray about it. I'll get back to you."

"Well, don't take more than a day. These are the last three units, and as soon as they get sold the well will be started."

The evening of the following day, Tom called and Stephen immediately relayed the news to Rock. "OK, brother. We're in for three! I'm taking one myself. My brother Tom is taking two for himself and our dad, jointly . . . tenants by the entirety."

"Hallelujah, brother Steve! I'll let know know how soon we can spud!"

Chapter 12

Not a River but a Flood

It was Thursday and Stephen had agreed to attend this one evening in Oral Roberts' weeklong crusade at the downtown civic center. He would rather have disengaged himself if there had been some way to do it graciously. . . at least without causing a ruckus with Faith. She liked to appear at these sorts of things as a couple, the model Christian couple, he figured. He could bet all the other model Christian couples would be there: Matt and Leah, Andy and Rachel, and, of course, all the evangelicals, John Mark, Billy Bob Baxter . . . all those types. And Oral was having Kenneth Copeland as special guest. Lydia had said she was going, so was Rebecca. Rock and his wife, Dorcas, would be there. Of course, KXAO TV board members Doc Parsons and Barnabas Childs, could be counted on. He could rest assured that Felix would not. Nor would Brother Leo, lest he steal some of Oral's thunder. He wondered whether Reverend Paul Masters would be?

Making slow progress through the constant hugs and Holy Kisses as they met people they knew, Stephen and Faith—and Andy and Rachel and Matt and Leah—finally made it up to the balcony to the right of the large stage, and settled in their seats a full hour before the designated time to start. Stephen desultorily scanned the hordes—the biblical 'seas' of people milling about to see if he could spot any familiar faces. He noticed again that this was a fairly well-dressed crowd, considering the temperature outside which was still insuperable when they came in. Although the modern center no doubt had its air conditioning up to maximum, that was beginning to equalize with the hundreds upon hundreds of bodies continually crowding in. It was a happy crowd; a lot of camaraderie, back slapping, embracing, hailing and going to and fro. He spotted everyone he expected to; even Rock was ushering. Stephen had gone over to Rock's office that morning and had written him out his personal check for $40,000 for the one share, and another for $80,000 on his dad's Merrill Lynch cash management account, for the other two. So, they were in Revelation 22:20 and the die was cast . . . as Caesar said as he crossed the Young & Rubicam (*pun intended*). No turning back. It would have been a better simile if he could have worked in Constantine's '*In Hoc Signo Vinces*,' . . . in this sign (the sign of the cross) you will conquer. That should stand for Revelation 22:20 : victory in the sign of the cross! Good old Constantine—old reprobate!

The evening's program was filled with singing by various groups and various soloists, including the rich baritone of Kenneth Copeland himself, and Richard Roberts, and it seemed like dozens of others. It went on and on, the audience not tiring for a minute and always anxious for more, clapping along where appropriate, and sometimes singing and praising along too. It was truly a spirited and Spirit-filled evening. The highlight, of course, was what everyone had been anticipating all week: Oral's big sermon.

And, none were in any way disappointed. They clung to his every word, his every action, his every intonation, every grimace, every entreaty, every gesture, every passionate plea, every beseeching of God's blessing, guidance, mercy, grace . . . some perched on the edges of their seats in rapt attention, some taking notes throughout. Oral had them all in the palms of his hands, his magnetism was mesmerizing. They would have done anything he wanted them to . . . and shortly they would do just exactly that! With the practice of more than thirty years—having earned his spurs in the dusty Gospel tent circuits of the forties— he had received a special ministry from the Lord for healing and had subsequently gained an ever widening reputation as a Faith Healer. Having been miraculously healed himself by the Lord at an early age, he went on to minister that power to heal with which God had endowed him until he had become one of the best-known preachers in the midwest. Stephen wondered for a moment *what, if anything, he had done in World War II, he would have just been of age to have been called for military service. Had he claimed 'conscientious objection,' he wondered? Or physical disability?—seems odd, if God had healed him. Stephen wondered about Brother Leo also, but he remembered the brother saying something about his miraculous recovery as a lad in the thirties. Maybe he had been 4-F as a result of that.*

Oral was a tall, imposing man, marvelously in his stride, talking about God's giving . . . and a Christian's giving . . . and how, "when a Christian gives to God and to God's works, God gives back so much more than anybody can ever give . . . and it all starts out like a trickle . . . and then the trickle becomes a river—You can never out give God!— and the river becomes a flood! And, you can't stop it! From a trickle . . . to a river . . . to a flood! You give . . . and God gives . . . and, Glory be! That trickle in your life turns into a river . . . turns into a flood!" And, he kept repeating it and urging those in attendance to shout it with him. To "speak it forth with him . . . 'not a trickle! . . . not a river! . . . but a FLOOD!' ! Praise God . . . yamma-sha-had-nana-oooh-ala-ha-shem . . . .Hallelujah! Praise God! God is Good! Yes! Praise Him on High! . . . and, now folks," he yelled over the microphone at the pitch of the crescendo of praises and hallelujahs from all over the auditorium . . .

140

"God wants to see that trickle right now! He wants you to start giving . . . so it can come right back to you the same way! . . . It doesn't have to be much—a penny, a dollar, a ring or a watch . . . just a trickle—Praise God! — just a trickle! Yes! Come right on down and just put whatever it is that God has put into your heart this night . . . hearing His Words . . . following His leading . . . right down here at the edge of this stage. God will accept anything you have to give to Him . . . to His works. And, he will give it back to you like a flood! The hundred-fold return. You can't out give God! That's right! Hallelujah! Step forward . . . bring whatever you have right down here . . . it doesn't have to be money.. it can be anything of value . . . or it can be money. God will leave that up to you. Praise God . . . now while you all are coming down . . . that's it, come right on . . . while you are all doing that, Richard, why don't you step over there to the microphone and give us a song to His glory to carry us on . . . Band, you give him some music and—Hallelujah! . . . this here trickle . . . I see it! I see it! . . . Already it's turning to a river! . . . Soon it's going to be a flood! Yes, tonight you are going to see a miracle of God right before your very eyes! God is going to turn a trickle to a river to a flood right here on this stage before your very eyes! Praise God! Richard, go to it! . . . "

The music engulfed the auditorium with Richard's manly voice booming and reverberating off all the walls . . . as the faithful filled and jammed the aisles, heading for the stage. Ushers tried vainly to steer them into some sort of traffic pattern, mostly down the center then splitting and returning both left and right. The music remained at crescendo level and everyone was totally caught up in the river now turning to a flood! Oral paced up and down the front of the stage, sometimes praying with hand uplifted, sometimes stopping and sinking to one knee, head bowed, other times strolling back and forth praying audibly in tongues, stopping now and then to give added encouragement with a few well-chosen words over the microphone he still clutched in one hand. The trickle of objects and coins and bills that had begun to clutter the apron of the stage had now covered it . . . and it kept building. People took watches and jewelry off their arms, rings off their fingers, wallets came out and money was withdrawn and deposited onto the stage. Some wrote checks. Others tossed more as the pile heaped and heaped and glittered under the spotlights from the ceiling. There was hardly a single soul in his original seat in the whole place..a place that seated perhaps ten thousand. The balconies began to move now.

Faith was strangely unmoved. Stephen asker her if she wanted to give something. She said she was waiting for a leading from God. Stephen was thinking it over himself. He suppressed the thought that he was witnessing mass manipulation, and asked the Lord to forgive him. He had too much at stake with the Lord to risk His displeasure and lack of faith. He began praying under his breath and in tongues, seeking some guidance from the Lord.

As the glittering pile of treasure mounted up on the stage, Stephen felt the urge to participate. Whether from the Lord's leading or an innate sense of covering all bets, he nevertheless got out of his seat and wended his way through the throng, down the stairway, and over to the stage. The crowd was thinning out now and Stephen deposited his contribution to the mass of valuables, two twenty dollar bills . . . all he had with him. He was satisfied that he had given it all to God. It wouldn't be long at this rate that he would, indeed, have given it all to God! . . . and he would look for that flood to come back to him . . . a flood of oil, maybe? He'd even settle for a river of oil !

It seemed that a series of bizarre events was taking place . . . no doubt attributable to the 'dog days' of August. Faith was all fired up one Friday evening over some guru, some health freak she'd heard about over in

Jenks who had some kind of special ability to see maladies just by looking into one's eyes, searching the tell-tale patterns of their pupils. Furthermore, his remedies were simple: all natural, health   foods . . . which he just happened to sell in his store.   Faith wanted to check him out . . . see if he were of God.   She felt an affinity to health cures, knowing that God's way was 'natural,' . . . that natural foods and the things that God had provided for us on this earth that He had made were better than all the chemicals and medicines that ignorant man had come up with. God and his creation was able to heal itself.

The next morning they drove across the river to Jenks.   The health food store was just off the main drag, on a side street in the 'one-horse town,' as Stephen condescendingly described it.   Jenks was just a cluster of older houses, a bunch of vintage stores and, farther out, a new shopping strip.

Before entering the health food store, Faith went to the corner of the weathered structure and laid her hands flat against it. "Hon, help me cast out the demons and cleanse this in the name of the Lord," whereupon she went into her practiced prayer of demonic exorcism. Stephen stood beside her, his hands also on the clapboarding and prayed dutifully in tongues.

The shop was an old, turn-of-the-century country store . . . remodeled somewhat, with a few newer shelves.   Whatever mix of products it had once carried, all now had been given over to the health kick . . . the usual capsules, potions, powders, herbs, vitamins, vitamin supplements . . . their packaging and labeling oddly incongruous with the worn and scarred counter and its antique cash register and some of the left-over relics of the past still on the walls now sharing space with bright new posters and pricing cards. Faith asked the young woman clerk if she could see the man who looked into your eyes and could tell if something was wrong with you.

Without a word, the girl turned and disappeared through a door for a moment and came back with the news that Mr. Jethro would see them. She led them through the door, through a dingy stock room back to another door, knocked once and opened it, standing aside to allow Faith and Stephen to enter the dimly-lit room.

Mr. Jethro mumbled an unintelligible greeting of sorts as the clerk motioned for the newcomers to seat themselves in the two chairs opposite his gigantic desk. Mr. Jethro was a mountain of a man, certainly topping three hundred pounds. Not exactly a walking advertisement for his health food business. He appeared to be about seventy years old; older, perhaps. Being so obese, the fat in his face no doubt tended to pooch out his wrinkles. He could have been eighty. It was obvious by his manner, his grimacing when he talked, by his shifting now and then, his heavy and irregular breathing, that he was not in good health. '*Physician, heal thy self*,' Stephen thought.

As the clerk stood at Mr. Jethro's side, to assist, evaluate, protect, interpret, whatever, the old man rambled on semi-coherently about good health and how he could tell if there was something wrong with you. Since Faith had maintained firm eye contact and seemed to project interest in the endeavor, whereas Stephen had retracted noticeably, the guru directed his remarks to her. After a while he told her to lean forward. Not moving his corpulent hulk himself, he then squinted and stared intently into hers eyes, first the right, then the left. His face was expressionless. Stephen thought to himself, *he's sitting over there, across the desk from Faith . . . a full twelve feet away . . . and he's claiming to be looking at the fine details of spots, specks and capillaries in her pupil? He must have 500 millimeter telephoto lenses for eyes . . . what a fraud! Even medical doctors get a spectroscope and put it right up to the eye to examine it. And, this guy, with ordinary eyesight from across the room! Give me a break*!

144

After some hemming and hawing and clearing his throat, the guru bestowed his diagnosis. Her bowels was impure. Yes, a lot of people's bowels is impure . . . and that is the cause of a lot of bad health. The solution? Take a coffee enema every day. That's right, an enema of coffee . . . and make sure you get it up . . . all the way . . . up into the small intes-TINE! . . . that's where the trouble should be flushed out.

Stephen was sure he saw the guru's impenetrable eyes widen, come alive for a split second.

After paying the ten-dollar fee, Faith and Stephen wandered around the store, ostensibly trying to decide on some purchase. Faith was obviously ruminating on the encounter. Stephen leaned over to her and whispered loudly, "We'd better stock up on coffee!"

Faith turned and glared at him.

"Pardon me, but I think that old geezer just got his jollies by telling you to take a coffee enema . . . dirty old man! I saw his eyes twinkle when he was telling you to get it way up in the small . . . "

"Can it!" Faith shot back.

Chapter 13   Apocalypse

When the news came it was electrifying.   Revelation 22:20 was being spudded tomorrow.   Rock had telephoned and asked if Stephen wanted to come out for it.   Too unnerved about the whole venture—and all that was at stake—Stephen begged off, pleading station duties.   He allowed as how, though, he would certainly be out there when they got close to total depth . . . might even come out in the van and spend the night or whatever it took.

'*So, Lord,*' Stephen reflected, '*This is it. I have every ounce of my faith that this is of You . . . that You led me into this investment because You want to prosper me . . . and I simply stand on that.   Thank You, Lord.*' Rock had estimated an overall six-day drill, so Stephen would go out around Friday afternoon. That way he wouldn't be missed at the station and what better and more exciting way to spend an otherwise dull weekend?

Preparations were progressing at a quickening pace now toward the telethon which would take place in early October.   Stephen allowed the personnel, mostly Lydia and Rebecca, to decide whether the theme should be "Oktoberfest" or "Harvest of Thanks," which he thought would have been more appropriate closer toward Thanksgiving . . . and Oktoberfest carried the connotation of beer drinking.   They finally decided on Harvest of Thanks.   It would be a seven-day effort . . . he thought *six days with the seventh as a day or rest might have been more appropriate. Nevertheless, seven days it would be . . . not a complete elimination of all programming, but promos between programs, and a good chunk of the live midday show, and then at 7:00 p.m. each night until 11:00 or till whenever the Spirit led to conclude, the telethon would take place. Only CBN's 700 Club would have to be really bumped and rescheduled after 11. This meant that Stephen would only be responsible for one, possibly two nights at most, where he had to emcee and keep it going. It was an exhausting task and one he did not particularly relish. But . . . he resigned himself to it. It had to be done . . . it was part of the backbone of station financial operation.*

The week plodded along with the never-ending sameness. It was becoming a chore, no longer a challenge, no longer the underlying excitement of running a complete TV operation or of dedicating all of this effort to the Lord. Was he just getting tired . . . needed a rest? Vacation? Or, was the edge really dulling?

Friday finally rolled around. He had arranged with Faith for him to take the van, which was not an easy task. She hated to drive the Bronco . . . and, of course, it did not have her ministry identification all over it. Stephen provisioned up with some cold drinks in the small cooler and a couple of bags of chips, snacks, candy bars, and, having been a field Marine, some toilet paper and a small shovel, and a couple of jugs of bottled water. He also tossed in a canvas folding chair and a couple of paperbacks, sweater, light jacket and an extra pair of jeans and boots. It was September now and you couldn't count on the weather, so he got out his felt western hat, his gloves and a parka . . . a pillow and a blanket, a couple of flashlights, and a first aid kit, . . . mustn't forget cleansing towelettes, the pocket radio . . . his dopp kit, portable electric razor, a towel. It sparked a twinge of memory of a decade and a half ago preparing for a patrol out into the boonies. He figured he had prepared himself for a good camp-out and he sure was going to wait this sucker out!

Stopping off at a McDonalds on the way out, he arrived well before sunset. The sight awed him. He had seen these types of larger rigs from a distance, but this was unexpectedly much more impressive up close . . . and he knew this wasn't even the largest type. They were only going down sixty-five hundred feet; he'd like to see one of those that went down to 20,000 and deeper! Those must be some operations.

This operation was no slouch, though. Four—no six—times larger than Logos and Genesis. The small air drill steel-grid tower used on those was truck-mounted. It just tilted upright, a section was added, and it was ready to go. This tall, tapered steel-grid tower-mast was in three large sections, each trucked in separately and when assembled, must be topping fifty feet. It was on its own separate, sturdy, good-sized platform, too. And all the support vehicles were nosed and positioned around it on one side in an orderly manner. There were stacks of drill pipe and more were being hauled in by giant flatbed eighteen-wheelers that arrived periodically. There were gigantic pipe connections going over to the inky olympic pool-sized sludge pit. The noise was overpowering—a consistently higher level than at Logos. He should have thought to bring ear plugs. He'd have to make some somehow. The spectacle was just that—a spectacle. The driller, toolpusher, roustabout, engineer—whoever they were—were swinging a long length of drill stem on a hoist from the top of the mast and with heavily gloved hands were guiding it onto one just protruding out of the casing hole in the center of the platform. One of the figures swung a short length of chain around it, gave it a tug, it turned and screwed itself onto the protruding pipe, they became one and the powerful rotary drive grappled the huge collar while the roaring generator strained and the whole apparatus turned and turned, noticeably working downward with each revolution, while a series of other powerful pumps circulated a proper mixture of mud and water down the center of the hollow drill stem with such force that it was flushed back up between the stem and the casing, thus lubricating the whole process, and flushing out through the large blouie into the sludge pit.

Stephen could envision that churning, chewing, drill bit with the diamonds studded in it, down at the bottom . . . maybe five thousand feet down there at the bottom of the stem . . . determinedly gnawing its way through dirt and rock. He wondered how many turns the top of such a long stem was ahead of the drill bit at the bottom due to the torque that twists the pipe as the power is transferred all that distance? Must be a dozen or so turns, he estimated.

He spotted Rock coming out of one of the portable shacks. "Rock! Bring me up to speed. How we doing?"

"Hey there, brother Steve, You gonna be here for the gan' finale. Eh?"

"Yep, going to stick it right out till the end. Ready to camp in the van."

"Atta boy! It's gonna be exciting! C'mon, lemme let you meet the guys what run this here show . . . this danged circus! Some circus! Whadda ya think?" Rock shouted ebulliently.

Rock strode at a goodly pace—he was 'in his element,' it was obvious— all decked out in heavy westernized work clothes, the muddy and dusty Dingos, jeans with a wide belt and big ornate buckle, checkered lumberjack shirt, dirty swede vest and his big Stetson. Stephen was at his heels.

A giant of a man with a full beard, similarly attired except for a hard hat, emerged from the door to which they were headed. "Hey, brother Moses, I want 'chu' ta' meet this here brother here . . . Steve, meet Moses. ' Moses' Steinberg—let you figure why they call 'im

149

'Moses'! . . . Moses . . . Steve. Steve, here, runs th' Christian TV station over at Broken Arrow. Treat 'im right—he's our biggest investor. Three shares!"

"Howdy, Steve. Welcome to our humble little world. If 'Moses' don't strike ya' right . . . then, jist 'Mo' . . . or my real moniker, Daniel. Daniel Steinberg."

Rock interjected, "Or, some people call 'im 'rocky mountain.' Guess, 'cause he's big enough, ya' think?" Stephen wondered if Rock had missed the double-entendre in his name, or was just putting him on.

But, Rock continued, "He ain't gonna tell ya', but this here guy . . . me'n him was green berets together back when you was living it up with all them pogey-bait Marines back chasin' all them nurses at China Beach," poking an elbow toward Stephen. "With a name like that, I keep tellin' 'im he's Jewish.."

"Just one of the lost tribes," cut in Moses. "A 'Jew for Jesus'! It's German, ya' dum' 'Okie'!"

"Look who he's calling an Okie! We both come from El Paso!"

When the playful banter subsided, the seriousness of the project was explained in great detail to Stephen. Rock took him over to a detached trailer house and, after a discreet knock, the door opened. "We got us a special engineer-geologist on this here well . . . Steve, meet Nick . . . Nick, Steve . . . big investor. He can come in whenever he wants to." Then, turning to Steve he explained, "We done closed this drilling . . . don't want nobody just a comin' wanderin' in here . . . we're paying a lot for this here guy and what he's watchin' for us . . . and when we hit—what we hit, and how much we hit ain't nobody's business but us ! . . . You, me, Mo an' Nick. We ain't gonna let people nose around here sort of spyin' and lookin' to see how good we're doin' and then goin' out an'

150

grabbing a lease close by and off-drillin' us. No, siree, we jist gonna keep our traps shut on this one . . . play it like you was holding a poker hand."

"Sounds good to me," agreed Stephen.

After Rock left to go back to Tulsa, before the sun began to set, Stephen walked the area and selected a camping site, off a way from the activity, on a slight rise among some short trees where he could look down on all the goings-on. Settled in somewhat, he put up the folding chair and drifted into reverie . . . thinking of all that led up to this . . . this grande finale of the oil ventures for the Lord. Gazing around, he wished he were an artist. It was a strangely compelling scene . . . the brilliant sunset was rapidly fading and the work lights all over the area illuminating the foreground paraphernalia and activity contrasting against the darkening landscape in the distance. It was that wondrous interval of twilight with its short lived balance between the lingering light of day and the inexorable advent of darkness. It always elicited a bit of uneasiness in Stephen; in the military it was referred to as BENT, 'beginning evening nautical twilight,' that brief period after the sun goes down while you can still see, similar to 'before morning nautical twilight' before the sun rises and the hidden rays beyond the horizon overtake the faint starlight— both critical times to mount surprise attacks. He was ingrained to be particularly alert around these times and he couldn't shake it off, despite the interceding years that had gone by. He sat for a long time staring into the darkness, savoring the vastness of the world and the tranquility he was experiencing.

He had brought a battery fluorescent light with him which he now used inside the van. The van really belonged personally to him. He had bought it from a friend in Connecticut right after the divorce when he had given the house and all of his worldly possessions to Diana in lieu of alimony . . . since he had explained that the KXAO-TV job paid so little that he would be strapped financially. Instead, they had agreed to her taking the house (with more equity than his profit-sharing —which, of course, he had shared with her as well) and a modest amount of child support . . . which he even had a hard time paying, always having to dip into the eighty thousand he had left—or used to have! That was down to less than five now. He really didn't want to know. . .probably more like four. So, he had come out to Tulsa in the van, sleeping in it on the way occasionally. It was a comfortable, customized 1978 Ford Econoline 150. Of course, when he married Faith, she convinced him that the van would be perfect for her ministry, so he let her use it, put it in the ministry's name for tax purposes, and traded her two-door chevy in on a used Bronco. So, the Bronco was actually Faith's; but it was too rough and truck-like for her.

With the four luxurious 'captain's chairs,' he could easily go from the front into the back without having to go outside, and he had a lot of room to sprawl out on the rear bench type seat. He could even draw the curtains over the screened windows for privacy. So, he was quite comfortable and looked forward to enjoying this semi-rough outdoor experience. He even brought a small battery reading lamp that fit right onto a book . . . didn't want to drain the van's battery . . . not out in the middle of nowhere. So, he felt he had his campsite in order . . . even had his .25 caliber automatic pistol tucked under the driver's seat, a precaution and habit he could not break despite his present pacifistic "walk in the Lord." He had mentioned it once to Faith, whose reaction was predictably negative. There was no need whatsoever for weaponry when you had the power over Satan in God's Word, she had insisted. He simply kept it out of her sight from then on.

By this time Stephen had so adjusted to the noise level that he had become totally unaware of it. He sat in the chair again next to the van overseeing the working scene below him for almost two more hours.

Then he ambled down onto the site, wandering unobtrusively watching with undisguised awe the methodical activity.

Moses stepped out of a door, saw him, stepped back, and again emerged with a hard hat in his hand. "Here, Steve, be safer for y' ta wear this aroun' here."

"Thanks. How's it coming?"

"Right on schedule . . . gettin' close to five-fifty. Lemme know if y' need sumpin'," he said striding off to something that required his attention.

After an hour of this aimless kibitzing and reverie, Stephen wandered on back to the van, took a leak in the bushes, and opened a coke and a bag of chips. He tried the pocket radio and after dialing through a bunch of rock and country-western stations finally found the PBS one in Oklahoma City. He really liked C & W but felt more like a little Mozart tonight —a little night music . . . Eine Kleine Nachts Musik. 'Hah,' he thought to himself, ' . . . try springing that on the charismatics!' Stretching out as comfortably as he could on the back seat, he drifted off after a while.

Stephen started upright! Wide awake. Momentarily disoriented, he was aware of something . . . the sound had stopped. It was eerily quiet. The lights still gave off an overall glow into the dark sky . . . but all was quiet . . . except for a shout here and there. The luminous dial on his wristwatch indicated three a.m.

He pulled on his boots, put his jacket and hard hat on and walked toward the head shed. No one there. All the activity appeared up on the platform. Standing below it, he waited until one of the crew climbed down and asked him what was going on.

"Bit's broke."

"The drill bit—busted?"

"Yup.   We gotta pull what's left uv it up . . . if we can and replace it . . . gotta git five thousand feet of stem otta there first . . . then put on a new bit and put it all back down there again."

"Holy smoke!" How long do you think that'll take?""

"Half a day. More, maybe."

Stephen was dismayed but assured himself that these sorts of setbacks were surely factored in.   So, he'd just have to roll with the punches. Slowly he wended his way back to the van and sacked in again, as a generator cranked up, he figured, to hoist the sections of drill stem out of the hole. That rhythmic staccato lullabied him to sleep.

When the light of day woke him he was aware first of still no noise but the generator. Shortly that stopped altogether and he guessed they had retrieved the broken drill bit. After performing his primitive ablutions, he set off to find Moses.

Moses was not around; he was still sacked out in his camper next to his trailer office, evidently taking advantage of the routine retrieval of the bit to grab a few winks. Sleep on this sort on an around-the-clock operation was catch-as-catch-can.

One of the engineers popped out of a tool trailer and hurried over to Moses' camper.   After a short interval, he and Moses came charging back, obviously agitated. A lot of scurrying about ensued, a huddling of figures, some shouting back and forth, and gesticulations. Stephen sensed something untoward had occurred.

Approaching Moses, he called out, "What's up?"

"Oh, we got us a problem . . . kinda big one. Ain't got the right replacement bit . . . not for this here formation that broke this 'un. Gotta send over to Oklahoma City . . . see if they got one. It's a kinda rare type. Didn't figure hittin' no rock like this. Gotta analyze it, see what we

got ourselves into. If it's what I think, 's gonna take one expensive sucker
— special diamond-graphite. Hope they got one."

"How long you think the operation will be down?"

"Well . . . hit bein' Saturday—that really don't make no
difference though—if we can git aholt a this here sucker . . . should be
putting pipe back down the hole by afternoon."

"How much deeper we got to go?"

"Less than a thousand. Gonna stick around?"

"Yep. Might as well."

Stephen thought he might as well also use the interim to go look
for a fast food place. A sausage biscuit and a hot cup of coffee would
taste pretty good right about now.

Stephen drove off in the direction of Enid and as he neared a Burger
Chef, which the billboard had indicated was only a half a mile ahead, he
passed a man walking along the the side of the road going in the same
direction. It was still out in the sticks, he hadn't come to any sort of town
as yet. The man appeared young, a bit mussed up, a growth of beard,
and a plastic garbage bag with something in it thrown over his shoulder.
His first inclination to give him a ride was overruled by his common
sense. As he looked at the figure in the rear view mirror, he thought what
Faith would have done . . . stopped at once, told him she was a preacher
and if he wanted a ride he was going to have to listen to what she was
going to tell him . . . Fair enough? She did that all the time, anywhere,
any time of day or night. He had warned her to no avail . . . she was
operating under the guidance and protection of God, Jesus and the Holy
Spirit . . . no harm could come to her as long as she was doing God's will.

He was hungrier than he had thought and ordered a complete
big egg and hot cake breakfast. As he sat down facing the window
toward the highway and began to eat, he saw the man he had seen earlier

155

walking directly over to the door to the Burger Chef. Instead of coming in, he lifted the lid off of the garbage container, bent over and rummaged around until he came up with something and began nibbling on it.

Horrified, Stephen dropped his fork and bounded toward the door. The few other customers looked his way curiously. Bursting through, he hailed the young man who by this time had turned back toward the highway. "Hey! Wait! Come in here and I'll buy you a breakfast. OK?"

The man stopped, turned and walked back, nodded to Stephen and followed him to the counter. Stephen said to the girl, "Give this gentleman anything he wants." And put a five dollar bill on the counter, "And give the change to him." He then went back to his table, expecting the benefactée to join his benefactor.

Instead, the man took his full tray over to another section of the room and proceeded to eat heartily and quietly to himself.

'Alas, we know not what motivates people,' Stephen reflected. 'Maybe this guy just got out of prison . . . he is certainly down and out . . . he didn't ask anything of anyone . . . he just took what he could scrounge . . . maybe he is mute, deaf —no, he heard me—and dumb. Oh well, we all have our problems. Thank You, Lord, for mine and not his . . . however, Father, I ask in Your Son's Name to bless this poor afflicted human whom You made in Your own image . . . and guide him and protect him as he wanders this day . . . and let him find You if he will . . . and at least let him get his life together . . . and prosper. Thank You, Jesus.'

Stephen looked over again at him and he was gone. Ate and left . . . back on his way. He craned his neck and caught a glimpse of him back on the edge of the highway once more. When Stephen finished a few minutes later he was overcome with an intense desire to go after the man and at least give him some money. He drove in the direction the man had gone and saw that he had crossed the road. Driving past him,

Stephen went until he found an opportunity to turn around and headed back toward him. As he slowed, he reached over and rolled the window down and pulled onto the gravel. As the man passed next to the window, Stephen held the twenty dollar bill out for him., saying, "God bless you." Without saying a word, the man took it from him and continued on his way. Stephen's emotion—or a filling with the Holy Spirit overcame him momentarily—and he wept . . . wept compassionately for the unknown wayfarer. "God, he is Your creature . . . Bless him, Father."

Rock was at the site when Stephen returned. He was noticeably agitated.

"Rock! Any late word?"

"Nope. We just got a real problem . . . that's all. The type of bit we need has to be flown in from Houston. Get here late tonight. Gonna cost a fortune and Moses says it ain't covered in his bid."

"Ouch! So, now what?"

"We just don't talk about it till this thing's over . . . then we'll straighten it out best we can."

"So, the drill stem will be back in the hole and we'll start drilling again . . . when do you think? . . . tomorrow morning?"

"Better be! We got the cementers and frac'ers coming tomorrow and Monday. Couldn't get Schlumberger . . . worse luck . . . gotta use some body I ain't never heard of. So, that plus the doggoned drill bit . . . and, brother, we are up to our necks in alligators . . . "

Stephen felt a chill envelop him . . . a chill of unadulterated fear . . . something he had not experienced in a long time. It sickened him.

" . . . 'cause . . . we gotta get off'en this here hole by Tuesday night. We only got money for two extra days . . . ya' know, this here circus is costin' us close to seventy-five gran' a day! That leaves just enough to set in the holding tanks . . . water and oil and set up the well head, pump jack an' all. Man, it's a gonna be close now!"

Stephen didn't respond. He just looked up at the derrick . . . then surveyed all the engines and vehicles that were set up . . . and the work crew . . . and the whole thing . . . and tried to get a grip on himself.

"Hey, c'mon, brother Steve . . . It ain't that bad! When we start pumping all them eight hundred barrels a day, you ain't even gonna remember any of this here crap."

The following hours were agony for Stephen. He couldn't concentrate enough even to read. He just wandered around watching with sightless eyes for some sign of activity. The crew was crapped out somewhere . . . resting up for the next phase, no doubt. He sat in his chair beside the van for an interminably long time . . . forgot to even think about lunch. The sun began to set . . . and still no change. He had been praying intermittently . . . reassuring himself that God was still the provider, the overseer, still had His hand on it and would still bless it. Exhausted with praying articulated thoughts after repeating himself over and over, he lapsed into tongues and let them flow softly with a calming, mesmerizing effect . . . which began to quiet his racing fears and racing heart. He lay down in the van and tried to sleep. His mind was too unsettled for that. He simply stared at the ceiling of the van long into darkness.

A truck raced into the compound around midnight amid whoops and hollers. Stephen guessed the new drill bit had arrived. He resisted the temptation to go down and see it and finally closed his eyes, as the familiar sound of the generator broke the stillness of the night. The drill stem was going back down. "Thank You, Jesus," he mumbled gratefully.

When he woke up, Stephen felt anything but rested. He ached as if he had been working out all night. He knew he could get a cup of coffee down at the driller's shack, so he headed in that direction after he painfully gathered himself together.

The coffee was strong . . . just what he needed. He detected the different sound and rhythm of drilling now and when he spotted Moses, asked what the prognosis was.

"Well . . . we shore had a rough night . . . waiting for that sucker to git here . . . and, yep, we got th' stem back down . . . and we're drilling through them rocks. We'll know sumpin' for sure by the end of the day . . . that's when we get near or into the zone . . . and from what I hear from our engineer-geologist . . . well, when Rock gets back we'll all git together and go over it. Gotta go . . . see ya'."

Rock showed up after dark. "Hey there, Stevie . . . had to look after my other wells or I'd a been here sooner. How's it goin'?"

"According to Moses, we're back on schedule . . . or at least drilling again."

"Good! Hear that bugger got here at midnight! Son uv a gun! That should not a happened! Dang!"

"Moses wants us to get together with the geologist," Stephen reported matter-of factly.

Moses, Rock and Stephen all bent over the geologist as he manipulated his computer screen and the EKG-looking printout. The screen was full of columns of differing heights with horizontal lines and numbers and symbols to the left and bottom. The tape printout was much like a seismograph in that the four vibrating needles had scratched jagged paths . . . evidently indicating formation densities and certain depths. It was all beyond Stephen's comprehension . . . and neither Moses nor Rock had bothered to explain it thoroughly to him. ..but, they were certainly intent upon it.

"You think it could be?" Rock inquired.

"Brother, if so, you is millionaires!" came back Moses in his loud, raucous voice.

"Hey, cut me in," piped up Stephen.

"Well, brother," Rock began, patiently, as if to a dull student. "We jist might'a hit something nobody thought was even in this part of the state—this part of the country, even —the Brownsville! And, if this here geo-ologist knows what he's a talkin' 'bout . . . and we hit this sucker . . . and it looks like we are pretty close! . . . man, have we got us a find! They's gonna be people all over this area . . . this could be another big pool like that one under Tulsa . . . and Bartlesville. Whoooee! Man, the Lord is shore 'nuff pulling this thing in! Hallelujah!"

Moses stood back and beamed, his white teeth flashing through his bushy dirty-blond beard. Stephen's heartbeat skipped a few then raced with excitement.

"Biggest thing is," continued Rock, " . . . is we gotta keep the lid on this! We cain't let one single word of this git out . . . everybody understand that? Man, this is now top secret! Not even the President of the Yew-nited States is got a need to know! This here trailer house is off-limits to every body but jist us four . . . got it?"

It seemed to Stephen that the pace picked back up and everything was right on track. They would TD now just after midnight . . . and the cementers and fracturing trucks would be moving in the following dawn . . . Monday. Monday! Good Lord! He would have to stay out here . . . simply could not go to the station right when the big event was to take place! He'd have to call Faith tonight and tell her he would be staying out here Sunday night and into Monday. He couldn't trust Faith to relay that information to Lydia in the right spirit to cover for him . . . and it was pretty evident that Faith had had no part in and would take no interest in Revelation 22:20.   Her 'nose was out of joint,' he supposed because the investment had been entirely his.   He hadn't so much as asked her advice or counsel but had asked for her prayers . . . for which she had been rather hesitant to bestow.   And, he had certainly not told her how much he had invested.   He hoped that she assumed it was the usual two thousand per unit.   No, Monday morning he would have to telephone Lydia and flat out tell her that he was not coming in that day. He would not lie about being sick or anything like that; she was simply to tell anyone who inquired that Stephen was away on business.   Period! And, she would—convincingly.   He hoped at that time he would be able also to tell her that some good news was about to come forth.

There was frenzied activity throughout the night.   Rock had stayed.   He and Moses . . . and frequently Stephen . . . had periodically visited the geologist's trailer to ascertain his findings . . . and further confirm the good news of the rich strike!   Stephen managed to catch cat naps in the van during all this and again, when dawn came, he felt dragged out.   He was tired of chips and sodas and being in the same clothes.   He did shave with the charged electric razor, though . . . as he had always managed in the field as a Marine . . . as an example to his men.   Nobody else at the site appeared to either have time for that sort of thing . . . or gave a darn about it.   He drove quickly down to the main highway to a pay phone at a gas station and called Lydia.

TD, total depth, was reached soon afterward and there was much conferring.   The cementers' and fracturers' trucks were arriving and the place began to look like the 'truck stop' Rock had predicted.

"What you see over there, brother Stephen, is a costin' us about fifty 'Gs'!"

161

Stephen saw no cause to doubt it.

The geologist allowed as how the zone was, indeed, showing strong hydrocarbons . . . in an uncharacteristic way for this part of the country . . . or at least the Mississippian.   It just had to be the Brownsville!

Rock explained that what had to be done now was get the sucker cemented . . . and then frac 'er . . . and she should flow like that flood ol' Oral was a tellin' us about! Praise, God!"

Stephen could scarcely conceal his glee.

The morning was pretty well consumed by the cementing operation . . . all those special pumpers and collectors and re-circulators . . . all driving that perfectly balanced mixture of cement and water down that incredible distance . . . beyond the intermediate casing cementings . . . down to the bottom of the hole to cement the bottom casing in place . . . all of that intricate operation done by estimation, practice . . . and guesswork. After all, how can anyone know what's really going on six thousand feet down there? What that formation is like and what it really has within it?   He just had to rely on experience and leave it up to the experts . . . and the Lord and His guidance . . . for which he fervently prayed the entire time.

After the cementers pulled off, the frac'ers got to work. This was also a tricky part. They were going to lower a cylindrical charge—several as a matter of fact—right down to the bottom through the tubing that had now replaced the drill stem until it was in the pay zone . . . a stratum of anywhere from a foot or two to a dozen or so in thickness of oil laden or oil saturated clay, sand and rock. Sometimes the oil was in liquid form in a pool or stream and when tapped merely gushed forth. Other times—

the majority—it was suspended in little droplets and pockets throughout the oil producing layer. In this case, to make the oil flow toward the path of least resistance, that is, up the tubing, it had to be made to flow toward it . . . and to forestall the weight of the earth crushing down and interfering with the process, the formation had to be fractured in all directions and sometimes flushed with water or nut hulls to keep the formation open and flowing. This is what the charge was going to do. When it was lowered into the exact position down there at sixty-five hundred feet depth, it— or they—would be fired and actual bullets would be shot in 360 degrees right through the casing and cement on into the formation, fracturing the small geological faults as far as their power would take them, thus opening the zone for the anticipated flow.

By evening several frac'ings had been performed and everyone was antsy waiting for the results. But, nothing came. There was again much stirring about, hurried visits to the geologist, animated conversations between Rock and Moses and the toolpusher. Still nothing!

Stephen decided to keep his distance. The constant worry back and forth . . . the positives countered by the negatives see-sawing back and forth had unnerved him completely. He almost preferred to not know what was going on . . . possibly because he suspected the worst.

Moses and Rock seemed to be paired off with everyone else circling them to watch. It appeared to be quite a heated shouting match. Stephen edged closer in order to make out what it was about . . .

" . . . the hell you will, brother!" Rock's voice rang in his ears, now in a tone and ferocity he had never heard from him before.

" . . . And, I said we gonna be off this hole by eight a.m.!"

"Damn—you cain't do that! We gotta break down through that cement and go three . . . four . . . six more feet! I'm ordering you to do that . . . put that drill back in there and let's go down!"

"You don't tell me what I'll do, brother Rock! I got a contract to be on another job with this rig at 0800 Wednesday morning . . . a hundred a fifty miles from here . . . and, I'm a gonna be there. I cain't help this here bunch a crap! I didn't cement the danged thing!"

"Well, you hired this no-good outfit . . . least you kin do is fix it!"

The two men were bent menacingly forward, like two fierce bulls, almost nose to nose . . . were it not that Moses towered some four inches above Rock's six feet two! It was a dangerous moment . . . everyone sensed it. The crew, who were used to this sort of thing were just settling in for a good one . . . they could care less for all this Christian crap . . . they wanted a good fight!

Rock landed the first one—right to the belly—catching Moses off guard!

As the force of the blow took Moses back a step and the wind out of him, instinctively his right fist came doubled up from his side catching Rock's jaw with a force that split his tongue. Stunned for a split second, Rock spun and crouched simultaneously, charging into the mid-section of his adversary like the line-backer he had been, causing the two of them to crash to the grimy steel decking of the platform. Now on top of Moses, Rock managed to get his right arm cocked enough to land him a powerful haymaker that even through the thick brush on Moses' chin everybody could hear.

At that point, Stephen thought it was enough . . . and, as he had swung himself up onto the edge of the platform when it had started. . . he now charged in to separate the two as they were struggling to get up. They tried to resist the smaller body that had thrust itself in between them and each attempted to cast Stephen aside.

"Knock it off!" Stephen yelled with all his might, "Knock it off!"

No one was sure just who had done it, but the next instant Stephen went reeling off the platform, crashing in a clump on to the hard ground and debris. That stopped the fight.

Seeing Stephen's crumpled form spread below them, Rock and Moses came to their senses, relaxed their up-raised fists and began to regain control of themselves. They disengaged . . . and jumped off the platform to where the rest of the crew had gathered.

Stephen raised himself up on one elbow, shaking his head as a long-haired dog would his wet coat. Rock reached him first and quickly tried to get his hands under Stephen's shoulders. "Hold it! No! Easy! I'm OK . . . just my hip. Don't move me!" With that, Stephen lay back supine . . . and gingerly straightened out. "It's my old war wound . . . my hip. Think I must have twisted it. Don't think it's broken . . . just need to stretch out here a minute and let it take it's time."

"You want us to get a doc?" Moses asked solicitously.

"No . . . thanks . . . I think I can move it . . . yeah . . . I don't think it's too bad . . . give me a few minutes."

"Shoot, brother, this here makes us feel real bad," Rock said, slapping a hand on Moses' shoulder in a machismo gesture of apology. "If'n you's hurt, Stevie, we ain't never goin' ta' git over this. Sure we cain't take you to a doctor? Do sump'in'?"

"No . . . you guys just get the well going . . . I'll be all right."

As they reluctantly left and went back to their several duties, Stephen managed to sit up, propping himself with his two arms behind him. When he felt he had survived that successfully, he rolled over on his good hip and one of the crewmen gave him a hand to get to his feet. Steadying himself against the platform, he practiced standing erect, then slowly rotating his hips. The injured hip was shot through with pain, but it sustained him . . . he could put some weight on it.

165

Moses' voice startled him, "Here, take this," and handed him three aspirin and a paper cup of water.

"Thanks," gulped Stephen.

" . . . and, this here might help you a while," and handed him a crude walking stick carved out of a tree branch. "I keep this around just in case. Hey, Steve, I want to apologize again . . . me'n Rock didn't have no right to be doin' that. We shouldda been the ones hurt, not you!"

"Forget it . . . just tell me when we start getting those eight hundred barrels flowing!"

As Stephen, leaning on the cane, limped off with Rock to his pickup he asked what it had all been about.

"Well . . . ," Rock struggled to answer while his breathing and pulse were getting back to normal, " . . . this here cementer outfit . . . that Mo done lined up . . . they didn't know their ass from that there hole in the ground we drilled. Them bastards went and cemented the whole frigging formation up . . . the cement was pushed right out into the formation like the frac'in' shouldda done . . . only we ain't got oil flowing in the fractures. . .we got solid cement! Damn!"

"Is it hopeless?"

"Not exactly . . . if we get the drill stem back down in there we could drill right through that cement and go on down below it . . . and frac' it right. That's gonna take another day, at least."

"And, Moses says he's under contract for another job."

"That's what he says . . . we got a contract for six drill days and two extra backup. We never figured he'd have another job backed up to ours . . . and those backup days we pay for! But, shoot! I offered to pay his penalty fine for showing up late on site. . .but it still was 'no dice'! He sez he's got to go way over to the panhandle somewheres . . . Hell, I don' know! . . . looks like we been screwed . . . by nature and by 'lady luck.' You was prayin', wasn't you?"

Stephen had moved like a zombie as he was breaking camp and getting ready to drive the van back to Tulsa. Moses and Rock had had further words and the air remained full of tension. It was now past ten o'clock Monday night. As a final shot Rock had yelled at Moses, "All right—get off'n the damn hole!" That was it, the final order from the contracting driller, formally concluding the project.

With that, Rock had stormed off. Everyone else simply skulked off in all directions leaving a hostility in the air that hung like fog. Stephen was in such a state of shock that he was almost catatonic. He had virtually no reaction at all . . . it just was not sinking in . . . his subconscious was refusing to receive the information his brain was sending it. *One hundred twenty-thousand dollars down a hole. Not a thing to show for it! Six hundred thousand dollars in all . . . gone! Evaporated! Surely some of that had not been spent. He'd ask Rock right away if there would be some sort of refund of the funds not spent. Surely he and Tom and dad wouldn't have to take that kind of loss. Something had to come out of this.*

Stephen was not even aware that he was driving back to Tulsa. The van took the right road and turns but Stephen had no later recollection of any of it. It was past midnight when he got to the apartment. His hip was really giving him fits now . . . especially after sitting so long driving . . . and he had difficulty climbing the stairs to the second floor. He made more noise than he had expected fumbling with the key in the latch. As the door opened, Faith called, "Well, how'd it go?"

Stephen flipped the light in the bathroom and tossed his dopp kit onto the basin. The light illuminated him and Faith caught the fact that he was limping. "What happened, Hon?"

"Just took a fall. Hurt my old war wound. It'll be OK in a few days." He started to undress.

"And, the well?"

"A bust," he admitted sheepishly.

"I knew God wasn't in it," said Faith as she turned over and closed her eyes.

The hot shower Stephen had taken before going to bed had served as a soporific. He slumbered deeply and restfully, his fatigue mercifully blocking out his thinking process. He was awakened the next morning as Faith got out of bed and went into the bathroom. He heard her run the water, which meant she was shaving.   Following that, he heard the shower but no flush of the toilet. He indulged a smile . . . Faith liked to pee in the shower instead.

He had almost drifted back to sleep when Faith emerged in all her pristine loveliness—naked.   Not a bad figure for 37, he observed appreciatively.

"Ta-Ta!" she fan-fared cheerily as she struck a cheesecake pose, fully displaying her fleshy crotch completely devoid of pubic hair. "Saddle time!"

Whereupon she pirouetted over to the bed, yanked the covers off Stephen and mounted him. "Get'er up, ol' horsey, get'er up! I want to ride a cock horse to Banbury Cross!

Chapter 14   Beneficiaries

Stephen had telephoned Prudential and they had mailed him the forms.   He sat in the living room filling them out.   For that amount . . . and because of his war wound . . . he would have to have a physical. Pru would arrange for it.

When he finished the forms, he laid them with the envelope on the coffee table and went into the kitchen to see if there were any ice cream left.   There was nothing else to eat, only a couple of cokes in the refrigerator.   Faith had stipulated very plainly in the beginning of the marriage that she was not entering marriage to be any body's cook and bottle-washer. She refused flat-out to cook any meal . . . any thing ! She refused to have any pots or pans in the kitchen, and, after all, most of the stuff in the apartment was hers.   He had moved in with her after the wedding. He had no furniture anyway; it had all gone to Diana. So, they simply ate all meals out, mostly right around the corner at one of the several delis and modest eateries at the major intersection.   Stephen was pretty used to it. It certainly made them both entirely independent. Of course, when Faith was caught somewhere without any money, she simply praised God and fasted.   More often than not, though, she managed to be with someone or at someone's home when the dinner hour approached and thus wheedled an invitation to break bread with them. She simply lived a hand-to-mouth existence, refraining from anxiety as Jesus had instructed . . . *'anxious not for what you should eat, or drink, or clothe oneself . . . for the Heavenly Father knows one needs all these things . . . But seek first His kingdom and His righteousness . . . and all these things shall be added to you . . . be not anxious for tomorrow . . . each day has enough trouble of its own.'* "I can say 'Amen' to that," Stephen let go audibly.

Faith walked from the bedroom into the living room. "Say something, Hon?" Then, spotting the insurance forms picked them up and read $200,000 . . . then her eyes caught 'beneficiary' . . . Tom Trevelyan and Abner Trevelyan! "Hon, what's this?"

Stephen came out with a bowl of ice cream. "Want some? What's what?"

"This insurance. That's a big amount . . . why isn't my name on it?"

"That's something between me and my brother and my dad. It's got nothing to do with you."

"Nothing? We're husband and wife . . . right? Don't we share everything?"

"I've covered you on my SGLI policy. This is something outside of and beyond our marriage. I'm simply covering some of the investments that Tom made for himself and for dad . . . in case they don't come through . . . and something should happen to me."

"Like what?"

"Like I get run over by a truck crossing the street."

"So?"

"So . . . I leave them something to cover any and all losses."

"And me ? Me , your wife, your biblical helpmeet . . . I don't get anything but that twenty-five thousand policy? I suppose Diana and your children . . . they get something, don't they?"

"Look, Honey . . . we talked about this when we got married. What I bring into the marriage . . . that is, the baggage I have to carry with me . . . that's separate . . . it has nothing to do with us, you and me. Our marriage is something set aside completely from these other goings-on."

Faith was silent, thinking. She walked and stared out the window. "So . . . that's all you think of this marriage . . . all you think of me, your true wife that the Lord brought to you, huh?"

"Look! A lot of things are falling apart around here . . . these wells have not come in . . . and where is God in all that? And the station is going to hell in a hand basket! What do you want me to do? Or, what do you think I can do?"

"Get right with God."

"Damn! Look, I don't know what 'right with God is.' I'm doing everything I know to do . . . and nothing is working out . . . everything is turning to garbage. What can I do? I'm worth more to anybody—to everybody—dead . . . worth two hundred thousand dead. So, if one of these days or nights I should get hit head-on . . . or fall asleep at the wheel . . . I'll be worth something to somebody !"

"You're planning to commit suicide, aren't you?"

"Sure, sure . . . that's what I'm planning to do . . . so I can leave the two hundred thousand to Tom and dad to pay them back for the wells . . . "

Faith closed her eyes, tears forming, and wandered around the room praying in tongues . . . visibly bristling inside.   As Stephen retreated back into his own thoughts, she suddenly turned on him, "That insurance company will never pay off on your suicide. I'll see to that!" she shouted righteously.

After a couple of days of telephoning, Stephen was finally able to pin Rock down for an appointment in Rock's office.

The building was as impressive as the one Faith had just gotten an office in. The gold embossed lettering on the frosted glass of the door was attractive, belying the lack of taste of Rock's usual demeanor. "Agape Oil, Inc. Peter Weller, President" 'Agape,' the charismatic euphemistic catch-all for God's love . . . the greek word for that specific type of Divine love that does not exist in English as a separate word.

Rock jumped up from his plush executive chair behind his desk when Stephen entered. "Hey, brother Steve! Good ta' see ya!" they exchanged the perfunctory hug and Rock continued, "Sit! Coffee?"

"No thanks. Just wanted to see you and chat about this disaster out at Revelation . . . see what the wrap-up is."

"Well, they ain't much to wrap-up, brother . . . 'cept pluggin' 'er."

"You mean we couldn't go back down there . . . with another rig and crew . . . and bore through that cement? . . . and get something out of it?"

" 'Fraid not. Hit don't work thatta way. T' git back up on that site? . . . cost a fortune . . . 'bout half as much as we done already spent. 'Tain't worth it."

"So, just how much was spent? Is there anything the investors can get back?"

"You know how this works, Steve. You're a businessman. As 'limited' partners, you was just that . . . limited in investment . . . and in liability. We— me 'n Agape—we was the 'general partners.' We done all the work and took our share of the risks . . . up to a point. You know this thing was an 'exploratory' well—a wildcat . . . nobody knew for sure what was down there—or, if anything was down there. We took a chance . . . "

172

"You didn't have a share, did you? . . . a personal share, I mean, limited . . . like I did."

"Didn't need to. Rare for a general partner to have a share, especially if'n he's the driller. Mine comes out of the overhead and the royalty side. . . you know that . . . expenses first, then a percentage on top . . . for overhead . . . this office . . . down time between programs . . . advance fees . . . you know, all that crap that goes along with it."

"So . . . you   got something out of it . . . personally, I mean."

" If ya mean did we pay ourselves . . . 'Course. So did Moses . . . 'Course, that's part of the expenses. Moses has to pay his crew and equipment rental—that stuff don't belong to him personally—and pay himself and his overhead . . . all that comes out of the four hundred thousand we already paid him . . . the extry drill bit . . . well, we still fightin' over that! . . . But, shore . . . I gotta pay myself or I don't stay in business . . . comes out of the mark-up . . . all adds up to the total of six hundred thousand . . . the entire cost of the program. Good thing we're able to use what we would a spent on gathering to plug 'er . . . instead a assessing th' investors extry for it. Y'know, it says we kin do that in the prospectus . . . Should a' read it, brother . . . 'N'other thing . . . you realize that the Limited Partnership drilling programs are designed under SEC rules for high rollers . . . big incomers —doctors, lawyers— professionals . . . who can afford to win or lose. They lose, they git a big tax write-off . . . Win— the well comes in—and they got gravy. These things ain't for these small investors . . . most of 'em most likely didn't even qualify financially. Guess I shouldn't a looked t'other way."

Realizing he would be unable to pin Rock down exactly as to how much he had gotten out of the deal, he reluctantly concluded the meeting and got up to leave.

"Say, brother Steve, I think I know you pretty well . . . we's fairly close brothers . . . in the Lord, ain't we?   Well, lookit, I know you been losing some big chunks.   Don't know what ta' tell you 'cept them's the risks in this here oil business. We'll never know why th' Lord didn't come in with us.   Maybe he'll tell us to our faces some day . . . but, look, brother, don't take it this   hard . . . I hear tell you gonna commit suicide . . . "

"Suicide? Where in God's Name did you hear that?"

"Hey . . . just a rumor's been going around. Dorcas told me . . . she got it from somebody at the fellowship. Any truth to it?"

"Hell—of course not! I just joked around with Faith about that being the only way to get more money . . . insurance money. That's all I'm worth now. Faith ! Good grief! Is she going around spouting off that I'm going to kill myself?"

"Appears what it is, brother."

"Well, stifle it whenever you hear it . . . is'n so," he said closing the door behind him.

For God's sake, he thought to himself, *what is this creature trying to do to him?*

On the way back to the station, Stephen ran over in his mind the discussion he'd had with Rock.   Something nagged at him and he couldn't quite put his finger on it. *The upshot in all this drilling . . . this wildcatting . . . is that the investor is the one who loses . . . not the driller. Right! Why had that not dawned on him before? Why had he not realized it? He was enough of a businessman to have figured it out . . . or was he? You didn't have to have much business knowledge to be in advertising—marketing, yes.   While he and all the investors kept losing, he had figured that the general partners were losing too . . . those who were generously given a share . . . like a ministry, a family member, the royalty land owner . . . they all lost too. But the general partner who put the program together,* *the driller in the case of Rock . . . why had he been able to continue from one well to the next? How had he managed to stay afloat while everybody else was sinking? 'You get it now, dummy'? Rock was paying himself all along. Perfectly rightly so . . . only Stephen had not realized it. A flash of insight illuminated his mind . . . of course! Rock had been excited like all the rest—that was the nature of the business—but he wasn't gambling like the rest. When you get right down to it, although his general partnership shares would give him a nice investment . . . true . . . and he hasn't made anything on any of the wells because they weren't pumping . . . he is still getting a healthy slice off the top—and then some! If the total subscription for a shallow well is thirty-two shares at two thousand apiece . . . sixty-four thousand to work with . . . Well, I'm going to find out, but I'd bet that the cost of drilling and completion is less than thirty . . . tanks, jacks and all . . . another five. So, that leaves almost . . . thirty-five thousand unspent! Three or four wells a month . . . they don't come in . . . be conservative: three times thirty thousand . . . ninety thousand this guy could be raking in off this thing each month! No wonder! His office overhead . . . one secretary, his wife bookkeeper, his brother the landman . . . couldn't set him back more than . . . seven, eight thousand a month. What a killing! No wonder he didn't seem particularly concerned when those wells didn't come in! He could really care less! . . . and, come to think of it, I really wonder if that old reworked field for Logos, Genesis, Hebrews . . . was any good to begin with? What if that was just the 'come-on' . . . a fabricated story just to suck in the investors . . . then actually drill the wells? But none of them come in—disappoints the poor saps who invested—but doesn't hurt ol' Rock . . . he walks away with ninety thousand a month . . . either way! Good God! That's it! That's what this whole thing . . . this scheme is all about! And, Revolution 22:20 ! What a killing Rock must have made on that one! Good act he put on with Moses . . . all that fighting at the end. Of course, he probably wanted those eight hundred barrels to flow—that would have put a bundle more in his pocket—and they might have if they hadn't been cemented in . . . but, either way, Rock won . . . he came out smelling like a rose. He pays Moses four hundred thousand. I wonder?—maybe more like $300,000! . . . doesn't have to finish, doesn't have to install gathering tanks, pumpers,* *heaters . . . all that . . . so he's under budget already, doesn't have to disclose anything to the investors . . . then the overhead goes into his own pocket anyway . . . and he pockets . . . out of two hundred thou left, five-ten thousand to plug, clean up . . . at least one hundred and fifty thousand dollars! Rock walks away with one hundred and fifty thousand dollars! More, most likely! A good part of that, mine and Tom's and dad's money! God! God! Why didn't You open my eyes to all this sooner? Where were You, Lord? Why did You let this happen to me—us? Is this Your way?*

After that rationalizing process had settled into his subconscious and seared those facts indelibly, Stephen let his mind drift toward a theme that had been recurring more frequently . . . the root cause of his lack of success . . . or of his always finding himself in these sorts of situations that somehow get botched up . . . and he invariably coming out on the losing end. *It was so even back on Madison Avenue. There had been a number of incidents, projects that had not come off right, where he had come out with egg on his face, so to speak . . . the things that lost you 'brownie points' . . . also raises and promotions. The . . . not exactly 'run-ins' . . . but awkward situations with the senior account executive Hank Worthington . . . and the impossible confrontations with Ruthie Cohen, one of the creative directors. Stephen had defended what he had been in charge of . . . the strategy, the campaign, whatever . . . and when something had gone drastically wrong, he—as he was brought up to do . . . at Sewanee Military Academy, in the Marine Corps—took responsibility for what had happened, being the senior man. He had naively thought that was the way it worked. A Marine captain takes full responsibility for everything everyman does in his outfit— takes credit and blame! He had noticed others covering their asses, though, and he had sneered at them; but they were the ones who stepped adroitly out of the way of mishaps . . . they were the ones who survived! He had not!*

It was only after he had gotten away from the ad agency that he had begun to reconstruct in his mind what the things were that had gone wrong, the things that were possibly sabotaging his career path . . . that subconsciously contributed to his souring on advertising when the religious substitute presented itself as a welcomed alternative. He was becoming aware of what his basic fault was . . . but he had never expected to encounter it once more in this world of true brotherly love, of God's Agape love . . . but he just had it thrown right in his face—*the basic fault: no 'street smarts' ! No street smarts. Moxie ! Chutzpa ! . . . good old-fashioned 3rd Avenue chutzpa ! It was as simple as that! Most people on Madison Avenue had them . . . got them, or learned them . . . from somewhere! Most ordinary people have them. And, he had just been outwitted out here in the sticks by a prime example of a street-smart put-on cowboy . . . who had just relieved him of all his earthly possessions—almost as easily as the slickest con artist of them all. Street smarts! No, he didn't learn them growing up in Atlanta; not at E. Rivers Grammar School . . . the Driving Club's social set . . . nor at Sewanee Military Academy. The academy had been the foundation for the basic fault—the structured system . . . the military system. The increasing authority step by step until you reached the top. That power, minor as it was for young boys and as beneficial at that formative age, was nevertheless a system instilled . . . that once ingrained . . . you figured everyone else was playing by the same rules . . . until you found out too late—as in his case. At Yale it hadn't mattered. There, everyone operated as an individual; there was no structure demanding authority . . . just some minor volunteer offices that required adaptability and tact . . . so that was at least some alternative training. Then, the good old Marine Corps. Officer . . . absolute command of those below you; absolute adherence to the command of those above you. The structure was clear, the rules clear, the system without flaw . . . and, obviously, no room for street smarts . . . except, maybe on the enlisted levels. But the officer ranks were above that sort of thing—or so Stephen theorized, having tasted only a small portion of it before being wounded in combat and reaching the end of that short-lived career.*

That's what they've all got that I don't have—street smarts ! That covers lack of formal . . . or highfaluting education, the Ivy League, the Junior League, the debutante crowd . . . a Yale degree . . . a commission in the U.S. Marine Corps!

177

These people are all enlisted . . . there's not an officer among them . . . and I stand out like a sore thumb. Who is the odd man out? Me ! Yours truly . . . El Estúpido . . . Stephen Trevelyan, that's who! Maybe if I could have stayed in the service, retired on thirty years, reached brigadier general or something—if I'd gotten that silver star I was put up for—I would have been able to survive in that system. I would never have had to confront 'street smarts' . . . the structure doesn't permit it—only allows for 'kissing butt' to get ahead, a good fitness report, regular promotions. Back then he had begun to see in the Marine Corps that it was the loyalty to your commander that got you ahead . . . and he would gladly have played the system to the hilt . . . like all the rest. If he had realized it sooner he might have been awarded that silver star combat medal.

That's what Faith has: no education, knows nothing about music, art, literature, history . . . any thing in the world that is considered important . . . but she's got street smarts! . . . and her Bible, and her God, and her Jesus. And, she is surviving. God, come to think of it, that's what Ham had when he didn't invest in Revelation . . . his street smarts tipped him off. Sure. He had a lot more money to invest than Stephen. Street smarts . . . common sense but more . . . an innate protective, looking out for number one !

Is this the one great lesson of life that You are teaching me . . . the hard way? I thought, Lord, that I was in a regulated society of good and righteous Christians that were led by You to behave properly. God! If only the Holy Spirit had given me the gift of 'street smarts' instead of a bunch of pious 'Praise Gods'! . . . and, to find myself to be a simple, trusting religious fool surrounded by sharks—God!

The next day at the station after the routine morning chores were out of the way, Lydia came in to Stephen's office and closed the door behind her. Stephen knew that meant a confidential tête-à-tête.

"Stephen . . . let me ask you something . . . that might be none of my business . . . but I think it is . . . cause it affects me . . . all of us, including you."

"Shoot. I'm all ears."

178

"Are you planning to commit suicide?"

"Oh, God! Not you, too! What the devil is going on? Rock asked me the same thing!"

"Rebecca told me she heard it from the fellowship . . . seems your wife Faith has formed a group of prayer warriors to bind Satan from leading you into this . . . "

" . . . Not, I can assure you, due to any deep concern for me or my life, but so that my brother, Tom, and my dad would not get the proceeds on my life insurance policy if I were to die! Faith's got it in her craw that I am going to go out and kill myself so that . . . Listen, I want you to do me a favor . . . a very personal favor. Give me a few minutes, then come back and I will have something for you to type for me . . . very personal. OK?"

Lydia left, obviously puzzled.

Stephen took his pen and put a yellow pad in front of him. He reflected, then began writing: 'Dear Tom, The reason for my writing— for having to write—this letter is incredible! Like something out of a bad dream! And, I want you to keep this letter in your safe deposit box, in the event something should happen to me, resulting in my death, and retrieve it and read it in court, should Faith attempt to do what she has threatened.

'As I was taking out the life insurance policy with you and dad as beneficiaries, as I told you on the phone I would, Faith found out and went into a rage seeing that she was not on it. And, somewhere in the ensuing argument and words that flew, I let drop in a fit of anger that, what with all the bad luck we have been having with the wells—and that God does not seem to be in any of this—that I would be worth more dead than alive, especially since I am now practically broke.

'So, what leapt into her distorted mind was the idea that I, therefore, was planning to kill myself . . . to commit suicide, so you all

179

could get paid back for the losses. You might well expect that I have been more than a bit despondent because of all this . . . plus the mess at the station. So, she's got it in her craw that I am going to commit suicide. . .and she has been going around telling all her praying friends that this is what I intend to do. Even Rock and Lydia, my secretary, ran me a playback of what's being said all over town.

'So, if it ever comes to this, that this letter has to be read in court to counter her charge to the insurance company that I planned all along to commit suicide, then, I want to state here and now, for all to read and understand: I do not intend to commit suicide, or to kill myself in any way; it is the farthest thing from my mind. I would not do such a thing under any circumstances; it is against God's teachings . . . and, besides, some day I want to be able to see and play with my grand children. I have no intention of departing this earth. Let the record so state.

'There is a whole lot more to my relationship with Faith. It is becoming a nightmare. She has spells that are indescribable, goes into all sorts of frightful accusations that I have demons of lust coming out of me toward strange women I never notice . . . and she carries this sort of holy condemnation for days and days with no letup. I think she's crazy. I had no inkling of any of this before I married her . . . no one did—or does—it doesn't occur around anybody else. So? My word against hers? Yes. That's going to be hard to prove in any case. But, I wanted to get this down on paper, as some sort of record to refute whatever she might take it upon herself to do. Lydia, who is typing this, can be my witness.

'Take me seriously. And, I will send you the policy. I've made you owner.'

Proof-reading it and making a change here and there, he called Lydia in to type it. "Make one copy only, please."

Twenty minutes later Lydia reappeared. "Steve . . . I don't know what to say. To give you my sympathy? What a heck of a situation to be in. I suspected something like this about Faith, but I would never have said anything. You know, women pick up on certain things . . . and I've thought I detected that she tries to control people, things, situations . . . and when she can't, she tries to destroy them. She's got a hate on Rock, too, I've noticed."

"You are right on on that! I am just beginning to realize that I am being subjected to an insidious form of mind control . . . through the bludgeoning weapon of the Bible! Can you imagine? The Word and God thrown against me constantly—and what have I done?— only tried to be a good Christian. Not to her, though! She and God are one . . . so, guess who I am left to be 'one' with? I never thought in my wildest moments that I would ever find myself latched up in such an incredible trap—a mental prison !"

"I'll get some of the 'good' team and we'll pray for you and hold you up . . . there are a lot of people around here, Steve, who do care for you."

"Thanks, Lydia. I treasure your support. Do me one more favor . . . keep the only copy yourself . . . just in case. I certainly can't keep it in my files."

After several unsuccessful attempts to focus his thoughts on station business, Stephen gave up and leaned back in his creaky executive chair, hands behind his head, and stared blankly at the ceiling, a posture that had become a virtual habit since there were no windows to look out of. His mind was a mush of disconnected thoughts and fleeting impressions, a kaleidoscope of long-past and recent events. Flashes of his office in New York . . . a muzzle flash in a jungle thicket . . . holding his infant daughter, Gloria, up in his arms for the first time . . . Darien, Connecticut . . . the house and the excitement of Christmas . . . the kids tearing open the presents. It was as if remembering bits and pieces of some movie or television show, now hazy in dim, imagined images. Ugly, intermittent flashes of oil rigs, Rock's and Moses' faces intruded. So did Faith's . . . contorted and fierce with condemnation of the evil spirits she saw in his eyes—but they were actually there, plain and fiery in hers, laughing at him. Felix's appeared; Cabada's and Barnabas' . . . and even Paul Masters'. Then, Lydias'—he had been so deeply lost in his nightmarish reverie that he was unaware that she had entered his office and was standing in front of him.

"Sorry, Steve. You've got a visitor. Says he has a prophesy for you . . . the Lord led him to bring it to you."

"Good God! I wish God would spare me—No. Wait a minute. You never know. Remember when Penny Gentile came in with a 'leading from the Lord' . . . a month or so after I came here? And, she said she was led to give me a thousand dollars?"

"Sure do. Wish the Lord had led her to me!"

"Remember? You were standing right there . . . smiling . . . as I was trying tactfully to refuse . . . "

"And Penny firmly told you not to 'rob her of the blessing' . . . "

"Yeah. I told her I might accept it for the station, and she said, 'No. The Lord told me to give it to you, Steve Trevelyan'! So, what could I do?"

"You learned. Learned how God blesses in mysterious ways. And, poor Penny, died just two weeks later. She wasn't poor Penny . . . she was rich in blessing in Christ Jesus!"

"Even if that was her last thousand dollars. 'Member her funeral? Over at Fishers of Men? No sad occasion, that! Singing and shouting and praising the Lord—happiest party— non-alcoholic party— I'd ever been to!"

"We were all happy that she had gone to be with the Lord. Nothing sad in that!"

"So . . . my dear sister-in-the-Lord, Lydia—not that I expect a repeat of anything like that—although after all this oil well business I could use a little manna from Heaven . . . in greenback form. What's his name? He a minister?"

"Cotton Mather Priestly . . . can you believe it? Roaming evangelist, I gather."

"Cotton Mather Priestly . . . well, his parents must have had his career chosen at birth. Either a shrewd insight or simple-minded religiosity. OK. Show him in."

Cotton Mather Priestly was a short, stocky middle-aged man . . . not muscular, more rolly-polly. His cheeks and neck slightly bulged over his tight, starched collar with its neatly-tied necktie perfectly centered at the top button of the "v" of his dark pin-striped vest, matching his wide-lapeled, bell-bottomed dark, conservative pin-striped polyester suit. His light tan Hush Puppies, while obviously comfortable, totally shattered an otherwise prepossessing image the little man projected. "Brother Steve . . . Brother Cotton Mather. Th' Lord bless ya' "

"Pleasure, Brother Cotton Mather. Have a seat. What can I do for you?"

"Not what you can do for me . . . the Lord spoke to me to come to you, Steve Trevelyan. I am to lay hands on you and prophesy. Sha-na-ma-ka-na-sa-la. Pa-sa-kee-ta. Mona-taka . . . Brother, the Lord has laid it on my heart to bring you His message. I don't know what it is . . . 'cepn' I come a long way to do His will."

Stephen remained silent . . . let him get it all out. This was not the first—nor would it be the last—of these sorts of Heaven-sent visitors carrying out an assignment direct from God. "What's your church, or ministry, Brother Cotton?"

"Church? Ministry? The world . . . the whole world, Brother Steve. I go where the Lord leads. Wherever He sends me . . . with a message, a blessing, an admonition . . . a prophesy. That makes mine the largest church under Heaven. A church, as you surely know, Brother, is not a building. Not a structure. A church is the assembly of the saints, the believers. We are all the church. Wherever we are, there is the church. We can gather in a building . . . in a fancy stone edifice with arches and stained glass windows . . . and it is a church when we are in it. It is only a pile of lifeless stones when we are not in it. We are the true body, the church, the Bride of Christ . . . and He will come soon for His bride. Let no one sleep . . . or tarry . . . or fail to keep the watch . . . for He will come as a thief in the night . . . and two will be plowing in the field, and one will be taken . . . the wise virgins will take enough oil for their lamps on the wedding night . . . " Seemingly caught up in his torrent of God-inspired scripture recitations, the portly little prophet stood up effortlessly from his chair, transfixed by some mental interplay in some other dimension, and with eyes half closed and arms outstretched, walked almost trance-like to position himself behind the chair where Stephen sat, trapped like the prey he was.

Stephen sat motionlessly as the faithful were supposed to do in such cases. Despite his lack of ease over the situation in general, he submitted only because he was really interested in hearing the prophesy. This 'gift of prophesy,' and the 'interpretation of tongues' were carismata, gifts of the Holy Spirit from First Corinthians 12 something or other. So was the 'discernment of spirits,' whereby one so gifted with that could separate true, Divine prophesy from demonic, satanic, deliberately misleading prophesy—even from hoax and fraud. In essence, if the prophesy were positive and up-lifting, it was obviously from God. If condemnatory or negative, it was surely not from God and could be refuted by binding the words—and Satan— on-the-spot in the Name of Jesus and casting them out. Both he and Faith had witnessed and participated in such prophesies time and time again.   It was a mainstay of the charismatic experience.

As the instrument of God's Spirit-tongues waned, his words followed a familiar pattern, "Oh, thank You, thank You, Jesus.   Yes, Lord. Yes! Yes! . . . Yes, Lord, yes." And then he was silent. When Cotton Mather spoke again, there was a change in his voice. It struck Stephen as not the voice he had been hearing. There was a mellowness to it, a richness in a lower baritone range . . . and an eloquence that belied its possessor. "Thou art My beloved and faithful servant . . . and thou hast demonstrated a pureness of heart that truly the righteous possess. Thou art proven . . . thou art, therefore, ordained to perpetuate my good works. Thou wilt be my harbinger. Thou wilt go before the multitudes and illumine their ways in the wilderness.   With thy instrument that I have given thee, thou wilt go forth in My Name in righteousness and honor and thy reward will be great . . . for thou art truly my servant before all. Thy prosperity will be as a beacon to My Word and the Glory of My beneficence. Thus saith the Lord. Amen."

Cotton Mather remained motionless and silent, hands pressed onto Stephen's head for an interminable length of time—until there was no doubt the spell was over. The portly prophet then heaved a deep sigh, mopped his brow with his handkerchief as he strode back to the chair and collapsed into it. He appeared drained of all energy.

Stephen sat quietly, hands folded on his desk in front of him, studying his visitor intently. The words of the prophesy had embedded themselves in his mind. He rarely remembered things as clearly as he did prophesies, possibly due to the self-fulfilling, wishful promises they offered. He was pleased with the words he had heard.

Recovering, Brother Cotton Mather gradually regained control of himself and resumed the conversation. "Hallelujah! Brother, that must have been a good one! Ya' know, I never remember what I said—

I'm only the instrument . . . for God to talk through me . . . through my mouth. His words come out of my mouth . . . and I'm off somewhere 'in the Spirit'! Praise God!"

"I thank you, Brother . . . and I thank the Holy Spirit for the prophesy. I needed that. Things have not been going too well of late . . . the station's got troubles—Big troubles. My life's got troubles . . . I lost all my money investing in oil wells for and with the Lord . . . "

"Praise God! Faith, Brother. Keep the Faith. He will never let you down. Trials, tribulations . . . it's all part of His testing."

"He did call me his 'beloved and faithful servant,' so I take heart in that. In fact, I do feel better. My mind is at ease again. Tell me, Brother Cotton Mather—are you a 'fire-and brimstone' preacher like your forebear? The Colonial New Englander, Cotton Mather?"

"Not exactly. I am a prophet . . . and I have the gift of prophesy. The two are not the same. You witnessed the gift—I was the instrument, God spoke through me. He also speaks through me as a prophet of old . . . as Isaiah, Ezekiel, Daniel . . . you know, in modern times He has sent many prophets—especially in these End Times.

"Pat Robertson with his CBN . . . to warn of the Second Coming and to prepare. People like that?"

"Yup. Many, many of us. You know that there are thousands more prophesies in the Bible yet to be fulfilled? Thousands of others have come true . . . but God had to take time out—God's seventy-week count-down had to stop so the Christian Age could be fulfilled and the Gospel spread . . . which has consumed almost two thousand years since the crucifixion of Christ . . . and His miraculous resurrection. Now, as the time approaches for His return, God has sent more prophets out to preach and prepare the people . . . because He is coming soon! At the end of this century! Just nineteen years from now—but, a lot has to happen in those nineteen years before He comes again . . . the Beast of

186

Revelation— 666—must arise . . . the one who befriends Israel and then betrays her—the Anti-Christ, has to appear . . . and there has to be a battle in Israel before all this . . . so the Anti-Christ can stop it and save Israel. You are familiar with Revelation, the Apocalypse of John, aren't you? Well, then, after the Beast, the 666 who betrays Israel, does so . . . he creates an abomination in the Temple . . . then the hoards from the east . . . armies of two hundred million—and where do the two hundred million come from? Iran? Iraq? Russia? China? Egypt? Arabia? It's all in Revelation. ! These hoards invade Israel from all sides!"

" . . . and Daniel . . . and Joel, Habakkuk . . . the Gospels, Peter . . . all foresee it," interjected Stephen, warming up to the subject.

"But, I get ahead of myself . . . jump around too much. He's coming—soon!—but there's lots to be done first. The Word has to be preached to every corner of the world . . . "

" . . . as we Christian TV stations are doing now . . . and will soon reach every spot on earth in our coverage . . . "

"The jews have already come back from their dispersion . . . back to the 'Promised Land.' Israel was created by the U.N. in 1948 . . . as prophesied by Ezekiel—but that U.N.! Got right into the hands of the Lord of this world, Satan! The U.N. is not of God! Run by pagan, demonic countries—ungodly! . . . "

" . . . but the dry bones now have sinews and skin back on them. "

"Jews all over the world have come back to their homeland . . . But, mark these words, as Jesus said, 'before this generation shall pass, I will come again.' A generation in the Bible is forty years, so, from 1948 till forty years later . . . puts it at 1988 to 1999 . . . give or take a few years . . . and you have the end of this century! 1999!"

"Even Nostradamus prophesied—correctly, I might add—all the events from his time . . . in the 1500s or 1600s . . . right up through

World War II. He had even predicted that men would fight above the earth and below the water in 1917. He also predicted that someone named Hister— close, wasn't it?—would throw the world into war . . . and he predicted the final, big war to come in 1999!"

"Nostradamus was not a prophet of God."

"Can't even the demons prognosticate?"

" . . . Anyway, three major things have to happen between 1948 and 1999 . . . before Christ will come again as promised . . . one, the Jews have to be back in Jerusalem . . . "

" . . . and that happened in the 'Six-Day War' in 1967. I was fighting in Vietnam at the time."

"Right.   For almost two thousand years before that, Jews everywhere at the celebration of Passover would end their prayers with 'Next year, Jerusalem!' "

"And . . . it happened! . . . "

"Number two big event is that the original temple destroyed right after Jesus said it would be . . . "

" . . . in A.D. 70 by Roman Emperor Titus . . . ."

" . . . has to be rebuilt. Only problem . . . the A-rabs went and built their own mosque right where the Jewish Temple used to be . . . "

"The Dome of the Rock Shrine, built shortly after Mohammed died in the sixth century A.D. The 'Wailing Wall' is part of the original foundation of the Temple that the Jews were anxious to recapture and be able to worship at . . . when they retook Jerusalem "

" . . . so, they have to somehow get rid of the Moslem mosque in order to rebuild the Temple—as the Bible says they will. Because . . . they have to reinstate worship—blood sacrifice— in the Temple in order for the betrayer, the 666 Anti-Christ, to do the 'abomination in the Temple' to incite the Jews to warfare . . . "

"Then, the Arab armies surrounding Jerusalem attack and Israel is crushed . . . "

"Almost," corrected Brother Cotton Mather. "The armies from Gog, Megog, Meshech and Tubal—all of which are Russia—and the hoards from the east . . . all try to crush Israel . . . and there is a bloody, final battle on the Plain of Esdraelon near Megiddo "

"Armageddon " interjected Stephen again, totally caught up in one of his favorite topics.

"Armageddon . . . the final battle with all the world's armies . . . that ends the age. But, regard this—it is not the end of the world! No. It is the end of the age, . . . by Jesus coming back down from Heaven with one foot on Mount Carmel just outside of Haifa . . . and the other over in Jerusalem . . . as the earth splits asunder across Israel . . . and swallows up the opposing armies!"

"And, the whole world witnesses it, as predicted, because of satellite TV televising it around the world . . . "

Brother Cotton Mather stopped for a moment, pondering. Stephen wondered whether his prophet friend had never seriously considered such a possibility as TV coverage of the Second Coming. At any rate, the modern-day prophet picked the thread of thought up and continued, "So, when Jesus— the Messiah—finally comes again, the eyes of the Jews—as prophesied—are opened from their Divine blindness inflicted for their earlier denying of Him . . . and at once they hail Him as their Messiah . . . at long last!"

"And, as also prophesied, the great, new millennium is ushered in."

"The 'thousand years of peace and prosperity' . . . which will be the entire twenty first century . . . where us Christians will be running things and Christ Jesus reigns as King from His throne in the Temple in Jerusalem."

"A millennium of peace . . . where Isaiah prophesied that 'swords would be beaten into plowshares . . . and the lamb would graze with the wolf', " reflected Stephen.

"And us Christians will live the thousand years—without dying! — as in the days before the Flood . . . "

"The true 'Sabbatical' thousand-year, seventh millennium of rest as God's work of the six preceding millennia are done," again offered Stephen.

"Until," warned Cotton Mather, "Satan is released for a time toward the end of the thousand years . . . to do his last evil deeds on mankind . . . and Jesus finally casts him and all his demons into the Lake of Fire . . . for eternity . . . "

"And . . . then the White Throne Judgment?"

"The White Throne Judgment by God, Himself. When Jesus came back to usher in His thousand-year reign, He conducted His Bema Judgment, that is, His separating the wheat from the chaff among His believers . . . so that He could appoint the faithful to ruling and responsible positions within His new Kingdom on Earth. When that Kingdom is over, then comes the final judgment . . . of all mankind who had passed away before Christ and outside of Christianity. God, the Father, conducts this one and writes the names of those who, without knowing God, Jesus and the Holy Spirit, nevertheless led righteous lives — their names will be written in the Book of Life. Those who are found wanting will be cast into outer darkness forever . . . "

"Then?" questioned Stephen, knowing full-well the answer but relishing the hearing of it again.

"Then, the 'New Jerusalem' comes down from Heaven to replace our world which has by then perished in flames."

"With streets paved with gold and precious jewels . . . "

"And, all shall live in the glory and presence of the Lord forever, A-men."

"Amen," echoed Stephen. "Brother Cotton Mather, the Lord has put it upon my heart to donate to your ministry." He pulled out his checkbook, wrote a check for a hundred dollars to Cotton Mather Priestly, tore it out and handed it to him.

""The Lord bless you, Brother Steve," he said, folding the check and putting it in his vest pocket.

When the door closed behind brother Cotton Mather Priestly, Stephen reflected on the prophesy and the 'alms' he had given to this anointed messenger of God. That's the way it worked, wasn't it? The Lord blesses or instructs His servant by messenger— sometimes—and the servant blesses the messenger . . . in the Name of the Lord? A never ending cycle. A preview of the great, new millennium to come. "Come, Lord Jesus," Stephen could not keep from uttering aloud.

Chapter 15   Tele-Harvest

The long-awaited—dreaded?— time had arrived: the Telethon was airing. The weather had cooled somewhat so that the studio was tolerable as long as the loading door stayed open. One could wear a suit coat, however, without wilting in perspiration. Three walls of the barn-like studio were dedicated to the gigantic effort. Eight-foot upsom board flats had been painted varying tertiary colors with large, simple designs of harvest, painted rather amateurishly, signifying the theme, Harvest of Thanks: pumpkins, cornucopia, apples, clusters of nuts, bundles of wheat, and so forth. These flats were lashed together in shallow saw-tooth groupings in front of the large, blue-gray cyclorama that covered a good twenty feet of one side wall. Spaces were left for interview areas, the 'tote' board, the announcer, and a large area had been set up on low risers for a long, elevated table with eight telephones . . . at which sat eight volunteers who answered the call-ins and noted the amounts and the names and addresses of the pledgers. All of the suspended ceiling lights were aimed around this periphery of activity.

The two pedestal cameras were operating in the center of the studio where they could spin in at least a half arc and cover quickly any event at any one of the on-camera set areas. The third, a minicam, was used as a roving, close-up camera. It also had a wooden adjustable tripod on wheels on which it could rest if an interlude went long. These were the only cameras the station had; there was thus no backup. The pedestal cameras' video tubes were reaching the end of their life expectancy. Of course, much could be done with a single camera, panning, zooming and dollying—if the operator were skillful enough—which more often than not was not the case. So, at least the telethon stood a good chance of staying on air one way or another . . . with God's help!

Rather than a hushed and controlled affair as in bigger commercial operations, the ambience here was casual, much milling about, directions right on camera to cut to something else . . . the informality was, in fact, its saving grace. Neither the crew, the volunteers, not the viewing audience expected anything more . . . any more polish. This was more fun . . . and more appealing. Especially, since there was much spontaneity from the volunteers and visitors that served to enliven the dead spots and keep the pace going. When at a loss for words or actions, whoever was emceeing at the time might just call someone out of the darkness of the studio to 'come on up,' sister, brother so-and-so . . . and tell us what God's doing in your life . . . that sort of thing. With these charismatics there was no reticence—most were not shy at all about testifying. This made it all one big family, too . . . it was more like a big church picnic. Stephen even thought that—'amateur night' though it certainly was—it was more interesting and lively than those dreary PBS on-air fund-raisers. Those poor secular people only had one basic pitch, and their attempts at variations only engendered early boredom and tune-out, whereas, for the Christian audience (hopefully there was one out there!) at least, KXAO-TV's telethon covered a wide range of interests . . . albeit religious. Content varied from testimonies to singing groups, to mini-sermons, to discussions with leading evangelists (whose ministries were not in competition and which could benefit from this kind of exposure . . . plus a portion of the donations). There was something new and interesting every moment—to the faithful.

The telethon had been going on for two nights. Stephen was scheduled to co-emcee it tonight, Wednesday, then to take it again Saturday. It would wrap up on Sunday with 'all the stops out'! . . . all the big guns, Doc Parsons, Barnabas Childs, brother John Mark, several other notables . . . and Stephen had even prevailed upon Faith and some of her cronies to participate. The projected goal was $50,000 . . . to raise in seven days . . . more than the station had ever set its sights on before. Doing such a thing two times a year was stretching things a bit; Stephen personally doubted they would hit this figure. And, he had told the board this at the last meeting . . . which he had survived, mostly, he thought, because Felix had not been there. He struggled to shake off his perpetual despondency of late . . . brought about by both the state of the broadcast operation and the demise of all the oil wells.

Joining the festivities in the studio close to seven p.m., Stephen made the rounds greeting people, thanking them for their assistance, and generally contributing to the necessary and vital public relations of the station. He would be working with one of the staff announcers, Jean Baptiste, who also doubled in the continuity department writing promotional spots. Lydia, in a typical display of loyalty, had volunteered to work the tally board. Jean would anchor the evening, so to speak, introducing Stephen and turning the interviewing and general continuity over to him . . . a chore Stephen had to psych himself up to. Once he got into the swing of it, though, it became second nature and he was at ease.

He was particularly interested in the special guest for this evening, a Biblical scholar and one of the followers of the Institute for Creation Sciences in San Diego. The work of the institute had fascinated him from the moment he heard about it and he began reading its publications. Their work in essence was a confirmation of the famous Scopes 'Monkey Trial' that had defeated the first round of the teaching of Evolution in the schools back in the '20s. Based on—or coincidental with the condemnation of "Evolution," Immanuel Velikovsky's scientific theories corroborated certain Biblical phenomena described in the Old Testament as 'miracles': the stopping of the sun in the sky for long periods of time due to the Earth's tilting off axis, Noah's flood relating to geological strata that are devoid of plant and animal life until a later age than thought . . . that sort of thing. Stephen would really like to pursue this sort of an investigation in depth some day.

"Good evening, folks. Welcome to the third day of KXAO-TV's Harvest of Thanks for the Lord. We can only harvest what He has sown out there, folks . . . so I trust that our gracious Lord and benefactor . . . who has blessed you all out there with His blessings and bounty . . . will put it in your hearts to share that bounty with us . . . help us bring in a harvest for the Lord and His works. Bless you . . . call the number at the bottom of the screen. Now, I want to introduce a special guest . . . and we are going to talk about something that I think you will find truly interesting . . . not the usual sort of thing . . . Meet Doctor . . . Ph.D. type doctor, that is . . . Timothy O'Daniel . . . Welcome brother O'Daniel.

"Pleased to be here, Steve."

"Now this is a large and involved subject . . . just how shall we get into it? What is the Institute for Creation Research?"

"I'm not actually a member but I am a follower of Dr. Henry Morris and his team . . . all highly accredited Ph.D.s in the scientific fields. They study the Biblical phenomena and interpret it in terms of present-day scientific fact . . . "

" . . . To confirm the Scopes 'monkey trial' that is ws God's 'Creation' and not blind 'Evolution'?"

"That too . . . which is one of the important factors since the theory of evolution has now replaced the God-creation model in all public schools. This is a bit off the track, but this is an insidious plot by the forces of 'secular humanism' to discredit Christianity and, in fact, replace it with this new secular religion. Actually, a 'Humanistic Manifesto' was written up and registered with the government back in the thirties. It is now so ingrained that no one notices it . . . but, in essence, 'Humanism' is the idea that God is replaced by the notion that man, himself, has everything necessary within himself to live on this planet . . . he, therefore, has no need for any concept of a god, an unseen, unproven god to guide him. It is not 'humanitarianism'—goodwill and help to all mankind. That is embraced by both sides. No, this is the term, Human-*ism*, and its basis goes back to Aristotle. It has has thus been the eternal struggle vis-à-vis Christianity from early on. It can be looked upon as the concept of anti-Christ . . . as a force rather than an individual . . . who is yet to come. It therefore, aligns itself with the forces of Satan, the deceptive forces of this godless world . . . and so on . . . "

" . . . *the fool hath said in his heart, There is no God*. Psalm 14." Stephen paused, reflected, and resumed, "So, the institute is refuting 'Evolution'. How?"

"Well, to begin with . . . everyone nowadays . . . informed people and uninformed people, scientists, professionals . . . all have a knee-jerk reaction when 'Evolution' is mentioned. It is presumed to be a fact of intelligent observation . . . a theory that has been accepted without, I might point out, the slightest shred of corroborating evidence. Even Darwin, shortly after he wrote an outline of it . . . repudiated it as being unprovable, except for the 'survival of the fittest' part. That is obvious in any stratum of existence. But, the great dichotomy—one that the scientific world lives by in every other area—chooses to ignore in this is the second law of thermodynamics. The first law is something to the effect that energy can neither be created nor destroyed . . . it all remains somewhere, in some state. But the second law is one that simply in and of itself refutes 'Evolution.' Simply, that accepted and basic law states that matter does not tend to create higher matter, to the contrary, all matter tends to decay . . . to break down to lower forms . . . order never arises out of disorder. Yet, subscribing to this without equivocation, the scientific community— those virulently opposed to any notion of a great super intelligence, a great creative force, a God—simply close their eyes when confronted with the illogic of their blind acceptance of evolution, believing it all came together out of chaos. It's really incredible when you think about it."

"Intelligence, therefore, is not random. By the way, where are the missing links? The transitional life forms? If the evolutionists are right, ever wonder how our eyes somewhere eons ago decided to work their way up on either side of the nose? Where are the examples of homo sapiens—or homo erectus—when the eyes were still down around the mouth . . . or on the back of the head? And, what about the emotions . . . sensitivity to beauty? . . . ethics? . . . what did these non-instinctual qualities 'evolve' from?"

"Couldn't happen. The second law of thermodynamics proves that the real world, if left to itself, will de-generate to randomness and disorder."

"You mean that if you set a monkey down at a typewriter and left him long enough, he would not be able to accidentally come up with a Shakespearean sonnet? Or . . . leave a bunch of mechanical parts in the path of a tornado . . . and find a Boeing 747 assembled when the storm is over?"

"That's about what the evolutionists think."

"Isn't it more logical to imagine apes descending from us rather than we humans evolving up from them?"

"To us enlightened Christians, yes. Evolutionists are blind to reason and proof."

"So, you people are throwing their own material right back at them . . . and by so doing, proving that the Bible is right all along. Beautiful! I've read some Velikovsky. What about his work . . . similar to the Creation Research group?"

"Yes. And, he was ostracized by the humanistic scientific community . . . nevertheless, he bears studying. What Dr. Morris and his group are proving are a lot of geological truths and disputing other entrenched fallacies."

"Like? . . . "

"I've brought some graphics with me . . . First, the earth is not nearly as old as geologists insist."

"No?"

"No. For a number of reasons . . . carbon dating is extremely inaccurate . . . decay factors only conjectural. Morris points out that the presence of Helium in the atmosphere and its decay or decline . . . which, fortunately, man has been measuring for over a hundred years now,..is much more precise. We put the age of the earth . . . as it exists in present form . . . at around ten thousand years at most. Not a billion or whatever had been claimed."

"How do you arrive at that?"

"From a number of directions . . . and, I'll try to condense all this . . . "

" . . . and don't get into any highfalutin' big words we can't understand!"

"Well, let's start with Noah . . . and the flood. Counting back in the Old Testament, we know exactly that Noah came a thousand years after creation and a thousand years before Abraham . . . who preceded David by one thousand years . . . who preceded Jesus by one thousand years . . . and it has been almost two thousand years since Jesus. Add it up and you get six millennia. Six! Mean anything?"

"As in six days ? God created the world in six days . . . "

"And Peter, in his second epistle, said '*a day with the Lord is like a thousand years . . . and a thousand years is like a day with the Lord*' . . . "

"And, you know, when you leave the earth into space, you enter another time dimension. I read where the astronauts on one of their moon trips returned a second younger than when they had left!"

"So, if a day is like a thousand and vice versa, the six days of creation could have been six thousand years in God's time . . . "

"Or, actually, six days . . . "

"And, on the seventh day God rested. The analogy now can be taken to a higher level and is that, referring to Peter's description, six days of creation could equal the six thousand years the earth has already lived . . . and we are now headed for the seventh millennium, the seventh day   . . . the day of rest . . . the Sabbath. Does that trigger anything from John's Apocalypse . . . Revelation ? The 'end times'— not the end of time—but Christ's Second Coming? At the 'End of the Age' . . . the end of the six thousand years to usher in the day—the final thousand years of rest with Him—the Great Millennium described in Revelation? At the end of which God calls all mankind to the final 'white throne' judgment?"

"Wow! That fits . . . but that's a whole 'n'other night's discussion. You can read about that in Hal Lindsay's The Late Great Planet Earth. Sure wish we could go on into that . . . but, back to the beginning . . . "

"The first thousand years before Noah would, then, be the Biblical time of the creation by God of the earth . . . so that would make the planet only roughly seven thousand years old . . . defying, of course, all scientific secular knowledge.   Now, you know all about what Genesis says about Adam and Eve, Cain and Able and the spreading of mankind and animals over the earth and how wickeder and wickeder they became . . . until He told Noah to build the ark to save himself and family from the destruction that was to come. Well, it's the flood that is the key to all geology and knowledge about the earth. From Creation to the flood, there is a good theory that there was a canopy of water vapor encircling the earth, giving it a moist and warm greenhouse effect . . . "

"Would that account for some of the early Biblical characters— Methuselah— all living many hundreds of years . . . and all that?"

"Could be. That canopy filtered harmful ultraviolet radiation and kept everything moist . . . good for growing of plant life, too. I guess you could say it was perpetual overcast and semi-tropical . . . and, the theory goes, the earth was relatively flat, not chopped up with huge mountain ranges . . . "

"I think I remember picking up somewhere in Genesis, they were all vegetarians, too"

"Right. So, God decides to destroy the sinful earth that He had created, saving only Noah to repopulate it with righteous people. He foretells that a flood will come . . . so build the ark . . . et cetera. Now, where does all that water come from?"

"The canopy of water vapor!"

"Correct! Allowed to fall. It inundates the earth for forty days and nights and was so much that Noah remained in the ark for three hundred and seventy-one days. When everything had finally receded and dried, the sky was clear for the first time . . . "

" . . . and God gave the sign of his promise never to do such a thing again—the rainbow!"

"Now, scientifically, the flood is of primary interest . . . for a number of highly technical reasons I won't get into . . . the theory of uniformity and other contrary theories. But the fascinating thing is that all dinosaurs and many other life forms—fish, amphibians, and mammals

—all appear in the same geological stratum . . . in the top of the Pleistocene . . . which is dated too early by secular geologists . . . it is much later. The coal deposits and oil and gas are in this stratum . . . all of which indicates a cataclysmic occurrence. I won't get into long drawn out details . . . but, if any of our viewers want to pursue this, I suggest you look up Dr. Henry M. Morris' books . . . especially The Genesis Flood.   He and co-author, John Whitcomb, analyze, refute standing theories . . . and with such authority I can't understand why the scientific community hasn't welcomed him with open arms . . . "

" . . . because it leaves all of the anti-Christian, anti-Creation, anti-Bible clique of self appointed authorities with 'egg on their faces'! That's why they turned on Velikovsky like a school of barracuda.   Also, this is the group that writes the textbooks . . . you can't see them allowing anyone else to invade their domain, can you?"

Reminded of a certain passage, Stephen picked up a Bible in front of them and flipped to the first chapter of Romans.

Dr. O'Daniel continued, "You are absolutely right.   But, some high school textbooks do begrudgingly give a separate page to Velikovsky . . . not exactly knowing how to handle him.   It is said that Albert Einstein—who knew him at Princeton—was studying his works when he, Einstein, died. So?"

"I think this verse from the first chapter of Paul's letter to the Romans is pertinent here, ' . . . *professing themselves to be wise, they became fools . . . and worshiped and served the creature more than the creator . . . that is, they did not like to retain God in their knowledge . . .* '   Getting a signal from the floor manager to cut the interview, Stephen picked up, "I know there is more to this . . . we have barely scratched the surface . . . but we have to go to Jean now and an update on our tally board. Stick around Doctor O'Daniel, and we'll try to get back into this later . . . I'd like to bring up something Velikovsky uncovered about the change of the earth from a 360-day to a 365-day year in Biblical times."

Stephen again looked into the camera and took his cue, "Hello there again, brothers and sisters and faithful supporters of KXAO-TV's Harvest of Thanks. As station manager, I can tell you what a boost this gives to the station . . . we simply cannot continue to operate without your generous contributions. Keep praying and asking the Lord to bless us—and you—and call a friend and ask them to call in and contribute, too. The number is at the bottom of the screen . . . We've been talking to brother— Doctor . . . Ph.D. type—Timothy O'Daniel whose particular ministry is on the Bible and how its words fit in and explain the scientific phenomena better than our learned secular scientists . . . who really don't know anything without God's Word as the basis."

"Thanks, brother Stephen. We had just gotten through Noah's flood and how the firmament of heaven—the canopy of water vapor— has poured down causing the flood all over the world . . . even ancient manuscripts—not manuscripts but cuneiform writing on baked clay tablets of Sumer and Assyria, for instance, depict the same flood. So do western hemisphere indian cultures and civilizations. So, it happened all over the globe at the same time . . . we know that."

"Well, it was indeed just that," interjected Stephen, " . . . and they had a year of 360 days as we can see from the Bible . . . until one day it changed to 365 days. Remember when Joshua slew the Amorites at Gibbon . . . and he had commanded the sun to stand still . . . 'and it did not hasten to go down for about a whole day'? Wasn't that about around fifteen hundred B.C.?"

"Yes, and another time for a fourth of a day. Velikovsky's theory, which explains a lot of unexplained phenomena, is that the earth was pulled by a gigantic celestial force off its axis and the earth actually tipped . . . or rotated over to another axis that spun it faster, 365 rotations rather than 360 per complete orbit."

" Thus accounting for Joshua's view of the sun appearing to stand still in the sky "

"And, equally important, explaining why those mammoths and mastodons were quick-frozen with tropical vegetation in their mouths and ended up in glaciers in Siberia . . . that were excavated, you remember? You know, glaciers only travel a short distance a year . . . and those creatures could easily have outrun an advancing ice flow—avalanche, maybe not."

"And, Jewish records—I mean, Israelite . . . they weren't Jews then . . . Israelite records show the change in the calendar with five extra days. So, what was the celestial force that changed it?"

"Velikovsky maintains that Mars and Venus back then were much, much nearer to the earth than now—so close, they appeared larger than our moon in the sky. And, he theorized, that there was an instability in their orbits that, when the bodies approached a proximity they had never reached before . . . presumably at the time of Joshua's battle . . . enough of gravitational or electrostatic charges built up that lightening-like flashes of energy sparked between them that it was interpreted by ignorant and awestruck humans below as the warring of the gods in heaven!"

"Of course! The pagan greeks could have gotten that notion from such a sight recurring in their heavens—day or night . . . and, they attributed to them all sorts of supernatural powers . . . what else would they have thought? And, they—and earlier civilizations—had seen these bodies and groupings of constellations and pictured them as signs of the zodiac . . . the first repeatable pictures that mankind discovered. Now we have television as repeatable pictures from the sky, the ether—of course!"

Dr. O'Daniel continued, "So, when these gravitational negatively and positively charged forces collided, Mars and Venus tugged at nearby earth pulling it off kilter a bit, but not out of orbit, before they flung themselves out to more stable orbits where we see them today. Conceivable?"

"Quite! Don't you in the audience agree? There is a lot more to all of this . . . which we can't get into . . . and, this is just a part of the prophesy of the Old Testament prophet Daniel that God would reveal more of His Divine knowledge in these last days. Thank you, doctor, but we have to get back to the business of raising money to do the Lord's work in our own little KXAO-TV orbit. Thank you, again, for coming. Jean, what's the tally now?"

The tally so far was a disappointing $5,240.

Chapter 16   Sheba & Satan

It was Friday . . . 'thank God it was Friday!'   The week of telethon had disrupted things around the station, routine—as much as there was of that—and personnel were a little cranky.   Overworked, perhaps.   Everyone was tired . . . tired of the whole thing.   Stephen despaired of the effort.   What had it brought?   A measly $9,000 something—mostly pledges—IF they could be collected.   That's hardly going to take care of the utility bill . . . certainly not debt service even for the month!

Lydia had reported the previous day that Felix's henchman, his sycophant accountant, had been over sticking his nose into the station's accounting office.   And, there had been some unidentified visitors . . . while Stephen had been out on an appointment . . . who had toured the premises with an interest more than casual.   They were dressed a bit formally, too, all in business suits.   Didn't strike her as local either.

As Stephen lethargically dug through a pile of papers to deal with a past-due bill that he had procrastinated too long over, his phone rang.   It was Rock.

"Hey, brother . . . jist thought I'd give ya' a bit of news . . . ain't gonna make ya happy . . . "

"At this point, nothing would," retorted Stephen bracing for the other shoe to drop.

"Guess who's drilling right across from Revelation 22:20?"

"No idea. Saint John of Patmos, himself?"

"Little earlier in the Bible than that—Moses!"

"Moses? Moses Steinberg? Our erstwhile driller-brother?"

"Yup. Seems he got hissef the lease across the road . . . somehow he and his landman was working on that thing when we was drillin'. Didn't know it . . . didn't even know the thing was leasable . . . thought my brother had checked everything around there. Moses must'a done some high financin' or palm-greasin' to git that lease!"

"So . . . when he smelled the Brownsville . . . he hopped on it . . . and knew he could go next door . . . drill . . . and hit the same thing."

"Or, off-drill . . . angle it, if'n he wanted."

"So . . . we had us a Judas in our midst all along. No wonder he wanted to get off that hole . . . wasn't interested in re-drilling . . . gave us that cockamamie story about having to be somewhere else . . . "

"He had an adjacent lease and let us pay for exploring it . . . "

"So much for the Christian brotherhood. *'Do unto others as you would have them'* "

"Ain't nothing' we kin do . . . 'cept see if'n he hits . . . jist thought you'd like to know."

"Yeah, just what I wanted to hear . . . to cheer me up. Thanks."

The news began to sink in after he had hung the receiver up. Now Moses stood a good chance of striking those eight hundred barrels a day. "God, how could you? How could You allow that traitor in our midst to . . . prosper instead of us? I really give up, God . . . I don't think I will ever understand all this . . . Your ways . . . anything . . . "

He swiveled his chair and stared at the blank wall for an interminable time.

Saturday evening finally rolled around and Stephen's spirits picked up a bit. This was his last chore for the telethon and he looked forward to his interviewée, brother Gabriel Levy, a converted Jew . . . a 'Jew for Jesus.'

The telethon opened with quite an unusual musical ensemble . . . unlike the typical Christian groups—even the more contemporary ones —this one went right into a rousing and rollicking, heel clicking, tambourine, steel guitar and high-pitched pipe and clarinet rendition of what resembled a fast country & western sound . . . but a bit strangely, a step away. Stephen recognized it immediately as good old Yiddish Klezmer music.

Stepping in the dark alongside brother Gabriel Levy, Stephen remarked, "What's this? The Catskills? The Borscht Belt?"

Turning to greet his old acquaintance, Gabe retorted, "This is Temple Beth Shalom, isn't it?"

"Shalom, yourself you Jew-Christian," and they embraced in the customary manner, except that Gabe kissed Stephen on the right then the left cheek.

Gabe took the arm of his companion on his right and introduced her to Stephen. "Sheba, I'd like you to meet Stephen Trevelyan . . . manager of this station and director of this extravaganza . . . Stephen, Sheba Herzog . . . Sheba's from Tel Aviv . . . a dancer . . . and scholar . . . and former soldier in the Israeli army . . . fought in the Yom Kippur war . . . back in '73."

"Shalom.   Na-im me'ud . . . which is the extent of my Hebrew . . . if even that is understandable."

"It is . . . nice to meet you. Gabe has told me a lot about you . . . and your wife . . . and your ministry."

207

"Sheba and her dance and musical group are touring the U.S . . . .sponsored by us Jews for Jesus . . . of which she and they have not fully come around yet to full conversion . . . but we're working on it."

The music was winding down and the floor manager signaled them to take their seats on the couch and chair in the interview set. Lavalière mikes were quickly snapped onto the three and Stephen looked up as the camera light came on.

After the perfunctory welcome and praise and telephone number to call in, Stephen turned to his guests and introduced them. "Gabe, before we get into a lot of other areas I know you and I want to talk about concerning the Jews, Jesus and the Second Coming, explain to us just what that music was . . . "

"Steve, that was Klezmer . . . a folk type of music typical of Yiddish . . . or the Ashkenazy . . . or European Jewish flavor."

" . . . as opposed to?"

" . . . the Sephardic, or Middle Eastern, North African, Mediterranean Jew."

"Something to do with the diaspora?"

"Exactly . . . the dispersal of the Jews out of Palestine to all parts of the world following the destruction of Jerusalem by Roman emperor Titus in 70 A.D. Then they were expelled out of Spain the year Columbus was discovering America. . .and took with them to North Africa that flavor of music."

" . . . fulfilling Ezekiel's prophesy? . . . leaving Israel the dry bones ?"

"Would seem so."

"So two basic groups became recognized," added Sheba, " . . . the western European and the eastern . . . or Oriental."

"And," quizzed Stephen, " . . . the Ashkenazi developed Yiddish? It sounds quite like German to me."

"A derivation . . . bastardization . . . flavored with some Hebrew."

"I know. Thought for a moment I was back in New York when I walked into the studio. Love it! . . . Well, Gabs and Sheba, we have a lot of time tonight . . . in between our tote board and other messages . . . so, I really want to get into some things about the Jewish religion and Jews for Jesus . . . and present-day Israel . . . that even a lot of our Christian viewers probably do not know."

Gabe responded, "The most basic thing to know is that both Jews and Christians worship the same God of Abraham, Isaac and Jacob. We born-again Christians know that, but you know, most Jews have no idea that that is so, and we are also the biggest supporters of Israel in the U.S."

"Now, what do you call yourself, Gabe, a Christian or a Jew? With that Yarmulke, I'm not sure!"

"I'm neither—or both! Jesus was a Jew . . . and He broke the barrier between Jew and Gentile by opening the way for all to His Father. In my own little church-temple I am a rabbi, but we worship as Jesus taught . . . mainly as at the 'last supper.' We have communion breaking bread and wine, operate like He and His apostles did . . . only He is an invisible presence with us. So, our group is more like the simple, emerging form of Christianity in the Book of Acts. We even have retained certain of the Jewish customs . . . like the Sabbath—today—is our day of worship . . . Friday sundown to tonight, sundown. Sunday is actually an error in Christian reckoning . . . Jesus was not crucified on a Friday . . . It was Wednesday . . . and He arose on Saturday, not Sunday."

"Interesting . . . but, look I want to pursue something here . . . and that is the long history of Judaism . . . of the Old Testament . . . No other civilization on the face of the earth has existed—or lasted as long—over five thousand years!"

"Right, this is the year 5742 in our calendar—1981 in yours. First, though, let's get 'Judaism' straight," said Gabe, warming up to his favorite subject. "Judaism—Jews—only refers to present day Israel . . . Jews, who come from the tribe of Judah . . . who, along with the Levites . . . were the only surviving remnants of the Babylonian Captivity in 450 B.C."

Sheba interjected, "You remember, after Solomon, the kingdom of the Israelites broke up into the northern and the southern kingdoms. By the way, they were called Israelites when they demanded of God a king and became a nation; before that, back in the days of Egypt . . . and Moses . . . and the desert, they were Hebrews . . . of the twelve tribes of Jacob . . . well, the northern kingdom of ten tribes was captured and destroyed by the Assyrians back around 600 something B.C . . . "

"And, the southern kingdom around Jerusalem, the tribes of Benjamin and Judah . . . and the non-land-holding priestly tribe of Levi . . . were captured by the Babylonians in 535 B.C.," volunteered Stephen, who then nodded toward Gabe for him to pick it up here . . .

"And, these people were taken to the ancient city of Babylon . . . which doesn't exist anymore . . . nor does Nineveh, its rival. Present-day Baghdad is between where the two were . . . and, remember, all this was fertile land back then . . . the 'fertile crescent' . . . not bleak desert as it is today. So, they stayed in captivity . . . and it wasn't necessarily a harsh imprisonment . . . more like a benevolent enslavement. The prophet Daniel emerged as a confident to the ruler Nebuchadnezzar . . . Well, to make a long story short . . . after seventy years Darius the Chaldean ruler overtook the Babylonians . . . and Darius, seeing his name mentioned by the prophet Isaiah two hundred years earlier, took it as a sign to release the captives . . . those who made it back to Jerusalem were predominantly the remnants of the tribe of Judah and the Levites. Therefore, the Judahs became Jews. The ten lost tribes of the earlier Assyrian invasion evidently intermarried with the conquerors and evolved into the Samaritans . . . and that intermingling of blood was what caused them to be so hated by the Jews at the time of Jesus. The Judah remnant, on the other hand, were forbidden to intermarry . . . and kept the chosen race pure as God had directed . . . "

"There is a lot to chew on here," interjected Stephen. "But, my cue sheet here says that . . . after we go to the tote board . . . Sheba, you and your group, are going to entertain us with a series of authentic Israeli folk songs and dances . . . then, we will get back into our discussion . . . All right, Jean, what do we have over there? How much have our faithful followers pledged up to now?"

After a lively interlude of spirited folk dances and songs by the group of a dozen colorfully-clad Israeli dancers, accompanied by the half dozen musicians, the cameras returned to Stephen and his guests, Gabe Levy and Sheba Herzog.

"That sounded so different from the earlier presentation . . . I take it those were in the Sephardic tradition—thought I detected an eastern flavor," observed Stephen.

"Precisely," answered Gabe.

"You know, that brings to my mind the gathering of east and west . . . of all the Jews coming back to their homeland . . . the sinews coming back onto the dry bones as Ezekiel prophesied . . . "

"Yes, thanks to the United Nations in 1948 when they recreated Israel. You know, at that time the Hebrew language was a dead language, like Latin, only scholars and rabbis used it. But Hebrew was instantly resurrected and became the modern language of reborn Israel— God's language spoken once more!"

Stephen added, " . . . Readying God's people for the Messiah's coming?"

"Would seem so . . . you know, the languages in Jesus' time were Hebrew and the popular, everyday language, Aramaic, a holdover from the Captivity. Of course, one had to know Latin and Greek as well to get around."

Stephen paused a moment to consider bringing up the Zionism and move of the Holy Spirit that he and Reverend Paul Masters had discussed. "Yes, that was surely a triumph for Zionism, the growing movement to stir interest in Jews returning the to Holy Land . . . but did you ever connect the fact that the present 'movement of the Holy Spirit' among us charismatics is actually God's way of preparing us Christians to be ready when Jesus comes again at the end of this century?"

"Hadn't connected the two," responded Gabe, "But that does make sense."

"Well, no doubt about it that the creation of the state of Israel gave the Jews their homeland back . . . the true one that God had promised Abraham and had given to Moses and Joshua . . . and they did come from all over the world . . . to reconvene in the old area of Palestine. The Bible says somewhere that a generation after that occurrence, that the Messiah will come—again! A Biblical generation is forty years . . . that makes it about time we started being ready!"

"True, but a few other things have to happen within that period to prepare the way—in Israel—for the Messiah to come. One, Jerusalem had to be back in Jewish hands . . . which happened in the 1967 Six-day War. You know . . . from the time of the destruction of the second temple, the so-called Herod's Temple, the one Jesus preached in . . . until the six-day war . . . Jews had no central temple in which to worship, to offer the blood sacrifice . . . only synagogues—and there is no blood sacrifice there! The prayer for almost two thousand years of Jews all over the world on the eve of Passover had always been, 'Next year, Jerusalem!' Then,Hallelujah! In 1967 they were in Jerusalem . . . at the only existing remnant of the Holy Temple . . . the 'Wailing Wall.' On the site of the original temple, the site where Abraham had been tested by God as to whether he would obey and sacrifice his son, Isaac . . . Mt. Moriah . . . and, then, in the seventh century A.D. the Moslems erected the Dome of the Rock shrine to Mohammed . . . thus complicating the Jewish situation vis-à-vis the site. I might add, parenthetically, that Mohammed was not Divine, he was a secular prophet. He did not ascend to heaven; he was buried in Medina."

Sheba added, "That U.N. creation of Israel was certainly not a clear-cut thing . . . we've had four wars there since . . . and I took part in the Yom Kippur one myself. That was horrendous . . . we fought two solid weeks for our very existence . . . and, I am sure that the Hand of God had been with us. The odds were too formidable not for it to have been"

Stephen jumped in, " . . . and you had to fight for strategic pieces of territory that you should have been given in the beginning by the U.N. in order to protect yourselves . . . the Golan Heights, the West Bank, the Gaza Strip . . . You know, when august bodies decree such partitions and demarcations . . . it is a very arbitrary thing. Take following World War I, the Balfour Declaration, which was the forerunner of the later creation of Israel . . . Lord Balfour and Lawrence of Arabia simply drew lines on a map of the middle east and thereby created Palestine, Syria, Iraq, Saudi Arabia . . . no rhyme or reason . . . no recognition of ethnic or tribal claims . . . just hypothetical lines drawn with a ruler which set in motion future conflicts. Too bad, the lines didn't include some of the rich oil reserves for Israel!"

"Odd that you should say that, Steve, because there is a group of Christian oil explorers who are negotiating right now with the Israeli government to drill in Israel. Seems they have interpreted a passage from the old testament where God says that riches, of a bitumen-petrol nature

213

will be found in the 'Foot of Asher.' Asher was one of the twelve tribes whose territory was along the upper coast including present-day Haifa and the fault line running through Mt. Carmel below the city . . . "

" . . . Mt. Carmel? Where Jesus is to return . . . with one foot on each side . . . astride the great rift that will erupt between there and the Holy City, Jerusalem?" Stephen quickly enjoined. "You know, I hope some Christian TV group . . . maybe Pat Robinson's which CBN is trying to establish in Lebanon . . . will be there to televise Christ's Second Coming . . . over satellite . . . to all the world, as the Bible says will happen! Exciting times, wouldn't you say?"

Gabe picked the thread back up, "But, as I said, Jerusalem has to be back in Jewish hands, then two other signs have to occur before the Messiah comes: The original temple has to be rebuilt . . . and sacrificial worship has to be reinstated in it . . . and, lastly, Jews have to accept a world leader as savior—who then betrays them and performs abominations in the temple, finally being disclosed as the anti-Christ— the 666 of Revelation—accompanied by the beast and the false prophet . . . the antitheses of God, Jesus and the Holy Spirit . . . before all the armies of the nations opposing Israel assemble for the invasion from the east and north to finally exterminate them . . . where 'the blood in Israel will run to the depth of a horse's bridle and it will take six months to clear the land of the carnage' . . . and the final Armageddon, the end time battle has to take place following that."

"I was on the Marine Corps advertising account at the time of the Yom Kippur war and happened to be in Washington at a briefing . . . and, do you know? . . . they were actually blocking out the valley of Desraelon? . . . Megiddo . . . to the west of the Sea of Galilee . . . now Tiberias . . . where the apocalyptic battle of Armageddon is prophesied to take place? And, that was not so far-fetched at the time, because we forget now, but the U.S. went on global military alert when the Soviets dispatched a freighter with nuclear warheads to Egypt and actually got two infantry divisions air-borne. That was truly close to Armageddon! Even closer than the 1962 'Cuban Missile Crisis', especially since the '73 crisis involved the armies of the nations surrounding Israel . . . actually invading her and the prophesied forces of Mesech . . . interpreted as Moscow . . . and Tubal . . . interpreted as Tobolsk . . . actually threatening! We forget these things so conveniently—but, at that time there was a very real threat of all-out World War III over Israel!"

Stephen could not contain himself, he loved this type of eschatology. He continued, "You remember that many of the minor Old Testament prophets predicted such things that up until now have seemed incomprehensible?   Like Joel's and Nahum's descriptions of these last battles, seeing giant iron locusts spitting fire out of their noses skimming across the land in swarms . . . Ever seen?—or can you imagine—a concentrated helicopter attack? . . . like some in Vietnam . . . or the tank battles in the Yom Kippur war? . . . how these attacking, flying-firing and charging monsters look? . . . and to someone trying to describe a vision thousands of years in the future? . . . what other terms could he have used? The Bible is full of these sorts of visionary descriptions . . . all of which must mean something, because, of the thousands of prophetic predictions contained in it, about three-fourths have come true. That leaves one fourth yet to come! Convincing?"

"What with the constant turmoil in and around Israel, there is no doubt that the only resolution will come catastrophically—as the Bible states in both testaments."

"Why don't we hear more of this, that is, the relationship to Biblical prophesies in terms of today's news events?" queried Stephen. "You know—you and I know—that the root cause of the Arab-Israeli conflict is not over the ownership of the land that was called Palestine . . . God was very clear in the Old Testament that He gave it to His chosen people—the twelve Hebrew tribes and their descendants, the Israelites, the Jews. No, the root of the problem is the legitimacy of Abraham's line . . . and the illegitimacy of one side of it. Remember? Abraham's wife Sarah, since she was in her eighties, lacked enough faith in God's promise that she would bear a son and begin Abraham's anointed line. Instead, she offered her husband her Egyptian slave girl, Hagar, who bore Ishmael. Ultimately—eighteen years or so later—Sarah did bear a son, when she evidenced faith in God's promise . . . who was Isaac. Ishmael beat up on baby Isaac and Hagar was jealous . . . so, you know the story . . . Abraham banished Hagar and her illegitimate son into the desert. As these two were about to expire, God took pity and did save them . . . and thus Ishmael became the father of the Arab race—the illegitimate offspring of Abraham. Thus, the four thousand-year conflict! The right of succession—primogeniture—of course, always went to the first-born of the legitimate line . . . Nobody ever brings this aspect up, naturally. It is too inflammatory an issue—but it is what the Bible says all along. One other thing, the Jews . . . who now comprise the end of that Abrahamic lineage . . . don't realize that we Christians are their biggest supporters . . . because of our understanding of the Bible . . . and our revealed knowledge that this is all fulfillment of prophesy."

"Steve, when you get right down to it, neither Jews nor Christians really know the Bible—only fundamentalists and charismatics like ourselves—who take it literally. Your liturgical churches don't dare get into end-time prophesy . . . eschatology. They stick to their saccharin homilies and other pablum so as not to disturb the lukewarm flock—it's hard enough to get them to come to church anyway—they sure don't intend to drive them away by throwing the Word at them!"

"You sound like me. And, the Jews?"

"We—they—are about the same. The 'reformed' Jews are like your Episcopalians— no deep commitment, go along with the social aspect, the ritual for weddings and funerals. The 'conservatives' correspond to your Baptists . . . pretty deep into making a show outwardly, but are not totally consumed inwardly. That leaves our 'orthodox'—who correspond to you charismatics in a sense . . . except that 'Orthodox Jewish' doesn't share it or spread it . . . they make a fetish of just practicing it, of holding it close to themselves—to preserve it. They are legalists, conforming to the jot and tittle of the expired Law of Moses . . . a continuation of the Pharisees! They keep it all in their little cliques . . . observing this and that kosher ritual, reading and tracing rabbi so-and-so who commented on rabbi so-and-so in the tenth century . . . who commented . . . ad infinitum. They perpetuate the learning but there is no outward life related to a practical or loving world in which they participate. You want to say to them sometimes, 'Get a life'!"

"Is Judaism, then, a viable religion?"

"Most Jews embrace it—until their eyes are opened . . . like mine . . . and they find that the Messiah really did come two thousand years ago . . . as I found out. But, no, Judaism is dead, really. It ceased to exist when the Temple was destroyed and the blood sacrifice stopped— only the Jews refuse to admit it. And, you think God has favored them? Well, He has kept the scattered remnants and given their homeland back to them as He promised. But, what about their constant persecution? . . . the Holocaust? Where was their God to help them then? Did they have the power to call upon Him? Do you think that was to open their eyes to something? To get their attention?"

"Makes you wonder! You know, Judaism is a dead end—it offers no salvation—no hope for the hereafter. The cessation of that animal blood sacrifice in the Jerusalem Temple was for a purpose . . . to rivet the importance of the substitute blood sacrifice of Jesus on the cross . . . 'By His shed blood was He made a sacrifice, once, for all . . . and by the blood of the Lamb—the substitute sacrificial lamb!—He was made expiation for our sins and we are washed clean and justified, that is, our curse of sin is lifted by His shed blood—the sacrificed blood—of Jesus and we are freed from the sentence of sin. And, this we attest, confirm and remind ourselves by the cleansing ritual, which He taught us, to eat the bread of His body and drink the wine of His blood in commemoration of these things . . . "

"Praise God, Steve . . . you wouldn't make a half-bad preacher!" exclaimed Gabe. "You're right about Judaism. And, God said in the Old Testament that because of their hardness of hearts, He would withhold the Holy Spirit from them and give the promised blessing to others . . . and since they missed the long-awaited Messiah when He did come . . . He would blind them until just before the Messiah's return. You remember, after the Jews came back from the Babylonian Captivity, they repeated their usual pattern of obedience and disobedience, trying God's patience once again, so that finally God forsook them and did not speak to them through His prophets for four hundred years . . . until He sent His Son, Jesus, the prophesied and long-awaited Messiah. In fact, the last book of the Old Testament, Malachi, ends with a curse . . . which the orthodox Jews naturally turned around so that it does not end with a curse on them. Alas, alas . . . the day will come—soon! Come. Lord Jesus!"

Stephen continued the train of thought, "Yes, the Messiah as Son of God and the Holy Spirit as the third person of the Holy Trinity of the God-head were stumbling blocks to the Jews . . . yet, the Messiah —and the Holy Spirit—were both mentioned clearly in the Old Testament. You know, when you read and study the entire Bible it makes so much sense, is so logical, so fool-proof despite criticisms to the contrary . . . that you know it is the work of God . . . even though He used His chosen prophets as His human instruments to reveal and write it. I've read other religions, the Koran, and all, and none of them track like the Bible. The others all seem as if someone—the writer—heard about this other great religion of the Jews and the Christians and tried to paraphrase it . . . but simply missed. To think that more than half the world is benighted by these spurious offshoots or false substitutes makes you wonder about Satan's power to deceive . . . or makes you want to get global Christian satellite TV up there working . . . and spreading the gospel to every nation and tongue and tribe and people on the earth!"

There was more general discussion of these topics and Sheba told in vivid detail of the ferocity of the Yom Kippur war in which she and every other able-bodied female and male had dropped everything on that Holy Day in 1973 and leapt into the heroic defense of their homeland, engaging in some of the fiercest and largest mechanized warfare and tank battles in history . . . until this small God-protected nation fought back the Egyptian, the Syrian, the Saudi and the Jordanian invaders— victoriously!

Stephen invited Gabe and Sheba to join him and Faith at a restaurant after the program for coffee and a late snack. He had telephoned Faith earlier to meet them there. He was particularly interested in finding out in more detail Sheba's combat experience—and incredible experience for a woman, he thought, since he had been tasting combat a few years earlier on the other side of the world . . . and he knew what it was like! And, for one who hardly looked the part of a soldier . . . slim, svelte, lithe . . . as the natural dancer she was . . . her shock of short hair framing the pronounced and sculptured features of her face in which were mounted her dark, intriguingly unfathomable eyes.

219

Stephen, Gabe and Sheba had been sitting in the booth for a short time; they had ordered and the waitress was bringing their coffee and grilled cheeses when Faith arrived, bright and cheerful.

"Praise God! Hi, Gabe . . . Hi, Hon . . . Hi, I'm Faith . . . "

"And, I'm Sheba Herzog."

"You didn't give me a chance, Faith," Gabe said a little awkwardly.

Faith slipped onto the seat next to Stephen and gave him a big, broad grin. Sheba was across from Stephen. "How'd it go tonight? I saw some of it . . . "

"Oh, as usual, we didn't have enough time to get into the subject properly . . . but, then, that's television for you . . . just skims the surface," replied Stephen matter-of-factly.

Faith motioned to the waitress and ordered a coffee. "Sheba, what is your ministry?"

"My ministry? . . . I guess it's dance . . . theatre. I have the Israeli dance group from Tel Aviv. We're here on tour."

"Praise God, I know God is calling me to go to Israel . . . I feel such an attachment for the land. I know I must be Jewish somewhere back in my line."

Stephen offered, "You could go over there and join the army . . . like Sheba did. You know? She fought in the Yom Kippur War?"

Faith studied her but said nothing.

"Sheba, did you get into the actual fighting? Did you carry a weapon? What kind of outfit were you in?" inquired Stephen.

"I was in a reserve communications unit . . . made up mostly of members of the Kibbutz I was living in . . . just below the Golan Heights . . . "

220

"Good grief!   That's where the Syrians broke through and almost annihilated the Israelis! As I remember . . . there were only four Israeli tanks that got up there at first . . . and they barely managed to stop them. Two or three of them were reserves who had quickly left wherever they had been and—not even in uniform—had jumped into their tanks and sped right into the enemy guns . . . one guy was in his pajamas, I think."

"Everyone jumped into action . . . we grabbed our gear in the Kibbutz and manned the perimeter—everyone did . . . except some of the older women who took the children into the shelters . . . It was scary!"

"I suppose shells were landing all around . . . "

"Some . . . but the Syrians were held up by pockets of our defense forces and some aircraft were strafing now and then . . . and one or two of our tanks rumbled up."

Faith established eye contact with Sheba with hardly a blink. Stephen was aware that she was praying in tongues quietly under her breath.

"Then, as some of the wounded came streaming in to our camp . . . they told us reinforcements were needed where they had come from. We hadn't had time to set up any meaningful communications in the Kibbutz anyway . . . so, our lieutenant ordered my section to take our radios, our weapons and ammunition . . . and a handful of rations . . . a couple of chocolate bars . . . and we headed up the heights."   She stopped. "You sure you want to hear all this? I was scared silly!"

"I, for one, want to hear it because a few years before that . . . on the exact other side of the world, I was in jungle skirmishes in Vietnam with my company of Marines," assured Stephen.

Sheba continued, addressing him directly, a bit unnerved by Faith's riveting stare. "We ran crouched . . . dragging our stuff with us . . . and jumped into a shallow trench one of our units was in behind a large boulder . . . The noise was horrendous! And, I realized the heavy squealing, grinding noise was tanks . . . Soviet-made Syrian tanks passing just to our right. More were coming up the hill on the far side . . . those that had just passed us fired their 105 mm guns down at our three tanks that were just coming up above the lake . . . the upshot is that we were surrounded for a long time. Our guys knocked out several of the Syrian tanks with bazookas . . . but we ran out of ammunition. A couple of jets came over and shot at the tanks . . . real close to us . . . so I had my head down a good bit of the time "

"Incredible! Here you . . . a woman! . . . were going through something like this . . . and I thought I had it rough! You know, Vietnam was nothing like the Yom Kippur war . . . you could put all the battles of the ten years over there and all together they would not be as tough as the two weeks of fighting you Israelis went through . . . We were never against enemy tanks, enemy aircraft . . . massive enemy attacks . . . ours was mostly just short skirmishes . . . company and platoon size . . . in some piece of jungle against an enemy you couldn't see most of the time . . . "

"Yeah," Gab interjected, "But it was rough enough to get you pretty shot up!"

"Thank God I wasn't wounded," Sheba said. "There's hardly enough of me to hit."

"So, how long was that action?" asked Stephen.

"We stayed up there for most of the two weeks . . . back and forth to the kibbutz for resupply . . . but as our forces stopped them . . . knocking out thirty or so tanks . . . you know, one of our reserve tank commanders just jumped from tank to tank as they got shot out from under him . . . and he managed to destroy more than twenty enemy tanks single handed! You never saw anything like it!"

"As I remember hearing and reading about it, you all held at the heights . . . while the big tank battles against the Egyptians were taking place down in the Negev and the Sinai. The final tank battle down there had more than eight hundred tanks engaged . . . before the Israelis chased the Egyptians back and crossed the canal right on into Egypt."

"We had a bit of a big one up our way, too. At the time the southern battles were taking place, our tank reinforcements were coming up and from the Golan our tankers simply looked down on the Syrians and Jordanians and Saudi . . . caught them in a classic three-sided trap . . . and had themselves a—what do you call it here?—a 'turkey shoot'?"

"There is no doubt that the Hand of the Lord was upon the chosen people that time!" observed Gabe.

The talk wandered from that subject to others and Faith joined in after a while . . . ultimately steering the topic around to something she felt comfortable with . . . something that she could lead and control . . . her ministry to the prisoners. The apparent gutsiness of this fearless evangelist barging into big penitentiaries and demanding that these great big hulks of evil humankind obey the will of the Lord actually fascinated Sheba. She mentioned how Faith should have been in her place on the Golan Heights . . . and maybe the war would have been over sooner! They finally concluded the evening, left the restaurant and parted company . . . whereupon, Faith wheeled around to Stephen, lifted her finger right up to his nose and . . . "

"Don't." Stephen said in a calm, strong voice. "Don't . . . do . . . it!"

"Hon, you know God is telling me to do this for your own good . . . You've got to get right with Him!"

"Faith . . . I said, 'Don't!' . . . and I mean it!"

"Those demons were coming out of you like a swarm of bees!"

"Stop it right now! Don't go into this . . . "

"Halla-ga-yamma-sa-nanna-sah-banna-sah . . . "

Stephen proceeded to the Bronco. "I'll meet you back at the apartment."

He was in the apartment undressing for bed when she came in. She slammed the door, flipped off the light, threw her purse onto the couch and stormed into the bedroom. When Stephen emerged from the bathroom, he met a formidable figure, hands akimbo, eyes afire, ready for battle,!

"You must get rid of those demons! I saw them coming from you to that woman all evening . . . "

"I said, 'don't pursue this' . . . let it drop!" He pulled the spread and sheet back and climbed into bed.

She glared at him in the reflection of the mirror, her face contorted with anger. "God told me to warn you. Get right with Him . . . or else!"

Stephen refused to rise to the bait and with closed eyes tried to shut the ugly sound of her voice out of his consciousness.

She persisted . . . walking about the room . . . pacing, muttering, praying in tongues under her breath . . . then audibly . . . punctuating it now and then by turning toward the bed and shaking her finger menacingly at the prostrate figure of Stephen, shrieking, "Demons of lust! I saw them! You can't hide them from me!" And, then she would go back to her pacing and mumbling.

Stephen mustered all the will power at his command . . . not to throw the cover back and stand up and yell back at her! He knew the pattern. It would go on unabated . . . .fifteen minutes . . . a half hour.

She retired to the bathroom. When she came out again . . . the same onslaught. After an hour of it, Stephen, by now thoroughly exhausted and shaken by the senseless ordeal, got up and went into the living room, closing the bedroom door behind him . . . and lay on the couch . . . first tossing her handbag unceremoniously to the other side of the room. Any latent drowsiness had departed him . . . his adrenaline was so high now and his heart was racing so that he was wide awake. Exercising an ingrained self discipline that had speeded his recovery from his war wound, he lay back, closed his eyes and concentrated on emptiness . . . on a big, black nothingness that would block out all attempts of his conscious mind to function. It soon calmed him appreciatively . . . and he began to drift off . . . his last conscious thought having been that it must be about one-thirty in the morning . . .

Stephen drifted in and out of a semi-comatose state of exhaustion and slumber. In one of those driftings, his conscious mind alerted his defensive sensitivity to something . . . and as it was enter twined in the deep, dreaming, rapid-eye-movement phase he had sunk into . . . he fought to waken himself out of it . . . out of the deep, dark chasm into which his mind and body had plunged. He became aware of a presence, his heavy eyelids struggled against their own weight and slowly opened . . . He started! He was sure of a large dark object above him. His right arm came instinctively and defensively up over his chest . . .

"Hon," Faith said, realizing that he was awake. "Get right with God. You can't go on like this. I've tried to cast these evil things out of you . . . but you've got to help me . . . help yourself."

Realizing that he was saying the wrong thing as he said it, Stephen barely audibly managed to utter, "I wasn't looking at her with lust . . . I was fascinated that she . . . a girl . . . had been through worse combat than I had . . . that's all . . . couldn't you see that? Leave me alone . . . I don't want any more of this."

The rest of the night was interrupted twice more in a similar manner. And, when he got up and showered, the barrage continued. He tried again to ignore it. She subsided from time to time and he thought it might be over. But, each time it came back with more fury. He knew that it was a thing . . . and ungodly obsession . . . that would not die . . . soon. The spell seemed to have a life of its own . . . undulating phases that crashed and receded. There was no surcease. He would have liked to read the paper and have a cup of coffee, but there would be no peace. He dressed and abruptly left.

Chapter 17   Fade to Black

Monday morning arrived, as Stephen feared it would. The constant barrage from Faith was continuing and wearing them both down. He had made himself scarce all Sunday . . . had not even gone to the station to participate in the grand finale. He'd had enough of all of it!

Dragging himself into his office, it was all he could do to collapse in his chair . . . and stare dumbly at the contents on the desk.

Lydia had caught sight of him entering and had the good sense to fetch a cup of coffee to bring him. "Where was the train wreck? . . . or was it a truck that ran over you?"

"Lydia . . . I've had it!"

Sympathetically silent, she handed him the coffee and waited for him to continue . . . if he wished to do so.

"Dear ol' Faithy . . . God's blessed . . . anointed servant . . . following God's Agape command . . . has put me through the ringer again. Started Saturday night . . . right after the telethon. Saw my 'demons of lust' again! Haven't had a night's rest since!"

"I figured as much. I don't know how you stand it . . . but I'm at a loss to tell you how to handle it. Look, you just take it easy. I'll run interference for you . . . and you try to pull yourself together."

"It's a deal!   Say, what was the final tally? Be gentle . . . give it to me easy . . . I can take just so much bad news . . . "

"Sixteen thousand four hundred and eighty-six dollars."

"Ouch! Worse than I thought. And, we know that we'll lose ten percent of that . . . the 'no-show-ers,' the broken pledgers.   I don't know . . . I just don't know . . . "

After lunch, when she thought Stephen would have been recovered sufficiently, Lydia once more entered Stephen's office.   This time she closed the door behind her.

"Oh, oh. I don't like the looks of this. You're serious when you close the door."

"You were in no shape for me to spring this on you this morning. I waited until now.   This was hand-delivered this morning. I think I know what it is."

Stephen reached for the envelope . . . then, changed his mind. "Naw. I'm not up to it. You read it to me. If it's a summons . . . you've never seen me."

Tearing open the envelope and fumbling with obvious nervousness unfolding the sheet it contained, Lydia began to read aloud, "From the board of directors, Christian Television of Broken Arrow, et cetera . . . Dear Stephen Trevelyan . . . It is my duty as chairman of the board of Christian Television and KXAO-TV to inform you that your services as Vice President and General Manager of KXAO-TV are hereby terminated this date" . . . a tear welled in her eye and she took a tissue from her pocket.   " . . . Although regrettable, the board was unanimous in its decision, and I am, as instructed, passing that information on to you . . . Unfortunately, under the circumstances of the deterioration of the financial status of the station, we can offer you no more than two weeks severance pay. All other benefits cease thirty days from this date . . . We wish you well in your future endeavors. Please feel free to call upon us if we may assist you in any way . . . " She folded the letter in her lap and continued to stare at it.

"I suppose it was inevitable, wasn't it?" was Stephen's lame reaction.

Lydia remained silent, struggling to hold back a sob, trying to compose herself.

"Well . . . well. I suppose it will sink in . . . but right now I feel nothing. I have no sort of emotion of any kind. I feel like a shell of me —of somebody else . . . "

"Stephen, I . . . " and she put her hands quickly to her face and wept.

"Whoa! I'm the one who should be doing that! . . . " He looked at her, penetratingly, perhaps sizing her up truly for the first time . . . as someone who had really been a friend . . . a true loving friend in Jesus. He leaned back in his chair and stared at the ceiling for a long time. "I suppose the honorable Christian thing to do would be to take this like a gentleman . . . to wrap everything up, tidy up all the loose details, write up a final report . . . for my successor . . . do everything in my power to leave the station in the best shape I can . . . as if I owed it to God . . . to you people who will stay on and continue it. But, you know what? I don't feel that at all. I feel that I have not only been unappreciated for my rather dedicated and almost Herculean efforts . . . but, more simply, there is not one ounce of 'thanks' for trying! Can you believe it? Just the old 'kiss-off'! 'You're out!— Scram!' "

Stephen reflected then continued. "So? Lydia, my faithful side-kick . . . I guess it's over. It's really been great," he managed to say before the break in his voice occurred and he had to clear his throat.

"Steve, I'll leave you alone in a few minutes, but let me go get us some coffee. There's a bit more to this . . . "

As she left, Stephen wondered, for God's sake, what else could there be?

As he picked up his cup and Lydia settled into the chair with hers, she began slowly,   "There is a lot behind the scenes that has been going on . . . that I didn't want to burden you with. Maybe, in view of this letter, I should have made you more aware . . . but, I could tell you were just about to come apart at the seams . . . what with the loss of all the oil wells and all . . . But, in a nutshell: those men who visited the station the other day . . . that I told you about. They were not the only ones . . . and Felix's accountant . . . a lot of suspicious things have been going on around here. In short, Felix has bought the station . . . from the Christian Television group, who have the license. From what I have gathered, Felix badgered them that they needed financing . . . needed to redo the whole operation . . . and he was the only person who could do it. He would be willing to accept all the accumulated debts of the station and buy it from Christian TV for what they had invested in the Construction Permit and License plus a very low figure for the run-down, un-disposable equipment . . . I think he got the whole shebang for around two hundred thousand. "

"Two hundred thousand! He's a bigger crook than Moses!"
"What?"
"Sorry. You could not be expected to understand that analogy."
"And, that's only the half of it . . . "
"Good God! What kind of a world is this?"

"Seems Felix Toombs already has a buyer!" Seeing the startled look on Stephen's face, she confirmed the statement. "Yep. What I hear is that he turned around and sold it for five million!"

Stephen's jaw dropped, "You've got to be kidding!"

"Nope!"

"So, before the ink is dry on the contract stealing it from the poor Christian saps, he turns around and makes a killing off of it! He'd had to have planned that for a long time!"

"That would be my guess. Why else all the nosing around by his accountant?"

"And, he got it through the FCC as a distressed sale. He and his attorneys had a lot of influence up there, congressional and otherwise. It's all very clear now. . .Felix actually welcomed my discouraging reports at the board meetings."

"And, the telethon tally just gave him—them all—the excuse they needed to blame it all on you . . . and give you the axe!" She buried her face in her hands again, and said, "You know, sometimes I am just ashamed to be a Christian . . . at least to be with this sort of Christians."

"So, how could the new owners compete in this market? Only if they upgrade the facilities . . . equipment . . . power—that's it! Up the power to maximum allowable to throw the signal out beyond Miami . . . and Tahlequah . . . down past McAlester . . . even overlap Oklahoma City and Enid. Could conceivably cover almost half the state! Change the format —drop all the Christian stuff—program an entirely different type of Independent format— all shoot 'em-up, guys and gals . . . raunchy stuff. And, there is a lot of new stuff being made that the three network affiliates can't handle . . . and the new KXAO could ! Go lean and mean, almost fully automated, state-of-the-art equipment—especially the one-inch videotape format . . . drop all the old dinosaurs . . . and, by golly, it could be done! And, it could eventually be a steal at five million.

Chutzpa ! Street smarts again! Felix . . . and, Moses . . . and Rock! God, it's depressing!"

"I followed some of that . . . but you lost me somewhere along the way."

"Old Jewish saying, 'Too soon old—too late, smart!' "

"Stephen, what do you think you will do? I mean, you have money, don't you? Can you get by? Think you will look around for employment around here? Stay in Oklahoma?"

"Oh, God, Lydia. How do I know at this point? But, what is there for me out here? . . . at least in television or advertising? . . . about the only two things I know anything about —and, I'm even wondering about them, myself, right now!" He lowered his head to his desk. "I don't know. But, I'll clear out of here by five o'clock. Let's stay in touch."

Lydia got up and walked over and rested her hand on his shoulder for a moment before leaving and closing the door behind her.

Stephen drove home slowly, in no hurry to encounter Faith . . . in no hurry to go anywhere actually. Where was there to go? Back to a dissolving marriage? To an unemployment office? What's the hurry?

His mind was plagued by several realities. He was down to about twenty-three hundred from all the eighty thousand he once had. With only about two thousand more coming in from the station . . . rent, utilities, gas, a bunch of unpaid bills . . . that would soon be gone . . . might last till Thanksgiving. 'Thanksgiving'! Yeah! Thanks . . . for what? . . . He had to consider what options he had . . . and what other resources, now that money had been eliminated. Friends? Personal networking? Yes, he would have to get into that right away . . . Paul Masters? . . . John Mark? Were they the only two he could come up with? Rock was out of the question, as was any board member. Ham Washington? . . . Good grief! He did not have any serious contacts, he had made no 'useful' friends out here in all this time . . . only a bunch of half-baked religious freaks! Gabe, maybe? What use would they be? And, did he want to stay in Christian broadcasting? What else was there? But, there was no other around these parts . . . if he wanted to stay in it, he would have to land a job somewhere else . . . And Faith? Would she up and come with him? Her ministry clearly seemed to be right here. What kind of a job . . . a meaningful, prestigious job . . . could he get around here?

Then it hit him with full force: he had been fired ! He was unemployed—the second time in his life! God, what humiliation! How could You, God? He narrowly avoided driving off the roadway.

Cautiously opening the door to the apartment, he was greeted by a cheerful, "Hi, Hon."

Stephen looked skeptically at Faith, who quickly sized him up, "What's the matter? Something happen?"

Her prescience disarmed him. *Could she actually have discerned what had happened to him? Could she actually 'read' those demons emanating from him? Thank God,* he thought, *the old demons-of-lust spell seems to have gone . . . evidently as suddenly as it had occurred. But, he would nevertheless keep his guard up and test the waters, so to speak.*

"Come on, let's grab a bite and I'll bring you up to date."

As they sat at a table in the corner of the little greek restaurant, they ordered two large iced teas.

"Want to share a Greek salad?" offered Stephen. "We're going to have to watch our pennies from here on out . . . "

"Oh? Some kind of change? What are you trying to tell me?"

"In a word, I am no longer VP and General Manager of WXAO-TV."

"They fire you?"

"If you had said, 'Did you resign?' it would have indicated a bit more wifely support and being on my side. Sounds like you expected that's what they would do . . . or ought to do."

"Well? Which?"

"For Pete's sake! I was canned! Unceremoniously, too! And, I'll give you fair warning right now—one word about my 'getting right with God'—and I walk straight out that door and I guarantee that will be the last you will ever see of me!"

Faith sipped her tea . . . thoughtfully. "Sorry, Hon. Now what? What do you do now?"

"That, I don't know. I'm trying to sift through my options . . . and my resources. Speaking of which—money—we are just short of broke."

"What? I thought you had a lot of money—from the agency in New York—your family!"

"Thanks to the oil wells . . . and your Lord's leading to invest in them . . . well, thanks to His leading . . . and my blind faith in Him and His leading . . . most of my money is down a dozen holes in the ground . . . or in a dozen pockets—none of which is any longer mine!"

"Don't blame that on the Lord . . . You—" She caught herself.

Stephen raised his eyes to hers to convey a warning to that effect. "We've got about enough to get by two, maybe three months, that's all! Then—it's over! Kaput! The welfare rolls!"

"They didn't give you anything?"

"Two weeks severance pay."

"Well, there's always my ministry . . . my oil wells."

"That'll be the day!"

"Really, Hon. Think about it . . . you could move right in . . . take one of the offices —the big one. Help me run the oil programs. Do your own thing. We could make a team. I think this is what God's plan is . . . what He has been leading us to. So, we can be together."

Stephen poked at his portion of the salad and pondered the new possibilities that Faith's plan offered. The first thing, he thought, is that it would restore his self-esteem . . . he wouldn't just be wandering around like a bum. The address and telephone would certainly be a better base of operations than the apartment. "How many more months free do you have?"

"Until the first of November."

"Three weeks. How much money have you made off the drilling programs of 'brother' Amos Godwin?"

"Money? Nothing's come in yet. We've drilled two and have most of the money to start on the third."

"So? What's your share of the general partnership?"

"You mean units? The two first wells were dry. There was no money . . . Look, I don't know. Why don't you come in on this and straighten it all out. Wanna be President?"

"I think I will come in . . . and look things over. But, I'll make no promise I'll get involved with you."

She didn't respond. Taking the last bite of her salad, she looked at him and with a signal he couldn't miss and intimately murmured, "Banbury Cross."

"Right here? Ok. Lie down."

"Pay the bill. We'll find the right place."

Since it was still light, they strolled arm in arm around the corner away from the commercial strip back into a modest, well-kept neighborhood where they made their leisurely, customary circuit, meandering finally as dusk overtook them to a little park at the foot of a small, suspended foot bridge over a gully that led to a similar subdivision. It was a star-filled darkness that descended on the already still community in the early fall night. Although there had been no further mention of code 'Banbury Cross,' it had been foremost on Stephen's mind the whole walk. Having sensed it, Faith at one point as they had reached an isolated spot midway in their stroll, reached over and grabbed his crotch. He had responded by a quick move of his left hand from her waist to her left buttock with a firm, full grasp. Then, checking to see if the usual trait was in evidence, he had lowered it to the hem of her skirt, quickly running his hand up under it . . . affirming, much to his delight—no panties. That augured well for the anticipated climax of the evening.

They wandered onto the suspended foot bridge and stopped in the middle . . . and leaned against the wood and steel cable railing. "Saddle time," Faith said softly, moving her hand to his fly, unzipping it and inserting her hand. After achieving her purpose . . . which had already been half achieved when she found it, she released it and turned and lifted herself up by the suspension cable to sit on the railing. Stephen, who was quite ready at this point to perform, stepped between her parted legs and hoisted skirt, clasping his hands behind her hips and drew her onto him . . . as her feet locked themselves around the backs of his legs. The height of the low railing was perfect, affording a partial support for both of them as they poised, coupled in a long, slowly undulating embrace. It was a nice fit . . . a physical compatibility made in heaven.

Stephen's troubles fast-faded into oblivion.

Chapter 18   A test of Faith

Stephen laid his briefcase on the empty desk and stood, scanning the office and the breath-taking panoramic view of the landscape. On the distant horizon were the tell-tale landmarks of Broken Arrow. Halfway there, the tall TV towers, one of which carried the antenna for WXAO. 'WXAO' . . . *'Christ, the Beginning and the End'. . . That sure was a short-lived beginning and end for me in Christian TV!,* he thought, stifling the slight twinge of remorse that struck him. *Why had all that turned to—no other word for it—crap ?*

As he sat comfortably in the elegant executive chair that would be his now, he surveyed the room. Spacious. Long. A 'conversational grouping' at the far end with couch, matching chairs, end tables and lamps. Six, seven large picture windows lining the right wall . . . vertical glass panels, the opposite wall. The far wall over the couch, tastefully decorated with a decorator-harmonious abstract. Really first class. It was certainly appealing, maybe this is where he should be.

He brought his reverie to a halt and turned to practical matters. Taking a yellow pad from the top drawer, he noted that all the accessories had been provided. *Must have been a 'packaged deal' from the office furniture rental place.* He jotted down: contacts . . . Paul M. John Mark F. Then, cogitating, wrote 'office': lease, utility contracts, furniture rental agreement, copier, typewriter, other. Under 'drilling' he noted: read Amos' prospectuses and agreement with Living Water.

Satisfied for the moment with those, he started thinking about his 'options.' Jotting them down randomly as they occurred to him, he soon had a list consisting of: oil business (administrative), advertising (account exec.), secular broadcasting (account-sales) . . . construction (admin? learn trade?) . . . real estate (sales, training, licensing) . . . stock brokerage (licensing, study course—cost?). He spent the better part of the morning filling in bits and pieces as they occurred to him. Faith had not shown up; she was off somewhere on God's business, no doubt.

He decided to call Paul Masters . . . to break the news to him and really sort of cry on his shoulder, he admitted to himself. Paul answered and Stephen told him all that had happened.

"So, my friend, you are momentarily faced with another of the trials and tribulations of life. How are you proceeding?"

"Logically, I trust. And, if the Lord assists along the way . . . so much the better. However, if He has put me in this situation—which it is pretty obvious He has—then do I turn the solution over the Him . . . and wait for a miracle? Or, do I go on and do the best I can?"

"It's not Biblical, but 'the Lord helps those who help themselves'."

"Well, at this point I have not reached a state of desperation. That may come . . . but at least I can survive for a couple of months . . . then, *le déluge* !"

"What options are you considering?"

"First, I have to decide whether to stay in something to keep working for the Lord . . . or to be practical about it, and get back into the secular world. That's going to be difficult because after all this brain-washing through the charismatic thing . . . I am really soured on the secular world. I don't know if I could go back to it. It would certainly be a last resort."

"Is there anything out here in this neck of the woods that would offer the kind of challenge the TV station did?"

"I sort of doubt it . . . I might have to go somewhere else . . . back east, most likely."

"And, Faith? And, her ministry?"

"That's one dilemma, of course. I haven't discussed it with her . . . and I don't know what her reaction will be to, quote, following her husband, unquote. So, looks like I've got a rocky road ahead.   As you might guess, I am more than a bit disillusioned by both the Christian and the secular worlds at this juncture. Toombs stole the station from the innocent believers and turned around and made a killing off of it. I was—forgive the expression—screwed out of my money drilling a bunch of oil wells that I thought were God's will . . . and beneficence. I've got a wife who turns out to have crazy fits . . . so, I really haven't sorted anything out as yet."

"Steve, I know you will come through.   Believe in yourself, if nothing—or no one— else! Sorry to have to conclude this, but I've got a luncheon to go to, and I'm running late. Let's get together and go into some depth on all this.   Sounds like you could use a little glass of sherry . . . for your ailments . . . right about now."

"Amen! I'll call you."

Around lunchtime, Stephen went down to the lobby to see about getting a coke and a snack . . . if there was a machine . . . or a lunch counter, or something. As he got out of the elevator, he noticed some activity in the swank, glass-partitioned ground floor suite near the entrance. Tastefully lettered in a unique sans-serif style was the name-logo, 'A. L. Williams.'

He wandered in, asked some questions and came away with a handful of literature before procuring his lunch snack.

He was reading the brochures and munching on the peanut butter-filled crackers when Faith came bursting in with, "Praise God! You look like the place was made for you! See what I told you?"

He watched her go about the office, into hers, to her desk . . . to the coffee nook, unload some provisions . . . stir about, humming pleasantly to herself. *'What really makes her tick?'* he thought to himself. *'She's got to be the world's biggest screwball—at least the biggest he'd ever come across. What other self is she hiding? . . . hiding under that thick veneer of charismatic Christianity? Karl Marx was right . . . this is all the 'opiate of the masses.' She is simply drugged—or tranquilized—out of reality into a world that she and her cohorts have created . . . as they conceive it should be . . . so they can exist in it—exist at all ! . . . according to some transcribed utterings of an ancient mystic.*

" I've got coffee brewing. What'cha up to?"

"Just getting adjusted to my new life style—unemployed! By the way, I think I should look over your drilling prospectuses with Amos. And, what about your banking? Is the ministry solvent?"

"I'll get you all that before I leave. After coffee I've got to go see Amos anyway. The ministry doesn't even have a hundred dollars in the account. Nothing to worry about . . . God always provides!"

"Well, He's got until the first of November to come up with twelve hundred smackeroos . . . or we're out of this beautiful dream bubble."

"That stuff about A.L. Williams? A lot of Christians are in that . . . must be good."

She went back to her office, dug around some drawers, gathered some files and books and came back and dumped them all on Stephen's desk. "There you go. Have fun! Gotta grab my coffee and go! See 'ya!"

The more Stephen perused the material she had left him, the more the old despondency began to return. The drilling programs were the first jolt. Just as he had feared, the ministry was not an operating partner . . . just a holder of a small, insignificant general partnership share . . . not even a limited share . . . but, that was fortunate in a way . . . she had not had to come up with a lot of money. But, the general partnership share gave the ministry practically nothing—yet it included it in the general liability! Good grief! And, more disturbing—the lack of an 'operating' co-participation with Amos meant that the ministry got no split of the overhead. Obviously the general share must have been in lieu of a commission on all the sale of units to her friends. *God! She had been taken . . . worse than he had! Boy! These leeches hide behind the cloak of Christianity and suck the blood of all the unwary who come their way. God, are they all like this?*

After reading the literature, Stephen decided to stay for the evening meeting of A.L. Williams which started at seven. He'd telephone Faith and tell her he would be late. He had discerned through the deliberate obfuscation of the literature that the Williams thing was a variation of multi-level marketing . . . which wasn't bad. He and Diana had looked into Amway when someone had approached them about it, and it had intrigued him. He could see the brilliance of eliminating the middle-man and going manufacturer direct to consumer. He had even envisioned building up a little empire that Diana could operate . . . but they really hadn't needed the extra money that badly. When he joined the TV station, the idea had recurred to him. But, it seemed a lot of work for such little return.

Stephen was a jump ahead of the presenter of the evening. He instantly grasped the enormous possibilities of the multi-level aspect . . . how you join someone's hierarchy . . . then build your own . . . until you have your own little empire. And, their schtick was better, he thought, than Amway—life insurance. Basically, talk people out of 'whole life' policies that they might be carrying . . . which, they pointed out disparagingly, only returned something like 3% in a market of 14% . . . and you could point out to them how much they were losing. Convince them it was better to dump whole life, buy term insurance, which is much cheaper . . . and invest the difference themselves . . . and make out infinitely better. Furthermore, the commissions on the sale of term life were a great deal more than anyone could make in Amway peddling soap products. In his continuing analysis of whether this would be the right thing for him to join, the positive factors were that he would be entirely independent . . . could work out of his new office upstairs . . . could be his own boss . . . an entrepreneur, in fact . . . and make a lot of money, quite honorably, when you get right down to it. The drawbacks seemed to be that it would take some time to build up that hierarchy below one so that it payed off well. It appeared obvious to him that the earlier one gets in on any kind of multi-level scheme like this the better the chances of big money. He wondered if those rungs were too far down now to make it worthwhile. Also, the thing that it would take . . . and the thing that least appealed to him . . . was the constant door-to-door canvassing that it required—mostly in the evenings. Even though the 'pitch' as they explained it, was very simple and straightforward, he really didn't like badgering people . . . and he felt it would be just like the Fuller Brush man . . . or a vacuum cleaner, aluminum siding salesman. He couldn't lower himself to that! He didn't care how much money there was! He knew he could sell, but something more like a high-tech product for a large corporation. Something more on that order. So, he concluded that this was an option that he would not exercise just now but would leave open. It gave him a spurt of confidence that he was tackling his problem positively . . . and, if this was only the first day, something was bound to turn up in the near future.

As the first week of his unemployment passed and the second began, a feeling of uneasiness crept over him. Despite the fact that he was looking into all sorts of things, even perusing the classifieds for employment opportunities, he had found nothing at the level which would interest him. He even went to the library on Monday and scanned the New York Times to see what was being offered back in the northeast. *Lots of things . . . but with his messed-up track record now . . . what kind of a chance would he really have? Besides, he still loved God's world and His work, he kept telling himself, and that's where he figured he's best stay. Once turned off to the secular world, it was awfully hard to turn on again. He knew he could never give it his all like he had given the Lord's work at channel 21.*

Tulsa no longer held the charm it once did either. It now seemed stark, forlorn, even ugly . . . *which came*, he surmised, *from his jaundiced outlook on things in general now. In fact, he had never felt more a stranger . . . more a fish out of water. ORU, Logos, Fishers of Men . . . none of those places intrigued him any longer. In fact, he hadn't set foot into any one of them since his ignominious ouster from the station. He knew people were aware of his situation and he just did not feel like facing them. After all, what explanation could he give? Everybody knew he'd been fired. That firing could be explained satisfactorily to a prospective new job opportunity . . . 'they wouldn't listen to me,' 'I didn't know they had sold the station right out from under me,' . . . 'constant fighting with the board,' 'couldn't do it my way' . . . all of those sorts of arguments he felt he could manage. But, why try with the 'faithful'? They no doubt would side in their ignorance with the larger entity as being that ordained of God. And, when the truth finally comes out about the resale, they will just shrug, dismiss it, and go about their business.*

With only a week and a half left before the end of the 'freebie' period and the real enforcement of the rental contract for the offices took effect, Stephen's uneasiness increased, especially since Faith seemed totally oblivious of the reality of it. She simply awaited God's miracle. He could not. Although he had not signed the lease, he was an officer of the ministry and, he feared, could be held liable. He would not leave it to chance. He would confront Faith. And, it would be better to do so on the premises.

Stephen had asked Faith to come to the offices right after breakfast so that they could have a serious discussion of the situation of the ministry, the offices, his prospects, their future and whatever else needed talking about. She had said that she had something else to do later on but that she would be there.

Stephen arrived around eight thirty and fixed a big pot of coffee, then washed out the cups that had accumulated over the past several days. This was all such a good layout for business—if only they had business . . . or he could get something going. But, time was running out. The next ten days would be critical.

Faith came bursting in, praising the Lord and singing. Happy as a lark! "Praise God! Isn't He wonderful?"

"Did He confide to you that He was going to pull us out of this?" Stephen said in a flat tone as he handed her a cup.

"Oh! Where is your faith ? Oh, ye of little faith . . . "

They went into his office and she paused at the window and stared at the scene beyond. "That's how I know there is a God. He made all that."

Stephen wondered if she had sensed the spectacular beauty . . . or was just struck by its awesomeness. He had never heard her articulate any of her innermost thoughts or feelings . . . only scripture paraphrases. He began, "We have only a few more days to face reality. Separating our

244

personal money, of which there is precious little left . . . we come to the fact that the ministry has nothing but a few dollars. The ministry was not cut into the co-partnership you described to me . . . so it got nothing out of the overhead figured into those three wells—and that could have been at least five thousand apiece. Good ol' Amos saw you a comin', Babe."

She sipped her coffee, not responding. Listening.

"The wells have all turned out dry . . . so, not even a measly penny from the general shares. So, where does that leave Living Water? You tell me . . . .and, on the first of the month, in less than ten more days, the first rent of twelve hundred dollars will be due on the offices, a hundred and fifty on the furniture, a hundred or so for telephone, copier lease purchase . . . and whatever else I have not discovered." He concluded and motioned that it was her turn.

She got up and strolled to the window again. "I just don't believe it's over. I know God is in this and will come through . . . hamma-sha . . . ba-a-nanna- . . . oooohh . . . alaa. ha she . . . " and tears welled up in her eyes as the ecstasy of her communication with the Lord overwhelmed her. She remained transfixed in her own other-world or out-of-body experience or whatever she was going through . . . for a long time. Stephen knew not to interfere. He simply finished his coffee and went to the coffee pot for a refill.

When he sat down again, Faith still said nothing.

"Well? He tell you anything? How to get out of this mess? How to pay the bills? How to render unto Caesar that which is Caesar's?"

She took a long time formulating the words for an answer. "My ministry is above all. He reaffirmed that. Whatever happens, I am to continue the ministry He ordained me for . . . and that I will. If this office idea does not work, He is not in it . . . and it would fail anyway. He is calling me to go preach. He gave me the word . . . Pensacola."

Stephen waited for her to get it all out.

"I must go . . . as soon as possible. Mother is there, but I don't know exactly what mission He has for me . . . oh, Hallelujah! Praise You, Jesus!"

"Then," Stephen broke in as tactfully as he could, "What I understand from all this is that God has told you to walk away from all these problems and go do His bidding in some place far away. Right? May I ask you simply, where does that leave this situation?   And my situation?   And, our situation? It may not have sunk into that brain of yours yet, but we are at the end of the line,"   Stephen said, his voice getting firmer and more forceful as his frustration mounted. "In a couple of weeks, we—which is I—will be practically out of money. Destitute! I've never been in this sort of a situation before. I don't know really how to handle it!   And, you are not facing it . . . you are waiting on some miracle to swoop down and rescue the situation . . . and, in the midst of it, your God tells you to bug out!"

"Maybe none of this was such a good idea in the first place. I mean, my ministry was going great and the Lord was blessing me . . . because I had my eyes only on Him. Maybe you and I should never have gotten married. I think God wanted me to be married to Him . . . and to do only His work. And, that's where I have failed Him . . . and why the blessings have not been coming."

Stephen froze, fearful of destroying this fragile moment of insight of hers—and his!

"No. I have failed God." She dropped to the carpet and wept.

Stephen watched. This brought an entirely new dimension to the predicament. He inferred from what she had said that the issue of the office was closed. They would not stay. Then, the matter of Living Water: that meant more to her than their marriage. That was an angle that had not occurred to him. He had surmised that she welcomed the breadwinner's role that he had assumed . . . and she, the Biblical helpmeet role that he thought she had assumed. But, it hadn't been like that at all. Her mind had been somewhere else the whole time . . . on the Lord . . . but more than just on the Lord—it had been obsessed with it all along. Nothing else had really mattered. He had sometimes wondered how long he could take the 'demons-of-lust' onslaughts, and, on those occasions, the idea of splitting from her had reached the point of possible action. So, now she, herself, was bringing it up. Un-do the marriage. Divorce! "You want a divorce?"

Her body did not move on the floor.

Stephen tilted back, put his feet up on the credenza and gazed out of the window. They both remained motionless in these positions for an interminable length of time, neither wanting to be the first to break the spell . . . or knowing quite how to.

Finally . . . "Yes."

They had talked it over some more that evening at the apartment, each one becoming more used to the idea as they talked it out. They agreed that a Christian divorce should be without rancor, without animosity . . . a civilized agreement mutually to end it. How they would go about it was discussed at some length, out of which came the solution that Stephen's only hope of regaining any sort of future was to try the big Christian networks . . . the ones in the east, PTL and CBN. Faith would give up the apartment, sell the furniture, and go around from place to place, wherever the Lord would lead her. She had been used to it . . . and looked forward to doing it again. She worried not one iota about subsistence. She had many friends she could move in with temporarily, single friends who would welcome the companionship.

As to possessions, there was not much to agree on, except the vehicles. Stephen was adamant on repossession of the van; she, as much so about refusing to take the Bronco.

"Look. The van was mine to begin with. It is just the size that will hold everything I own, and I don't know where I will be going or where my next meal will be coming from. I might have to live in the thing. How about this? You trade the Bronco in on an efficient foreign compact station wagon. You don't need such a gas-guzzler like the van to drive around in . . . and you don't take much stuff with you. Seems to me that would be a much better solution for you. We can go out tomorrow and visit some car dealers. We would have had to do something about it anyway."

The idea was working on her, and she nodded approval. "Now, what about money? Are you going to leave me with nothing?"

"I haven't got much left, myself. But, we'll spread it all out on the table and I'll split it with you the best I can."

With that, they retired to bed, silently lost in their own separate thoughts.

As they lay in the dark, Stephen asked, "You really want to go through with it?"

"I don't see how it can be any other way. I am certainly not going to give up my ministry that God called me to . . . and follow you back east . . . to where ever you can find a job."

"Well, at least we can sleep on it . . . want to sleep on it?" he said, putting his hand gently on her breast.

"No, Hon. It's over."

They spent the morning looking at used cars and finally found a clean three-year old Toyota wagon with not too much mileage. The trade was made . . . not exactly advantageously for Stephen. He still had to cough up almost nine hundred dollars to close the deal and finance the rest—in his name. But Faith seemed satisfied.

As they had been looking at the cars, Stephen brought up to her the only way he could see of getting out of the lease . . . 'skipping' on it. Packing everything up and skipping out in the middle of the night before anyone knew it. He reminded her that she had actually signed the lease and was committed to a three-year rental agreement. There would be a penalty . . . if they were not taken to court. And, he was in no position to contend with something like that—neither was she. He said he would take care of it and to meet him back at the office late in the afternoon to help him separate and pack what she wanted to keep.

When the Toyota was prepped and everything signed, she drove off and Stephen headed in the opposite direction . . . to the furniture rental . . . to negotiate a repossession. His talk with the manager was successful . . . as he explained how his wife, without his knowledge, had entered into the thing . . . implying that she was a religious nut, 'you know what I mean' sort of thing . . . and was doing this for her so the furniture would not be damaged and nobody would get hurt. Those sorts of reassurances. His charm—or sales ability—or something had worked, because the manager saw no problem in taking it all back. Stephen told him the exact date and the precise hour to have his men at the office. The manager nodded his understanding, suppressing a slight smile.

Back at the office, Stephen spent the entire afternoon stacking files and sorting things. It was amazing what all Faith had managed to put in the office already . . . and he had added a lot of his things, mostly from the station, that he thought he should lug with him. He called the telephone company and told them to disconnect the phones anytime during the day, October 31st. His plan was to take such items as the copier and fax out, one at a time, down to the van, which he was now driving, and take them back to their rightful owners and default on those contracts, saying that his wife had left and they would do better to take them back than to pursue the contract. He would do the same thing with all the files and papers, loading them into two briefcases, and walking casually out with them, unloading the contents into the van, then returning with the empty cases for the next load. He knew that the TV camera surveillance in the front lobby would spot him and he wanted to attract the least attention possible. It was a hell of a thing to have to do —completely against every shred of decency in his body—but, it was either that or be stuck with the debts. He considered this his first application of his newly found 'street smarts' . . . engendered by necessity. At least he was not stealing the stuff and was being very decent about returning it. The big deceit was the unauthorized vacating of the premises. He wondered whether that might constitute a misdemeanor . . . or even a felony. No, how could it? They get their offices back . . . in perfect shape. All they lose is two month's time, and now they would have to go out and find another tenant. And, that was not going to be very easy to do, not in the present economic climate. Rumor had it that four other companies—oil companies —in the same building had gone down the tube this month, too. He was sure the landlord would be understandable.

Stephen lost track of the time and it was beginning to get dark. So what? He wasn't hungry and there was more to do. He'd forgotten about Faith. He would save the IBM Selectric typewriter until the last, also, because he would be writing letters. As a matter of fact, he should whip one off to Tom right away and tell him about the whole situation. He had not even telephoned him after the firing . . . wanted to save money on telephone calls, because he knew he would end up talking a long time to him. So, he sat down at the secretary's station on the little swivel chair in front of the typewriter, inserted a sheet into the carriage and began to type . . . losing himself in concentration. So much so, that he failed to notice the door, which was to his back, open quietly.   Faith entered silently and strode across the lush carpet, unheard, and went to the small alcove where the coffee maker was. Deftly doffing her dress and bra—no panties, of course— she struck a provocative pose against the doorway . . . and gave a low, almost imperceptible whistle.

Stephen stopped typing for an instant, listened . . . then resumed typing.

Another low whistle, this time a tiny bit louder. Stephen halted again and glanced over his right shoulder toward the door. Seeing nothing, he once again resumed.

This time, a '*tweet-twooo*,' plainly audible. Stephen turned all the way around . . . and to see a nude female figure. He started! Then, looking up to her face, recognizing her, smiled appreciatively, made a broad gesture of licking his lips, and gazed from breasts to navel to clean-shaven, baby-like pubic region to upper thighs and, slowly, back up again.

"Hah! Venus on a half-shell! To what do I owe this totally unexpected . . . and most pleasant—I hope—intrusion? . . . and, just what is a Christian gentleman to do in a situation like this? Deny the Christian lady the pleasure of the flesh in which she has come to indulge?" he said as theatrically as he could, lest she wrongly interpret the pagan elements therein and self-destruct what portended to be perhaps their last wild encounter, as he walked over to her."

"Bring the chair with you—and lock the door."

Becoming aroused in anticipation, he wheeled the small chair over, and she positioned it in the alcove.

Then, looking up into his eyes with a lascivious grin on her lips, she unbuckled his belt and with one fell swoop, dropped his trousers and undershorts.

"Aha! Horsey out of stable!"

Gently pushing him onto the chair, she then straddled him.

251

"Giddyap, horsey . . . to Ban bury Cross! . . . to Ban-bury Cross!" . . .and she cantered gracefully all the way!

Chapter 19   In the Wilderness

Tulsa was now far behind Stephen. He was deep into Arkansas in the van, which was loaded to the gills with everything he owned that he wanted to keep. Approaching Memphis and tired of listening to his classical tapes, he turned the machine off and drove in silence, recounting past events . . . pondering them to find some sort of connection . . . some underlying reason . . . for all that had transpired. He recounted the departure. It had been less than pleasant . . . in fact, disturbingly hectic!

Faith had arranged to sell her furniture while he was abandoning the offices. He had to hand it to her, though, right after he had vacated, she had boldly stomped right over to the owner—not the agency—and charmed him into releasing her from the contract . . . explaining how she had thought God had been leading her, or something to that effect . . . and that now her ministry was being called elsewhere . . . and so and so . . . and he released her. Talk about chutzpa—AND fluttering eye lashes and a cleavage that would shame Dolly Parton!

She had also let it be known around her circles that she and he were splitting because God had unmistakably called her back to full-time ministry—her original calling from God— as if she had not always been full-time. So, she naturally elicited the sympathy and support of her ilk.

As a consequence, he guessed that was why not a soul had contacted him to say how much they'd been glad to have known him . . . or to wish him well. Not John Mark. Not a single member of the board. Only Rock, who had telephoned and stumbled awkwardly, encouraging him 'to hang in, there' and hung up. He had called Reverend Paul but had not been able to get over to see him. And, Lydia, who had wept openly on the phone and told him he could count on her . . . count on her to be his contact back here, if need be. He thanked her, blessed her and, as he hung up, experienced a twinge of remorse or something that almost brought him to tears. All the old ties were being broken, but what kind of ties had they been, really? This had just been a passing interlude . . . a disastrous turn of events . . . a horrendous mistake in his life. So, now the question: would he be able to rectify it? With or without God's help?

Just before he had left, Faith had gone off on one of her more predictable off-the-wall tangents . . . not 'demons' exactly . . . but a nasty, confrontational demeanor that poisoned their final moments together. They had agreed that he would file for divorce once he got to Virginia Beach; that she would not contest it. But the episode had been so upsetting, that Stephen realized he had overlooked a number of minor, but important, details . . . like getting her to sign with him, in the name of the ministry, the title of the van over to him. Also, how to reach each other, should that be necessary. One good thing, though, that he had managed to achieve was to get her to contact one of her friends at CBN, Eve Lovejoy . . . who then gave him the name of one of the executives on the top rung and promised to pave the way for an interview there with him. So, at least, that was a positive note—albeit the only positive thing at all that he had going for himself. And, that was a mighty tenuous thread.

Perhaps Faith's ugly disposition at the end reflected a wavering on her part. He had sort of expected it. As for himself, once the logic of the decision had settled in him, he was adamant not to let it change. He had been fast coming to the conclusion that the marriage was not by any stretch of the imagination a success . . . any way he looked at it. Furthermore, he knew how difficult it would be to hold to his convictions if she had lifted her skirt just once more. He hated to admit it, but sex was an illogically strong drive . . . and he was prone to succumb to it. Thank God she had—except for that last incredible tussle on the carpet in the office—been in no mood those last days. He wondered, though, *just how much he was going to miss all those wild, serendipitous romps with her?* He thought, *most likely, that after that aspect cooled down and he was able to think straight once again . . . that he would analyze their marriage as having been a blind mistake in the first place . . . he, seeking a substitute for the life he had given up . . . as well as a sign of some approbation by the Lord for his sacrifice . . . and, she, for a helpmeet in her ministry . . . if not an instrument to satisfy a too-long suppressed sexual urge, herself. Had there been any real love in it? A line from the Broadway musical, Finian's Rainbow, came to him, '..when I'm not ne-ar the gir-l I lo-ve . . . I lo-ve the girl I'm near . . . ' Was that the real Stephen, he wondered? Could he have been that callous? He doubted there had been any true love on her part.*

His situation was now quite critical. After paying off all bills—and Faith getting the deposit refund on the apartment—and splitting the remainder with her fairly, he had less than six hundred dollars left . . . now in travelers checks. That and the Merrill Lynch debit card on his father's account. Plus an Exxon gas card which he had never used. That would just take him to Virginia Beach and allow him to set up in a motel or something and get through the month of November . . . perhaps. If anything should happen to the van . . . blew a tire . . . needed engine work . . . any unexpected thing could blow him out of the water!

He had alerted Tom that he was coming through Atlanta . . . that he would be staying a day or two and then be on to Virginia Beach. He wanted to talk things over with Tom, and he wanted to see dad. He checked the map. Atlanta . . . less than five hundred miles. He'd like to drop by Sewanee down in Tennessee—but some other time. Ought to make it in eight to ten hours. Can sleep in the van along the way, although it's so packed, there isn't much room to stretch out. But, he'd make do.

The next day around noon, Stephen found himself entering the northern outskirts of Atlanta. He hadn't been here in a long, long time . . . not to drive around, at any rate. Diverting off Interstate 75 onto West Paces Ferry Road, he traveled east and slowed as the landmarks rang familiar. This is where he had grown up . . . the 'right side' of the tracks . . . the wealthy estates . . . the southern Episcopalian elite. As he approached a long, high hedgerow, he slowed to take a brief look through the bricked gateway down the long, tree lined driveway. Hadn't changed a bit . . . just as it was when he used to come home from Yale. Resisting the temptation to turn in, and pressured by the buildup of traffic behind him, he drove on to the main intersection in Buckhead . . . where he turned right onto Peachtree Road and headed south.

It was all so familiar . . . all so reassuringly the same. This kind of high quality neighborhood never would change . . . the stately mansions, the large, grand old apartments built back in the twenties . . . the Episcopal cathedral on the promontory above to the right— many memories there!—then, on down just before Peachtree Creek and E. Rivers Grammar school on the right. Completely changed now. The old Richardsonian collegiate Romanesque had given way to a modern, functional style after it had burned to the ground. He wondered how those escape tunnels in each of the classrooms had actually functioned during the fire—or, had it occurred at night? Had happened while he was up east; couldn't recall.

Crossing Peachtree creek, he looked for the familiar left turn before the shopping strip and turned onto Brighton Road. God! Not a blade of grass had changed. The entire neighborhood was frozen in time . . . this could be now . . . or ten—forty years ago . . . it had remained absolutely unchanged—and would remain so. This was not a part of Atlanta that was likely to be 'block-busted' by blacks. He wouldn't mind someone like Ham Washington for a neighbor, but he had seen some of the deterioration of those once lovely old Washington, DC, neighborhoods when he was stationed there. What a shame! Always considered upper middle class, these homes, he estimated, had doubled or maybe tripled in value since his college days. They had moved here during his last year at Yale, when his mother, Rebecca, had come down with cancer . . . and the medical bills had forced dad not only to sell the business but the house on West Paces Ferry.

Fortunately, dad had been able to get a house here. Mother had lasted just two years. Following her death, dad had had his stroke. Tom was just finishing at Emory, so he was able to stay right with him and look after him. Later, with the help of a practical nurse who was hired to take over the chores for a good ten hours of the day, Abner was moved down to the first floor bedroom which had a full bath. When Tom married, Martha had simply moved right in with them. It was a very practical thing to do. The house was certainly big enough . . . even when the children started coming.   Tom had not done too well for himself, anyway; held a non-challenging, dead-end job as a minor manager in one of the big insurance companies. Stephen had urged him time and time again to get on the sales side. That's where the big money was! Maybe he'd tell him about A.L.Williams. Tom wasn't a risk-taker, a go-getter, though. Preferred to punch a time clock and dutifully bring his paycheck home. It was a god-send that he was able to live in dad's house. Martha was a good southern wife and mother, wrapped up in the children, the

Junior league, and various church activities. She had had two years at Sweetbriar, and her family were fairly well-to-do. The limit of her conversation was the periphery of the world she experienced, which Stephen found made conversation difficult. She didn't read; watched television, of course . . . epitomized the empty-headed 'southern belle' syndrome—a real anachronism nowadays. She had been the Belle of the Ball as a debutante at the Driving Club country club, the center of the Atlanta social whirl. Now Tom, Martha, and he were like so many good southern families who had dropped from wealth, from prestige, but who still managed to maintain that innate patrician dignity that loss of wealth could not strip. In genuine Southern society, like this, the cream of the old lines looked to breeding, not to money. There was always a lot of new money coming in, but the crassness that underlay it was subtly not accepted. His and Martha's families were considered to be the old, accepted breed—had to be to have survived "Sherman's burning of Atlanta"—despite their present circumstances. Of course, none of this 'southern heritage' mattered in New England or New York.

Stephen turned up the steep driveway and parked on the apron beside the garage in the backyard. Knocking on the kitchen door, it was opened by the practical nurse, a rotund black woman about his age, he guessed. "Hello, I'm Mr. Trevelyan's other son, Stephen," he said stepping inside. "How's he doing?"

"Jus' fine. I'm Alzonya,"

"Pleased to meet you. I'll just dump these things here for the time being and go in and say 'hello.' Mr. Tom's missus here?"

"Naw-suh. She over at th' church. They said you'd be comin'."

Stephen walked quietly into his dad's room. His dad was asleep on the bed with a crocheted afghan over him. Stephen had always known that afghan. It had belonged to his grand-mother . . . and he had been wrapped in it often as a baby . . . and had cuddled under it as a youth when reading on chilly evenings. His mother had loved it. He hoped Martha would as well . . . and that it would always stay in the family.

He sat in a rocking chair next to the bed and looked affectionately at his father. *'Poor soul.' I wonder what dreams his injured mind is conjuring up? Do I suppose that this is the state of being that he is most comfortable in now? Unaware of his infirmities? Awake, he can't talk, can hardly walk . . . cannot use his right hand and arm. God, that sudden aneurism . . . or whatever it was . . . that caused that cerebral hemorrhage and irreparable damage in the left side of his brain . . . paralyzing the function of the right side of his body and affecting his speech. And, so sad . . . to have happened right after mother died . . . I was just about out of college . . . and Tom was just going in . . . So sad not to be able to communicate with either of his sons . . . nor to share in their triumphs . . . or exchange thoughts and ideas, hopes and dreams. To miss those greater times in life when the father is able finally to know the progeny he has sired . . . the young lion who has finally developed into an adult . . . not to be able to share that . . . God! What a tragedy! I was never able to discuss anything with him . . . I was always too busy running around with my own concerns . . . never sat down with him father-to-son . . . man to-man . . . never let him know that I had turned out OK . . . thanks to him . . . and that I loved him. I never told him I loved him! . . . and, now . . . I don't know whether he would even understand me if I tried to tell him. There are times when there seems to be the glimmer of recognition in his eyes . . . but, I wonder.'*

Stephen sat and rocked for most of the afternoon contemplating the father he had never known as an adult as he slumbered peacefully in front of him. *Had he had the same dreams, aspirations? . . . the same desires . . . foibles that he had? Had his father ever made the same horrendous types of mistakes his first-born son had? Had his life been a happy one . . . a fulfilling one? Had he achieved what he had set out to do? He had been fortunate to have inherited the family shipping business; had walked right into the job there before even finishing college. But, he had not managed it well in a changing world . . . well enough to gain much more than three quarters of a million dollars when he sold it. He had not been quite sharp enough, either, to shelter the proceeds properly beforehand . . . so took a big tax hit. Then, with all of mother's medical expenses—which insurance had not covered— and there was left only two hundred and fifty thousand when she died. Now he, Stephen, had eliminated almost half of that. Thank God the house was free and clear.*

Stephen settled in, as Alzonya had instructed him, in one of the kids' rooms, which doubled as a guest room when needed, since his dad occupied the one downstairs which used to be the guest suite. He showered in the bathroom down at the end of the hall—that was so familiar to him—then closed the door to his room and stretched out to try to catch a nap, which he sorely needed. Martha came home with two of the kids around late afternoon. He would come down when Tom got home.

Around five thirty Tom drove into the garage, and he and daughter Anna, in ballet costume, gave Stephen's van—which still had the ministry markings on it— a curious once over, before continuing into the house. Stephen gathered himself together and went to the bathroom to splash some water on his face.

Stephen appeared at the doorway to the kitchen and greeted them all. The kids circled him, calling in their innocent excitement, "Uncle Steve! Uncle Steve!" Tom smiled and offered his hand; Martha turned from the sink and gave him a "Hello," and, shrugging her shoulders indicating that she had work to do, went back to her chore.

"Come on," said Tom. "Alzonya's giving dad his supper."

There was a momentary flash of recognition, Stephen thought he detected, when his dad saw him. He walked over to him and put his arm awkwardly around his shoulders and hugged him.   As Alzonya resumed feeding him, Stephen stepped back and studied him.   "He's aged a lot since I last saw him," he confided in a stage whisper to Tom.

"Yeah. He used to be able to feed himself to some extent. He's going down hill, no doubt about it."

He and Tom stayed in the room while his dinner continued, chatting about things in general, the trip, the kids, school, work . . . inane stuff. After Martha fed the kids and sent them off upstairs, during which Tom excused himself a couple of times to assist, Martha finally announced dinner. She had set the table in the breakfast room next to the kitchen rather than the formal dining room. He couldn't blame her. "Hope you like spaghetti. The maid only comes once a week now and it seems I never have enough time to do anything properly any more."

"Fine with me," responded Stephen.

"I think we could use a little red wine for such an auspicious occasion, think so, Martha?"

"You know where it is."

"Steve, you're not so charismatic that you won't touch a little wine, are you?"

"Only when Faith is around . . . but, that's over, thank God . . . "

"Oh?" chimed Martha. "You two break up?"

" 'Fraid so. Thought Tom would have told you."

"Well..he sort of . . . hinted . . . I don't know . . . I guess I wanted to hear it from you."

"Just one of those things . . . didn't work. She's gone back to her ministry . . . chasing demons . . . and I am headed for the east coast, chasing . . . I don't know what— just a job!"

Conversation was an excruciating effort. Discounting the vacuity of interests with Martha . . . not to mention her obvious coolness . . . which he attributed to her knowing about the oil investment losses—

which, no doubt she held him   responsible for—Tom was less than cordial at times himself.

After dinner, after dad had been put to bed and Alzonya had driven home, he and Tom were able to converse alone in the living room. Her tidying up finished, Martha disappeared upstairs.

"You know we only have less than a hundred and thirty thousand left? On twice that —a few months ago—dad was getting almost twenty-five thousand. Now, his income is cut in half! Barely a thousand a month. We can hardly keep Alzonya for that and get some of his medicines. You know, with the trust, Medicaid is out. I just hope to God he doesn't get real sick. We do have a policy but it costs like the dickens!"

"What do you want me to say? I'm sorry?   . . . You don't know how sorry I am. Remember? We both put our entire trust in the Lord in all this—You just as much as me ! So, it fails . . . and guess what? God doesn't get the blame . . . No. Old Stevie does! It figures."

"Well? You were the one out there . . . you seemed to know what was going on. I was way back here a thousand miles from it. How could I really know? I was pressured "

"We were all pressured . . . pressured by faith . . . by promise . . . by trust . . . but, as I see it now, mostly by greed. But, then, the Bible promises the hundred-fold return . . . to bless the faithful. I don't know! I've been over this till I'm sick of it. You think I wanted to lose all that money? You know what I—personally—lost? Eighty thousand! I haven't got but a few hundred dollars left—and I am out of a job. Unemployed! How does that grab you? At least you have a roof over your head—a free one, I might add—and you have an office to go to every day and a pay check every two weeks. Want to trade?"

Tom sat in a glum heap. He knew he was as much to blame as Steve . . . but, then again, no he wasn't. Steve had really talked him into it, when you get right down to it.

"Look. It isn't much, but it is the only thing I can do. I have the insurance policy with me. $200,000 with double indemnity. I'll sign it over to you. The first six months are already paid. But, since I don't have anything, you will have to pick up the payments to keep it from lapsing. It's all I can do."

Tom nodded acceptance.

"One last thing, though. I've got to keep the debit card. That's my only insurance against disaster. I promise I won't use it except in a dire emergency. But, if I'm up against the wall . . . I don't know what to do otherwise."

"I'm not so sure . . . we both have power of attorney, but either of us can do anything for dad without consulting the other . . . "

"Well? Did I consult you about the wells? Or, did I go off and do it on my own?"

"How about next time?"

"That's a hell of a thing! Don't you trust me?"

"After all this, I really don't know."

"For Christ's sake!—forgive me, Jesus. At least I stepped out and did something. It's always easier to let someone else take the action . . . the risks . . . and then sit back and criticize. When the old radio comedian Fred Allen was criticized for one of his shows, his reply was 'Where were you when the thirty pages were blank?' That's about the way I feel! You know, twenty percent of the people in this world are leaders, doers . . . producers . . . the other eighty percent are followers, consumers. I thank God I am in that first group. Tom, I couldn't be like you. You're a flat-out wimp! Look, life is tough all over! I've lost a family—now my second wife. Frankly, I'm not too pleased or happy about anything at this point. These are strange times, I don't know what's going out there any more . . . I've lost touch—lost my touch! Here I am middle-aged . . . with a big problem. No family . . . no money . . . no job . . . no future. I'm terrified! . . . At least, you can hang on to your piss-ass little job and come home to a big, mortgage-free home . . . and look forward to a pittance of a retirement some day and social security. My   retirement's gone—and social security ?—in the ministry we don't have FICA withheld . . . so at 65 I'm liable to have a big zero for income . . . be living under a bridge—on welfare! Want to trade places?   You'll have the house, too, remember?   Suppose I relinquish my share?..give mine to you to compensate for the loss of the oil investments? That sound fair? You take it all! What use have I got for anything? I have nowhere to go . . . nothing to do! What would I need a big house like this to come back to some day to wait out my years? . . . So, I give it all to you!   Wouldn't that   be bending over backwards to set things right?"

Stephen had felt himself rise to a pitch that he though bordered on loss of self-control. He grabbed his head in his hands and slumped down on the sofa. Tom didn't respond. After a few moments, Stephen added, "At least—at this point—I think I still have the gumption and whatever it takes to start life over . . . and believe this time I may do it right. I'm barely treading water, though . . . one good-sized wave and that might just be it !"

Tom appeared somewhat assuaged by the tirade.

Then Stephen went on to describe more of the details of the mess at the wells, and of the station and how it had shaken his faith —the entire experience had shaken his faith, but he would give it one more chance. He pointed out that Tom had not had his faith tested so he could well afford to go to John Bellman's charismatic Episcopal services and 'feel good.' But, he chided him as an older brother is wont, when he got right down to it, was Tom really going out and doing God's will? Getting his hands dirty? Proselytizing and evangelizing? "

Tom feebly countered that his time was restricted, what with the kids, dad and all.

Stephen lost all respect for his brother at that moment.

"I'll be on the road in the morning.   If I miss Martha, say goodbye for me. I pity you, Tom."

Stephen left later in the morning after everyone had gone, but not until he had had a long soliloquy with his dad. Alzonya had sat him in the big easy chair in the living room and put the bib around his neck. Stephen had forced himself to talk cheerfully about his life . . . how things were going . . . how his children—dad's grandchildren, who missed him so much— how they were growing . . . how well they were doing in school. He was making most of it up as he went along and had to get up occasionally and walk around to hold back the tears. But, eventually he was able to articulate many of the things he had often wished he could have discussed with his dad. He told him what a good upbringing dad had given him . . . how happy his childhood had been . . . how appreciative he was that he had been sent to Sewanee Military Academy and to Yale . . . and, how he wished he had lived closer so that he could have shared all the many things from day-to-day that he would have liked to . It was a catharsis for Stephen, and he thought—imagined ?—that he detected a glimmer of comprehension in dad's blank eyes. He prayed to God that the essence of this precious time had registered within him somehow and he asked God aloud to bless his dad and help him get better. For a moment, he wished Oral Roberts could have been there to lay hands on him— to heal him. Stephen rose and went behind the chair his dad was sitting in and laid his left hand on his left shoulder and his right on the top of his head. In an audible but low voice he first bound the forces of Satan and sickness and infirmity in the Name of Jesus, then prayed to the Father through Jesus to release the healing power of the

Holy Spirit on his father. He repeated it in several variations, claiming it to be done in the Name of Jesus, and launched into prayer in tongues.

Alzonya was about to enter the room when she saw Stephen praying . . . hung her head reverently and turned back, uttering "Lord have mercy! Lordy . . . 'Alleluyah!'"

There had been no immediate effect, no change, no apparent movement. It may come later, Stephen rationalized. He kissed his father on the forehead and left, telling Alzonya goodbye and thanking her for taking such good care of his dad, as he headed for the van. The empty feeling in the pit of his stomach almost caused him to throw up. As it was, he lowered his head onto the steering wheel and succumbed to convulsive sobbing.

Stephen neared Charlotte at dusk, cutting off just before the state line between the two Carolinas and headed for PTL's 'Heritage Village USA'. Paying his $6.50 fee at the gate and receiving his window ID card and directions, he headed for the camp grounds where he found the vacant slot assigned to his ID. After wandering around the camp site and finding a snack bar, he used the bathroom facilities and climbed back into the van to make the best he could of the night. Tomorrow—with luck— he might approach personnel and, who knows? A turn in his career could be awaiting him.

When he got out of the van at the studio, a red barn-like 'Butler' type structure nestled artfully amongst the trees, he noticed an absence of activity. Not what he had expected. He went right into the auditorium-studio with its plush living room set where Jim and Tammy Bakker and their co-hosts and guests held forth daily . . . except today, evidently. He had met Jim and side-kick, the affable Uncle Henry Harrison, at a National Religious Broadcasters confab in Washington the previous year. Stephen walked around in awe.   The place was enormous and the suspended lighting, first-rate, state-of-the-art—like Oral's operation—as were the big, pedestal cameras. How he would love to operate with this kind of set-up!

As he wandered toward the control room, a figure emerged from a door. Stephen recognized him, "Uncle Henry! Steve Trevelyan . . . KXAO-TV Tulsa. Don't expect you to remember but we met at the NRB last year!"

Uncle Henry, ever tactful and used to this sort of thing, hailed back, "Good to see you, brother! What brings you to our little part of the kingdom?"

Seizing an opening that flashed across his mind as God-planted, Stephen quickly replied, "Maybe God meant for me to find you. Isn't there a show today?"

"Everybody's off on a remote, except yours truly."

"Henry, time is of the essence. Can I ask you something flat-out?"

"Sure can, brother. Shoot!"

"I just got relieved as GM of KXAO-TV-21 . . . Christian station in Tulsa.   Station sold—really stolen from the Christians. Big mess. Upshot—I'm looking ! What do you think the prospects are for me here at good ol' Praise-The-Lord TV?"

"Sit down here for a moment, brother. Look, I'm not in this end of the business— you know what I do . . . all I do. Just the comic relief, sort of. But, maybe this is the Lord's leading . . . I don't rightly know . . . but, someone your age, obvious background . . . I don't know where you'd fit in.   We're already pretty top heavy with executives and preaching heavy-weights. And, brother, take a good look around you . . .

drive over and see the village under construction . . . the hotel and all. Some great things happening here—but something scares me. Jim and Tammy are the powers here—undisputed—but I worry we're going too fast. We're like a house of cards . . . "

Stephen read between the lines and the implied negatives had already served as a turn off for this line of pursuit. He wrapped up the chat as politely as he could and got back on the road to Virginia.

Chapter 20   Promised Land

Doubling back up through Charlotte, Stephen veered to the east on Interstate 85 across North Carolina. He then cut off toward Roanoke Rapids and took the back roads up over through Suffolk and Chesapeake, the southern loop, over to Virginia Beach, thus avoiding the heavier traffic in Portsmouth and Norfolk. A low level flight of Navy F-14 Tomcats, with wings configured dart-like, reminded him that this was a Navy-Marine town. They were landing at the Oceana Naval Air Station, he surmised.

Taking Eve Lovejoy's suggestion from a telephone conversation with her before leaving Tulsa, he checked several less touristy motels, the ones that catered to long-term guests, especially over the winter. The Clipper Ship looked OK, a block from the water, with parking directly behind the building, which afforded some protection against the corrosive effect of the salt-saturated air sweeping constantly off the Atlantic.

He checked in. Two hundred and fifty a month didn't seem bad, especially for an efficiency with daily maid service. He was fortunate to be able to choose the corner room on the second floor with a small balcony over the sidewalk and a picture window where he could catch a glimpse of the water between the two high-rises on the waterfront. Seemed secure and comfortable enough, under the circumstances. The

269

bed wasn't exactly double, but appeared adequate. The accommodations were usual motel: the one easy chair facing the TV set. A closet with a cloth curtain. A small gas stove and an well-worn bath. He could put up with the musty smell, since he didn't count on staying here too long—he hoped!

After unloading the van and settling in, he took a long walk up and down the beach front, the main commercial strip . . . the honky tonk dives and gin mills . . . the dens of Satan's iniquity. Of course, he would have none of that. He went over in his mind what preparation he had to do for tomorrow. *First and foremost was to telephone Eve Lovejoy and set up the introduction over at CBN.*

He telephoned Eve and arranged to meet her at eleven thirty the following morning at the main entrance to CBN. With that concluded, he succumbed to a deep sleep that resuscitated his state of exhaustion.

The Christian Broadcasting Network at last! Like a pilgrimage to Mecca . . . he should say, Jerusalem! CBN! Veer-y impressive! All pseudo Colonial Williamsburg Monticello-esque style architecture . . . huge colonnaded portico with tall columns and classic portico . . . on the main building . . . other similarly impressive buildings situated in an orderly fashion. All new. He only knew about the largest Christian network from what he had read and heard in the CBN bulletins and from what he'd seen on the 700 Club, which was his favorite of all Christian programming. Pat Robertson was the conservative evangelist —the one he felt most akin to. Son of a Virginia senator, had been in the Marines in the Korean War—a combat hero, as the story went. After the war, living in Brooklyn or something . . . got the 'call from God' . . . God led him to Chesapeake where the Lord also led him to buy a run-down TV station . . . turned it into a totally Christian station . . . the absolute first,

270

he imagined . . . ran it for twenty years. Channel 29. Wrote a book about it, "Shout it from the Housetops!" . One of the first to get a satellite transponder. Intellectual, erudite, articulate, business man—real contrast to the country bumpkin Bible-thumpers out in Tulsa, or Jimmy Swaggart down in Baton Rouge. Jim and Tammy Bakker had started out with him, he thought he recalled. Anyway, as the charismatic movement had grown, captured the minds and hearts—as well as eyes and ears of the faithful in TV church-land, Robertson was able to expand and build this giant complex . . . now including a University offering four or five disciplines, he thought he had read. Truly mind-boggling! This is the way this sort of ministry should be. This was on a par with any of the secular networks. Stephen would wager, too, that audience size was comparable. He had read somewhere, also, that yearly contributions from the faithful amounted to well over a hundred million . . . which might seem a lot, but this is a big operation to run, a large staff to pay, and to get on all the other Christian TV stations and cable, CBN has to buy the air time for the 700 Club, its flagship offering. On KXAO-TV, CBN paid three hundred and fifty an hour five days a week . . . and that was a low figure. In larger markets, it could be well over a thousand an hour.

"God! This is magnificent! I am renewed! This is obviously where You have sent me as the place You wanted me all along! I praise and thank You, Lord!"

"You must be Steve," said an attractive blond woman standing beside one of the columns as he mounted the steps. "I'm Eve."

"Good to meet you," said Stephen, offering his hand. "How'd you spot me? Am I such a hayseed now that I stand out?"

" 'Living Water' all over your van did give me somewhat of a clue. Look, I've only got a half hour for lunch—I don't eat—and we all have prayer promptly at twelve. Let me give you a quick tour, take you

271

by and introduce you to Dave King and you can set up a later appointment with him . . . then you and I can get together for dinner or something and chat."

The tour took Stephen's breath away. He was like a kid seeing the tall buildings down town for the first time. Even the colonnaded entrance where he had met Eve was overpowering . . . gigantic Greek columns . . . must be four stories high! The openness of the interior was obviously meant to impress, but also to accommodate large crowds without a cramped feeling. The main studio was humongous. He had never seen one of this dimension —or calibre—at any of the commercial networks in New York. All of the equipment was new, types he had never seen before and the steep banks of theatre seating must easily accommodate fifteen hundred. Eve pointed out the control room, explaining that the tape editing and all that were farther behind . . . and they had just gone over entirely to the 1-inch video tape format—state-of-the-art stuff.

She then led him up the broad, carpeted stairway to Executive Row, past doors with a couple of names he hoped soon to meet . . . Pat Robertson, Ben Kinchlow . . . Kinchlow was like Ham Washington, black, handsome, articulate, who often took over for Pat when he was away. On the one with the name David King, Eve entered and greeted the secretary. "Hi. Doris, this is Steve Trevelyan. Just need a quick 'hello' with Dave so Steve can make an appointment to talk to him later."

Doris smiled pleasantly and buzzed the intercom. "Eve Lovejoy and a Mr. Trevelyan to see you for a moment . . . OK. Go right in."

David King had gotten up and met them at the door. He was younger than either of them—in his mid-twenties. "Hi, Eve."

"Dave, meet Stephen Trevelyan. Remember? I mentioned he was running the Christian station in Tulsa . . . what was it . . . KX . . . ?" she looked to Stephen for help.

"KXAO-TV, channel 21. I was general manager until last month . . . when the chairman of the board pulled a fast one, bought the Christians out and turned around and sold it—had a buyer in the wings, real plot—for a cool five million."

"Hmmm. Staying Christian format?"

"No. That was what was so upsetting—they're dropping religious and going secular Indy. So, there was no place for me—I have dedicated myself to the Lord and His work . . . and I want to continue that."

"Eve told me that you had been on Madison Avenue?"

"Yep—before I got born again and baptized in the Holy Spirit. Once that happens to you, you can't stay pushing soap and headache pills!"

"College?"

"Yale . . . and I was also in the Marine Corps . . . captain, Vietnam. I hear brother Pat was a Marine. I'm looking forward to meeting him."

"Well, great, Steve. Here's what I suggest. Let Eve show you where Personnel is . . . go through all that rigmarole and testing and stuff, then call me and we'll have another chat in greater depth. Good to meet you. Look's like you've got a good background."

"Lord bless you, Dave. I'll be calling."

Stephen made arrangements, address and all that, to pick Eve up at six that evening.

Stephen located the modest neighborhood, found Eve's house, and they headed off to dinner. "I'll be honest with you—I'm on a tight budget. It'll have to be something not too fancy."

"There are plenty of good seafood houses at the beach. I know just the one. We'll go dutch."

As they seated themselves at a table by the window overlooking the dock and boats moored on the inlet, Stephen had a chance to study Eve as she was perusing the menu. She appeared about Faith's age. Quite the opposite, though, physically. Eve was a long-haired blond . . . possibly helped by a bleach bottle . . . tiny . . . maybe a couple of inches over five feet . . . a faint touch of coarseness . . . roughness around the edges. Buxom—very buxom! The lines of her face were beginning to crease indelibly, especially the crow's feet at the corners of her pale blue eyes. Her makeup—if it was makeup she was wearing—was a natural shade, the lips almost natural . . . just a hint of shadow on the eyelids. Any heavier and it would have tipped her toward cheapness. He gave her credit for holding back instinctively from that.

"I'd love a beer to go along with this," said Eve, "But, I don't dare. If someone from CBN were to see me—and you never know, they pop up everywhere."

"Don't know if I could handle one myself. It's been, let's see, three . . . almost four years since I've had anything alcoholic..even wine . . . if you don't count a glass of sherry with an Episcopal priest in the rectory . . . which, if Faith had found out! . . . she'd still be standing over me burning my ears about it now ! Just how did you and Faith hook up?"

Eve hesitated. "During her prison ministry. She was ministering to the prisoners . . . one of which was me !" Seeing Stephen's change of expression . . . "Shocks you, doesn't it? I was in the women's prison over in Hampton, doing time for a drug bust . . . I had the misfortune to be sitting in the passenger seat when my boyfriend got busted. I didn't have anything on me . . . but I had been smoking . . . pot. Well, the judge threw the book at us. I got six months. It was rough, but not all that bad. Faith came along . . . led me to the Lord . . . set me up with the right people when I got out . . . managed to stay clean . . . got a new boyfriend

274

—you'll probably meet him—and the Lord opened up this job for me at CBN. I'm in the traffic department . . . .did some of the buys on your station. By the way, my boyfriend . . . don't refer to him . . . I mean, when you talk to anyone at CBN . . . we have an off and on relationship. I go to live with him for a while, then he gets cold feet. He's separated. Won't divorce . . . won't make a commitment to me. So, we go round and round. CBN would frown on that."

As the seafood platters were placed before them, Eve continued, "How 'bout you and Faith? How come she's not with you? You two really split?"

"Sure did . . . and I need to get the name of a good—cheap— lawyer from you. I'm filing immediately. No contest. She's gone off on her own thing again. Just as well . . . it was getting pretty crazy. She saw demons of lust in me all the time . . . and constantly condemned me for, quote, not getting myself right with God!, un-quote."

"Tell me about it. Same ol' Faith. She pulled that on me a couple of times . . . the 'right with God' bit . . . and 'cleaning up my love life.' You ask me? She's the one with the demons! I'll bet she was wild in bed! Eh?" she leered, as if sharing the intimacy.

"No complaints on that score . . . gonna miss it, too."

"So, you're getting a divorce? Let me give you some advice: keep that to yourself. Don't discuss it with Dave King . . . or, personnel. Get around it somehow. There's still a lot of holier-than-thou around here. You know . . . Pat himself's clean as a whistle . . . expects everybody else to be a saint, too."

"Thanks for the tip. What about you? Your situation?"

"If it weren't for CBN . . . don't know what I'd do. They like the 'repentant sinner' like me who's come to the Lord. If they found out about my relationship with Jerry . . . or caught me having a beer?" She made a slicing motion across her throat.

"All these Christians . . . I've noticed . . . very judgmental. You've go to be as clean and pure and holy as they are—think they are—or they kick you out of the club. I had thought that was left up to the sinner and his personal relationship to God . . . his own asking for forgiveness . . . that sort of thing."

They discussed all aspects of the Christian experience and Eve disclosed more of the inner workings of the network, the cliques, the petty jealousies, the intrigues, the ego clashes . . . all the usual things that take place where people work together—sacred or secular.

He drove her home and she invited him in for a beer, but he declined. A rain check, perhaps. He had a lot to prepare for: go for the interview at CBN Personnel, check in to the unemployment office for Workman's comp.—see what that amounted to—and contact the lawyer to get the ball rolling on the divorce.   One of the nice things about the Commonwealth of Virginia, she'd told him, was that all you needed was six month's residency as separated and not cohabiting, and it became an automatic 'no fault' final decree. He'd certainly go for that, but it would be ticklish skirting the truth if confronted by Personnel or Dave King.

The Virginia state unemployment office, which he got to a eight a.m. with his tie and coat off, was a humiliating experience. He never in his wildest imagination ever thought that he, Stephen Trevelyan, would end up in an unemployment line. After an hour of waiting, his number came up and he was processed. He almost blew it, too. The interviewer, a black woman, had remarked that he must be another poor victim of President Reagan's policy, to which he had quickly, without thinking, countered, 'No. Carter's!' Seeing she was obviously taken aback and noticing a cross dangling from a small chain around her neck, he added quickly, "Jimmy is a born-again Christian, though . . . I see you are too,

276

with that cross. So'm I." Later he reflected: *all I need to do is alienate a little government clerk and to the bottom of the file my case goes! Street smarts! Big deal, though, he walked away with the maximum allowed . . . a paltry $190 a week for thirteen weeks. The check would be in the mail . . . soon! Sure! Well, he'd soon be at CBN and this would be ancient history.*

The application and interview at CBN Personnel was cordial and thorough. It took an hour to fill out the forms, another to be interviewed, after which followed a half-hour psychological test. He hated those; they were so obvious. Who the heck couldn't figure out the right answers? The ones he could easily imagine the network wanted to hear? That was followed with an essay to state his reasons for wanting to join the network, et cetera. Working into his best 'Prayer and Praise' frame of mind, but tempering it with good sense and obvious educated literary expression, he felt rather good about it. He would give a few days for the evaluation to get up to David King, then he would give him a call for an appointment.

The short session with the attorney was encouraging, as well. No problem to institute a Decree *A Mensa et Thoro* for the separation, then, at the end of six months, merge it into a Final Decree of divorce . . . so long as the situation remained status quo: Faith didn't change her mind and attempt to cohabit . . . and Stephen had proof of residency and a witness to testify to that effect. The charge was a reasonable four hundred and fifty dollars.

Two weeks passed since the interview with Personnel and his call to David King's secretary to line up an appointment. She had called back and given him a date and time . . . the week before Thanksgiving. He had subtly hinted for an earlier date but Doris seemed inflexible. He guessed Dave did have a lot more pressing things on his mind than a job applicant, one of how many, he wondered, he had to see every week. At least the definite appointment indicated that Personnel had passed his file upstairs.

During the interim, Stephen sought out the Episcopal church at the upper end of the beach, within walking distance of the motel. This, he reasoned, could well be *my anchor in the Lord while I'm here . . . whether it is charismatic or not. At least I will be on familiar territory.*

When he went around to call on the pastor, Reverend Beauregard Rivers, he discovered, much to his delight, that several of the CBN big-wigs worshiped there—even Pat, himself, on occasion. *What good fortune! Again, God's leading.* There was also a men's breakfast and fellowship every Saturday morning, as he looked forward to making friends and establishing contacts. He felt more reassured now that he was going to be able to put down permanent roots here. Thanks to the grace of God.

Stephen had looked forward to the CBN interview with so much anticipation that he had to stifle his mounting nervousness . . . which was unusual for him. He had prayed long and hard when he got up that morning and now, as he parked the van, went into another five minutes or so of prayer and praise—and tongues—to prepare himself for this most important moment coming up. He asked the Lord to give him a clear mind and an uncluttered tongue, and he implored the Lord to make David King receptive to him and to open his heart to discern his, Stephen's, true anointing and how he would be God's choice for the job —any job!

Vice President David King welcomed Stephen cordially. There wasn't the spontaneous Holy hugging that the Tulsa and PTL'ers ingenuously engaged in; this was a more formal, a more business-like atmosphere. That appealed to Stephen.

Eve had told him a little more about Dave . . . as much as she knew. He had gone to some little, obscure junior college in the southern part of the state . . . then had started out as a floor manager at WYAH-TV . . . then became a switcher-director . . . and, when Pat developed CBN, he had tapped Dave for ordination to these higher realms.

The interview got off to an awkward start, with King flipping through the folder that had been compiled on Stephen by Personnel, asking routine and mundane questions, all of which were answered in the file. This led Stephen to the thought that he had better grab the reins of the meeting and guide it so that he made sure he got his points across. Settling comfortably in the chair, he recounted in a casual and disengaging manner, injecting some light humor in how he had found the Lord in the Episcopal church (indicating he traveled in the right crowd) in Atlanta (indicating that he was not a Yankee, like Yale would imply)—and how, incidentally, he was thinking of joining the one at Virginia Beach—and of the trials and tribulations of the station in Tulsa (thus eliciting kinship in down-to-earth station operation). He adroitly made analogies and comparisons—negative, of course—of KXAO-TV to WYAH-TV, which he had made a point of visiting prior to the meeting. And, he talked technical details, station operation, the sorts of things that he thought Dave would warm up to . . . at least, loosen him up to. He had the intuitive feeling that his Sewanee, Yale, Marine Corps, Madison Avenue background was a bit intimidating, so he strove deliberately to gloss over that and, instead, to build a base of common, shared experience with Dave.

As this apparently began to work and Dave's slight reserve turned to a more at-ease exchange, Dave asked him what exactly was he looking to do at CBN?

Eve had prepped him on some things, so he smiled and started, "I'm so impressed and overwhelmed with the whole operation . . . I wouldn't mind just taking out the garbage!" Quickly passing on, he said, "I would hope that some of what I've done in the past could fit in in an area of responsibility here that the Lord would lead me to: production, administration, programming, promotion . . . I have a good deal of experience in all of those areas. And, I hear there are big plans to create and air a daily Christian 'soap opera' . . . maybe there's something in that area that you need someone with my type of qualifications." He was taking pains to be sure he pitched himself for an executive level commensurate with his age and experience that he wasn't at all sure a person like Dave, who had been elevated to such a lofty position at so young an age—with so little track record to justify it—would be all that sensitive to such amenities and subtleties. Stephen felt instinctively that he had to get past Dave successfully and win the final round above him— with Pat, himself, most likely. He felt there would be rapport there.

David pondered while Stephen extolled his virtues, strengths and qualifications in each of the areas he had mentioned. "Steve, we have something a little unusual . . . and we're looking for someone to head it. Think you would be interested in a foreign assignment?"

Stephen's shift of posture and facial expression affirmed his interest.

"We're setting up a Christian TV-radio operation in the near east, in lower Lebanon . . . just across the Israeli border. Rather primitive operation. Couple of trailers; one for living, one for switching and transmitter operation. Three hundred foot tower, but it's all located on the ridge of the Golan heights so that gives increased elevation. Ought to spread the signal over all Israel, Lebanon, half of Jordan and Syria. It's situated in an area under control of the Lebanese-Christian militia colonel Haddad."

"Wow! That would be an opportunity! Praise God! You'd be there to cover the Second Coming!"

"As I say, rather primitive.   Mostly a playback operation. Probably a minicam to cover anything important.   It would be isolated. How'd you think your wife would take that?"

Stephen had rehearsed his answers about his marriage in a number of variations: *technically*, he reasoned, *they were still married; Faith was still his wife. When the six months were up while he was working at CBN, he would just say she had decided not to live in Virginia Beach—which was the truth— and so he had filed a no-cause divorce . . . his wife had left him . . . and that would be announced as a fait accompli.* So, he quickly responded with a broad grin, "She's an evangelist, you know.   So, she's off all the time, going with others to prisons all over the country, herself.   But, I would imagine I would get to come back here periodically . . . to report . . . be interviewed by Pat . . . to update the operations, air tapes . . . that sort of thing?"

"Yes . . . about every six months."

"I think that would present no problem.   After all, during Vietnam I was out in the field for almost a year. A good field Marine is used to that. Also in my favor is my Marine Corps background; I would not be upset being that near to a war zone. So . . . yes, that does sound like a promising prospect. I have always wanted to go to Israel . . . to make a pilgrimage to Jerusalem. I'd like to learn Arabic or Hebrew, too. Hallelujah!"

Standing up, Dave offered his hand to Stephen, an obvious indication of the conclusion of the interview. "Good to see you. I'll talk this over with the others involved, and I'll get back to you."

"Thanks. God bless you, brother. I've got a good feeling that I am the man for that job.   The excitement—the potential—the possibilities . . . are already working on me!"

Stephen left with his head reeling with visions of his being CBN's representative in the Holy Land—well, just north of it. Obviously the

Israelis would not sanction a Christian TV station on their soil . . . he had heard that the Israelis arrested any Christian caught proselytizing Jews. Spreading the Gospel from just across the border on invisible, unstoppable air waves was the obvious solution to that. God's perfect plan, no doubt. He had heard, too, that American music, especially Country & Western, was popular throughout the middle east, and that Arabs could be found listening to it on their Japanese made walk-mans as they rode their camels in the desert! What a way to spread the Gospel to prepare that part of the world for the End Times that were upon us. And, He— Stephen Trevelyan—was going to be God's chosen instrument right in the midst of it! He felt his spirits had never been higher.

He lost no time in calling Eve and telling her the whole story. She thought that warranted celebration and suggested that he get a six-pack . . . and she would come over to his motel and they could lift a couple while they explored the ins and outs of this new opportunity. He agreed wholeheartedly.

The beer was stashed in the small refrigerator, the room was tidied up and he was ready when she knocked on the door a little after eight.

"Say, it's such a nice warm night out," she said upon entering, "Let's have a beer, then take a walk."

"Good idea." He took two bottles from the refrig and started rummaging through the drawer with the mismatched silverware and utensils.

"What cha' lookin' for?"

"Bottle opener . . . don't think there. . ."

"Boy! You sure haven't had a beer in a long time! You twist the cap off now. Here . . . " She took one and demonstrated, handing it to him.

They clicked the bottles together in toast-fashion and then took long swigs.

"Hmmm," sighed Stephen, savoring the long-denied taste and licking the lingering foam off of his lips. "That do taste good! I've got to rationalize this as harmless . . . like wine, when you get right down to it . . . not the hard stuff. Don't see why Christians can't drink it in moderation. You know, I even heard of an order of Catholic nuns who have one beer daily. Monks used to make it in the middle ages—still do wine, out in California. Sometimes, I think these self-made restrictions are simply re-instituting the legalism of the Pharisees."

"Amen. This is one thing I never let bother me . . . this and sex. This is all between me and my God—not me and CBN!"

"Right . . . as long as one doesn't make a spectacle of himself and embarrass either CBN or the Kingdom."

The walk was pleasant and he and Eve talked like good friends, brother and sister. Confiding things that they ordinarily would not have so openly and on so short an acquaintance. They felt compatible, at ease, and uninhibited. It was refreshing for them both, especially since Eve was having boyfriend troubles again.

They finished off the six pack when they got back to the room. The two that Stephen downed had left him quite woozy and he admitted that he was glad that he was not the one driving home. That was punctuated with a hiccup which sent him into a spasm of laughter that was totally out of character.

"You certainly are out of practice. Better sleep it off . . . want your mummy to tuck you in, sonny?"

"Hey, I'm not tipsy . . . (hic!) . . . oh, yes I am . . . Bye! You'd better leave so I CAN sleep this off."

She departed and Stephen slept it off.

Chapter 21   Hand of the Lord

The better part of the next day Stephen spent in the library, digging up everything he could on the middle east. He consulted and copied maps, measured distances, familiarized himself with the major cities, the major geographical areas, the deserts, the seas, the lakes and rivers. He perused several bookstores for titles pertaining to Israel; there was not much to offer at the beach, hardly more in downtown Norfolk. But, he did come up with a couple of things that he would study and, when the next interview came, he would naturally astound them with his knowledge.

Thanksgiving was getting close. Of course, that meant nothing to him with no family or friends. He'd just go get a turkey sandwich somewhere. Eve, he supposed, would be all tied up with her family . . . or with Jerry. So, he decided study was the best way to get his mind off things and help the time go by.

The day before, however, Eve called him and invited him over for a family get together, turkey and all the trimmings . . . an invitation which he accepted with alacrity.

It was one of those cold, clammy November days, overcast . . . not at all cheerful. He arrived at Eve's and parked on the street in front, since the driveway had three cars in it. She greeted him at the door and gave him a brush on the cheek with her lips, turned and called out for Jerry to come meet Steve, then scooped up a toddler off of the floor and cuddling it next to her chin, introduced Tootsie, her daughter's baby. Her daughter, Alyssa, hadn't come back yet . . . she had gone off with some friends somewhere.

After shaking hands with Jerry, Stephen wandered into the kitchen where Eve was tackling the turkey dinner and the baby was playing contentedly in a small playpen. The aroma was divine. He hadn't smelled a roasting turkey since he couldn't remember when.

"I've got a little wine . . . or a beer . . . or, I've got some apple cider. What's your pick?"

He settled on a little glass of white wine and did his best to join in . . . or offer his assistance . . . or, even get out of the way. The kitchen was small. He took her hint and went back into the family room where Jerry had the TV on to a football game. Jerry made a perfunctory attempt at conversation, asking what he did at CBN. Stephen corrected him . . . that he was hoping to land there. And, by the way, what did Jerry do? Construction. Build houses. With that, their mutual interest in the game acted as a tenuous bond of their presence. Stephen nursed his wine as long as he could . . . to drag the time out . . . then slowly got up and went to the kitchen for a refill.

"Anything I can do to help? Sure smells good. You know, in the whole time I was married to Faith I never had a home-cooked meal."

"You're kidding!"

"Nope. She said she was a servant of God . . . not man. Bang! That was it."

286

"Must have been some life."

He watched her a while then wandered back and sat at his place before the TV set as the game continued on . . . well into the early evening. Eve had offered encouraging calls from time to time that it wouldn't be long.

As he had just about finished his second glass of wine, the front door opened, there was a lot of commotion, shouting—'whoopin' an' a hollerin' as they would say down south. The door slammed and a large, female teenager dressed in black leather and bangles and boots came prancing into the room. "Hi, gang! Ain't you two dudes cute!" Without waiting for any reply, she whisked into the kitchen and confronted her mom, "When's din din, old girl?"

Stephen heard some muffled talking, a sing-song pattern of rising and dropping tones, after which the girl grabbed the baby out of the playpen and stomped up the stairs with it.

"OK, guys. Din-nah is being served . . . in the dining room."

They all squeezed around a small table which had been decorated to some extent with small cutouts of turkeys and pilgrims. The was a centerpiece of an autumn-colored floral arrangement, nice looking tableware and a fancy lace tablecloth. Stephen complimented Eve on such an elegant outlay and he reassured her that the turkey would be as good as it smelled. Jerry mumbled something to the same effect. The fourth chair remained empty. Eve explained that she had told Alyssa that she could damned well go feed her baby herself and get her act together if she wanted to join them. She never reappeared.

The evening went as pleasantly as could be expected. He and Eve did most of the conversing. Jerry evidently felt ill at ease . . . jealousy? . . . muttered something every now and then, but really didn't have much to say. Again, Stephen felt that he was somehow the intimidating factor.

After helping with the dishes and finishing off the wine, Stephen thanked Eve profusely, tactfully bade his farewell and drove back to the motel. He had to hand it to Eve, she seemed to be putting up with a lot. He figured the daughter was high on something . . . it was obvious that Eve did most of the caring for the infant . . . and boyfriend was no great shakes. Then again, that was her milieu, she knew no better . . . and did the best she could under the circumstances. She went up in his estimation; she displayed some true-blue qualities. He wrote Jerry off as a jerk. No doubt treated her boorishly. He would bet that the front seat of his pickup was cluttered with beer cans. *'God! There I go judging again! Forgive me, Lord!'* Anyway, it was a break in an otherwise very dull routine. He would telephone her tomorrow and thank her again for including him in such a marvelous, family celebration . . . he really meant it, too.

Stephen figured that the call from Dave King would come right after Thanksgiving. He wondered if he would run into him by chance at the church that Sunday? He hoped so. That would keep his face and situation fresh in Dave's mind and might even trigger a positive sign from him that things were working out.

At the service on Sunday he didn't see Dave or anyone that he thought might be from CBN. He had stayed for the social time following the service and had met a few people . . . but had found it awkward trying to explain his presence and just what it was that he did. He decided that he should fabricate some truthful but more plausible story that would engender respectful interest, such as he was a consultant (the code word for unemployed) sizing up the possibilities for locating his next venture in the Tidewater area. It really was not worth the effort, though . . . he would soon be telling them that he was off to Lebanon to set up a CBN TV operation . . . and then their jaws would drop.

288

When he got back to the room he thought that he had better check his situation money wise against the calendar. When he did start at CBN, there would be a thirty-day period before his first paycheck came in . . . or maybe they paid on a bi-weekly basis . . . anyway, he'd be wise to plan very carefully. With December's rent he would have gone through the entire five hundred dollars he had left when he arrived here. The unemployment checks had started coming in; he'd gotten two so far and most of that had gone to clear up the utility bill back in Tulsa and the Exxon charge for gas coming out here . . . and the van was far from economical. By the middle of December he would be scraping bottom . . . and actually living off the unemployment check. If he needed a new suit or something to start at CBN . . . well, maybe he could set up a charge account based on his intended employment . . . or, in a pinch, he could use the trust debit card.

There was nothing to do now but wait . . . sweat out the call from Dave King.

When the end of November passed and so did the first week in December with no call from King, Stephen began to be apprehensive and telephoned Eve one evening. She had heard nothing, but then she was virtually out of that loop. She promised to go up and see Doris and see if she could find out anything. She'd call him back.

Early the next evening she called and told Stephen that the systems seemed 'Go,' . . . that Doris had indicated that there was an office down the hall being readied for him. So, it looked like he was 'in', fella!'

Stephen promised that they would celebrate big when the news did come in, and he settled back to a comfortable complacency, imagining all the great things he was going to achieve for CBN in the near east. 'Oh, Hallelujah! This was it , Lord. Thank You . . . thank You . . . '

Stephen remained a virtual prisoner in his room, tied by anxiety to the telephone. He got up early, showered and breakfasted so that by eight thirty, the beginning of the business day, he would be manning his telephone watch. And, he didn't budge from it all the day long. He wished he'd had an answering machine, but that would not have done anything but get the message and he might have a hard time reaching him back. He did all his errands well after six o'clock when he knew they'd all be gone from CBN.

Days passed. The fifteenth came and went. He called Eve a couple of times to check if she knew anything.

No. Same as before, no change. His office was still there.

It was approaching the 20th. Soon everybody would be tied up in all the Christmas goings-on. He would have to remember to get a couple of presents for Gloria and Michael. He couldn't afford to buy them much, and he would have to get it in the mail rather quickly. He was sure the post office stayed open late at this time of the year . . . so he wouldn't chance missing the call. Worse, too, if they delayed much longer, then there would be the temptation to delay until after Christmas . . . which would just prolong his agony, not to mention throw him into some real financial squeeze. He was beginning to panic. He was thinking about it too much—then, what else was there to think about? He spent most of the days now pacing, back and forth, with the TV on, oblivious to it. This was down-right nerve-wracking. He had no choice but to call Dave.

Spending more than an hour calming himself down and rehearsing very carefully what he would say to Doris, he finally made the call.

"No, I'm sorry, Mr. Trevelyan. Mr. King is not available at the moment."

"I understand. I just thought that I might have missed his call . . . I don't have an answering machine where I am . . . so I thought I'd just give a call and see when he wants me to get back with him."

"I'll pass that on to him. I'm sure he will be back to you before too long."

"Thanks, Doris. You have a good day."

He hung up the receiver and collapsed on the bed. He went over the short conversation in his mind. Had he said the right thing? Convincingly? In a way that would spur Doris to action . . . to get Dave to get back to him? 'God! God! Where are You in this? Help me, Please , I beg You!'

Two more days passed since his call to Doris—still no call from Dave. Stephen was becoming totally unnerved. He consciously knew that he should grab hold of himself . . . but his anxiety got the best of him. He couldn't eat . . . he just paced the room. "God!" he cried out, "Where are You? What are You doing to me?" and fell sobbing onto the bed.

The morning of Christmas Eve, the phone rang. It startled Stephen so that his heart felt like it would jump out of his throat. He let it ring twice to make sure it was an intended call. Clearing his throat and mustering up the calmest voice he could, he picked up the receiver and said, "Hello, this is Steve Trevelyan."

"Steve, Merry Christmas. This is Dave . . . Dave King."

Stephen's heart raced. He grabbed a pencil to write on the pad next to the phone. "Hi, Dave. And, a Merry Christmas to you . . . I was hoping to hear from you."

"Well, Steve, I was putting off this call to you as long as I could . . . in hopes that the picture might change . . . "

With that foreboding, Stephen sank onto the bed.

" . . . but, we have had a little setback in the Lebanon project. Because of the Israeli occupation at the moment . . . even though that, everyone feels, will be only temporary . . . until they clean out all the guerrilla bases they invaded in order to do . . . President Gemayel has asked Pat to hold up on advancing the broadcasting project we talked about."

" . . . That would mean a temporary setback," interjected Stephen, " . . . but I would imagine plans would continue to go forward for when the time is right again . . . which will need planning, that sort of thing . . . "

"Well, that's true to an extent . . . but we have all taken this under a considerable amount of prayer . . . and we have all come down, basically, to the same leading of the Lord . . . that this is a message to us from the Lord that . . . you are not the right man for the job . . . Sorry to have to put it that way . . . "

Stephen scarcely heard the rest . . . if there was any more. He was stunned! He managed to come back weakly, "You mean . . . you are turning me down . . . because of a temporary halt . . . and you are interpreting that to mean that I am not the right person?"

"Sorry to have to put it that way . . . but that's the looks of it. There may be something else that will open up . . . never can tell. Keep in touch. Drop by Personnel again . . . "

"Merry Christmas." Stephen said dryly, not masking the bitterness in his tone, and hung the phone up and lay back on the bed. '*I just don't believe it. God . . . I just don't believe it. I don't believe that You would treat me this way, God. This can't be real. I'm just imagining this. That phone didn't ring . . . I didn't talk to Dave King . . . that was only a bad dream. I'll wake up. There'll be a tap on my shoulder and someone will tell me to get dressed and come on down to the office . . . to my new office at CBN. And, I won't even remember this nightmare.'*

He rolled over and buried his face in the pillow. He cried for hours, it seemed. Well into the afternoon.

Stephen Trevelyan was so crushed . . . so despondent . . . that he could hardly function.   Mustering all his strength, he telephoned Eve. No answer. *Of course, Christmas Eve . . . out shopping . . . or over at Jerry's preparing for all the festivities.* He had gotten a card for her . . . to deliver to her personally on either Christmas Eve or Christmas day. He'd give it to her some other time.

He sat in the stuffed chair and looked out at the darkening night and the holiday scurrying about. He was absolutely catatonic. This was the end. Dave had offered no hope . . . no positive follow up. *A real kiss-off* . . . then, the thought occurred to him, *they must have checked his references, KXAO-TV . . . maybe Felix himself . . . God knows what might have been said about him . . . despite his explanation of the circumstances of his departure. Or, someone might have dropped the fact that he and Faith were getting a divorce . . . and he had not put that plainly on paper on his application. But, he could explain that if confronted . . . Yes, they had discussed it . . . but had decided on his landing with CBN and seeing how that could fit in with her ministry . . . that sort of thing. 'God, it must have been something like that . . . how can You let these people serve You . . . and be so judgmental?'*

He gazed off into the darkness again.

'Wait a minute . . . No! . . . this is incredible! What Dave said . . . They had prayed to God! . . . They had talked to God! . . . They had heard from God! . . .

This is Faith all over again! They are all on the side of God ! So? Where does that leave me ? On Satan's side . . . obviously ! God! How do I fight that? Is this always the way it's going to be?'

"Screw it!"

Stephen sat in the chill of his dark, dank room . . . hearing occasionally strains of Christmas carols coming from far away . . . down the street. The bustle of activity, the automobile traffic . . . all that had tapered off to quietude . . . except for the cars that were heading up to the traditional midnight Christmas Eve services at the Episcopal church . . . that he would not go to this night. He looked at the illuminated digits on the clock face . . . a few minutes til midnight . . . until the glorious birth of the Savior. *'Savior—my ass! The Mithraic cult . . . a pagan bacchanal, that's what it really is. So, You think, Lord . . . that, after all You have put me through . . . that I would actually go and worship and praise You? You got another think coming!'*

'I really think the time has come', Stephen thought to himself. He had wondered earlier if he would ever get this close to it . . . but he had always shut the idea from his mind. Not now. He felt numb. Drained. There was nothing more to his life.

He got up painfully. He had sat in one position for so long that his joints ached, especially his hip. He turned the reading lamp on and went over to the tiny closet and rummaged around the bottom until he came up with a small metal box. Taking it over under the light, he thumbed the little wheels on the combination lock until three threes lined up. The top came up and he picked up the zipper bag encasing the .25 caliber automatic pistol. He checked the clip with a practiced hand. Full. He closed the top of the metal box and left it on the table. *'Trusty little thing . . . been in the family for over sixty years. Used to be dad's . . . and his dad's.* He grasped it, took aim out the window and lowered it. *Not like a .*

45 Colt like he carried in Vietnam. That would really leave a hole! This, though, if it hit the right spot . . . it could do the job.

He put on a small jacket then an army surplus jacket over that. He grabbed his gloves and stuffed them in one pocket, the automatic in the other. He crammed a crummy rain hat down on his head, checked for his key . . . that would be the only identification necessary . . . and laid his wallet on the dresser—no need for somebody to get the credit cards—and scotch taped a list of emergency contacts on the mirror.

The beach was quite cold; he pulled the zipper up around his neck as far as it would go without strangling him and descended the steps down to the sand. There was a faint glow spilling over onto the beach from the Christmas lights that sporadically blinked from various windows and from the street above. He turned to the north, where he usually strolled, up to the deserted end of the beach, beyond where the hotel lights were. This was where he had walked many a night, especially recently, since he came here two months ago . . . talking to God, praising Him, pleading with Him . . . questioning Him . . . sometimes doing nothing but praying in tongues as loud as he could as fast as he could . . . believing some kind of prayers for something were getting through by the spirit, which would take care of whatever it was he should be praying for . . . but, obviously those had been to no avail. *Here he was . . . cast out . . . rejected by CBN—and by God, as well!* What else could he think?

He entered the dark part where the bulkhead jutted out narrowing the beach to a few paces from it and the edge of the surf. He looked out into the dark water and the breaking waves. *Maybe it would be better just to walk out there and continue on. Christ, it would be cold. No, not at first, not bundled up like this. Yeah, but then it would be when the clothes got all soaked . . . and dragged him down. So what? That's the point, isn't it? But, God, would that be the way to go? The body stone cold, washed up somewhere down the beach? What if it weren't found for some time? After all, who would know I was missing? Nobody knows me. Only Eve. A description might appear in the paper . . . anyone can miss a paper . . . she doesn't even read the beach paper anyway. So, after a while . . . she can't reach me by phone . . . stops by . . . nobody's heard from me . . . the maids say his bed hasn't been slept in . . . his van is still there . . .*

Stephen shuddered and looked up the beach. He took his right glove off and stuck his hand into his pocket and grasped the pistol. *This is going to be quicker. Not cleaner, but quicker.*

He thought first whether a bullet to the temple would be surer and quicker . . . especially with this small calibre, or whether up the roof of the mouth. That, too, would lodge in the brain . . . none of them would go right on through tearing out a whole chunk like a .45 would . . . assuring success on the first shot. Either way, he would have to get off two shots in rapid succession . . . before his reflexes ceased . . . to be sure he did the job right . . . and there would be no lingering . . . no coma . . . or prolonged agony by life support systems. He had to make sure he killed the brain right away.

Or, if push came to shove . . . maybe one right smack into the old heart? He'd have to open his jacket and his wool shirt to do that. But, that would surely do it; he would bleed to death there on the beach before anyone found him. And, of course, after the first instant, he would feel nothing. It would be all over . . . then they would have to identify him. They'd find the key, then the notes in case of emergency stuck to the dresser mirror. Then what? They'd contact Eve, maybe; pity to put her through that. They'd make a lot of calls and end up reaching Diana, or maybe Gloria or Michael, if Diana weren't at home. What would their reaction be? Disbelief at first. Then, some kind of shock . . . but, would there be any tears? He doubted it. Perhaps Michael. He was the youngest, and when Stephen had found the Lord . . . he had showered that love onto Michael who was young enough to receive it . . . Gloria and Diana had rejected it . . . that agape love. The others rejected it because he had never shown his love to them before . . . didn't know how until that rebirth freed him emotionally. But, it was too late for them . . . all they really remember is my cussing and drinking and yelling and beating them. God, if I had only been able to erase all that! Now, of course, they don't understand it. But, then, did I cry when mom died? I was an adult at the time; no, I didn't . . . maybe because she had suffered so much with the cancer and the operations and the chemotherapy. She was really better off dead. "No," Stephen cried aloud, *'I didn't cry for mom until ten years later when I visited her gravesite for the first time. I was alone and I stared down at the headstone and tried to picture her as I had remembered her best . . . and the most uncontrollable sobbing overtook me . . . and I cried like I had never cried before. I must have bawled for fifteen minutes or so—everything that had been pent up came out. And, I talked to her just as if she were there and I knew she wasn't because the Bible teaches that the spirits of the dead immediately go to heaven to be with the Lord or to hell to await the final judgment. I knew mom was in heaven, up there with Jesus. Yeah . . . even though the dead in Christ shall rise first at the last trump, it didn't mean that in God's time frame mom's spirit was still down under the ground, waiting to rise.'* He didn't think he had separated those thoughts at the time, he thought to himself now. But, he remembered that through all the crying he kept asking his mother to forgive him for not loving her more and showing her so . . . *that's* why he had been so glad to have had those moments a couple of months ago with his father . . . so this would not be repeated.

Stephen cried again, standing on the beach recounting to the cold night wind his feelings for his parents. *God, would his own children someday feel the same remorse at his grave?—if he ever had a grave! Maybe they would never find him . . . or they would have to cremate him if the deterioration were too bad.* He fell to one knee, weeping. "Why, God? Why have You brought me to this?"

He pulled the pistol out of his pocket. He couldn't see it in the darkness, but he knew guns and knew how to get a round into the chamber blindfolded. *I'll bet this friggin' thing hasn't been fired in twenty years. I should have thought of that and at least cleaned it. Oh, what the shit!*

H pulled the slide back and let it snap forward, putting the first bullet in the chamber ready to fire. He raised it deliberately to his temple and slowly squeezed the handle causing pressure on the trigger and . . . the explosion broke the silent air over the low muffle of the surf. Hordes of sleeping sea gulls squawked in sudden frenzy and added their flapping cacophony to the now dying echo of the shot. A double echo caused by the sound bouncing off the seawall reverberated again over the waves.

Then . . . all was silent again; a few gulls squeaked overhead as if to chastise for the rude disturbance. Quickly, everything settled down and only the motion of the waves broke the stillness in their incessant rhythm. A light breached the darkness up the beach . . . and another, in response to the unusual sound that had come from the water.

Stephen's body lay motionless on the sand.

Damn!

      I couldn't do it.

Chapter 22   Christmas Present

It was not too long after midnight when Stephen stumbled, drenched and shivering, back to his hotel room.

Passing the paltry strands of fuzzy gold-like tinsel Christmas decorations the manager, Mr. Weisenberg, had perfunctorily put across the front door—along with a Hanukkah menorah cutout—and finding it locked, he went around the building and up the back stairs onto the outside-inner balcony where his door was.

Inside, the sense of loneliness hit him. So did the stale smell of the room which, oddly, was warm. *'My Jewish friend must have had a turn of heart for us goim on this religious holiday of our false celebration of the birth of our false Messiah,'* he thought. He shed his coat and let it drop on the floor in front of the closet. The clunk of the pistol in the pocket startled him; he'd already forgotten about it. *Screw it!* He didn't bother to pick it up. His mind continued to race from one torment to another. *No guts after all —or, was it God's hand? Come on, Stevie, old boy, 'git a holt a yo'sef!'* He hit the on button for the TV as he kicked his shoes off and plopped down onto the bed to see how the lost, pagan, humanistic world was ushering in this sacred day. . .that had turned into a horrid binge of buying and partying and a half-hearted, hypocritical nodding toward the Christ child. *Just enough of that sweet, syrupy shit to make all those organized-church Christian assholes of the Church of Laodicea pious until Easter . . . when they could be pious again.*

  Damn! The Jews really have us by the gonads. Hah! Goims by the Gonads ! There's a slogan for 'em. They don't celebrate this crap but they own all the toy manufacturing . . . all the gift manufacturing . . . all the advertising . . . all the media . . . all the retailing . . . So? What do they do? They hype Christmas up so all us dumb, slob 'holier than-thou' worshippers of a young Jewish rabbi who died two thousand years ago—whom they never accepted as the true Messiah—will succumb to an enormous gilt trip of gift giving in the spirit of some Santa Claus—from some obscure early saint named Nicolas— who nobody remembers anything about now . . . or cares . . . but the whole Christian world —damn! And the Japanese now have Santa and Christmas, too!—the whole dumb-ass Christian world goes off on this spending spree while the Jew merchants sit back on Christmas day, doing whatever it is they do that day . . . and howl with glee and count their shekels. Another prosperous year . . . thanks to those stupid goim. 'Sadie, pack the bags! We're going to the Catskills again! Oy-veh !'

  'I . . . stupid goy that I am . . . couldn't even buy Gloria and Michael presents this year. Imagine! Not enough money to buy your own kids a Christmas present! Thanks a lot, God! Just a card to them all with a wholly inadequate note wishing he could have been there . . . and all. He could telephone them . . . in the morning . . . but the pain would be too much for him. It would be too awkward explaining. He knew he would break down on the phone—

  —Two light raps sounded at the door.

  Startled, Stephen glanced at the clock. Twelve thirty a.m. He swung off the bed and took the step over to the door to open it . . . without his usual precaution of leaving the chain latched. It was Eve.

  "Called you . . . no answer. Decided to drive by . . . saw your light on and figured you needed some company on Christmas eve —'Christmas' . . . 'Eve.' Get it?"

  He smiled and ushered her in.

"God, I needed to get away! Had about a whole six-pack to try to blot out a terrible evening. Lover boy decided yesterday to go visit his wife and kids. OK. So, I can't fault him on that, not at Christmas. Then, Lissa invited some girl friends over to sit with the baby . . . on his first Christmas. And . . . you got it . . . they called their creeps over . . . and somebody lit up a weed. Then I suspected more . . . and I wanted outta there!" She stopped, sniffed the air and exclaimed, "What's that smell? That's . . . that's gunpowder. What the hell? What have you been up to? You got a gun?" And, she looked around.

Stephen picked the coat up and took the pistol out of the pocket. Of course, it smelled like it had been fired.

Eve grabbed his hand and took the pistol from him.

"Watch! There's a round in the chamber! I forgot to unload it."

Eve popped the little magazine out of the palm grip and flipped the slide back, sending the bullet in an arc onto the floor. "Christ, Steve! You try to shoot yourself?" She picked the bullet up and deftly reinserted it into the magazine.

"Got some bad news this morning. Dave called. They're not hiring me . . . God told them Stephen Trevelyan is not the man for the job. Can you imagine? Shades of Faith again . . . So? . . . I just sort of tried to end the whole damned thing . . . didn't have the guts, when I got right down to it!"

Eve deposited the gun and clip on the TV set and picked up the paper bag she had set on the floor when she came in. "Then . . . all the better that I brought this . . . some Christmas cheer. I think we could both use some of this . . . " she said taking two bottles of champagne out of the bag, one with a big, bright red Christmas bow stuck to the neck. "Chilled and ready. Cheap brand . . . but, what th' hell! After six beers, who cares?"

"Merry Christmas," she lisped slightly, handing him the one with the bow and opening the refrigerator to put the other inside. "Go ahead, don't wait for New Year's. Break it out!" she commanded, reaching into the small cabinet for two suitable—clean, at least—glasses. "Some fancy living, huh? No champagne glasses . . . not even wine glasses. So, these dime store, low class motel ones will have to do."

She held them out as Stephen poured. Lifting hers aloft, she proposed a toast, "Here's to us . . . good people are scarce!"

"I'll drink to that!"

After a few healthy swigs by each of them, Stephen, surveying the awkward situation of only having a semi-stuffed chair and the single bed, motioned with a broad sweep of his hand, first to one , then to the other. "Guest's choice. I'm a bit grungy. Gimme five to hop in the shower and we'll finish this elixir of good cheer."

The hot shower felt good but he didn't want to linger too long, lest it ruin the slight and pleasant buzz the champagne had given him. Sure didn't take much alcohol for him to feel it anymore. *Four years without —yep, you do build up a tolerance when drinking—and, lose it when you stop.*

After toweling off he slipped into a loose sweat shirt and jogging pants and slippers. He gave his face a quick going over with the electric razor. Well, I guess spending Christmas eve with Eve is better than nothing, he thought as he opened the door to the room.

The sight that he encountered stopped him in his tracks. There . . . just three steps from him directly opposite the bathroom door was the bed and on it was Eve . . . stark naked . . . hind quarters up in the air over her slightly spread knees, feet toward him, her shoulders down on the bed, her ample breasts showing between her knees . . . her head covered by her hair which was down and long and hiding it. There she was, bare-ass naked, butt up ready to be humped from behind . . . with the bright red ribbon from the champagne bottle stuck right over her anus. "A special Christmas present just for you," came Eve's muffled voice from the pillow.

Stephen roared with laughter! "How did you know to give me just what I wanted?"

He lost no time untying the string on his warmups and letting them drop to the floor. As he did so he stepped out of them and reached over and clasped her nude behind and pulled it to him. He didn't enter but began stroking her sides and reaching for her breasts. She started to turn and he grabbed the bow off of her buttocks. "I will keep this souvenir forever!"

Eve rolled over, brushing aside his firm erection and presenting a quite well developed and alluring body to him . . . as he had expected she would look. "I'm on the pill, so don't worry."

"I've had a vasectomy, So, don't you worry."

Stephen reached for some more champagne and filled their glasses. As he stood by the edge of the bed, his virility at peak, Eve's hand firmly grasped it and, holding her full glass of champagne directly under it, guided his penis into the bubbly liquid. The sensation was immensely pleasurable. Then, she withdrew the glass, bent forward and put the dripping flesh into her mouth . . . *oohing* and *aahing* as she sucked and licked and otherwise eliminated all vestiges of the champagne. Not wanting to take that startling exercise too far too rapidly, she then gently grabbed one of his love handles with her free hand and drew him over onto her . . . still managing not to spill much out of the glass. When he was comfortable in place astride her . . . between her upright knees but not in her yet, she gently dribbled the champagne over her breasts and down her tummy. He pulled up a little so she could continue down to her crotch.

"Now. Your turn."

Stephen bent down and kissed her on the lips . . . which developed into a vigorous contest of tongues. Then he kissed her neck and cheeks and ears and, adjusting his body, worked his way down to her breasts, lapping tantalizingly like a kitten. She purred responsively. After thoroughly pursuing every vestige of the bubbly liquid from these areas, his tongue traced its way down to her navel and beyond. Her hips were heaving now and he found it somewhat difficult to find her clitoris with his tongue. She was writhing now and he hadn't even entered her. It was an ecstasy he had not experienced for a long, long time. They moved harmoniously together when he entered . . . not in and out, but with an undulating, fluid motion that he could feel was putting just the right pressure on her *mons venus*. Her gyrations became more intense, the motions more rapid, and, suddenly, they both hit that supreme moment of delight at the same moment. Eve uttered uncontrollable gasps and little cries of delight; Stephen emitted similar ecstatic shudders. As it subsided, they both embraced and buried their heads in each other's shoulders. After a lengthy and pleasurable interlude of quiet rest, Eve whispered, "You ain't so bad, fella."

"You ain't so bad, yourself. Thanks for the present. This is the best Christmas I think I ever had."

They lay side by side as the TV tube carried on with its incessant nonsense. Stephen opened the second bottle and by two . . . two-thirty . . . who cares what time it was? . . . they were both very tipsy. Stephen had caught up to Eve's state by mere fact of lack of practice.

Eve stroked him ever so gently all the while until he was erect again. Pouring some champagne right out of the glass over his penis, she went down on him. It was mutually delirious. He swung her backside over his chest and massaged her vulva, now and again pulling her toward his mouth. His erection lasted and lasted. He felt no urge to ejaculate.

It was incredible! The sensation was there—he must have developed a Priapus complex!

Eve found it even more delightful and used him—used it—in a score of highly imaginative ways. Some, even Stephen had never envisioned. It was a most refreshing and delicious romp. A catharsis for both of them. The release of pent-up hang-ups and tensions that had gnawed for far too long.

"So much for the favored 'missionary' position," Stephen could not resist remarking.

"Listen, don't you believe it. Those missionaries tried a thing or two despite their cover-ups. They were probably horny as hell—especially if the wives were prim and proper—or Baptists !"

"Thank God the charismatics believe in good sex. Although—forgive me for bringing her up—but Faith preaches against oral sex."

"Tell me about it! She had the gall to confront me one time and flat-out asked me if I engaged in oral sex. I didn't answer her, of course . . . which she took for an admission of guilt . . . and lectured me on God's insistence on wholesome sex. No oral. Where does He say that, I asked her? She just went on condemning and admonishing and I just tuned out."

"What about Oral Roberts?" Stephen tipsily quizzed, gulping the last of his champagne.

After Eve left, which was as the sun was rising, Stephen allowed a thought to come forth that he had sublimated during the incredible encounter with Eve. *He had committed adultery. Technically, the divorce he'd filed against Faith was still in the works. Technically, he was still married to her. Therefore, technically, he had committed adultery. He knew she would not have done such a thing. His train of thought took him to the fact that if Faith were to find out, then the tables would turn. She would lose no time in suing him for divorce on grounds of infidelity—and put him through the wringer. She could defeat his grounds of 'desertion' by finding him and moving back in, although his attorney had told him he could bar her from doing that. But, he knew what Faith was capable of once she got something in her craw—or, worse, when God spoke to her! He'd have to discuss this with Eve.*

"All right, Jesus, You forgave the woman caught in adultery that others were stoning, and commanded her 'to go and sin no more.' OK, Jesus, forgive me for my adultery with Eve. I will go and sin no more. I stand on my faith that You heard me and it is so. I am forgiven. Amen." *Who am I kidding? God doesn't give a shit about me . . . or I wouldn't be in the mess I am right now. Screw it! Why should I be restricted by something vague, an abstract idea that has obviously no bearing on reality?*

He spent the day trying to keep his mind on finding a solution to his problems . . . his utter catastrophic predicament . . . only to have multiple images of Eve and the previous night constantly erase them.

An idea formed in Stephen's mind. It had nothing to do with his situation but it took shape and finally prompted him to telephone Eve.

"Hi. This is Steve . . . or what's left of him . . . "

"Come on . . . you didn't strike me as so out of shape."

"Well . . . I forgot to wish you a Merry Christmas. So, 'Merry Christmas.' And, thanks so much for the present . . . I couldn't have appreciated anything more."

"My pleasure," she chuckled.

"Now . . . I would like to reciprocate . . . in the only way I know how . . . I want to take you out on New Year's Eve . . . dinner . . . dancing . . . the whole works . . . and you must spend the night with me . . . that's part of my present. I don't care if you already have plans or not—break 'em. I'm going to make this a special evening for you . . .

Oh, one more thing . . . you've got to promise not to see Jerry until afterward . . . that's got to be part of the deal. How about it?"

"Well . . . sure . . . that sounds good to me. Jerry hasn't asked me out or anything . . . but, why not see him?"

"I'll explain when I see you. That's part of the deal. Promise?"

"OK. Promise."

"Now, this is going to be fancy. Dress up your prettiest . . . not a long dress—I don't have a tux—but as close to that kind of dressing up as you can get. This is going to be an elegant dinner and dancing . . . and then afterwards . . . my place. That's got to be the whole deal. So, prepare an overnight bag or something, and a change of clothes for the next day. OK?"

" . . . I guess so . . . "

"No guessing. Promise?"

"Promise."

"Now, I won't see you until New Year's eve . . . but be ready right after noon. Bring your dress-up stuff along. I'll pick you up about one o'clock. You're off then, aren't you?"

"Yes, we have a half a day off. This sounds kind of mysterious to me . . . just what am I getting myself into?"

"Hah! You'll see . . . and you're going to be most pleasantly surprised! I guarantee you that!"

Extracting a promise once more not to see Jerry, he hung up and began to formulate his plan and go over his finances. It was the loneliest Christmas he had ever spent in his life and, since nothing much was open . . . just some eating places . . . he just walked around the beach area looking in shop windows and sitting on the cold waterfront on a bench gazing lost in thought out over the uninviting water. One thing came to mind that he would have to take care of the first thing the next day.

Chapter 23   Surprise!

Getting up early, dressing and breakfasting quickly, he set out in the van up the freeway toward Norfolk then took the turn north that would take him across the river over into Hampton. Getting off I-64, he picked up U.S.17, went past Yorktown, then turned east on Route 3 and hugged the coast, veering onto Route 200 until it dead-ended. Driving around the area along the coast of the Chesapeake for upwards of an hour, he at last came upon what he was searching for.

Satisfied that it was, indeed, satisfactory, he made a deal, signed a paper and drove back toward Norfolk.

Along the way he spotted a Home-Builder type discount place, went in and purchased a large can of gold spray paint and a paint scraper that held razor blades. He then drove around the back of the Home-Builder center . . . where the wood line and the trash dumpsters were. *The time has come*, he told himself, *to make a change*. Getting out his small tool box, he took out a screwdriver and a pair of pliers. Going to the rear of the van, he unlocked the small padlock on the rear tire cover which was mounted externally on the left rear door, unscrewed a bolt and removed the cover. Shaking the paint can as he carried it over to the woods, he reached the base of a tree and leaned against it the large round cover with the elegant lettering, 'Living Water Ministry . . . If any man is thirsty, let him come to Me and drink. John 7:37.' Vigorously shaking the can again, he removed the cap and began a back and forth motion spraying the lettering lightly. In a short time he had completely obliterated them and the gold had blended imperceptibly into the gold-beige of the original paint job. He let that set to dry for a while and went back and picked up the scraper. He then carefully scraped under the stick-on lettering of the ministry names that were on both of the rearmost side windows. Having removed all traces of ministry identification, he replaced the tire cover and drove back to Virginia Beach.

The week went slowly and uneventfully. On Saturday, he pulled himself together, put on his best face and took advantage of the men's breakfast at the church . . . where he could have a hearty breakfast for a buck . . . which would last him till supper. He would have to take advantage of all these little corner-cutters in order to save what little resources he had left. The unemployment compensation would run out in just three weeks . . . and then there would be nothing! A big, fat zero. Then, it would be over for real. Besides, he was supposed to report to the unemployment comp office the number of job interviews he had sought each week . . . when and where. He explained a couple of time that things were cooking at CBN and, anyway, the type of high level job he was looking for . . . you just couldn't go in for an interview every week. That had satisfied them . . . since, he figured, they had no experience dealing with anything but hourly and low-salaried workers.

New Year's eve finally rolled around and the night before Stephen telephoned Eve to confirm the arrangements. She got off at noon and it would take close to a half hour for her to get home and dress. He told her to come as she was from work, bring her party stuff and something for the next day in a hanger bag.   He'd pick her up at twelve thirty.

He was there on the dot, and as she got in she remarked, "What'd you do? Give up the ministry?"

"In a big way! Didn't need all that baggage to carry around . . . especially with the way the Lord has been treating me lately.   I'm not going to ask you how things are going at CBN . . . cause I don't give a damn . . . and I want this to begin the most pleasant time you will have had in a long time . . . at least, I trust it will. So, no shop talk."

"Where are we going? This isn't the way to the beach."

"You just watch the scenery . . . sit back and enjoy . . . don't think about anything . . . except how much you are going to enjoy being away from everything . . . and living in a little fantasy world for a couple of days."   He then switched on the classical radio station and undergirded the experience with the soothing strains of a Chopin piano concerto.

Eve rested her head back on the seat and closed her eyes. "I like it already.   Where we headed?"

"Secret . . . but I assure you I am not taking you across the state line . . . for immoral purposes. I want to keep you an honest woman."

"Sure . . . like protecting my virginity."

Fortunately the day turned out bright and sunny and pleasantly warm. Having just beaten the usual traffic tie-up at the tunnel, they sped up the route Stephen had taken earlier in the week.   The countryside was charming . . . with the glistening glimpses of water every now and then and as they crossed little bridges. Eve's curiosity was fully piqued. "Will you tell me where we are going?"

"Keep your pants—panties—on. You'll see in a moment."

In a few moments, he turned the van in to the parking area of an elegant new three story motel-marina-yacht club on the water's edge and parked near the front entrance. "Now . . . Mrs. Trevelyan . . . and don't forget the 'Mrs.' part . . . we are here at our little 'honeymoon hideaway' . . . at least for the evening and tomorrow morning. I won't carry you across the threshold . . . just yet."

Stephen checked them in as Eve waited discreetly in mid lobby. He used his Merrill Lynch debit card. Picking up his and her hanger bags, he led her to the elevator and to their room at the end of the hall on the top floor . . . overlooking the water. The room was large and tastefully furnished and had a walk-out balcony on the other side of the enormous sliding glass doors. He hung the bags up and opened the glass doors. They stepped out and beheld the view. They could see far across the bay . . . over to Tangier island, which he pointed out. The air was invigorating.

Eve threw her head back and inhaled deeply. "Marvelous! I just love it."

"Now I suggest you freshen up, then we'll go down on the dock . . . out to the end there . . . and sit at that bar and have ourselves a nice quiet afternoon drink and watch the sun go down. Then, come back up here . . . take ourselves a nice little nap . . . before bathing and dressing for dinner. Dinner isn't until eight. Plenty of time to relax . . . and do all sorts of things."

Eve nuzzled him affectionately. "This has all the marks of a very nice present."

Stephen was very attentive, opening doors for her, holding her hand, affording her every courtesy a gentleman could think of. He held her chair as they seated themselves in the enclosed cocktail lounge out at the end of the dock, all decorated with ship's bells, hawsers, lanterns, anchors and other nautical accoutrements. It was a thoroughly charming ambience. They had beers. Stephen knew anything harder for him and he might not make it to dinner, so he was very careful. As they drank and made small talk, they watched the boats come and go . . . and the setting sun behind them cast its golden glow on the clouds in the sky far across the bay. Eve seemed younger, relaxed, content, which was his whole point. He had only seen her before at CBN escorting him around . . . or fussing around preparing Thanksgiving dinner . . . or in the semi-darkness of his room. Here, in this setting, she was strikingly attractive . . . and it gave him a very nice feeling inside. He would make sure the rest of their time together was as nice as this. This was his present: to treat her like a lady . . . a queen, to do his best to give her a fairy-tale evening that would not be spectacular . . . but, if he were any judge of character at all, would be one she would cherish always.

He complimented her . . . as these observations flowed from him . . . on how pretty she looked . . . and how pleasant it was to be here with her. They explored a range of conversational topics, Stephen purposely steering away from anything remotely connected with CBN, Faith or anything that would rob either of them of these precious few moments of escape from reality. Stephen asked her what she really wanted from life . . .

. . . and she couldn't answer right off. "I suppose . . . when you get right down to it . . . a good life . . . to find someone I really love . . . and who really loves me. I mean love, not just sex. You know, I've led such a rough life . . . had Alyssa out of wedlock when I was seventeen . . . and she's gone off and done the same thing. I guess it runs in the family. You know we . . . you and I . . . hardly come from the same back—"

—"Tut tut, don't talk like that. I am looking at you as a person . . . a deep and tender person . . . who has been wounded . . . not what your background might have been. It's what you are now . . . and that impresses me. You have pulled yourself through a lot of hard times. That takes an extraordinary person. I don't know many who could have pulled through like you have. So, give yourself a compliment. You deserve it. And, I like to be with someone like you . . . I like being with you !"

"That's mutual. I have to admit, I have never had anyone talk to me like you have. You are educated . . . refined . . . genuine—you didn't make a pass at me when we first met— in fact, I was the one who made the pass at you!" She laughed. "I hope you won't hold it against me."

"Not until we get back up to the room!"

She caught it and puckered her lips at him in a mock kiss. "No. All I've got is that loser, Jerry . . . who treats me like dirt sometimes . . . "

"Ah, ah. We aren't going to talk about things like that . . . I have hereby established a 'problem-free' zone around us. This is all pleasure time . . . no ties with reality. Tell you what, let's always refer to this as our 'problem-free zone' . . . code name: PFZ. Anytime you want to get away from it all, look at me—or call—and say, 'PFZ.' Deal?" He put his hand gently on hers as he said this and a twinge of excitement ran through him. He wondered if it had had the same effect on her.

As five o'clock passed and they had finished two beers each, he suggested it was time to go up to the room. Casually strolling up the dock, Stephen put his arm around her waist, as he was used to doing with Faith . . . and Eve did the same. There was evident bonding taking place.

When they got to the room, Eve stepped into the dressing alcove next to the bathroom door and removed her clothes. Stephen, gazing out of the glass doors, turned and watched her with great appreciation. Stepping into the bathroom briefly, she emerged and lay down on the bed. "Want to take a nap?"

"Come to think of it, I have never felt sleepier." And he followed her example, undressing and lying next to her. "Wake me when it's time to go home."

"Ho, ho ho! See how far you get with that one!" she chortled, turning on her side with her back to him, nudging her backside into him as an overt signal for him to turn and cuddle . . . both locked in coupled fetal positions. Her warm body felt marvelous against his . . . and the faint fragrance of her femininity . . . not to mention the proximity of his organ to her receptacle . . . led to an erotic embrace. They remained locked thusly until they dozed off to a sweet bliss that lasted until the darkness overtaking the room gently awakened them.

Rolling her gently onto her back, Stephen began a series of soft caresses with his hands . . . ever so lightly . . . up and down her body . . . lingering periodically on her breasts and titillating her nipples. She complimented his actions by her own, stroking him gently and titillating his nipples as well. When the moment seemed ripe, he entered her and there ensued a long, gentle rhythmic interlude which prolonged the inevitable to the point of uncontrollable eruption. Exhausted and thoroughly satisfied, they lay in each others arms, savoring the moment. She kissed him on the ear lobe. "You are some lover, Mr. Trevelyan."

After a while Stephen got up and went to the small refrigerator and withdrew two small bottles of champagne—'Splits'. Popping them open, he poured the bubbly contents into two proper glasses that were set out for that purpose. Eve propped herself up on the pillows and he handed her a glass, while he sat on the edge of the bed and sipped his. He dribbled a little over her tummy playfully and bent down to lick it up, causing her to giggle. When they had finished, he bent over and kissed her passionately. Then, disengaging reluctantly, he announced, "Shower time! I'll run the water . . . you come right with me."

She did as told and they embraced long and hard under the cascade of hot water, wriggling ever so slightly, arousing each other to potentially another round of love-making. Stephen put a halt to it, lest there be nothing for later. She chided him and said, "Chicken."

They entered the dinning room and the Mâitre d'Hotel escorted them to the table which he had carefully arranged for beforehand. It was by the window, overlooking the water, upon which the reflections of the lights of the dock were rippling in hypnotic cadence. The room was lit only by the huge chandeliers, three of them, and the individual small shaded lamps on each table. There was a big streamer with the words, "Happy New Year" on it strung across the ceiling, and each table setting had a paper hat and a paper horn for use later. Of course, many people donned the hats immediately, which helped to shed inhibitions they might have been harboring. Low background music wafted through the sound system, which added to the feeling of elegance. The clientele was nicely dressed, some ladies in evening dresses and men in tuxedos. A good crowd . . . a cut above what one might expect at a public place for New Year's. Again, Stephen's instincts had proven right . . . he had made a good choice. And Eve was thoroughly enjoying it. Since neither one of them was used to drinking hard liquor..and he certainly didn't want this evening to be spoiled with too much alcohol . . . Stephen suggested they each have a frozen daiquiri . . . then either red or white wine with dinner . . . and, of course, champagne would be 'on the house' at the bewitching hour. He figured all the physical activity of dancing, too, would dissipate any untoward buildup of alcoholic effects.

Their drinks came and they stretched them out until their dinner was served, savoring every moment. Eve often looked at him . . . right into his eyes . . . then turned away self consciously, smiling to herself. He felt her companionship was so pleasant that he took her hand as he had before and told her so. This time, he held it and stroked the top of it with his other hand . . . then, lifting it a little, bent toward it and kissed it tenderly. Eve blushed and smiled in appreciation.

Eve had seafood and he had roast beef, with corresponding white and red wines. Everything was delicious. Toward the end, before the desert was served, the small orchestra set up and began to play good old dance tunes of the Big Band era.

They danced, Stephen holding her close and guiding her through steps with which she was not all that familiar. . .fox trot . . . the things he had learned at Miss Brim's dancing school when he was in the seventh grade. She had a natural grace, though, and caught on quickly, for which he complimented her and nibbled her ear once or twice while giving her meaningfully gentle squeezes and rubbings with his hand on her back.

As the evening progressed, the music got livelier and they picked up the tempo in their dancing, improvising and stumbling occasionally . . . not falling . . . but recovering amid gushes of mirth. In all the evening was a total delight.

Just before midnight, the waiters and waitresses flurried about the room filling glasses with champagne, then leaving the bottles and their remains on the tables. Everybody was anticipating the stroke of midnight. The countdown began with the whole room counting in unison as the drummer struck the tick-off . . . then, the fanfare, the whistle tootings, the yells and shouts, the shrieks and laughter.

Stephen had positioned his chair next to Eve's and when the moment came, reached over and kissed her long and hard. As the strains of Auld Lang Syne started up from the orchestra, Stephen took her hand and led her to the dance floor. There they locked in an embrace and swayed to the music as the lights had dimmed and the horn-blowing and confetti-throwing continued. They stayed that way through the end of the number and a bit afterward as the band began to wrap it up. The floor was still crowded with people in similar stances.   As they approached their table, a raucous 'HAP-pee NOO Ye-ar!' behind them, startled them, and a very middle aged bald-headed man, obviously in his cups, grabbed Eve and laid a big kiss on her . . . just missing her mouth, which she turned when she sensed it coming.   Stephen instinctively grabbed the man's sleeve, pulling him back, "Right, fella.   Happy New Year . . . yourself!" At which point the fella's wife . . . or lady friend . . . grabbed his other sleeve and with a frown on her face, led him off. "That was a close one!" murmured Stephen.

They did not go back up to the room but strolled along the water's edge, on the lighted walkway along the bulkhead.   The night air was crisp and the stars were out in sparkling brilliance.   Stephen wrapped his coat around her.

"Just lovely, Stephen.   I've loved this evening so much.   I can't think of a present I have ever enjoyed as much.   You are so sweet.   You know, I think both your first wife and Faith are crazy to let you go . . . I wouldn't! . . . have let you go."

"You're just taken by the charm of the evening and by our little 'honey moon' . . . and that's the way I intended for it to be.   You deserve to be treated this way.   You are a lovely person . . . a lady . . . and I am attracted to you . . . I feel affection for you . . . I love you in a way that is not . . . exactly in love with you . . . but I love you.   I can't make love to you . . . without loving you.   It's not in my makeup just to have casual affairs . . . I really have never had any.   And, I can't just make love to you . . . know you intimately . . . and say, thank you, M'am.   You gave me something of yourself, and I gave you something of myself . . . there was love involved in that, not just carnal pleasure—although I'll say that was great, too! But, now that I have tasted you, taken a part of you, I care about you . . . care about what happens to you.   I can't just turn my back and walk off . . . I don't know what I'm going to do . . . because I know this can't last. I'm at rock bottom . . . I am down to nothing . . . but I don't want to drag this in that direction . . . let it suffice . . . I like you, I am fond of you, I care about you . . . and I want to make life pleasant for you . . . for both of us . . . as best I can . . . while I can."

She hugged him tighter. "I love you, too . . . the same way. That is the greatest thrill to me simply that you care for me. I've never had anyone tell me that before. And, the guys that have told me they loved me . . . they all had pricks for brains. No, Steve, you are the first man . . . .gentleman . . . decent and honorable . . . person I have ever known. You have treated me in a way I had only dreamed about. You have restored my dignity. I love you, too, Steve, and I care what happens to you. And, whatever . . . I will never forget you."

The chill of the night air forced them to go back up to the room.

Eve clung to him . . . and he to her . . . for most of the night. Their slumber was tranquil and in unison. Occasionally, she snuggled, not waking, adjusting herself, shifting in whatever dream state she had lapsed into. Several times Stephen awoke and didn't move . . . opening his eyes only enough to see the silhouette of her profile in the ambient light from the window. He watched her shallow breathing . . . and thought how lovely she was . . . she was a thing of beauty that God had made . . . and that ought to be cherished. He felt an attachment to her unlike any he had ever felt for Diana or Faith. This was purer somehow . . . not in the sexual sense, of course, but in his feeling for this lovely human being. He knew that he had made a brief moment in her life just a tiny bit better . . . and that was all he had intended.

When the light of dawn streamed through the glass doors and awakened Stephen, he opened his eyes and found Eve leaning against her two pillows with one hand under her chin, gazing intently at him. "You were sleeping so peacefully . . . just like a little boy. You were so cute."

"And you, my dear, were sleeping like a little kitten yourself . . . as I observed several times during the night."

"Steve . . . It was so wonderful . . . last night. That was the best idea you had. Let's not let it end just yet. Make love to me . . . and then let's stay in bed all morning . . . till checkout time."

Stephen accommodated her with all the tenderness he could command and their copulatory embrace melded their flesh as one, protracting the ecstasy and carrying it to heights neither had experienced before. It was both exhilarating . . . and exhausting. When it subsided . . . they lay in an afterglow of another dimension. "Stephen," she whispered, "I do love you . . . in my special way."

"And I, you, Eve."

After showering, they ate the breakfast he had ordered in bed. It was most pleasurable.

"We're getting just like an old married couple, aren't we?" observed Stephen.

"You think married people get as comfortable as we are?"

"I know it wasn't quite like this in either of mine. I don't know . . . maybe this is how it is supposed to be . . . but . . . marriage is one thing I cannot be thinking about right at this time in my life . . . not until some things get sifted out. You know, I wonder if I will ever marry again? Two haven't worked out . . . why would I think a third wouldn't be a strikeout too?"

"You never know. Time will tell . . . and time heals all wounds . . . as the Bible or something said."

They lay together propped up on the pillows . . . her head resting against his shoulder . . . nude. The morning sun was streaming at a shallow angle through the doors and fell across their bodies illuminating them brighter than their surroundings and penetrating their skin with its warmth. It felt so good to lie like that. There was nothing to say . . . to be said . . . they simply languished in the beauty of it all. Some time after the suns rays had travelled to higher angles and the roof blocked them, Eve stirred and turned toward him. Without a word to break the spell, she held his face in her hands, looked at it and into his eyes long and hard . . . then kissed his mouth fervently as if it might be for the last time. Then, she kissed his neck and ears . . . and chest and shoulders . . . his stomach and navel . . . and his now erect symbol of manhood. Stephen lay perfectly still, letting her get her fill. She went down his legs as well . . . then, kneeling upright, she tossed her left leg over him and sat on him, inserting his penis deep inside her as she did. Bending forward prone on his body, she rested her head on his chest just under his chin. She lay for a long time without moving . . . then began an almost imperceptible undulating circular motion as Stephen gently fumbled to find her nipples. As he did and her response intensified her motions . . . he placed his hands on her buttocks and assisted. Soon, the intensity reached a level of thrashing and writhing until it exploded in simultaneous convulsions of orgasmic pleasure. They lingered coupled thusly for as long as they could before facing the reality that their time was running out. Their golden coach was going to turn back into a pumpkin at mid-day.

Reluctantly they showered together, caressing and kissing in the spray . . . desiring to take each moment up to the hilt.

On the drive back they were quiet. Each hated for it to end. Stephen dreaded going back into that tiny room; Eve dreaded the debacle she surely faced at home. God knows what those kids might have done.

"Why didn't you want me to see Jerry?" she broke the silence.

"Because, I was planning for this to work out exactly like it did . . . and, frankly, I don't like the idea of sharing you . . . especially with someone like Jerry. Do you love him?"

"Not really. He's just my boyfriend . . . I guess I am fond of him. Or, he's just the only thing I got going! Lose him, and what have I got?"

"Well . . . to be brutally frank, if you and I continue . . . feel like continuing this affair we are having . . . you are going to have to make a decision about the two of us. I simply will not share you with him—do you know whether he's seeing other women?"

"I wouldn't put it past him . . . "

"Well, that's reason enough there. He looks to me like the type who would shack up with anybody . . . and where does that put you? Suppose he picked up something . . . some disease . . . and passed it on to you? And, you passed it on to me. You know for sure that I am not fooling around . . . and that is safe for both of us. If we can't keep it this way . . . we won't be able to keep it."

"What are you going to do . . . now that CBN is down the drain?"

"That, my dear, is the big question. Fortunately, this soirée of ours has taken my mind off of it . . . but, I guarantee you it will hit me hard once I get back into that stinking little cubby hole at the motel. And, to tell you the truth . . . after I pay January's rent . . . that's it. My unemployment compensation ends the fifteenth. Then, its all over. Money gone . . . I'm out in the street.."

Eve was quiet for a long time, then she said matter-of-factly, "You want to move in with me?"

". . .You mean it? How would we work that?"

"I've got four bedrooms. Tiny, though. I've got mine; Lissa, hers, and the baby, next to Lissa. I could rent you one . . . just between us . . . pay me what you can when you can . . . to make it legal."

"You think that would work? I mean, my being so close to you? . . . under the same roof?"

"Well . . . you would have your own bedroom . . . but you could find your way over to mine, if you wanted to."

"Would you give up Jerry."

"Yes."

"What about Lissa? And, the baby?"

"Lissa won't give a damn . . . she has a boyfriend over most of the time . . . most of the time she's not shacking up somewhere else . . . and the baby, she won't mind." Eve added with a smile.

"So . . . we'd be setting up house . . . baby and all. I never would have believed it!   Whoa! What about CBN?"

"What about CBN?   I only know one or two people who would ever come by . . . or who know where I live. My little circle of friends . . . such as it is . . . isn't included in the CBN clique. And, I doubt Dave King would find out—and if so, so what? You're not there, are you? Anybody ask—not that it's anybody's business—but you are a boarder . . . paying to rent a room. Nothing wrong with that . . . happens all the time."

"Hmmm. That IS a possibility. That would keep me going for a while . . . until I decided just what I could do . . . or am going to do in this world.   But, then, when and if I should leave . . . and we have developed an attachment? Then what?"

"We take it as it comes . . . in the meantime, enjoy!"

When they got to her house, she invited him in to look at the room. Neither Lissa or the baby was there. The house was a pig sty, especially the upstairs. "See what my going away for two days does? I make no apologies . . . this is the way it is most of the time. I would be so happy if that child would just find a life somewhere and take that poor child with her . . . like I had to do."

Stephen held Eve in his arms in a long embrace, capping it off with a tender and passionate kiss. They were reluctant to disengage. He promised to see her at least every other day, one way or another. She invited him over for supper two days hence. While he desired to be with her, he also wanted to make darned sure she had no further contact with Jerry.

He psyched himself to return to the motel.

Chapter 24   A Family Affair

It seemed strange to both of them: lying in her bed . . . in her bedroom . . . in her house . . . which she told him really belonged to Jerry. He was renting it to her at a very reasonable rate.   He'd built a lot of houses . . . sold most of them . . . except a few, like this one. Since he had a small mortgage on it, he had done her a favor and let her rent it for just what it cost him . . . not much more than she would have to pay for a good apartment anywhere. And, it was in a new subdivision, so it made it nice and she didn't have to worry too much about crime and drugs— and noise, although there were a few motorcycles and beefed up pickups shattering the peace every now and then.

So, Stephen thought, there is still a binding thread leading back to Jerry. Although he was unaware of it, he virtually had them at his mercy . . . if he wanted to get ugly about it. He could just take the house back. "Maybe it would be a good idea if you didn't tell Jerry that I have moved in."

"I don't intend to. The only way he'd find out is to drive by all the time and wonder what your van was doing here . . . or decide to pop over one day. We'll just face that when it comes."

"What's your routine in the morning? Get up . . . leave for CBN?"

"I have to be in my car . . . driving away at eight. So, I get up at seven. That gives me plenty of time. Quick bite."

"How about Lissa and the baby?"

"Lord, they get up anywhere from five on. It's a little easier now that she's not breast feeding . . . just pops a bottle in the kid's mouth and she's back in the rack . . . until Tootsie cries to be changed . . . poor thing. But? It's her mess. Lissa made it . . . she's got to lie in it. I did the same thing, but I think I had a little more sense . . . no, there just weren't drugs then. We just boozed it up. I thought I was in love with this guy . . . we were seniors in high school. I got knocked up . . . he lost interest . . . I didn't graduate . . . and so— Alyssa! That's just too damn young for motherhood. Of course, the thought never crosses your dumb little airhead until it happens . . . and back in those days the pill wasn't something teenagers thought about . . . and abortions were too risky. She could have had one but I guess, somehow, she must have really wanted the baby. She isn't even sure who the father is—little slut! Wow! Listen to me—look who's talking!"

"Whoa, now. None of that. Our relationship is different. It just happened . . . and, remember, it is a commitment . . . that's a hell of a lot different."

"Thanks, Steve . . . keep reminding me."

"Listen, I'm here . . . and I'll be here for you . . . and with you . . . and whenever you need me." He gently kissed her good night and rolled back on his side of the bed. "I'm all yours . . . whenever you want me . . . but I'll leave it up to you. I won't press it. Good night, my dear, sweet bedmate . . . Eve."

The morning routine was obviously going to have to be worked out. There was a bit of rushing and bumping into one another. Stephen shrank back letting Eve do her thing, then when she went downstairs to put the coffee on, he hopped in the shower.

Lissa was feeding Tootsie and Eve was finishing her toast and coffee, all watching one of the morning shows when Stephen appeared.

"And, a good, good morning, one and all." Spotting the cup set out for him, he filled it with coffee and sat down next to Eve. "I'll be out most of the day . . . a lot of things to tie up. Oh, gotta call my brother right away and give him your phone number. He'll be my only contact with the other world . . . in case of emergency, that sort of thing. I'll give you his number, too. What time do you get back from the office?"

"Around five-thirty . . . but I'll have to do some shopping . . . groceries . . . so I may be a little late . . . probably six thirty . . . seven."

"Anything I can get for you while I'm out?"

"Don't think so." She got up. "Gotta go. Bye." She bent over and kissed him on the lips and left.

Lissa gave him a curious stare and resumed feeding the baby.

Stephen went to the hall phone and dialed Tom. After the perfunctory inquiries about the holidays, he told him of his situation . . . of having lost out at CBN and was now going to look into advertising or something around the area. When he gave him the telephone number, he stressed that he was not to give the number out, especially to Faith is she should call. If anything was important, please just take a message or the caller's number and then call him and relay it. He told Tom that he had rented a room in a private house . . . and he just could not have calls coming in for him. He told him that he was using the same PO box. Finding out how his dad was, he said he'd keep in touch and hung up.

Grabbing his coat and briefcase, he stuck his head in the kitchen and said good by.

He headed for the public library in downtown Norfolk, which turned out to be a beautiful new contemporary building. It hadn't been open for even a half hour yet when he entered but there was not a seat to be had. All of the lounge chairs in the general reading area were occupied, each by a heavily clad figure, most with a hat of some sort on and a magazine in each lap. Of course, it's like this everywhere one goes nowadays, it's cold outside so the street people come indoors. All the vagrants. No law against it—it's a public place and they are the public and are entitled to come in to this public place. Makes it a little hard, though, for the serious people who want to read or research. The aroma was none too attractive either.

In the reference room, Stephen pulled out the Advertising Register . . . the good old 'Red Book' . . . the one that gives the names of every advertising agency, its officers and senior personnel, and its account list. The ones in New York . . . in the libraries, the agencies themselves, the Yale club . . . and even those who subscribed to it privately . . . were well thumbed. It was the main reference for job-hunting and job-jumping. He thumbed to the regional section . . . in the category of agency's gross billings . . . well, he might as well start with twenty million. That sounded about the ceiling for this market. No, that would mean . . . ten people per million billing . . . that'd be two hundred people. There wouldn't be any agency that size here. Atlanta, maybe.

So he went down by geographical index, found the Norfolk, Hampton, Portsmouth, Virginia Beach area: four listings. Four advertising agencies. Only one had total annual billings of over one million dollars; one point two million. That meant that they placed for all of their clients a total of one million two hundred thousand dollars in various media and they retained the media discount of fifteen per cent as earned commission. The client didn't pay them, the print and broadcast media simply charged the agency less and they pocketed the difference.

So fifteen per cent of a million two is a little over one hundred fifty thousand. Nobody can run a decent agency on that . . . overhead . . . four or five staff and less than fifty thousand for the boss. These small agencies simply can't operate that way. He wished he knew more about small markets. They must be on a fee basis. Charge flat yearly rates and rebate the media discounts back to the clients . . . then tack on .1765 per cent on all production. Maybe they could survive that way . . . but, it is obvious that he was going to be confronted by one- or two-man shops, with very small staffs . . . most of the stuff contracted out on a per-job basis. So, his chances of landing anything would be better, perhaps, as a freelance . . . copywriter . . . radio-television producer . . . marketing analyst . . . account executive . . . bringing in his own account—as if he could come right in and find somebody who needs to advertise and who hasn't been approached as yet. Fat chance!

He then looked up in the broadcast annuals and wrote down all the relevant statistics on the local radio and TV stations, and their facilities . . . whether they did 'production' . . . what their hourly rates were. The same with the print publications and the commercial photo studios. He was highly amused at some of them . . . it sure wasn't New York! All of this also meant that without big bucks, there would not likely be any big markups that he could put on deals that he could package as a freelancer. Well, he'd give it the old college try . . . but his heart really was not in it. He honestly did not want to get back into the secular, commercial world, especially in some half-assed, unsophisticated operation out in podunk ! Even Tulsa had more things going for it.

Nevertheless, considering carefully how to approach this market, which he had also researched as to Metropolitan Statistical Area, demographics, income and other vital statistics, he composed a general 'bait' letter to mail to the ad agencies and a slightly revised one stressing the sales side for the broadcast stations—excluding the religious ones, of course. He doubted that he could land something right off the bat on an executive level. The 'form' letter went something to the effect:

> "Former VP of major New York advertising agency seeking
> to relocate in Tidewater area for personal reasons. Would
> be happy to discuss whether credentials and wide range of
> experience in creative-copy, production, and account handling
> would add to the effectiveness of your agency.
>   Contact at PO Box so-and-so."

Having inquired at the desk about a public stenographer, he located one, had a half a dozen of the letters typed up, envelopes addressed . . . signed them, sealed, stamped, and posted them. Not entirely thrilled with what he thought his efforts would portend, he nevertheless felt a small sense of accomplishment . . . something he had not felt in a long time . . . retrieved the van from the all-day parking lot and headed for his new 'home.'

When he got to the house, Stephen went to his room and stashed his coat and briefcase. He didn't feel quite free as yet to put his things in the downstairs hall closet. That might appear a bit presumptuous—he would wait for an invitation. Freshening up a bit, he went down to the kitchen where he had heard some indications of feeding time at the baby zoo. It was close to five.

"Hi, gang," he greeted as warmly as he could, heading for the refrigerator to see if there were a soft drink.

Lissa finished feeding, wiped the messy little face and got up to rinse the plate and spoon in the sink. She turned and looked at him expressionlessly. "Like . . . you're fuckin' my mama. Wanna fuck me, too?"

Stephen, wheeled, looked at her fiercely. *This was a shocker! He knew he had to win Lissa somehow, but he had figured he would do it gradually . . . over time, as she got to tolerate him and even to know him better. He had visions of acting as surrogate father in a way . . . to help Eve. But, this was totally unexpected— and he couldn't let it go. Firm action was needed, regardless of the consequences.* "Sit down!" Stephen ordered firmly.

Lissa tossed her head back defiantly and continued her chore.

Stepping up to her, Stephen raised his voice and with a look straight into her eyes that he meant business, pointed to the chair she had been sitting in, and sternly ordered again, "SIT DOWN!"

Sullenly, Lissa obeyed, avoiding his glare.

"Let's get something straight right off, young lady! I am living with your mother for a very basic reason—I care for her—I love her. We have both made a commitment. You know what a commitment is?"

No response.

"Well, I'll tell you. It means that your mother and I are pledged to stay with each other . . . to help each other . . . to be a friend and companion to each other . . . to hold and caress . . . and cherish each other. She and I . . . at the moment . . . are all each of us has— each other ! You don't seem to care very much for her . . . Jerry used to come and go . . . how many friends does she really have? Do they come over . . . and give her encouragement? Ever stopped long enough—ever gotten that empty little mind of yours off yourself long enough to think what kind of a life she has? Do you ever stop to think if she's happy? That she likes having to put up with somebody like Jerry . . . and you ! Here you are . . . too young to be a mother . . . living off your mother . . . and giving her crap for thanks! And, ever stop to think just where you would be if you didn't have this house to live in? A roof to keep over that little life that you brought into this world?

Lissa squirmed in her chair and kept her eyes down on the table.

"Well, just look at it this way. I care for your mother . . . and I care that she is happy . . . I want to bring something nice into her life for a change. Wouldn't you like something nice in your life? No, you are not mature enough to want anything but some worthless strung-out junky . . . who's cool . . . and who struts around in his blind ignorance and stupidity, showing off like a young pup. What future do you think some creep like that could offer you ? Just more of the same. Well, let me tell you, young lady, the real world has no place for that kind . . . your kind. What do you expect to do all your life? Just grow up through a haze of dope smoke and watch innocent little Tootsie here make the same mistakes you did?"

Lissa still remained quiet. She mopped Tootsie's chin with her bib and looked at her.

"Now . . . all that said, we can do one of two things. Either you and I can exist in a state of open hostility . . . or, two, we can be friends . . . and live together in some state of harmony. If you are worried . . . don't be. I am not moving in here to squeeze you out." He reached over and put his hand on top of hers. She didn't move it. "If you let me, I can be somewhat of the father figure that is missing around here."

Tootsie began fussing and Lissa stood up, unfastened the tray and lifted the baby up into her arms, and said to her impatiently, "OK, miss nasty . . . change time."

When she took the baby into the powder room to change her, Stephen went into the living room and ensconced himself in the big easy chair in front of the TV set. Using the remote, he searched the channels for the local news. Lissa put Tootsie back in her playpen and turned the tiny black and white set on in the kitchen. Stephen could hear the baby playing, making little noises and throwing something every now and then.

331

Pretty soon it turned into fretting, then whimpering . . . and finally outright crying. "Beddie bye!" he heard Lissa say, picking the squalling child up to take her upstairs.

"Lissa," Stephen called out in a warm, friendly voice. "Let me hold Tootsie for a minute."

Lissa came in with the baby, observing him warily.

"Put the burp diaper on my shoulder . . . and let me cuddle her for a while," he said extending his arms to take her." Placing the infant comfortably on his chest over his heart, he then asked Lissa for a little light blanket to put over her. With that, he gently patted the baby on the back and whispered soothingly to it, until it whimpered, took some deep sighs and settled in sleep. Stephen lowered the sound of the TV to barely audible.

Lissa returned to the kitchen and tidied up, then, after a long interlude, came into the living room and sprawled on the couch. Soon she was asleep like the baby.

It was dark outside when Stephen heard Eve's car drive up . . . and the front door open and close as she entered the living room. He turned his head slightly to smile at her as she took in the scene that she beheld.

"Well, if this isn't a sight of domestic bliss!"

Putting his forefinger to his mouth to indicate not to wake the sleeping babe, he then motioned for her to come to him . . . as he puckered his lips . . .

. . . to which she obliged.

Lissa opened her eyes and Stephen gave her a big wink, motioning with his head to come retrieve Tootsie. She took the child gently from Stephen, rewrapped her and took her up to her crib.

Observing this, Eve said, "Well. I guess you two hit it off . . . to some degree."

"Not without a bit of a wrenching. I'll tell you about it later. Let me help you with dinner. How was your day?"

Later, as they lay in bed, Eve said, "Lissa asked me before we came to bed what kind of weirdo did I bring into the house? She had never seen a real guy take a baby and hold it like you did. Jerry's never even touched Tootsie . . . none of her boyfriends will, either. You struck her as quite different."

"I love babies . . . children. I miss my own. Michael's ten . . . Gloria's thirteen. Haven't seen them in almost two years now . . . I guess I was imagining I was holding Gloria, in a way. And, you know as well as I that infants—anybody, including Lissa—need love. Constantly. It didn't look to me as if Tootsie was getting much from Lissa."

"Stephen, you're a gem. Let's christen our bed . . . our new life together . . . no matter how long it lasts. Let's just live for the moment."

They christened it in appropriate fashion, concluding it with the usual pillow talk. "Did Lissa tell you how this all started?"

"No. There's more to it? How?"

Stephen told her in great detail of the incident and what he had done.

"Thank you, Steve. That's just what she needed. Jerry would never have done that . . . he simply ignores her . . . both of them."

"Well . . . I've got to get my family together, haven't I? I really hope I can get through to her. An afterthought . . . if you see us together a lot, don't get the wrong idea. I wouldn't lay a finger on her."

"I know you wouldn't. I love you, Steve."

Chapter 25   Confrontation

There were two responses to Stephen's letters to local Norfolk advertising agencies. He telephoned each and made appointments to meet the agency heads . . . who would also wear the hat of Personnel Director, he presumed.   One agency was in a small suite in a downtown office building; the other, in a refurbished old mansion in the renovated 'Old Town' section just beyond the dock and warehouse areas, themselves being razed to make way for plush condos out over the water and the new waterfront renewal project itself.   Each agency head exhibited a strong wariness about this New Yorker at first, until Stephen stressed his Atlanta upbringing.   The smaller one thought they could use him possibly to direct some radio spots.   The other, Renaud Advertising in Old Town could use him, almost immediately, to produce TV car commercials for Manila Honda, a local dealership with branches in Richmond and Baltimore.   This offered more encouragement because the commercials were changed and re-taped every week, as well as modified slightly to tailor them to the other two markets.   It would also involve creative strategy, copywriting, production supervision, and editing. It could amount to two and a half to three days a week, but it was strictly freelance, temporary, with no benefits. He was unable to negotiate a very satisfactory rate, either. Only fifteen dollars an hour or around three hundred dollars a week at most. However, the unused part of the remainder of the week could be looked at as productive time in which he could do other things—if he could find anything else to do.

He shook hands on it with Perry Fox, the president and owner of Renaud Advertising, and made an appointment to join him on Monday for the creative conference with client Salvatore "Sal" Manila at the dealership.

Stephen's Unemployment Compensation was due to run out in two weeks, but he certainly had no intention of reporting this job to them. It was, he reasoned, a temporary, per-hour job . . . which was not assured, could change, vary, decrease, and he would just use some street smarts and look our for 'Number One.' In fact, he would ask for an extension if that were possible. Anyway he looked at it, he stood a fair chance of seeing a little money trickle in . . . and not being totally broke. Plus, he could contribute more toward housekeeping with Eve. He promised himself his first pay check would go to her.

Stephen and Eve spent their evenings together, alternating with conversational periods between selected television programs. Lissa sometimes joined them but more often than not she was off either baby sitting to earn gas money for her second-hand heap or out with her empty-headed cronies. Tootsie slept through the night so presented no problem. Whenever Stephen and Eve wanted to go to the movies, it almost had to be a night Lissa wouldn't be baby sitting. Eve simply insisted that she earn some money to help feed the baby and pay for her gas. Fortunately, Lissa and the baby were both covered under Eve's health plan at CBN.

The routine became familiar and comfortable. The periods of conversation soon became longer than those of TV-watching. Stephen and Eve were becoming more like a couple of marrieds as time went along. Their friendship and companionship grew as did their love, although they were not exactly aware of it. They would, of course, exchange stories of the day's happenings . . . which didn't seem to vary much at the network, while Stephen's accounts of Sal's car commercials varied from week to week and were often amusing. One idea Sal wanted to do was have a Brink's armored truck drive up and money to go flying all over the place. Stephen had pointed out that the only way to do that was in a studio with an electronic blue-matte drop-out technique. Sal was all for it. Fortunately for all, though, Stephen had the foresight to check the weight of the armored truck and the stress-factors of the floor at WYAH-TV, the only studio large enough to handle it. He knew the floor was not poured concrete on the ground but was elevated. So, he averted a double disaster—which went over Sal's head . . . Perry's, too.

The one thing that Stephen could not quite get used to was the constant profanity at both the agency and the car dealership. He had been used to a lot of it in the Marines . . . a little of it on Madison Avenue, then none in his Christian walk. Here, suddenly, he found himself thrust into the secular sewer of vulgarity that seemed to be the norm everywhere. He and Eve had gone one evening to see On Golden Pond, with Henry Fonda and Katherine Hepburn – and had been totally taken aback by the foul language—four-letter words—that filled the dialogue. Actually, he had not seen any motion pictures at all during his tenure with KXAO-TV, so this struck him particularly hard—especially to see Fonda and Hepburn engage in it! The agency head and the client often had friendly shouting matches on the phone—which everyone in the agency could hear—with such a constant stream of expletives and scatological descriptions . . . that he wondered how the women put up with it. He, himself, was honestly shocked . . . and didn't consider himself a prude.

And, so it went . . . virtually the same routine week in and week out through January and into February. One thing Stephen did manage to do was visit a good Christian book store and find one or two suitable books he thought Lissa could master . . . and possibly benefit from. She was not alone as a teenager, he presumed, in choosing TV-watching over reading.

A week after giving Lissa one of the books—something on God and the Family—he found himself in the kitchen after she had finished feeding Tootsie lunch. He got the pad and pencil from next to the phone and sat down at the table, motioning Lissa to do likewise. Not a bad artist of sorts, he drew the outline of a person . . . silhouette, legs slightly apart, arms and hands away from the body . . . like a paper doll cut-out.

"Lissa, let me share something with you . . . that I have learned from life and from the Bible." Putting the pencil tip on the head of the figure, he said, "This, of course, is a person's head . . . we all know that is where the brain, the mind is." And, he printed to the side of it, MIND. "Now, the mind is a lot of things . . . it is your thinker, of course, but it is where a lot of other things take place, too . . . things like knowledge . . . understanding . . . knowing to come in out of the rain . . . reading, and so on. Really, your mind is the you . . . your soul." And he printed SOUL in letters larger above MIND.

"Now, let's take a look at the rest of the body." He wrote BODY off to the side at the bottom. "Your body needs . . . food. Right? And, water. Right? And, it needs to stay healthy . . . and if it gets broken . . . it hurts, right? Now, which do you think is more important?"

She didn't answer, merely shook her head, 'she didn't know.'

"They are both important . . . and there must be a healthy balance between to two. But, which one would you want to rule ? . . . to be in charge? Body . . . or Soul?"

She shook her head again.

"Which rules Tootsie?"

" . . . Body?"

"Right! Tootsie's mind—her soul—is just starting to develop. She has to put things . . . impressions . . . ideas . . . into her little brain so she can know what this world you brought her into is all about. Soon she will be putting her first words into that brain and then she will be able to understand your thoughts and tell you hers. Right now, though, she is just a tiny body that instinctively wants milk and food . . . and fills her diapers to get rid of it. It's all a basic animal-nature . . . natural function . . . or we wouldn't live. With me?"

She nodded, actually attentive.

"Now suppose Tootsie didn't develop that little mind . . . thought it would just be easier to eat, sleep, and poop! She would be letting her body rule her mind, wouldn't she?"

Another nod.

"Tootsie's just a baby. Adults—you and I—have many more bodily functions and appetites . . . because we have grown up and are much larger, for one thing, and more complex. Some of those mature things are called appetites. One you already know is the sexual urge . . . which is perfectly natural and respectful. God made us with it . . . so that we could find a mate . . . stay with that mate . . . and have children to keep the race going. Another appetite is for things that taste good . . . Coke, Pepsi, pizzas . . . beer, booze. Or, appetites for things that make us feel good . . . warm sunshine, having sex . . . rock music . . . sometimes too much booze . . . or marijuana . . . or worse. We think we feel good at the time, but we feel awful later. So, we end up taking more to feel good longer . . . and we can't quit. Now . . . you tell me : which rules in these cases, the soul or the body?"

"Th' body?"

"Does that make sense? When you have a mind—a brain—the most incredible of God's fabulous creations . . . to let that stupefy and let your body tell it what to do? Doesn't . . . does it?"

"Guess not . . . when you put it that way."

"So, you would agree. The intelligence . . . the brain, the mind, the soul should rule the body?"

"I guess."

"Well . . . you're right so far. Now, you know the blacks all talk about . . . and sing about . . . soul . . . soul food, soul this and that . . . but they are all stopping just short of the greatest thing of all!"

He had her undivided interest.

"There is a dimension greater than either the body or the soul . . . that is even beyond the mind. Got any idea what that could be?"

She shook her head, 'no.'

"That . . . is . . . spirit !" And he drew a valentine heart on the torso of the figure and lettered if SPIRIT beside it. "Now, what do you think the spirit contains?"

She shook her head again.

"How about . . . feelings? Emotions? Love? Anger? Hate? Pity? Compassion? Do you think those come from 'reasoning'? No, they come from the 'heart,' don't they? Your love as a mother for Tootsie . . . that comes from your heart, doesn't it? And, my love for your mother . . . that goes beyond the physical sex side of it . . . to affection, caring . . . which is in my heart." And her drew a heart around the word spirit to the side of the sketched figure. Pointing to each of the three things he had designated, he continued, "So . . . you see the body is made up of three parts . . . body . . . soul, and spirit. Agreed?"

She nodded.

"Now, if you let the body control the others, you are giving in to basic appetites . . . sex . . . gluttony, food gratification . . . booze . . . drugs . . . like an animal . . . and your mind is overpowered—sometimes ruined!   So instead, you can let your mind rule and you will think everything over before you act . . . and experience your mind keeping you higher than an animal. Then . . . the heart. If you can balance your mind with your heart, you become an intelligent, warm, loving human being. There is always that struggle between heart and soul . . . heart is your conscience telling your mind right from wrong. Follow so far?"

"Uh huh."

"Well, I'm going to share a secret now that a lot of people know . . . but most people don't. In order to stop the struggle between your mind—your soul—and your spirit—and your body—you have to get your spirit in tune with God's Holy Spirit . . . "   And he drew the outline of a cross with a dove below it above the head of his outlined figure and labeled it HOLY SPIRIT.   He then drew a connecting arrow down from the dove to the heart in his figure, and another from the heart of the figure up to the dove. "You see? When your heart— your spirit— is in tune with God's Holy Spirit . . . and His with yours . . . there is a two-way street of right-ness . . . righteousness . . . and goodness . . . and love . . . and power . . . and then your spirit, following God's spirit, becomes as one and your good spirit then controls your mind-soul and your body . . . and you become a good person . . . like God wants all of his children to be.   And, your life becomes good . . . and you and everyone around you become happy and good . . . and life has some better and higher meaning. Life is then worth living. Does all this make sense?"

"Un huh"

"Well, I want you to think about all of what I have told you. I'm going to stick this drawing up on the tack board there over the phone. You think about it. And, one day, if you want to know how to awaken your spirit and get it in tune with God's . . . I will show you how."

He patted Lissa's folded hands on the table. "Think about it . . . " He looked at Tootsie. "That's a precious little life you have in your care." He got up and left.

Lissa remained seated for a long time. Silent. Lost in contemplation . . . until the familiar frettings of her infant daughter demanded her attention.

Chapter 26   Emergency

It was well into March, in early evening, that Stephen got the telephone call from Tom.   It was only the second call he'd gotten from him; the other, to complain about Stephen's use of the debit card for what appeared to have been a New Year's Eve binge.   Strictly business, Stephen had assured him then; entertaining a potential client. The call this evening sent a cold chill throughout him when he recognized Tom's voice—Oh, God! It's dad.

It was worse—it was his daughter, Gloria!

Tom had called to relay a message just moments ago from Diana, who had contacted him since she knew no other way to reach Stephen. Gloria had had a ruptured appendix and peritonitis had set in.   It had been discovered only this morning and she had undergone emergency surgery.   And, there were complications.   She was in intensive care and her condition was listed as critical.

"Oh, God!   I'll go at once. Thanks, Tom.   Dad OK? Good. . .yeah, I'll let you know."

Upon hanging up, Stephen immediately opened the yellow pages and called Delta.   Their next flight to New York, with connections, departed at 11:30 p.m. Yes, they could book him. He said he would pick his ticket up at the gate.

He met Eve's inquisitive stare when he returned to the dining room. "You heard? Gloria's appendix burst—she's in intensive care. I've got to go to her. I was able to book a flight at 11:30 . . . so, it's now 7:30 . . . I can toss some things in a bag, shower . . . and be there by dawn. I'll have the pastor of the local church put me up somewhere. Think you could drive me to the airport? No, I could park the van long-term."

"No, sweetheart . . . that would cost too much. I'll take you. Might be wise, though, to park the van around in back of the garage on the grass. Be less conspicuous there for any length of time."

Stephen quickly implemented the plan—even thinking to telephone Perry Fox and telling him of the emergency and that he'll have to miss this week's production.

On the way to the airport, Stephen reminisced a lot about his children and admitted that being around Lissa and Tootsie, while really pleasant, was a painful reminder that he was missing the critical years of his own children. He was anxious to be at Gloria's bedside to help her through this, and it would be good to see Michael . . . and see how much he had grown and changed. He told Eve that he dreaded seeing Diana— she could be such a bitch.

He kissed Eve long and tenderly and got his bag out of the back of her car. "I'll telephone you. Sorry we couldn't have sealed this properly, but I'll make up for it when I come back. Tell Lissa bye for me. Love you." And he disappeared into the terminal. He had borrowed a hundred dollars from Eve. She had stopped at an automatic cash machine, and he had given her a check. He would charge the ticket on the debit card.

Stephen deplaned at LaGuardia, clutching his carryon, and made a beeline for the limo. It all seemed eerily familiar. How many dozens of times had he traversed the grungy terminal, crossed the parking lots to the long-term, gotten into his VW 'Beetle' and headed up the turnpike to Darien? This time there was no car waiting; he'd have to take a limo—if they were still running this late—or a cab into mid Manhattan and take a train . . . the milk run . . . out of Grand Central. The last limo for Connecticut had left before midnight.

'Dear God,' he thought, *'it's not easy taking the 'red-eye,' then hassling to get to where you're going by dawn. I won't be good for anything.'*

It was sheer compulsion now. The thing was driving within him, whatever it was that kept urging him with a totally all-consuming desire to get to his daughter's bedside, that overcame the spasms of weariness and his heavy eyelids that closed even as he stood waiting for the limo. The frigid blast of air from the revolving door jarred him wide awake. Zombie-like, he grasped his bag, pulled his muffler tighter around his neck, jammed his hat down snugly and boarded the van.

The ride into the city was oblivion, as was the ride to Darien; dozing was fitful but it was loss of consciousness which allowed for replenishment of sorts. The slowing, jerking motion of the train began to pull him back from the fathomless darkness into which his mind and body had slipped as the hand of the conductor firmly shook his shoulder. "Darien."

'Thank God it's almost dawn,' he muttered as he arched his back and stretched his arms, turning and savoring the familiar landmarks in the cold, still morning air. The thought of a cup of hot coffee instinctively took him in the direction of the lighted diner across the street. It was too early to go to the hospital anyway.

The ordeal of the trip had churned his stomach to the point he felt sick. He needed something more than coffee; he ordered eggs-over, toast and bacon. Also, he needed to come to grips with the situation . . . he had no place to stay. His first thought had been *that he could just sit up somewhere at the hospital and use the bathroom facilities there . . . but not for too long. He couldn't afford a hotel and to even suggest to Diana that he stay at the house was out of the question he knew. So, he would, after all, have to call the church and see if there weren't someone who'd give him a room for a few nights.*

The cab ride to the hospital was another couple of bucks and a buck tip. He would have to watch his expenditures very carefully. The new entranceway was quite an improvement; gleaming, modern-efficient, warmly prophylactic. Both Gloria and Michael had been born here and over the years sundry childhood maladies had brought them back once or twice, fortunately for minor things—at least compared to Gloria's current tragedy.

The elevator stopped on the third floor. Stephen looked at the visitor's card. Room 377. At least the digits are a good sign . . . the Trinity and God's number twice. He tapped lightly on the door and waited. After what seemed several beats too long, it opened and Diana, seeing him, stepped out of the dim light into the hallway, closing the door behind her. "She's resting now."

They walked slowly down the corridor to the waiting room. It was the first time Stephen had seen Diana since the divorce. He sensed it was painful for both. The infrequent telephone conversations during the past two years had been unmistakably hostile—at least, he thought, on her part. He, of course, had long ago given the whole thing over to the Lord and had asked forgiveness, and, of course, had forgiven her, too, in his own heart. So, he had an inner peace about it. There was a marked difference about her when compared to either Faith or Eve; Diana possessed an innate dignity . . . an indescribable quality about her that both of the others simply lacked. He glanced at her face as they walked; she, staring absently at the floor, expressionless. Her eyes were red. He remembered they had always been red . . . from crying. She had always seemed to be crying . . . over the least little thing. He used to wonder for what all the time? Now the crows' feet had deepened into crevices and the skin of her face seemed to sag into other wrinkles around her mouth and the sides of her chin, which he had not remembered. She seemed shorter, or was it that her shoulders drooped more? She had visibly aged in such a short time. Was it on account of the divorce or the present trauma with Gloria? She still looked attractive to him; for a moment there was a swelling, it seemed, of the old love. *Could that be? . . . after Faith and now Eve? Could he and Diana ever get back together? Or, was it only pity? Surely his love was all-consuming now for Eve. Nevertheless, Diana and he had known more years of it . . . the growing years . . . where the glow of romance should have transformed into the patina of comfortable companionship . . . but could not . . . during those tumultuous sixteen years. He realized he still loved her a in a way, maybe . . . but was not in love with her anymore. But, he knew he could never totally desert Diana and the kids—they would never not be a part of him. Maybe the wounds he had caused would heal in time. At least with Gloria. He hoped so. Her reaction to the divorce . . . even at ten . . . was devastating; she hadn't really spoken to him since. He wondered if Gloria would speak to him now. Surely having come this far . . . after so long . . . she would see his love and concern.* He prayed in tongues under his breath.

Diana sat down. He sat opposite her. They were the only ones in the room. Paper cups and littered ashtrays from the previous night smothered any vestige of charm. "I thought she was getting along all right after the operation?"

Diana's eyes began to redden as she looked into his for the first time. "She was . . . at first . . . then complications."

346

Stephen prayed in tongues as she cried. Tears came to his eyes also. "The operation went OK? How long will she be in intensive care? She'll be alright. I've been praying. The Lord . . . "

"Oh, can that, will you? If there were a Lord, why would he allow this to happen? You thank Him for this? Just keep your newfangled religion to yourself, thank you. Leave us out of it! . . . You and that two-bit floozy evangelist   can wallow in that born-again nonsense all you want. Just leave me and Gloria . . . and Michael out of it!"

Stephen remained mute; he knew not to push it.

"Furthermore, buster, if God is in all of this, maybe this is how he is punishing you . . . all of us . . . for what you have done!" Sobs interrupted her; chocking, she continued, "Breaking up our marriage . . . running off to Tulsa . . . hooking up with that (drawing out the word with biting derision) evangelist . . . all in the . . . " and she paused, staring him straight in the eyes with unmistakable contempt . . . "in the name of Jesus ! God! Is that what you two preach?"

Stephen followed Diana through the door. He didn't feel at all led to pray or to ask God for anything. His uneasiness had been building since Diana first spoke. He tried to separate the sickening urge within him from the emotional stress the meeting with his former wife had put upon him; perhaps that's all it was: anticipation and nervousness over the impending first encounter with both Diana and Gloria since the divorce. The figure in the bed lay still, an I.V. connecting to the suspended bottle next to the bed.

Diana touched her daughter's hand gently and the figure stirred. "Hi, Mom," whispered from her lips as her eyes adjusted from the darkness of light slumber to the dim light of the room. They searched the familiar face of her mother then became aware of the presence of someone behind her. "Who's there?"

Diana stepped aside as Stephen took her place and placed his hand on hers. "Sweetheart . . . it's Daddy."

The hand beneath his tensed and his daughter turned her head away from him.

Stephen turned dejectedly and strode quickly through the door. Ignoring the passing nurses and others, he paced aimlessly up and down the corridors, pleading first with God to heal her, then letting the prayers in tongues take over in the spirit in order to let these spirit words accomplish in ways he could not fathom whatever strange words of prayer were the proper ones for this occasion. As pained as he was, his faith in the Lord's healing was undaunted. Gloria would be all right.

He was startled to awareness by the loudspeaker booming up and down the corridors calling for Dr. Rosenstein. Seeing Sid Rosenstein walking toward him, he greeted him, "Hi, Sid. Good to see you . . . but not exactly under these circumstances."

"I know, Steve. We just had a close call . . . very close! We almost lost her . . . but she pulled through . . . and I know she'll make it now."

"Thanks, Sid. I knew she would too. And, I appreciate all you have done . . . and I prayed for God to be with you as you cared for her."

Sid patted Stephen paternally on the back. "You know I'd do all I could. After all, I did bring her into the world . . . and Michael, too. They're like my own."

"God bless you, Sid."

Stephen collapsed in the chair again as the doctor turned and left. Although his mind was groggy, confused, the thought managed to get through to his consciousness that he needed a place to stay. He limped across the room to the pay phone . . . his joints—especially his hip—and his whole body were stiff . . . from the trip. He flipped through the yellow pages under churches and held his finger at the number for the Church of the Apostles as he dialed it.

The customary three rings. "Hello? May I speak to Pastor Shepherd, please?" Pause. A voice came on. "Hello? Chris? . . . Hey, this is Steve Trevelyan. Hope I'm not persona non grata having tried to step into your business with all of those Tulsa Holy Rollers!" Stephen explained his situation and agreed to meet Chris at the church late in the afternoon. By then, Chris promised, he would have a place to stay.

Leaving his carryon at the hospital information counter on the first floor, a well as a note for Diana that he could be reached through the church, he set off to wander around town trying to repress the pangs of nostalgia as he walked among the familiar landmarks, the details of a storefront here, a break in the sidewalk there . . . the local tavern where he had spent so much time. He frankly hoped he would not run into anyone he had known. It was a weekday so the commuters would all be in the city; he might run into their wives, those in Diana's circle of friends, or a merchant friend or two. Just being in Darien again, though, opened the wounds that had begun to heal. It was as if he had never gone away—time had stood still—nothing had changed. There was no Tulsa, no Faith, no TV station, no oil wells . . . no Eve. He had stayed home from New York today because Gloria was sick; tomorrow he would have to get up at the crack of dawn, drive to the station, take the 7:40, grab a donut and walk through the lobby of Grand Central and take the elevator up to his floor at J. Walter Thompson advertising agency . . . to a routine day filled with meetings, screenings, strategy sessions, lunch at the latest bistro with a couple of healthy belts . . . the stimulation of the city, the fast pace, the chic styles . . . the people who were setting the pace . . . doing the things that the world followed with interest. Stephen's adrenaline began to flow. He took a long lunch in an out-of-the-way diner he knew and killed the time until school let out.

Walking the six blocks or so over to the intermediate school, he checked with the principal's office to find out what last period room Michael would be in and waited in the hall outside of it for Michael to come out. He would be walking home . . . or on his bike. It would give them a good chance to be together.

The bell rang and kids flooded the halls. Stephen spotted Michael and hailed him. "Hi, pal. Good to see you."

Michael was a bit reserved, most likely because he was terribly embarrassed that his father had come to get him . . . had actually entered his peerdom . . . where his friends would laugh at him.

Nevertheless, they walked out together as Stephen tried to strike up a conversation with his son. It was awkward. The 'whatcha' been doing ?' . . . the 'how ya getting along in school' . . . to which Michael responded with stubborn brevity.

Finally, as they neared home, Michael began to warm up and to share some of his achievements and to ask questions . . . 'was dad coming back to stay? . . . ' did he come because of Gloria? . . . 'How was she?' 'Did he want to come in?'

Stephen's heart thumped in agonizing beats. He dare not go in . . . they could just sit on the steps and chat . . . 'How about that?' They did and Stephen studied his son carefully. He was so different . . . he had grown so much in the two years. He was no longer the little boy he had left. What had he done in those intervening years? They were lost to Stephen now—a total blank in the life he had brought into this world. He would never know those two years . . . they were gone, irretrievable. With Gloria as well. *God, how cruel! How cruel life can be!*

Stephen probed into all the areas that young ten-year-old boys are absorbed with . . . baseball . . . his bike . . . TV . . . his friends . . . what he liked best to do . . . how about pizzas?   Stephen put his arm around his shoulder and hugged him next to him. "I've missed you so much, son. And, you know I love you . . . just like your mother does. We both love you. I just cannot live here with you all right now . . . some day you will understand . . . I hope. But, I would give everything to have you with me always . . . we could go places . . . to ball games . . . do all sorts of things . . . " He trailed off as he choked up . . . and the time was nearing when he had to meet Chris Shepherd at the church . . . which was a good twenty minute walk from the house.   So, he stood up and hugged Michael . . . for a long time. Michael reciprocated.

"I miss you, Daddy."

"I miss you, too, son. Hang in there . . . we'll be together some day soon . . . I promise." He waved back at him as he walked up the driveway. That image of Michael burned into his memory . . . *God! How would he look the next time he saw him?* Tears gushed from his eyes and he took out his handkerchief to daub them.

It was dark at five-thirty when he entered the church office. Lights were on but everyone had left for the day. Pastor Shepherd's office door was open.   Inside a burly, bearded figure in black was hunched over a typewriter behind a gigantic, heavy oak desk, cluttered and littered with papers, pamphlets, letters, bulletins . . . disorder of the first magnitude. The figure looked up over his half glasses. "Steve! Come in, come in!" he repeated as he rose and in one step crossed the room and grabbed his visitor in an enormous bear hug.

"Praise God . . . it's good to see you, Chris!"

"How's Gloria?   I went to see her yesterday.   We've all been praying for her."

"She's having a tough time of it, but she's pulling through . . . with God's help" He slumped in the hard-back captain's chair with the Yale crest on it as his host sprawled across the well-worn couch, propping his foot out in Stephen's direction as if to give room for the corpulence as it settled into his lower abdomen.

"We've all missed you, Steve. How're things going in your service to the Lord? Your new bride's an Evangelist, I think I heard . . . maybe Diana told me. Somebody did, anyway."

"Yep. She's an ordained evangelist all right. Got her own ministry, Living Water Ministry . . . a healing and deliverance ministry mostly . . . and she goes to a lot of prisons. Been to a few myself. That's all over, though."

"What? What happened there?" The pastor shifted his weight and ran his finger around the inside of his stiff white collar. "Whew! This thing gets tight sometimes. But, that's what it's for . . . to remind us that we are priests . . . not mortals. Would you like some coffee? Glass of sherry?"

"Sherry would be fine . . . would make me feel right at home in the Episcopal church."

With undisguised effort, the giant cleric got up and rummaged around for a couple of clean sherry glasses. "How'd your meeting with Diana go? You two speaking at all?"

"It was a bit bitter, but, yes, we are. It's Gloria, though, who's hurt the worst. She wouldn't speak to me and I'm afraid my coming has not helped."

"Keep the faith . . . she'll come around . . . some day."

"I don't know, Chris, do you think my divorcing Diana went against biblical teaching? You know, I stood on First Corinthians 7:15 . . . *'if the unbeliever leaves, let him—her—leave . . . you are not to be under bondage in such cases . . . for God has called up to peace.'"*

"And, Diana was an unbeliever . . . and left you, or you let her go, is that it?"

"Well, yes. She would not accept Jesus as I had done. She wouldn't even let me explain what to be 'born again' meant—much less to be baptized in the Holy Spirit. And, she wouldn't follow me when I took over the TV station in Tulsa and moved out there. That's leaving me, isn't it? A couple of passages earlier, Paul says that the Lord says that a wife should not leave her husband. Look, Chris, I didn't do this thing on the spur of the moment. You know I was born-again and spirit-filled for a year before I went out to Tulsa. And, I grew and studied in the Lord . . . while she refused and even went the opposite. I sometimes even thought she was demon-possessed, and I tried to cast the demons out! But, I really didn't know anything about that then. I surely do now, what with Faith's ministry. She tackles them all the time!"

"Stephen, you're an educated man. Do you really believe in demons and demonic possession? This is the twentieth century—not the twelfth! . . . or the First! In Christ's time it probably meant something else . . . a sickness, schizophrenia, or something unexplainable back then. Perhaps some day you and I can get into it . . . but, suffice it to say that a lot of damage can be done . . . going around discerning demons and trying to cast them out."

"Tell me about it! I've been put through the wringer myself." And he proceeded to synopsize his KXAO-TV demise, the oil investment debacle, the CBN disaster . . . and how close those had driven him to ending it all . . . and how destitute he now found himself . . . all in the 'service of the Lord'!

Chris picked up . . . "CBN? Say, I believe Joe Carpenter—you remember him? . . . "

"Sure do. We commuted together . . . got to be good drinking buddies."

353

"Well, you know, he went off to serve the Lord, too. And, I believe I heard he was a professor down at CBN University."

Stephen's eyebrows shot up. "No. I didn't know that. God, I'm glad you told me— that's a contact I'll follow up the minute I get back! Thanks, Chris. And, by the way, old chum, I'm dead ! I sat up all night on the plane and train getting here and spent the whole day at the hospital. I'd just like to collapse right here and now. Don't mean to be rude, but I can't even function."

"I can either give you last rites . . . or the guest room down the hall. It's a little spartan, like a monastery. I'll walk you down there. Got any bags?"

"Left it at the hospital. I'll just crash like I am."

"OK. There's shaving stuff, shower, towels. We'll get your stuff in the morning. Did you have dinner?"

"No. Just show me the room. And, thanks, Chris. We'll have a long talk tomorrow."

Still in his same clothes, but freshened by the shave and shower and the deep ten-hour sleep, Stephen headed for the hospital. He decided to walk the mile or so; the sun was out and it was not terribly cold. Michael would have gone on to school by now. How glad he was to have had those precious moments with him yesterday.

He felt considerably better, like some burden had been lifted. He had been praying under his breath in tongues. Spotting Diana at the nurses' station, he asked, "How's Gloria?"

"It was nip and tuck last night. Has Sid told you?"

"No. Haven't seen him today. Is she out of it yet?"

"Enough to have called for you."

"Gloria called for me ?" Stephen was stunned . . . pleasantly so.

"Yes. Let's go in."

354

Gloria lay still with her eyes closed. He father approached the bed and gently cradled her hand in his two. He fought to hold the tears back.

The supine adolescent's eyes opened and a faint smile of recognition crossed her lips. "Daddy . . . " her weak voice filled his ears. "I missed you."

"Sweetheart. I miss you. I love you . . . always will. Your mother and I both . . . we love you . . . and we'll be with you. Shhh. you just go on back to sleep. We'll be right here."

"Daddy, I'm all right now." Her eyes closed again and her hand clutched her father's more tightly. "I know you love me."

Stephen buried his head in his forearms and wept silently. Diana put a tissue to her nose. "Thank you, God," he said under his breath. As a final gesture, Stephen leaned over and kissed his daughter on the forehead, then buried his face in the pillow beside her, inexpressible joy and thanks to God welling up in his heart.

At the airport, Stephen found he had a couple of hours to kill before boarding time. In better past times he would have flashed his private airline Flagship Executive Lounge card and passed the time in comfort. It was early afternoon so he telephoned Hank Worthington, his former senior account executive at J. Walter Thompson in New York. Fortunately, Hank was in and accepted the call when his secretary told him who it was. "Steve, old boy! How are you?—where are you?"

"At LaGuardia, Hank, on my way back to Norfolk. Had to come up . . . my daughter had an emergency."

"Well, tell me about yourself. Haven't heard from, or about, you in . . . what? . . . a couple of years?"

" 'Bout that . . . to put it briefly, I've been through the wringer. I realize now what a mistake it was to leave Madison Avenue . . . and, frankly, I'm calling you to see just what chance I might have of landing back there—I'm about to chuck all this religion stuff . . . and get back to work." Stephen forced himself to say, fearful that the lack of conviction in his tone was betraying him.

" . . . Uh . . . I don't know, Steve. I'm not on the Marine Corps account any more. There's been a lot of shuffling around here . . . reorganization . . . shaving staff a bit. It's not the same old place you knew. Times are different, too . . . "

Stephen's mind wandered to other things as the transparently lame excuses rolled off Hank's glib tongue. He knew when he was getting the polite brush-off—at least, it was 'polite' as compared to the way the Christians seemed to handle it. But, it was becoming such a pattern now that he was actually becoming inured to it, insensitive to it; his response automatic without a twinge of emotion any more. He thanked Hank, remarked how good it was to talk to him again—quickly interjected, "If you run into my favorite Creative Director, Ruthie Cohen . . . tell her to stick it!" He laughed at their long-forgotten joke and hung up.

Turning the events of the past days over in his mind as he reclined in the airline seat, Stephen characterized them as unsettling. *He knew now that the Holy Spirit had led him to his daughter's bedside for that sublime crisis she went through and the miraculous healing of not only her little body but their father-daughter relationship. 'Thank You, Jesus.'*

But, to once again be with Diana and Gloria and Michael . . . in Darien . . . was more painful that he would have imagined. And, there was still something gnawing at his spirit, disturbing the 'victory' that the Holy Spirit had just accomplished. *Was it the conversation with Chris? Or, seeing Diana again? Or, relating all this to Faith and Eve? He ruminated on the explanation to Chris about his having stood on scripture—the Word of God—for the rationale for his divorce . . . Chris' reminder at dinner of Jesus' own words regarding divorce . . . in Matthew 19 something or other . . . 'that a man shall leave his father and mother and shall cleave to his wife, and the two shall become as one' . . . and even though Moses allowed divorce because of the hardness of the hearts of the Israelites, Jesus admonished that 'whosoever divorces his wife, except for adultery, and marries another woman commits adultery.' All right, Stephen argued with himself, Jesus' words are more direct . . . and less open to interpretation than are Paul's in Corinthians. But—and here he interjected his argument that he never could seem to get anyone to engage him in—that in the Gospels Jesus was talking always to Jews, not to Christians. Even his disciples had not been converted to Christianity or to being full believers in Jesus' Gospel of the Kingdom of Heaven until Pentecost . . . fifty days after the resurrection . . . when the Holy Spirit descended and imbued them all with power and knowledge and tongues. So, in reality, Jesus' words about divorce had been directed at Jews under the Law . . . and Jesus had brought the new Law, the New Covenant. And, even so, in the Gospel of John, eighth chapter, Jesus forgave the woman caught in adultery, saying, since no one is not without some deep sin and cannot therefore honestly accuse you . . . or something of that sort . . . then, 'I forgive you. Go and sin no more.' Therefore, if the only cause for divorce is adultery and adultery is a sin which Jesus specifically says He can forgive, then isn't Paul picking it up from there under the terms of the new testament of the Gospel of Christ—not the Law of Moses —and telling what Christian believers can do? . . . and not be in conflict with Jesus' previous words? How did that apply, he wondered, to his present adulterous relationship with Eve vis-à-vis Faith? He'd been over it time and time again in his mind . . . but he felt Chris had not accepted this (Seminary party line?), although he seemed to ponder it. Why was it so hard for the traditional church to understand 'revealed knowledge' in these last times, he wondered? And, he continued to himself: so maybe Paul realized that while divorce was not good, the adulterous aspect of it that Jesus had pointed out was simply a pardonable sin . . . not to be undertaken too often, but pardonable, nevertheless . . . that would assuage the Eve situation. And, hadn't he and Faith, like so many other born-again, spirit-filled Christians remarrying, gotten together on their knees and asked God's forgiveness on the wedding night if they were in God's eyes indeed about to commit adultery? And, hadn't they by confessing and asking forgiveness and seeking God's blessings in their new, now-for-the-first-time truly Christian marriage erased forever any such stigma? Of course, as far as they understood it they had, and he and Faith had had a peace about it. Still, Stephen was disturbed and confused. Seeing Gloria, Michael—even Diana—again raised conflict in his spirit. He had almost erased Eve from his mind these past two days. Faith was like a distant memory; he realized now that there had been no love there at all. With Eve, now that he was thinking of her again, yes, there was a feeling of love. Seeing Diana again had triggered no resurgence of that old love. His feelings for her emerged as remorse that it had not worked out, since they had brought Gloria and Michael into the world—but he was the one who had destroyed that! God, too, maybe?*

His train of thought faded as he lapsed into the less than restful slumber of the weary traveler.

Chapter 27   Out of Order

Stephen opened the back door of Eve's car and tossed his bag in, then got in the front and leaned over and planted a big, passionate kiss on her receptive lips. "Miss me?"

"Oh? You been gone somewhere?   Seriously, I'm glad Gloria pulled through so well. Appreciated your call."

"Yeah . . . it was all rather upsetting . . . seeing her so sick . . . actually seeing them all again. It was very painful. I saw the hurt in their eyes—all the children's eyes. Recrimination in Diana's.   I was never really any more than a meal ticket to her . . . and, basically, she's upset because she lost her meal ticket.   Good thing there's family money and she is dabbling in real estate.   She still has the big house though.   Don't know why she doesn't sell it. It's got a tremendous capital gain on it."

Eve let him wind down.

"Oh, another thing—found out that a friend of mine . . . fellow New York commuter friend . . . is down here on the faculty of CBN University.   I'll call him first chance I get.   Maybe he can open a door over there for me. Who knows where this might all end up? Think that's where the Lord has wanted me all along?"

"Never know."

"If I did land there . . . guess I'd have to make an honest woman of you," he said, tickling her side.

When Eve got to work the next day, she looked in the CBN directory and located Joseph Carpenter's direct extension number, then telephoned Stephen at home and relayed it to him.

Rehearsing carefully how he was going to handle a number where he could be reached and where he was staying, he dialed the his friend Joe. After speaking to a secretary and explaining that he was an old friend from Connecticut, Joe's voice came on the line, "Steve Trevelyan! That really you?"

"What's left of him. I just found out you were at CBN U."

"Yep. Been with the network four years. Moved over here when the University was formed. What in the world beings you to these parts? Last I heard was when I left the big city—you were still commuting. Think I heard . . . from Chris Shepherd, or somebody . . . that you had left Madison Avenue and had gone into some ministry . . . television?"

"It's a long story. Been here a short time. Got an application in at CBN . . . doing a little advertising on the side . . . waiting. Had to go back to Darien . . . my daughter, Gloria, had a ruptured appendix. Chris Shepherd did tell me you were down here."

"We'll have to get together. I'll call Mary and see when we can have you over— how's dinner?"

"I'd love it . . . haven't seen Mary in ages."

"How do I reach you?"

"Let me call you back. I'm staying with a friend temporarily . . . I'm in and out. Want me to call you at home this evening?"

"Yes, that'd be great." And Joe gave him his home number.

Stephen called at ten minutes to eight that night so as not to interrupt the 700 Club which he presumed they would be watching, and he had a nice chat with Mary, accepting her kind invitation for the next night at six. She gave him the address and a few directions.

The next evening toward six, Stephen pulled up in front of an attractive development house on a man-made lake in the center of the subdivision. *Not bad*, he thought; *certainly well over a hundred thousand. He wondered what Joe's salary was. Pat Robinson's was publicly reported at fifty thousand a year, so he supposed everyone else was below that . . . although that didn't necessarily hold because to attract some of the heavy weights at the network and the university, these days, you were not going to get very high quality types at those prices. Maybe at ORU . . . but CBN was higher class—and first class. Besides, that fifty thousand of Pat's didn't reflect the perquisites . . . the palatial mansion, the fleet of cars, wardrobe provided, and, he had heard, a stable of thoroughbreds. He had figured other evangelists for two-, three-, four-hundred thousand a year . . . Oral, Price, Copeland. But, then, why not? They were running—they were the CEOs—of multi-, multi-million-dollar operations. A half a million compensation for raising one hundred million was not out of line with corporate compensation.*

His reverie was interrupted by the front door opening and Mary's greeting him. "Steve! It's so good to see you!" They embraced in the Holy hug. Joe walked up and performed the same ritual.

"Wow! This is a lovely house," Stephen offered, surveying the tastefully decorated interior.

"Our timing was just right . . . God's timing, that is. Let me offer you some tea . . . or apple juice . . . coffee?"

"Apple juice would be fine. Far cry from our club car days drinking our way back from the city, eh?"

"Another world. One, I thank God everyday I left."

Mary poured the apple juice and handed Stephen a glass. "Joe told me you said Gloria was ill. She all right now?"

"Yeah. It was a close call . . . " and he explained in detail how he had gone up . . . stayed at the church. How Diana was cool . . . as could be expected. What a wrenching experience it was to leave them again.

Motioning the gentlemen into the dinning room, Mary further inquired, "Tell us how you ended up here."

Stephen 'allowed as how,' since they were old friends and knew Diana, and all, that he would give them the whole, bloody story—just for their consumption. Not to be referred to outside of these walls, because if he should land at CBN some of these things might be misinterpreted. He had nothing to hide, but he didn't like people talking. So, he told them about KXAO-TV, moving to Tulsa . . . marrying Faith . . . her ministry . . . the oil wells . . . the lousy station operation . . . the demise of the wells—all dedicated to the Lord and His work—the split with Faith . . . and his pilgrimage to Virginia Beach . . . to get with CBN. Then he asked their absolute confidence and told them the harrowing story of David King and the Lebanese operation . . . and King's interpretation that it was God's will that Stephen was not the right man. How that had utterly devastated him . . . to the point of attempted suicide.

Groaning from time to time with obvious sympathy, Joe and Mary shook their heads in disbelief. Joe observed, "You surely have gone through the 'Job' experience. Since you have been struck down like Job, have you managed to keep your faith in the face of all odds . . . and inflictions of evil . . . and testing?"

"So far . . . but I'm no Job!"

"Praise God! He's up there . . . He's got His hand on you! Now, what do you plan to do?"

"My last chance is CBN U. And, frankly, that's where I thought I would use our friendship—if you will pardon my candor, but I'm desperate at this point . . . and I feel I can level with you. I know I've got what it takes to teach . . . and I know something about business . . . and the liberal arts. So, I thought I might be able to get on here—even as an instructor if not a professor—even earn a masters degree here, since it is all graduate school. And, I've already gone through the application process . . . so, I thought I'd sort of pick your brains . . . see what you thought my chances were . . . and see if you could steer me to the right person, along with an introduction—an introduction, not an endorsement. I wouldn't put you on the spot for that!"

Stephen finished his little speech and before resuming his meal, added, "Forgive me, Joe . . . Mary . . . I've been so wrapped up in my own messed up little world . . . I haven't even had the decency . . . the courtesy . . . to ask you all . . . how you got here—I know your kids were already in college when your 'life change' came about. But, how did you land here? And, how . . . over here at the university? What do you teach?"

Joe and Mary hesitantly pieced together their finding the Lord and His deliverance from the secular world of New York. How one of the commercial network people here, whom Joe had known in New York in charismatic circles, had suggested Joe's name to the right person at the right time . . . and they came, loved the idea, joined and have been here ever since. Joe had an assistant professorship teaching in the Business discipline. Marketing was his forte.

The dinner was excellent and the ambience was most pleasant. Stephen felt comfortable and reminiscing about bygone days on the 'avenue' was a bit of fun, especially now since they could both see it through the rose-colored filter of the charismatic experience. They laughed derisively at the cares, the concerns and problems of their erstwhile commercial world now that they were in touch with the truly important things of this world . . . and their new lives in Christ.

As the evening drew to a close, Joe reintroduced the subject of Stephen's quest at CBN U. "The only person for you to see here is Dean Ezra Elihu. You'd have to go through him eventually, so you might as well start with him. I'll check first thing in the morning with him for an appointment. You give his secretary a call," and he wrote a name and number on his business card, "And you can set it up. In the meantime, I will talk to him and give him a run-down on you—just the highlights. You ought to have a one-page resume to give to him. And, a word of caution: he's a bit of an odd duck. While he's a charismatic . . . tongue-speaker and all that . . . he got his undergraduate degree from Luther Rice Baptist Seminary in Jacksonville and his graduate degrees from Bob Jones University—deep, hardshell Baptist! And, although he has seen the light in the Baptism in the Holy Spirit . . . and appears one of us . . . there's something of that ingrained Baptist 'sin-and condemnation,' 'judgmental' . . . 'angry love' and legalism that is still under the surface. Good man, though. I just wouldn't go too much into the breakup with Faith—the first divorce is going to be hard enough to convince him of."

Stephen offered his profuse thanks for the lovely dinner and bade his farewell. On the drive back to Eve's he thought long and hard about his strategy for the forthcoming meeting with Dean Elihu. *He would have to flat-out rehearse some responses to obvious questions . . . including why David King had not hired him. That would be tricky, since King would be the first one Dr. Elihu would certainly contact.*

After recounting the whole evening to Eve in bed that night he concluded with, "If this thing does come through at CBN U . . . and I join the faculty . . . I'm going to have to make an honest woman of you. Will you marry me?"

Eve had said nothing in reply but snuggled closer to him.

The next morning Stephen telephoned Perry Fox at Renaud Advertising to find about the next strategy meeting on the Honda account. Perry told him rather abruptly that in his absence they had, in essence, found that they really didn't need his services . . . and, thanks for all he'd done . . . his final check would be in the mail . . . etc. That was a staggering blow! His unemployment comp was long gone and he looked to that measly two-fifty to three hundred a month as the only thing between him and destitution. His only hope now lay with Dr. Elihu and his landing with CBN U.

Fortunately, the interview with Dean Elihu came before the end of the week, on Friday morning. Stephen arrived at this best, dressed in his most elegant and conservative dark gray flannel suit (he resisted wearing the vest) with white, buttoned-down-collar shirt and conservative paisley necktie. He looked like a banker. The image was what he wanted to convey: solid, conservative, authoritative, a model of excellence . . . one which students would look up to and one which would convey the first-class image of CBN U faculty.

Dr. Ezra Elihu was a tall man in his early sixties who exuded great dignity. He reminded Stephen somewhat of Oral Roberts, as he stood to shake Stephen's hand and offer him a seat in the conversation corner of his impressive, tastefully decorated Williamsburg-esque office.

Stephen handed him his resume.

Scanning it, Dr. Elihu began, "Well, Professor Carpenter has some nice things to say about you. Tell me, yourself, why you are seeking a faculty position with us."

Stephen began by relating the Madison Avenue-commuting grind in his and Joe's other lives before they found the Lord. And, how blessed Joe was that Mary came to the Lord and the Lord's work with him. He, Stephen, had not been so fortunate; his wife had not. He then told about KXAO-TV, his meeting with Faith and their marriage and ministry —and that she was off with her group preaching to the prisoners around the country while he was relocating at CBN. He noticed Dr. Elihu's expression change slightly as he explained that. Continuing, he described his meeting with David King and the Lebanon possibility . . . and how that was put on indefinite hold. (He dared not tell the reason King had given him; maybe that would never even be mentioned by King when Elihu contacted him) He went on to explain how he was dabbling in advertising at the moment to make ends meet, but that he would like to get back to the Lord's work . . . and find his true niche to work for Him—he felt a calling to teach. He thought that his summary had been quite good and articulate.

Dr. Elihu probed, "Getting back to your first wife; how many children did you have?"

"Two: a girl, thirteen, and a boy, ten. Gloria, my daughter, just had a close call . . . ruptured appendix. I just flew up there to be with her in intensive care. Saw them all. We're all on good terms."

"And, this television station you were in charge of?   Like WYAH?"

"We tried to be . . . but it was really a shoestring operation. We ran deeper and deeper in debt each month. We only had the Tulsa metropolitan market to draw from—and, of course, we were in competition from Oral Roberts, Kenneth Hagin, and about a dozen other well-known ministries. The chairman of the board didn't turn out to be much of a Christian after all—he virtually stole the station by buying it at a ridiculously low price, then sold if for a four and a half million dollar profit. That's when I was ousted."

"And, these oil wells?"

"Unfortunately, I learned a lot about the oil business—too late! I lost everything . . . I mean thousands and thousands of dollars . . . even though we had prayed over them, dedicated them to the Lord and the proceeds to His work . . . and cast out demons and lingering indian spirits. All of us Christians went down the tube!"

Dr. Elihu continued to sit back in his chair with one leg crossed over the other, elbows on the arms of the chair, fingers touching lightly in prayer-like fashion. His eyes focused intently on Stephen's under a slight frown that conveyed the seriousness of his reflection. "And . . . your ministry . . . with your second wife?"

Stephen would have liked to have avoided this line of questioning and talk about his credentials and what he thought he could teach. But, he bravely expressed his rehearsed answers . . . in the present tense so as to cover or throw off track any suspicion of their impending divorce. "Oh, she's a real hard charger. Always hearing from the Lord to go off here . . . or there . . . and do His bidding. She concentrates on prison ministry. She's got a lot of guts—plus the Lord's protection—to go to those places and minister to those guys! I've been with her a couple of times. She's something else!"

"And . . . where do you live?"

"You mean where do we call home?" Seeing him nod, Stephen continued. "Up until a couple of months ago, Tulsa. Then we decided there were no opportunities for me out there . . . and I thought—I believed it was a strong leading from the Lord—to come to CBN. When you come right down to it, I was a fish out of water out west. I belong back east . . . and with a first class operation like CBN."

"What is she doing?"

"She's totally peripatetic . . . I couldn't tell you exactly where she is at this precise moment. She has friends all over the country . . . just goes from one to the next . . . whenever she feels the Lord is leading her!"

"Is it a good marriage? Do you love one another?"

"There can be no doubt of that," he responded with as much conviction as he could muster. In case he failed to sound convincing, he used the question as an opportunity to launch into one of his favorite mini-topics in hopes that this exercise of his erudition would weigh well in his favor as a potential faculty member. "You know, Dr. Elihu, your question touches on an interest of mine in etymology of the Bible. I've studied a little greek and, you know of course, the four Greek words for love : agape, phileo, sterge and eros."

The dean acknowledged affirmatively.

"That all-encompassing Agape love of God is truly marvelous. And, to know it and to bask in it is to know true happiness. Next strongest I would think would be sterge, that familial love of father for children, mother for children . . . the natural, instinctual tie of affections that hold the family unit together . . . as God intended. Then, phileo . . . .that, to me, approximates the embodiment of agape love in us as we then express it outwardly to our fellow man. I know how it affects me sometimes . . . " And he recounted the brief tale of the poor mendicant eating out of the garbage can at the Burger Chef back when they were drilling Revelation 22:20. "I don't know whether I can really finish it . . . it affects me so . . . but, I caught up with him after he had finished eating the breakfast I had bought him . . . and I gave him a twenty-dollar bill . . . " And, Stephen began to weep as he told this part. "That poor soul . . . a creature of God's making . . . his one chance that God had given him at this life . . . and, I don't know what he did to get where he was . . . but . . . what a tragedy to have only one go-around on this earth . . . and to mess it up . . . by not knowing God! If only everyone could come to Him and find life! . . . "

"And the fourth word?" Dr. Elihu asked.

Stephen snapped out of his overt display of phileo-compassionate love, choosing his words carefully, remembering Joe's admonition about the dean's Bob Jones-Baptist underpinning. "Eros . . . the word does not appear in the Bible. Only the other three. One wonders whether Jesus deliberately ignored it . . . as not worthy to discuss . . . or not necessary to discuss . . . since it expressed the physical love of sex, everyone knew it and He did not have to dwell on it . . . except to admonish not to be fornicators . . . and for the adulterers to 'go and sin no more.' There was so much unfettered erotic love in those days . . . in the pagan world around them—which was one of the reasons, I suppose, why God wanted Joshua to slay all the idolatrous and fornicating Caananites! So, in essence, Jesus probably had no reason to preach on the eros kind of physical love, because it was taken for granted that that was the love of man for woman expressed in marriage . . . which results in offspring. Come to think of it, I never checked the Song of Solomon. I wonder if in the greek Septuagint the word eros occurs there? Meaning that it does not occur only in the New Testament?" He looked to Dr. Elihu for possible enlightenment.

The dean did not respond directly. "So, will this wife follow you here?"

"If I land with CBN . . . I'm quite sure." His face flushed slightly at the words and he left the next line for the dean.

Dean Elihu closed his eyes and reflected a moment, then recited, " . . . *'Surely he shall not feel quietness in his belly . . . The increase of his house shall depart . . . and his goods shall flow away in the day of his wrath . . . this is the portion of a wicked man from God . . . and the heritage appointed unto him by God' . . . "*

Stephen looked at him quizzically.

" . . . *'Far be it from God . . . that he should do wickedness . . . and from the Almighty . . . that he should commit iniquity' . . . "* The stately man remained lost in prayer and reflection. " . . . *and Job confessed . . . 'Hear, I beseech thee, and I will speak . . . I will demand of thee, . . . and declare thou unto me . . . I have heard of thee by the hearing of the ear . . . but now mine eye seeth thee . . . wherefore I abhor myself and repent in dust and ashes' . . . "*

The dean was silent again. Then he said, *"And Paul instructed his pupil, Timothy . . .'For if a man know not how to rule his own house, how shall he take care of the church of God?' "* Having thus concluded his leading from the Lord—or whatever had transpired— Dean Elihu opened his eyes, stood up and strode to his desk, addressing Stephen but not looking at him. "I am sorry, Mr. Trevelyan, but your house is not in order. We expect our faculty to be like bishops, and they can't look after the church — CBN University—if their own house is not in order. Good day, Mr. Trevelyan."

That was it—that was it ? That had been the interview—the final interview—his last hope . . . the last door that he had faithfully knocked on and which he had faithfully thought that Jesus had opened for him . . . 'knock and it shall be opened unto you'?

Stephen had to sit down in the anteroom. The secretary asked him if he were all right. "Yes, thank you." But, he wasn't all right—he was far from all right! He started shaking. His stomach felt queasy . . . a knot was forming in it that almost caused him to wretch. He bolted up and out of the building . . . back to the van. He heaved in the grass in front of it. It wasn't real! *This could not have turned out like this! What was it? What was it, God? Was it adultery with Eve? Was that it? But, that hadn't happened when Dave King shafted him . . . .Or, do You just not want me at CBN? Why the fuck don't You just tell me? . . . Stop leading me on . . . wasting my time . . . getting my hopes up—then dashing them to smithereens! I am no Job! Dammit! Haven't I suffered enough? Haven't You brought me down to absolute nothing . . . crushed me completely? Isn't that enough for You? You and Satan bet on me—and he won! Is that it? Sorry 'bout that . . . I tried to be your faithful servant . . . and believe in You in all adversity . . . like Your faithful Job . . . but I guess I'm just not like him. Sorry! Now, bug off! I want no more of You . . . You want me to confess my sins?*

All right! I confess them—I'm a sinner . . . a dirty, fucking sinner! OK? So, now what? Do I ask forgiveness . . . and get forgiven? And, then do I just go on to the next crushing defeat? When is it going to end? What the fuck do You want from me? Or, am I beginning to get it . . . for real . . . You simply do not want me at all! Fine with me! I don't want You! It's a deal!

Stephen started the engine but couldn't see to drive until he wiped his eyes with a tissue. He didn't know whether the tears came from losing his last opportunity or because he felt conclusively that he had lost all favor with God. Either was bad enough—combined, they were devastating!

Eve detected his mood when she came home. "It didn't go well?"

He looked at her with red eyes filled with tears. "Nope. It was worse than with Dave King. I don't know what's going on anymore . . . or what I'm going to do." He dissolved into tears, hiding his face in his cupped hands.

Eve dropped her coat and bag and sat on the arm of the chair and put her arms around him. Kissing the tears on his cheeks, she gently spoke to him, "Steve . . . it's not the end of the world. There's something else out there. I'm sure something will turn up. And, whatever happens, you have me . . . I am with you. It'll work." And she held his head snugly, caressing the back of it. "I'll make you forget all this tonight—later."

After dinner Stephen telephoned Joe. Telling him the whole story and not being able to prevent the crack in his voice . . . and only with great effort able to keep from breaking down by taking occasional big breaths of air, all of which translated through the telephone line a distraught, not-his-ordinary-self Stephen. Joe expressed deep disappointment and offered any other assistance he could. Stephen asked him to convey his regards to Mary, told him goodbye and hung up.

He knew he would never see or talk to them again—to anyone at CBN. That was the final door closed—no, slammed in his face! UN-ceremoniously, too! None of it with the slightest iota of Christian charity. *If these are Your people, Lord, You can have them—and those in Tulsa—and everywhere! They are all the same . . . and he, Stephen, had had enough of them. He wanted no part of any of them— ever again. Screw 'em all—kingdom of hypocrites! Holier-than-thou Pharisees!*

Stephen and Eve lay in each other's arms long into the night. The next day was Saturday; they could stay in bed late. They didn't talk. Stephen broke down a couple of times and she cradled him all the more tenderly, sensing the anguish that was tearing his insides apart. After a long period of this his tension seemed to ease. She began kissing him lightly around the head . . . ears . . . cheeks . . . the eye lids, nose . . . then on the mouth. One of her hands caressed his abdomen and pubic region and thighs, accomplishing its purpose. Showering his torso with her warm, wet kisses, he reciprocated and the two of them rose to a pitch of passion that could only be relieved by the thrashing consummation of the act. It did wonders for his frame of mind as well as his body. "Eve, I don't know what I would do without you . . . I know I could not have gotten through this this time. You remember how close I came to ending it all last time? I'm not so sure that wouldn't be the best solution in the long run."

"Shhh. We'll talk about it in the morning . . . in the full light of day . . . where things will be clearer. "Nite."

Stephen was not much company for the next few days. Even Lissa noticed it and asked her mother if they were breaking up or something.

When told it had nothing to do with her, Eve . . . or them . . . but that CBN had turned him down again, Lissa had simply said 'Oh.'

Stephen's mind, however, was racing . . . alternating between spurts of abject depression and glimmers of hope when a new idea or option occurred to him . . . only to be dashed in the cold light of reason. *What in God's name was he to do now?* he agonized. *All Christian and secular doors are closed for me here in the Tidewater area. My six months residency has six weeks to go before it's final—and I will be out of money in a week or so. Some street smarts! If I had reported the agency job, I might be able to draw unemployment comp again. Maybe A.L. Williams?* No, he couldn't bring himself to sell insurance.

God, what were the options? He could not let his relationship with Eve affect them. He couldn't do anything for her—she was doing everything for him . . . and she had a good job . . . that he was possibly jeopardizing by living with her. He would have to move . . . somewhere where he knew the area, had contacts. Without money, he could not go anywhere cold . . . he had learned that here. That left: Tulsa, Atlanta, or the New York area. New York was out, after the telephone talk he had with Hank Worthington while he had been in Darien. In effect . . . told that he had dropped too far out of the loop to entertain any idea of re-entering. Besides, with the recent, periodic shake-up in the world of advertising, what hope would he have over the hundreds of more qualified people walking the street already? So, that 'avenue' was dead-ended. He ruled Tulsa out . . . categorically and without a second thought.

That left Atlanta. *God! I know . . . 'you can't go home again'! And, 'a prophet is only without honor in his own home town,' so to speak. But, what else is there? At least there, he could demand to live in the house with all of them until he found a job. Maybe he could replace . . . what's her name? . . .the practical nurse and take care of dad in exchange for room and board. Not 'board.' He could just picture Martha cooking for him! Just his moving in would earn her utmost hostility. That was enough to contend with. But— screw it!—he had as much right to the house as Tom; he had promised but not actually signed the house over to him.*

Now, what would he do? He had to go back to the commercial world . . . either advertising or broadcasting. There were excellent branches of the big New York agencies in Atlanta: J. Walter Thompson, BBDO, Grey . . . and top regional ones like Tucker Wayne. In broadcasting there was a Christian station, channel 50, but he was repulsed by that idea. The secular stations were no doubt loaded with young, low-paid types who thought they were in the big time. And, Stephen's credentials at this point were not likely to impress anyone. That left the Ted Turner Group . . . the station, WTBS, and the new satellite network . . . and a news operation that they were inaugurating. Maybe that's where the potential is. At least there ought to be something that will keep me out of the bread lines. 'Hope springs eternal in the human breast'! And, that's not biblical.

So, a plan began to form. It had to be implemented the moment his final decree was merged . . . which would mean he would have to manage his remaining finances very, very carefully in order to reach that point. He still had three hundred to pay the attorney. At this point, he didn't know where that would come from— maybe he'd have to knock over a gas station, he thought, half-jokingly. He would have to break this to Eve very gradually and as gently as he could. He honestly couldn't bear to think of leaving her. They had become as one. He knew he loved her and cherished her . . . and didn't want to hurt her. He thought he was really in love with her now.

Realizing that he had been distant of late, he began warming up, first to Eve, then to Lissa and the baby. He especially took time to play with Tootsie and to hold her. The opportunity to talk at length again to Lissa, though, never presented itself. Eve sensed with female intuition that Stephen's mental struggle was being reconciled and was bracing herself for what she feared that portended. She had known all along that it would not last; that a day would come. She had just hoped it would not have come this soon—she was definitely in love with Stephen now. She looked forward to coming home to him every night, looked forward to their time together, to companionship she had never experienced before. Their relationship was still at that stage where it was all new, refreshing, exciting . . . the discovery phase. She did not kid herself, though, that there would not come some day when the things they talked about . . . and that interested them now . . . would start being repetitious . . . and that he would need more stimulation . . . more intellectual repartee . . . more sharing of things to which he—but not she— had been exposed by background, by education, by experience. There would come that time, she knew instinctively, that the bloom of whatever degree of youth and beauty that she now possessed would fast fade, and, as her mother's did, her genes would turn her into an overweight, frumpy, ordinary middle-aged woman, if not with curlers in her hair, slippers on her feet and a rump-sprung house coat, certainly an ordinary soul who would be an embarrassment to Stephen. She made no pretenses about their differences; they were from vastly different worlds. Their fling, while genuine, had been just that: a sexual fling . . . mutually satisfying . . . but not meant to last . . . no matter what their hearts were now telling them.

Stephen would have been thinking along these same lines had not his great sense of honor and loyalty intervened. Just as in earlier days at the ad agency, his personal integrity, his strong sense of responsibility had overshadowed his common sense and innate sense of survival . . . his dormant street smarts. Refusing to picture the two of them in other than a rosy future life together, *he swore to himself that he would come back for her . . . no matter what. He would get on his feet—make it somehow—and take care of her . . . as his wife. To hell with all that Atlanta class crap anyway! That was all anachronism in this day and age. Besides, getting back into Atlanta 'sass-si-ety' was the farthest thing from his mind. But, make no mistake—he would take care of Eve . . . possibly Lissa and Tootsie, too. His mind was also telling him he had to take care of Gloria and Michael as first priority. 'All right! I'll take care of them all, by God!'*

Chapter 28   Fare Thee Well

It had been a little over a week since Stephen had had the disastrous interview at CBN U; there were just a little over four weeks before the legal separation from Faith could be merged into the final decree of divorce. But, he had reached a critical point—his money had totally run out. The final check from Renaud advertising had virtually all gone to Eve for rent and household contributions. And, he'd paid the Exxon gasoline bill, He was down to less that three dollars. The only thing he knew to do was to withdraw cash on the debit card.

He drove over to Virginia Beach to his bank where they knew him. Stepping up to a teller's window, he presented the card along with a cash withdrawal slip, smiling pleasantly at the young woman as he did so. She looked at the card, then walked back into another room where she stayed for three or four minutes. When she returned, she handed the card back to him—without any cash—telling Stephen that she was sorry, but there seemed to be a denial of authorization of use on the card.

Stephen was stunned! He asked her to check again . . . there must be some mistake. He was definitely . . . authorized use of it . . . under power of attorney for his father. The teller did so again and returned with the same verdict: 'unauthorized.'

Stephen had trouble walking out of the bank. He stumbled, disoriented. Instead of shouting in a blind rage, he said softly to himself . . . *'so this it it. I am brought down to this. I am absolutely broke. I have only a couple of dollars . . . and a van—all I own in this world! This lousy, frigging world. I am too stunned, Lord, to even talk to You . . . to even plead or praise . . . or cuss You out. I throw in the towel. You win—somebody wins! But, it isn't me !'*

He walked aimlessly down the main strip of stores, most of which were still closed for the season. Everything had been taken out of him. He simply wandered . . . slowly, looking down at the pavement. *If he were not with Eve, he would be homeless . . . no, he could live in the van . . . wash up at public toilets—ugh! How he detested them! And, he could string the Exxon card another month or two . . . and that would be it.* He had five bullets left in the pistol.

As he stopped at a corner to cross the street, a bright shiny Mercedes slowed and turned in front of him. Driving it was a middle-aged black man, neatly dressed in suit and tie. Stephen eyed him and a sense of abject rage overtook him. *'Look at that black bastard! Where does a guy like that get the kind of money to drive around in a fifty-thousand-dollar Mercedes? If he were a drug dealer . . . he'd be younger and that would be a white Lincoln Continental. Here I am . . . Stephen Trevelyan . . . fine old southern family . . . Yale . . . Marine captain—dumb-ass broke as a beggar . . . at the prime of my life . . . while some goddam black ass-hole, probably never graduated from high school . . . driving around in a Mercedes! Jesus!'*

Circling back toward the van, he approached a group of street preachers on the back of a pickup parked at the curb in front of an elegant art and frame shop. Their loud voices could be heard a half a block away.

As Stephen approached, he heard words so familiar that he mouthed along with them. Below the banners admonishing 'Repent and Be Saved,' there was the name of a Baptist church. The preacher yelling at the moment was doing so while thrusting a well-worn Bible (King James, Stephen surmised) out toward passersby.   There was righteous anger etched on his face and a glare in his eyes that bordered on pure hate. *'God, these poor saps . . . these hard shell Baptists never do get it . . . It's not only fire and brimstone and sinners repent that Jesus wants taught, it is love. Come to Christ in love . . . and receive His love . . . and you will be a new, born-again creation in Christ and you can receive the gifts of the Holy Spirit to operate in His power . . . as well as enjoy the fruits of the Spirit—Hah! Yeah! Just like Steve Trevelyan. Use the power of the Holy Spirit like me ! Sure! How 'bout the fruit that I am enjoying? Here, look at me! Here's what your 'coming to the Lord' does to people!'* He wished he could out shout the preacher.   Instead, he strode right up to him and stuck his fist up in front of his face, middle finger extended in the universal sign and said straight at him, "Up yours, asshole!"

He proceeded on down the street to the trailing calls of the preacher. "Bless you, brother. God will forgive you . . . if you just repent and ask His forgiveness . . . "

The time had come to lay it all out to Eve. He waited until after dinner. Tootsie was in bed and Lissa, out baby sitting. He asked her to sit down on the couch beside him. He put his arm around her shoulder and she snuggled up to him cozily.

"OK," she said, "I've known it was coming. Let me have it."

"Yes, I know my behavior has been obvious and strange lately. No need to tell you why . . . except that today—the final coup de grace— Tom cut off my debit card. I think what he did was illegal . . . but I'm in no position to fight it . . . simply because that leaves me absolutely broke. I don't have but two dollars to my name."

"Oh, darling, I'll help you . . . we'll make it together . . . "

"No. It's not only that. I know now that I love you. I'm in love with you . . . and I'm frustrated because I'm in no position to do anything about it. And, that tears me up."

She hugged him tightly.

"And . . . I have no other conclusion but that everything is finally over. My career . . . pursuit of a career . . . whatever career that was. I am obviously out of God's favor . . . so I can scratch all this religious stuff. Anyway, I'm sick of sticking my neck out for the Lord and having it chopped off. Twice at CBN was twice too much! Furthermore, I find that at age forty-two—at the peak of my productive years—I am unemployable. And, with no more resources . . . there is no way for me to find employment . . . the kind of employment that, unfortunately, is commensurate with this goddamned sense of worth that my life has programmed into me. I would simply die having to do something that was inferior to my education and abilities. Damn Atlanta! . . . damn Yale! . . . and damn the Marine Corps! And, damn Madison Avenue!"

Eve did not comment, absorbing what he was saying with her heart filling with anguish.

He told her of all the options he had been considering. How many doors besides CBN, like New York, had been closed to him. How he felt now trapped . . . with no escape. How he was truly sorry that God appeared no longer in his life—if He had ever been there in the first place. So, the only option . . . especially now that he was destitute . . . was to get back to Atlanta and barge in on Tom and Martha . . . until he could land something at one of the ad agencies there or with Turner broadcasting. That seemed to be the only avenue left. Once on his feet there, he would come back for her. And, unfortunately, because of the money aspect, he had better leave as soon as he could. He would have to drive back to Norfolk for the date with the lawyer for the final decree and she would have to go with him to witness his having lived the whole six months in Virginia. The Atlanta trip would not have to come up . . . after all, it would be just a short trip as far as this situation was concerned.

He thought, too, that he could make it down there on fifty dollars, what with the Exxon card—if she could lend him the fifty. He would pay her back . . . tenfold, he promised. When home in Atlanta he would just have to sponge off Tom till he landed something.

They sat together on the couch without speaking for a long time. A tear slid down Eve's cheek as her heart told her this was the last time she would ever see him His situation would change . . . he would get on his feet again . . . make protestations about his coming back for her. Even then . . . if that did happen, their relationship would have changed. She was sensible enough to know that the old fire would be hard to rekindle after the passage of time. She would eventually get over Stephen, but it was going to be a heart-wrenching ordeal, she knew. He had become a part of her now . . . and she truly loved him with her heart—while her head kept telling her it would never work. Now, it had come down to less than twenty-four hours left; he would leave in the morning. Their last night together!

They made their last night as memorable and as pleasurable as they could. Their love-making was protracted . . . and tender . . . and all-consuming. There was genuine love in it . . . the mutual expression of a burning love that had been prelude to this final consummation.

They knew they had to get some rest; she had to go to work the next day. He had a long drive ahead of him.

They woke up early, though, and made love for the last time. At the end of it, Stephen sobbed uncontrollably, holding her in a tight embrace.

"I don't want to leave you, Eve. I do love you! Why, oh why, couldn't this all have worked out? Why did my life have to end up in such a mess?"

She stroked him gently, trying to imbed every second of time and every inch of his body into her subconscious. If she could only relive these precious moments in that blank future that lay ahead of her. She savored it, memorizing it, and forcing it indelibly into her heart.

The alarm rang as she disengaged, not bearing to linger or to look at him, and went into the bathroom. Stephen continued to sob into the pillow.

Before Eve left after breakfast, Stephen held her long and tenderly, not wanting the moment to end. He took a gold locket from his pocket and put it around her neck. "It was my mother's. I want you to have it." Eve wept and kissed him for the last time. Lissa watched them from the kitchen.

When the door closed, Stephen dashed up stairs and threw his belongings into his travel bag. It took a few trips back and forth to the van to pack everything, and when he was finally ready to leave, he went back into the kitchen. From his jewelry case he had also taken a small gold bracelet. Reaching for Lissa's wrist, he snapped the bracelet on and told her it had been his mother's. She had been a lady . . . now he knew that she would have wanted another lady to have it.

Lissa held her arm up and admired the gift . . . with a sad smile on her face.

Stephen took her arm and guided her onto her feet, then embraced her warmly. "Lissa . . . you are a sweet, young lady. Have a good life . . . and take care of Tootsie. I want to come back and see a beautiful young girl and her beautiful mother."

"Please come back, Steve."

Stephen released her and picked Tootsie up, looked her in the eyes, smiled and hugged her and kissed her on the cheek. Putting her back down in her playpen, he could not hold back the tears and left, leaving Lissa watching with tears filling hers as well.

Chapter 29   The Trek

Stephen had great difficulty forcing himself to pay attention to the traffic. He found it harder to convince himself that the familiar landmarks that he was passing would be the last he would be seeing of them for a long, long time. Yet, just a few miles away, ebbing farther and farther back behind him was Eve, settled at her work table . . . probably having shut him completely out of her mind as she did her routine air buys.

He traveled the same route he had come: the back roads down into North Carolina, then due west over to I-85, then straight southwest toward Atlanta. He had tanked up . . . filled both tanks, so that meant he could go close to four hundred miles without refueling— four fifty if he had to. He would use as little of his cash as possible; eat only junk snacks, and a big bottle of Gatorade and some bottled water. He drove the van slightly under the speed limit. No need to push it, besides, he couldn't afford a breakdown, or a flat tire.

His mind worked overtime, recounting recent past events. By the time he neared Durham, he was able to keep thoughts of Eve out long enough to review his options over and over. Then the thought struck him: *he had never contacted Reverend Paul Masters. He had really meant to . . . never even dropped him a note to tell him where he was. Now the thought was so strong, he thought it must be mental telepathy—or that old 'leading of the Lord' that he used to feel. It was nearly five o'clock . . . that would be four Tulsa time and he was nearing Spartanburg, South Carolina.*

He pulled off at a motel-gas-stop area. Always finding it better to go into a motel lobby to use the pay phone than gas stations, he got a bunch of quarters in change at the desk, and, looking the number up in his pocket address book, dialed All Saints church. After a couple of rings, a familiar voice answered, "All Saints, Father Masters speaking."

"Paul—Steve Trevelyan here—long distance . . . way out in the middle of North Carolina. How ya been?"

"Steve—would you believe? I was just thinking of you. Wondered what had become of you? How are you doing?"

"Not so good, I'm afraid . . . " and he recounted briefly the disastrous events at CBN . . . and his heading for Atlanta and trying now to break back into the secular world. He had no other choice."

"Alas . . . as the saying goes, 'the Christian army is the only one that kills its wounded'! Have you ever thought about teaching . . . in a prep school, I mean?"

"Well, no, not exactly. But, off the top of my head, it would offer some benefits, I suppose."

"Especially, a boarding prep school. Live on campus, room and board. Twelve months pay, summers off. Also, free tuition for your children. Lots of good things to say about it . . . not to mention a certain degree of prestige . . . self-esteem . . . an all-around honorable profession. Interested?"

"Yes, of course. But, where do I start?"

"I got a call the other day from a classmate of mine who is now headmaster at a little Episcopal prep school in western Maryland, Saint James. He called me for a recommendation for someone who could handle Development . . . you know, alumni and fund raising . . . as well as

384

teach one course . . . English, I think. Could start almost right away . . . on the development side of it. Got something to jot this down?"

The operator interrupted for four more quarters, whereupon the conversation continued and Stephen jotted down the name of the headmaster, the telephone and rudimentary directions on how to get there.

Stephen asked Paul if he would be kind enough to call the headmaster and tell him he'd found his man . . . that he would turn around right this minute and be up there by mid-day tomorrow. He asked for Paul's home number because he was sure to think of a bunch of questions he would want to ask him after he started thinking this over. Thanking Paul profusely, he told him he felt renewed and that he would keep in touch.

Before they hung up, Paul's final remark left Stephen uneasy. A lawyer friend had called asking if Paul knew where Steve was. Seems a warrant was being prepared for Stephen's arrest. Faith had charged that he had stolen the van from the ministry. She had, it seems, wrecked her station wagon, and the van title was still in the Living Water ministry name. Unless Stephen returned it to her she would place a felony charge against him.

The operator interrupted again. This time Paul asked for the number he was calling from and he'd call back.

The ring came and Stephen picked up. "You've got to be kidding! She and I made a deal . . . and I frankly forgot to get the title signed over to me. God, what a bitch! Paul—do me this favor. Let me get to Saint James, then I'll get back in touch with that lawyer and try to work things out. Obviously, I can't come out there . . . I've got less than forty dollars to my name . . . and the van at the moment is the roof over my head. I'm desperate!"

Paul agreed; promised to call the headmaster and the lawyer, and wished Stephen well. He would expect to hear from him . . . this time."

Stephen decided he needed a breather. He got a map of the eastern United States out of the van and brought it into the coffee shop in the motel to study it. He was just over the South Carolina border northeast of Spartanburg. There were two possible routes: either up 77 at Charlotte to 81 and up the Shenandoah valley, or back up 85 to I-95 and up, short-cutting the Washington jam by taking US 17 to US 15. That promised to be all flat and level . . . less wear and tear and he was more familiar with it. He ordered coffee and sat for a good rest break, jotting down ideas for this new prospect that Saint James offered.

Recalling his Sewanee Military Academy prep school experience, he transported those memories into a non-military co-ed series of images and envisioned himself as a member of the Saint James faculty, living in an apartment in one of the dorms . . . or in one of the private houses on campus. Paul Masters had given him a brief description of Saint James . . . a small nineteenth century cluster of buildings in the center of an expanse of rolling, manicured lawns and playing fields. A modern but matching chapel and similar academic building and a giant new gym building had augmented the quaint, rural eighty-acre campus out in the beautiful gentle hills surrounded by mountains of western Maryland at the lower end of the Cumberland valley. Stephen envisioned an orderly student body of well-behaved sub- and teenage boys and girls in blazers and ties, a respected faculty who, as masters in the English tradition, each heading a table in the scholastic-gothic paneled dinning hall with fine specimens of bright, well-mannered youths . . . growing and maturing into educated ladies and gentlemen well set on the pathway to superior colleges and lives of distinction and leadership. This was just the sort of environment Stephen now had a growing excitement to become a part of. They were his people and he would fit in like a glove. And, regardless whether it was low, high, non-charismatic Episcopalian, that no longer mattered. His former religious zeal had faded . . . and he felt he could assimilate once more into the liturgical traditional church . . . of Laodicea, even! More importantly, he could see Gloria and Michael attending . . . if Diana could be convinced. With free tuition, he didn't see how she could object. Also, not entirely out of the realm of possibility either, was the fact that this would be a good spot to bring Eve—maybe even Lissa and Tootsie. Eve would probably like it and could no doubt find employment either with the school or in nearby Hagerstown. So, at least things were looking up. And, since this wasn't intensely evangelistic or charismatic like everything he had touched since leaving New York, maybe he could just land this one—with or without the Lord's help. To be truthful, he no longer felt that constant camaraderie with the Lord and felt no desire to call upon Him any longer.

Having recuperated sufficiently from the long day's drive, he freshened up in the men's room, gassed the van up, and searched out a McDonalds for a hot hamburger and fries for dinner.

It was well after dark by the time he got back on the road. He had a long way to go . . . but he would break it up by a series of short naps along the way . . . and should get up there by noon the next day. He would ask the headmaster if he could shower in the gym's visiting team's quarters—or, perhaps, they had a guest house or something where they could put him up overnight or for a couple of days. He would make no bones about his present predicament and, if this Episcopal priest-headmaster was anything like Paul, he would be sympathetic. And, he would like nothing better than to be able to start on the payroll right away. Too, he could tell him that he had some unfinished business back in Norfolk and would have to take one day off to go back (a Monday so he could travel on the weekend) . . . back to once again be with Eve . . . tell her all about Saint James . . . .and take care of the final decree. This business about the van, though, that might be sticky. With Paul putting in a good word for him, he would just bare his soul and tell the attorney what his and Faith's deal had been . . . despite the failure to transfer title.

It was full nighttime, no moon, and Stephen had to restrain himself from pushing the van and himself too hard to get up to Maryland. He caught the speedometer over the limit several times . . . the last thing he needed was to be stopped for speeding. What if the van's license was already on an 'all-points bulletin' or whatever they call it? Would have to be real careful. . .keep it on cruise control.

Exhaustion was beginning to tug on Stephen. He pulled into a rest stop and tried to sleep for an hour, but the noise and lights and the fact that he was so loaded up that he couldn't stretch out, precluded real rest. The thoughts racing through his mind didn't engender slumber either.

Chapter 30   Violation

The drive was beginning to take its toll. He ached all over and the old war wound made his hip throb; no repositioning—such as he was able—relieved the incessant and increasing discomfort. Sleep fought to overcome him and the last caffeine stop was wearing off. And to boot, the junk food he had gulped at the last rest stop was beginning to rumble in his bowels. *Damn*, he needed to take a crap soon. *'I'll hold off as long as I can. Despise these frigging, filthy rest stops . . . and, this time of night—morning— three-thirty a.m., they ought to be pig sties!'*

He drove on. Pitch black. No moon. Only a few vehicles at this time of morning. More going south. Nothing in the rear view mirror; not even a glow on the horizon. The road all to himself. *'Better not doze. Keep awake, keep thinking. Put on a louder tape; Mozart's not even making any sense any more. Wish I had something Jazz—even rock if it would blast my eyes open.'*

The van headlights picked up the familiar white lettering on blue, "Rest Stop 1 mile."

'Hell, might as well dump this load, Maybe that'll take some of the pressure off.

Easing off the accelerator, he coasted onto the exit ramp. He was more conscious than ever now since he was jobless and broke about conserving, conserving even the brake linings. *Why brake? Just judge it right and coast in to the final necessary light tap of the pedal.*

389

As he did so, he quickly surveyed the parking area. Dimly lit; two of the floodlights were out. There were no cars, only a shadow of one—or a truck—back on the other side near the tree line. Or, maybe it was just his imagination. Maybe the trash dumpster or something. He was too groggy for anything to register in his numbed brain. He was totally exhausted. *'I don't think I could have driven one more mile,' he confided to himself.*

He didn't pull right in front of the small building with its single front light. Instead, he glided down to the end of the line of marked-off spaces. He figured after he took a crap and washed his face, a quick nap would help, and he'd be less likely to be disturbed by the next car to come along.

Coming to a halt, he switched off the ignition, took the keys, stretched his arms and clumsily got out, giving in to the injured hip with a single painful limp. Putting the key in his pocket, he took out the two tens and a five that he had left and stuck them over the visor; he then locked the door and instinctively looked around before proceeding toward the men's room. It was painful to walk and he felt like an old man. *'Only 42 and I feel like this? God, I'll never make it to 60!'*

There was a bit of a chill in the air and he clutched the lapels of his light parka as he pushed open the door marked "Men." The stench struck him as he expected. Obviously the cleaning crews came in early but not this early. His footsteps echoed on the tile floor. Glancing down to the end of the stalls, he leaned over to see if any feet showed. Satisfied he was alone, he pushed back the door to the first stall. The dim overhead light, the sole yellowish fluorescent tube that was working, barely illuminated the toilet bowl, but he gagged. Feces all over it; urine all over the floor. Paper, a long, twisted stand of it half wet on the floor snaked up over the edge of the seat and into the unflushed bowl.

390

Stephen backed out and quickly checked the adjacent one; a little better. *'Well—what I expected. I hate these damn public places. But, I doubt if I could find a decent motel at this time of morning to use theirs. Maybe a splash of cold water will help.'*

He turned the faucet handle—which immediately sprang back. *'OK, gimme a hard time.'* He held it with his left hand while holding his right cupped under the stream, then splashed it up over his face. He reversed the procedure and began to come to life. Then, he got as much in his right hand again and dipped his head into the sink and doused his head. It felt good. He would take his time . . .

A movement in the mirror caught his eye. He wiped the water away and saw a dark face behind him. He straightened, obviously startled, and turned around.

Whatever struck him in the pit of his stomach felt like a sledge hammer. He reeled back against the sink, bent over. His head began to come up and he saw a second dark shape. He registered shock. No real pain; the wind just knocked out of him. Instinctively his hands came up as a knee went into his groin. The pain was excruciating, stunning him and doubling him back over again. Instantly he felt his neck in a vise grip, a steel-like arm over his nape and back under his chin where the other hand grasped it firmly. His head was locked in an armpit, a sweaty, stinking body and armpit. He tried to catch his breath; he was choking. The sweaty, muscular hulk at the same time swung him away from the sink, bending him down almost to the floor.

"Hiyoulak dat? Muhfuka!" the husky voice above him muttered.

A second voice, on beat, chattered, "Man, you gon' git it! Honkey!"

"Gid de money, nigga."

Steve felt his hip pocket being torn out. The action wrenched his old injury and he winced. He was less aware of the pain in his neck and was dumfounded that he could not get his arms to swing, although they seemed to be free. The pressure on his neck had virtually nullified any feeling in his extremities. With a great effort he managed as hard a blow as he could muster with his right fist at the groin of his assailant.

"Muhfuka! You gon' pay fo' dat!" the voice proclaimed in a threatening, heavy tone at the same time wrenching him so that he fell to the tile floor.

Both figures kicked him—in the head, in the side, in his hip and his upper legs. Then the first one grabbed him in a headlock again and lurched him up as if he were a rag doll. He had never felt such strength; he began to be terrified, now that the first few seconds of this incredible episode had passed.

"Fu-uck! Dis sombitch honkey ain't got nuthin'! Three fuckin' greens."

"Yeh, he got it hid'n his truck. Muhfuka!"

"Fuck dat. 'M gon fuck 'im. Need me-a piece-a white ass. You like dat, white boy?"

The vise grip was like steel. He couldn't budge. He wasn't sure he believed what he thought he heard, but a sudden wrenching of the back of his trousers, as a knife tugged up under his belt over his backbone causing the buckle on the opposite side to dig deep into his belly, almost collapsed his lungs. His jeans and underpants came down with one powerful jerk, crumpling around his lower legs and ankles.

"Man, ain'dat nice. Whoooe! Dat mos' lak white   pussy. Whoooe-man! Looky here!"

Two enormous hands grasped his hips and he felt his buttocks lifted and jerked backwards. *At the same time he felt it! It could not be happening! He felt his legs being spread apart and, unmistakably, an enormous, hard penis was being groped to find his anus.*

He cried out, "Satan, I rebuke you in the name of Jesus!. In the Name of Jesus! I rebuke you Satan! I bind you, in the name of Jesus!"

"Hey, man. Watchu sayin'? You betta call Jesus. But he ain' gon hep you, baby, you white meat. You gon!"

The thing found its mark and jammed its way through the sphincter muscles, tearing skin, causing the victim to wince and scream out. To no avail; the thing plunged brutally, seemingly violating his whole insides. The strong hands pulled his buttocks back and forth, inflicting agony each time and causing the neck-lock to tighten. Stephen passed consciousness into delirium.

Suddenly, the thing stopped plunging, withdrew halfway—then all the way. "Sheeeit! This muthafuka fulla shee-it! Looka dis. ShEE-it!"

His neck was loosened and Steve felt himself sink to the floor.

"Cocksucka honkey. You shit, boy! You fukkin' shit!—Dis stinking muthafukka got shee-it all ova me!" the attacker cried in a high-pitched sing-song whine.

Semi-conscious, he felt a heavy Nike strike his naked buttocks. Then, his undershorts were ripped from his soiled pants, rending as the pieces separated from his legs. The angle of his head resting on the floor allowed one eye to catch a glimpse of the figure which had stridden him, with his pants around his ankles, wiping his genitals with his undershorts. That wasn't enough. The figure yanked the edge of his parker and continued wiping the feces from his penis and thighs. "You shee-it, white muhfuka!"

"Hey, man, I ain' gon poke no shitty white asshole!" With that, the one who had held his head gave him a rib-crunching kick and spat on him. Then, he flipped open his fly, pulled out his black pride and urinated on the fetally crouched victim.

"Les git th'fuck otta here."

393

Stephen had no idea how long he had lain in the puddle of feces and urine on the dirty tiled floor of the Men's rest room at the rest stop. It was probably not more than ten minutes or so. The realization of what had happened was slowly dawning on him, yet a part of him was trying to tell him that it was just a dream. *That he would wake up and this would be a nightmare. Then, why did he ache so—all over? Especially his anus?* The putrid stench in his nostrils suddenly overwhelmed his consciousness. Without opening his eyes he knew he was on the floor, that it was cold and filthy, that it stank—reeked of piss and shit. And, he realized he was in it. The warmth of the urine of his first attacker had now cooled; he was just coolly and stickily wet—and half naked, and caked with feces.

He thought he heard a noise at the door. *"God, are they coming back for more? God— yes, God, I called on you . . . used the power of the name of your Son, Jesus, to stop Satan. Why did You forsake Me?"*

"Herman, I told you we shoulda stopped at that last motel anyway. It would have been better to just park there than get out here like this in the middle of nowhere . . . "

"We'll get there all right. I'm just gonna stop and go to the bathroom right up here at this rest stop."

"Herman, we shouldn't stop anywhere at this time of morning . . . for anything"

"Well, we better stop now or we can float the rest of the way!"

Herman pulled the sedan right in front of the building. "Now, you lock up and sit tight. There ain't nobody in here, 'cept that van over there and he's probably sleeping. I'll be careful. If anything happens, you blow the horn—and keep blowing!"

Herman looked all around him as he walked to the door of the men's room. He cautiously pushed it open—couldn't be careful enough these days, especially for an old fart in his seventies, he thought. The smell hit him first—it was revolting, causing him to gag. Then his eyes caught the crumpled, lifeless figure in the mess of filth on the floor in front of the basins. The hair stood up on the back of his neck, his heart skipped a beat, then fluttered. A sudden engulfing fear caused his sphincter muscle to loosen and his bladder to react, soiling himself.

Stunned, silently he spun and panted back to his car, trying to regain control of himself. His wife saw him coming hurriedly and had the door unlocked for him. Herman collapsed into the driver's seat, turned the ignition on and was in reverse before his wife could shriek with dismay at the officious odor that now overwhelmed the interior of the car.

Gunning the car for all it was worth, the excited old man assured his wife he would explain a soon as they got out of there.

Stephen managed to get himself up off the floor and look in the mirror. The sight startled him. *That couldn't be him. Not him, Yale Class of 60, Marine captain, TV station manager—servant of the Lord! Every bit of him was a mess. His face was black and blue. And, there was no shower, of course . . . and that dammed faucet with a spring on it!*

He stepped out of his jeans, what was left of them, and took off his parka. Fortunately, the parka had absorbed most of the urine of his attacker, so his shirt was reasonably wearable. The jeans were caked with feces, his own, and, he noticed for the first time—blood. "God, I'm bleeding! God! How could You let this happen to me?" he pleaded into the fetid air.

The pants were unsalvageable. And, there were no paper towels, of course. He struggled along the stalls to find one with some toilet paper at all left. With it, he scraped off his feces and blood; his hands becoming so filthy with both that his actions defeated themselves. Delirious with pain—and now a churning anger—he took some tissue back to the basin and tried to wet and wash, except that with the stupid spring faucet he only managed to get it greased slippery with the fecal-blood mixture. Weak from the ordeal, he had to lean down on the basin to keep from collapsing. His mind was a hellish nightmare, still. The thing would not stop; they were still attacking him. The pain was still excruciating, he was still bleeding . . . all over his legs, his socks and one shoe that had stayed on . . . and all over the floor.

He staggered over to the second stall and almost fell onto the seat. His usual fastidiousness about lining the seat of any public toilet with tissue was farthest from his tormented mind as he closed his eyes and sank into despondency. The stench was commonplace by now. He managed to relax for a moment and allowed his bowels to evacuate. Through this he dimly perceived that that black semen would be flushed out of him. *Black!* "*My God*, he thought—*black ! I've had a black penis up my ass! I've been raped by a black man ! Man, hell, Ape! A black ape! God, how could You not hear me? I called out to You in the name of Jesus— and You still let it happen!* His mind reeled, *just grasping the enormity of it—the horror of it! The shame! He would never be the same. He had been violated, violated in an unnatural way—the way the Bible condemns—and, even if no one else ever found out, he could never forget it!* His colon ached; there were uncomfortable seizures, diarrhea, the bowl red with blood. The thought shook him; *he'd have to get a medical exam. You could lay odds that the raper was syphilitic—if not worse . . . AIDS?* "*God, how? How? Could You?*"

Mustering all his remaining strength, he got up, picked up the parka by the collar, held it somewhat protectively in front of him and made his way to his van as a set of headlights turned off the Interstate into the rest area. Fortunately he had stashed an extra ignition and door key in a magnetic box under the left fender, since the two attackers must have taken his keys also. He wondered why they just didn't come right to the van and take it, too.   Maybe the keys were still in his pants he threw away.

He opened the sliding door on the far and dark side of the van and switched off the interior lights. He hoped his assailants had left. He couldn't think straight.   The new arrival didn't stay long; the new headlights swung and caught his van momentarily, then sped by and off into the darkness as if chased by something unseen.   Seeing a roll of paper towels he had brought, he tore off two sections and stuffed them in the crack of his buttocks to absorb the continuing bleeding.   He then rummaged slowly and carefully through his duffel bag and brought out a large towel and another pair of jeans. Fetching a plastic bottle of water, he soaked the towel and sponged himself off as best he could, put on the clean jeans and tossed the towel onto the grass.   "No need for that to stink up the inside; I still stink like a shithouse!" He took a long swig from the bottle and dashed some more on his face and hair. A couple of dry towelettes got his hands cleaner, but it would take a real soaking to get rid of all this crap.

Painfully and carefully hoisting himself up into the driver's seat of the van, not wanting to turn on the interior lights, he groped around under the seat to find his .25 automatic. Taking it in still grimy, unsteady hands, he pulled the slide back and let it go, thus ramming one of the five rounds into the chamber and cocking it.   He then flipped the safety up with his thumb and set the pistol on the floor between the seats.

Recovering a bit, he checked the gas gauge. Three-quarters full. He felt woozy, light headed but not sleepy. He was wide awake now. It would be better to be on the road and get on the way.   No wallet, no driver's license, only two tens and a five-dollar bill under the visor and an Exxon credit card. Nothing to do but be careful and get there.

His eye caught the flicker of a dim light. A car's parking light that just went on. A car parked way behind the building by the trees and now slowly moving around the other side of it. He turned the ignition, eased the van into a backing turn and, without hitting the brake lights, slowed and threw it into park. He was now parallel, the right way on the road to exit, but totally dark with the engine running. The two parking lights crept up closer behind and to the left of the van in the passing mode. He rolled down the window and palmed the pistol.

The darkened car passed slowly, sounding like it was old and needed some engine work. It stopped, backed up, its backup lights illuminating the van and himself. A dark face and right shoulder leaned out as it came abreast. "How you feel, muhfuka?"

In an instant his right hand swung up, his thumb pushing the safety lever down, and the pistol was pointed out of the window. Instinctively and in quick succession, he squeezed the handle and trigger, cranking off two shots into the general area of the passenger window. A howl issued from the darkened vehicle and a string of curses. Calmly, he eased the van backward and, this time with the pistol in his left hand, aimed a shot down at the right rear tire. There was a small pop followed by a hiss. He quickly lurched forward to the right front tire and did the same thing. The howls inside grew louder. His left arm arced backward and he sighted on the windshield on the driver's side and let go his last shot. With that, he clicked on his lights and gave it the gas.

His heart battered his chest, his breathing was hard. *What had he done? Had he hit them? What if he had? What if he had killed one or both? So what! They deserved it. It was self-defense—he intended to kill them!* He actually felt a little pleased with himself. *He had been attacked, horribly violated . . . could not get them at the time . . . but, then had managed to get them after all. Sweet revenge. Revenge, he thought. Revenge is mine, saith the Lord.* "Yeh, but this is the real world, *God, one You don't seem to have anything to do with anymore. Where were You when I needed You? Huh? Besides, God, You don't say in Exodus 'Thou shalt not kill . . .*

You say 'Thou shall do no murder.' You told Joshua and a whole lot of others to go out and kill . . . and Jesus implied as much as the embodiment of the commandments. So, God, did I just kill in self-defense—or, did I murder? No matter what Your judgment—I'd do it again!'

As the miles wore on, his drowsiness returned. His anger over the incident, however, gnawed at him fitfully, in spasms, sporadically jolting him upright, wide awake. *'I still don't believe it! And, God, how come Your Words did not work? Those Words were supposed to have all the power of the Holy Spirit when I invoked them . . . Unless . . . You have forsaken me. You know, I'm beginning to think that's what this is all about. You don't give a shit about me— maybe not about a lot of people. Maybe, not about any of us. Maybe You just set this thing in motion and backed off and are just watching . . . or, maybe, You have just dusted Your hands of us all. You sure have dusted me off . . . and pissed me off, too!'*

Fifteen minutes passed, twenty miles. It was still dark. Dawn would break in about an hour unless the heavy overcast settled in as predicted. *He knew his soul was not right. His body was not right. Nor was his mind. The stark realization of what had happened to him kept thrusting through his consciousness like a hammer on an anvil. Clanging, reverberating throughout his whole body. He shook uncontrollably, shuddered, almost to the verge of sobbing. He wished he could. It would not be for supplication either, it would be from downright hurt. Hurt of the first order, first magnitude. Nothing could ever rectify this. No soft words, no good feeling of being with the Lord, no confession, no suppliant acceptance.* "I am not me any more," he thought. *'I have been mutilated into someone . . . something else. The rage that is in me will never be assuaged. Even if I got even—I didn't get even. I'd have to kill a hundred of those black mother-fuckers to even come close! God damn those black bastards, anyway. They're animals. A sub-species. They're inhuman; they ought to be exterminated. What in the hell did You make those creatures for anyway? They're scum. God damn fuck 'em!'*

This litany began to build as Stephen drove on, swelling up inside of him like a tidal wave that could not be stopped. "God damn, You, too, God. You mother-fucker. And, that goes for You mother-fucking Son, too. Fuck You, too, Jesus!" he shouted at the top of his lungs.

Tears flooded his eyes so that it was difficult to see the road. "Both of You sonsa-bitches have wrecked my life. That's right, you have royally fucked me. Here I came to You . . . in all humility, gave You my body, soul and spirit, dedicated my life to You, gave up everything for You . . . lost family and home—twice— three times for You . . . and, what do I get? A kick in the ass! A prick in the ass! A goddamn black prick up my ass. Is that Your idea of the fruits of the Spirit? Hah! Where was the promise? The love, the joy, peace . . . patience . . . kindness ! Your kind of kindness ? Shit! Goodness ? Gentleness . . . self-control ? Bullshit!

Stephen conjured up images of Diana and Gloria, early in the marriage. Gloria an infant. *'God, there had been so much hope then! It promised to be the storybook marriage, the vine-covered cottage, picket fence. Breadwinner coming home to loving family. Just like the movies— Donna Reed.'* He fell silent while the parade of images flashed through his mind like fast-forwarding a videotape. *'Those Halcyon days—were they really Halcyon now in retrospect?— war hero, Yalie, starting out with a bang on Madison Avenue in the Big Apple. That damned commute, exciting at first, then a drag. Leaving before daylight, before the kids were up . . . coming back after they were gone to bed. Usually loaded with six or eight drinks by then. Was all that fair to Diana? Shit! She didn't have to fight that stupid fight daily, that insidious, back-stabbing, dirty street type that I never mastered. Maybe if I had, this would not have happened to me—I could have handled those two nigger assholes. Maybe. No, I never could have mastered it. Good guys come in last—even in the Christian world!'*

400

He calmed somewhat as he drove. *God! How could he tell Eve about this? She would be sympathetic, though. She loved him . . . and he loved her. But, God! . . . to ever be able to get cleansed from this black scum! He'd have to go to a doctor and have him run a series of tests to make sure he hadn't picked up something from that horrid, filthy, dreg of humanity! That would make it difficult to ever make love to Eve again when he went back . . . if all the medical tests hadn't come back negative. But, he himself, felt he could never scrub his skin clean enough to eradicate the touch of that black skin on his. He would never be the same.*

He blurted out loud, "**And . . . I am not Job ! You can test me—if that's what you're doing—all You want. You seem to have done a good and thorough job of taking away all my possessions, my family, my wife and children. I had thought that that was the Job test . . . and that You then gave me Faith, that angel—angel, hah! Demon incarnate! Satan disguised as an angel of light! God what utter horror—mind control in the name of God to a degree incomprehensible! . . . and now Eve. Are You-all going to try to fuck that up too? . . . So, You all were testing me ? Sure, I believe that! Bullshit!**" His eyes glazed with a fury that had anyone been looking at him straight on, he would have sworn he had seen the evil of Lucifer himself in their depths.

Like a maniac, he suddenly yelled at the top of his voice, "**Well, fuck You, too, Mr. Holy Spirit! There, I said it—Go shove it up Your ass and see how You like it! Shove a big black prick up Your goddam holy asshole and see how that grabs You!**"

The rage boiled and seethed uncontrollably. "**. . . and, since I have cussed You out, all three of You, I guess I have committed the unpardonable sin—blaspheming the Holy Spirit. OK. Hear me: all three of You sons-of-bitches be damned! Go to Hell! Stick all this religious crap, this horseshit up Your chocolate speedways—sideways!. . . . Now,**

I want You to hear me carefully—if You do exist at all—but I am so sick of this goddamned religious crap that—just in case it is all true, and You do exist, and there really is a heaven up there—I hereby soberly and solemnly declare that I do not wish to have anything at all to do with it or You ! And, I can think of no greater horror than to think that I would join those asshole do-gooders and back-stabbers like Faith, Doc, Felix, John Mark, Rock, David King, Dr. Elihu . . . You name 'em . . . go right down the line. If they are going to get to heaven, I don't want any part of it—or them! I'd rather go to the other place and fry forever. I hereby reject You—all three of You—since all three of You have seen fit to reject me. So, fuck off!"

He pounded the steering wheel, wailing out loud, sobbing and cursing an uninterrupted string of invective, the foulest chain of epithets he had ever known, could ever remember . . . in every language he could think of one. His eyes teared and reddened. The bodily pain faded to nothingness compared to this new deeper pain of the soul.

'How in hell could I have gotten myself in such a fucked up mess? Second marriage a nightmare. Lost the children. Lost my job—livelihood. Where could I get another? Who in Hell's name would hire me? All in the nam—

"Unit 507 to Chesapeake . . . " "Chesapeake. Go ahead, 507."

"This is trooper Connolly. My location is rest stop 8, I-85. Have an apparent homicide victim . . . second victim wounded . . . critical. Shot in neck . . . small calibre. Both black males, early twenties. Request back-up."

"Roger, 507. Will notify supervisor."

"Roger that. Victims driving 1972 Plymouth, South Carolina plates KZD-443."

"Checking registration, 507."

" . . . 507 to Chesapeake. Wallet found belonging to Stephen Trevelyan, 5210 Sheridan Road, Tulsa, Oklahoma. License number 004247707. It's got a vehicle registration for a 1978 Ford Econoline 150 van, to . . . Living Waters ministry, Tulsa, Oklahoma . . . .Also, the two victims appear pretty fouled up. Human feces on clothes. Also, evidence of fight or struggle in men's rest room. Place filthy with human feces and urine. Only other evidence . . . large towel and parka in grass with heavy smears and smell of urine and fecal matter. Request crime scene van and investigator. Also suggest send an 'all-points' to be on lookout for the '78 Econoline . . . "

"Chesapeake to 507. We have a ten-fifty 'P F' . . . location . . . between McKenney and Dinwiddie . . . on I-85 . . . "

"Check . . . that's about . . . sixty miles north of here. Think it could be our Ford van?"

"Dispatching Unit 240. Notifying Dinwiddie. Will advise. Ten-four."

There was no sound—at least none perceptive to Stephen. All was a different consciousness. The roaring of the fire sounded as if it were in an echo chamber, far away. He surveyed the scene of the inferno detachedly; it was directly below him. Twisted and charred metal, colorless, was heaped in one jagged mass at the abutment of the overpass. Some bits and pieces, articles of clothing, a shoe, a box, broken glass, even strewn farther past the overpass giving mute evidence of the force of the impact. He had the innate knowledge that his body, his remains were in that mass. All charred beyond recognition. That almost athletic body, those decent good looks, those slightly grayed temples—no more. No more that torn rectum, the humiliation of that wretched encounter. There was no feeling, no pain, no emotion, no pity, no sorrow attached to his vision. He was simply a disinterested onlooker. An onlooker at his own funeral pyre. The dawn was breaking and the light of the sun overtook the illumination from the dying flames. It had been an immolation of the first degree when the twelve gallons of gas in the tank had burst forth on impact.

As he—or whatever he had become—hovered over the wreck site seeming to wait for a prescribed period, a car screeched to a stop short of the site and two people jumped out. Their voices joined that emptiness that resonated meaninglessly, futilely.

From the other direction, partially blocked by the overpass, came the louder sound of a warbling siren and alternating red and blue flashing lights added an eerie mobile cast to the macabre scene. A state trooper got out, still attached to his radio and speaking into it, he then walked nearer to the now cooling wreckage. Other vehicles began pulling up, rubberneckers talking excitedly to one another—and snapping photos.

There was no concept of time to Stephen although he did witness phases; the wrecker arriving, the cautious poking with long rods at the mangled metal, the ambulance arriving with its lights swirling, dozens upon dozens of cars stopping or slowly creeping by, occupants gasping with horror.

Most finally left and the uniformed ambulance people and the troopers, a half a dozen now, poked around in the debris, picking up something now and then and putting it carefully in a plastic bag. After a time the ambulance left and the troopers left and the wrecker people hauled the junk heap onto the bed of their truck and swept up as much of the debris strewn along the roadside as they could before departing.

Stephen became aware of a presence in the distance to which he was attracted and toward which he moved with ever increasing speed. It became a source of light, brighter and brighter, overpowering the sun . . . until it engulfed him.

Chapter 31   Payoff

Tom was just getting out of bed when the phone rang.   The emotionless voice on the other end asked if this were Thomas Trevelyan who had—(had ?)—a brother named Stephen. After this confirmation it proceeded with a perfunctory detailing of the accident that had occurred on Interstate 85 in southern Virginia. From a wallet found at a rest stop, et cetera, and piecing what few clues there were, the registration and all . . . and how that fit the description of the vehicle in the wreckage . . . that there is reason to believe that the remains—

"—The remains ?" Tom broke in.

The voice continued evenly;… "the vehicle had burned up in the crash and the remains had been sent to the local coroner in Petersburg. The accident is still under investigation.   For further contact, call the State Highway Patrol" . . . and the voice gave a number which Tom jotted down. "If we can be of any further assistance, please call," the female voice dispassionately concluded.

Tom rested the receiver back in the cradle. He was emotionless —or so he analyzed himself. *Steve—no more. Doesn't even exist. No body . . . only remains, charred fragments of bone, he imagined. Probably couldn't even put a skeleton together for burial. Just a second cremation. A small one at that.* He shuddered but no tears came.

He turned to go into his father's room. The motionless figure was stretched out under the bed covers, eyes opened and staring at the ceiling. Tom sidled up to the bedside and looked down at his father. "Dad, can you hear me?" No response. "OK. I know you're awake. I just got some bad news . . . " and he slowed, deliberately enunciating his words so that any comprehension in that stroke-damaged brain might have some chance of getting through. " . . . Stephen . . . has . . . been . . . killed . . . in . . . an . . . automobile accident . . . in Virginia." No response, not a flicker in the eyes. "I am going to have to go down there and take care of things. I'll get somebody to look after you."

Before dressing, it occurred to him to call Diana.

Diana thanked Tom and put the telephone down softly. She was stunned, momentarily shocked. After all she would feel the same about such news of any human being— especially someone she knew. Yes, that was all there was to it. It happened to someone she had known . . . and didn't know any more. She felt comforted that he must not have suffered. Even she had enough innate Christian charity to feel that.

Gloria came bouncing in, dressed and ready for breakfast, then school. Gently, Diana put her hands on her shoulders and stood her daughter in front of her as she sat on the edge of the bed. Looking into her eyes, she attempted the warmth of a smile but it came off phony. "Honey. You dad's had an accident."

Gloria looked intently at her, "Is he hurt? Bad?"

Her mother stifled a choke and cleared her throat. "He died. You daddy is dead."

"I won't ever see him again?" A puzzled expression developed on her face. "Is he in Heaven?"

"I suppose, Honey." And she embraced her young daughter.

"Oh, mummy!" the adolescent cried sadly. "Will you tell Michael?" Then she turned and went downstairs to breakfast.

Not a tear came to Diana's eyes. Even if she had tried, she would not have been able to create one. She had no feelings for him. She felt no loss. He was simply gone, gone forever. No longer existed. Chapter over.

'But, he had been right,' she remembered. 'He said that if he ever died, he would bet that she wouldn't shed a single tear. That she had never loved him. Worse . . . that she had cried uncontrollably for three full days when Tigger got run over by the garbage truck.'

The call from the state police finally reached the TV station. The receptionis/typist/goffer at the front desk forwarded it to Lydia.

Informed of the tragedy and that they had not been able to reach anyone at the ministry, whose telephone had been disconnected, and that they had finally traced Stephen Trevelyan back to KXAO-TV, et cetera, et cetera; was there anyone, any family, spouse, that should be notified? Et cetera . . . " Lydia only vaguely heard the recitation. Her heart was filled with such sorrow and overwhelming grief that she hardly realized that she had not gotten a number to call back when she hung up. Her eyes swelled with tears and she let her head fall to her desk. "Oh, God! It can't be true! Why? Why? He was too good to die! Why, God, why?" She sobbed quietly but uncontrollably and began softly to pray in tongues in the rhythmic, melodic chant that characterized her particular form of the gift. Her glossolalia soothed her and calmed her spirit, uniting it with that of God, and she drifted in almost a comatose state which masked and healed the hurt that the news of Stephen's horrible death had dealt her.

As she lay head-in-arms across her desk, Charlie saw her in passing and quickly came in. Putting a comforting hand on her heaving shoulders, he asked gently what was the matter.

He collapsed in the chair next to her desk, bent over and lowered his head into his hands. "Jesus, Jesus, Jesus . . . have mercy on his soul. We'll miss him, but—" He sat up straight, " Praise God—we know he is with You, Dear Lord, and that he has found that mansion that You have prepared for him. Hallelujah! Death where is thy sting? There is none to him who is in Jesus Christ. . .Praise God, Praise Jesus, Praise the Holy Spirit!"

Lydia raised herself up. "Yes, he was God's servant. He was righteous in His eyes. He was saved, born-again, and baptized in the Holy Spirit. There's no better way to go than that. He gave his life to Christ. He led the Godly life . . . and he is getting his rewards right at this moment in Heaven . . . at the throne of The Almighty! Hallelujah! Praise God!"

"Now," she said matter-of-factly, "we have got to do his death rightly. Notify the faithful, have a memorial ceremony . . . do something for his memory. He was such a good man." She wept silently. "It has to be done. I'll call Faith in Charlotte and tell her."

Eve was casually skimming through the newspaper. A small headline caught her attention: Fiery Crash Victim Identified. Possibly a twinge of morbid curiosity led her to the lead paragraph. 'The charred remains of the driver of a Ford Econoline 150 that crashed and burned against an abutment on I-85 in southern Virginia on March 15th has been positively identified as Stephen Trevelyan, formerly of Tulsa, Oklahoma.' Eve trembled. 'No, not Steve.' She read on.

'The Virginia State Highway Patrol and Brunswick county police have linked the accident to a previous shooting that occurred a short time previously at a rest stop sixty miles south of the crash site.'

'An unidentified man was shot to death and another was wounded. Evidence at the rest stop indicated some kind of trouble or fight had taken place. Bloody and feces-smeared clothing were found in the men's room . . . '

Eve crumpled the newspaper and ran into the kitchen with it. Thrusting it at Lissa, she then shrieked, "No! God! No! No! No! Not Steve! Not Steve!" . . . and slumped into a chair, letting her head fall onto her arm on the table . . . and wept uncontrollably.

Lissa put her arms around her mother and broke down, sobbing as well. Eve kept protesting: "No! No! No! It can't be! No! No!" And she pounded the table with the flat of her hand.

"How could it happen? He was such a good man, mom!" cried Lissa. "He loved you, too. I saw it. And, he loved me and Tootsie. He was so good—I never saw a man cry before. Oh . . . Mamma!"

Jerry's voice sounded over the noise of the TV set from the family room, "Hey! What's the matter with you two broads?"

Faith listened on the phone to Lydia's telling of the tragic accident and began praying audibly in tongues.

When Lydia had finished, Faith blurted into the air, "Satan I break that bond between Stephen and I in the name of Jesus! Hallelujah! Praise God! Satan, your power is broken, I speak it forth!" Turning back to the receiver, she said pontifically to Lydia, "You know, he never did get right with God. That's why God took him."

Lydia tried to interject, "Faith, you can't . . . "

Faith cut her off, "Hon, God spoke to me that He would take him if he didn't get right with Him. Those demons had him and he did not have faith enough to cast them out. God knows, we all tried to cast them out many times. Stephen's life just was not the spirit-filled life of the true Christian. He let worldly goods and things interfere with his relationship with God. We had many go-'rounds about this, but he just never could see it. And, God revealed it all to me. He was not really filled with the Holy Spirit. By his mouth he spake the Word but his heart was a deceiver! I knew him. I knew this. I knew God would take him. And, God did not prepare a heavenly mansion for him. God cast him into outer darkness until the time of final judgment."

Lydia slammed the phone down!

Realizing the phone had gone dead, Faith put the receiver down, closed her eyes and began spinning around the room in a dance to God, singing the incomprehensible and private language that God had given her. Singing and dancing and praising the Lord . . . the ultimate experience for her. God would speak to her now . . . confirming His favor on His faithful servant, Faith. Slowing the pace, she felt the unmistakable idea form in her brain that was coming from God. She gracefully swept her lithe body over to her writing desk and sat down.

Fumbling through a notebook until she came to an address. Taking out a sheet of stationery, she wrote the date on it and slowly began to write in a careful hand:

Prudential Life Insurance Company
Hartford, Connecticut.

Dear Sir,
My husband took out an insurance policy with your company a year ago for
$250,000, two hundred fifty thousand dollars, which would go to his father
Abner Trevelyan. My husband's name is or was Stephen Trevelyan. He just
died in an automobile accident. I don't think you should pay the money to his

father because I know for sure that my husband committed suicide. He said that was the only way he could pay anybody back for the money he lost on the oil wells. He told me that one night. So, I know that was what he intended to do. He went out and deliberately had a wreck so he could kill himself quickly and his father could collect the money.

Don't give it to him. I know you don't pay off for suicide and this was suicide.

I'm just telling you as a good Christian should because I could not live with a lie.

His death is a lie. He was not right with God so he killed himself.

Don't pay it.

Yours in Jesus,
Faith Chapelle Trevelyan

www.ingramcontent.com/pod-product-compliance
Lightning Source LLC
Chambersburg PA
CBHW060141260626
47160CB00001B/68

* 9 7 8 0 9 8 4 6 8 8 3 1 9 *